CU00468011

The Star Cross
(The Star Cross Series, Book 1)

By
Raymond L. Weil
USA Today Best Selling Author

DEDICATION

To my wife Debra for all of her patience while I sat in front of my computer typing. It has always been my dream to become an author. I also want to thank my children for their support.

Raymond L. Weil

The Star Cross

Chapter One

The Earth's eight-hundred-meter-long heavy battlecruiser *Star Cross* slid silently through empty space, the ship's powerful sensors scanning everything ahead and around it. Her four light cruiser escorts were in screening positions, protecting the massive battlecruiser from attack. The six-hundred-meter-long light carrier *Vindication* followed closely behind, protected by six small destroyers. Each ship was on high alert, and tensions were high among the crews. Everyone glanced anxiously at one another, wondering what was awaiting them at Earth.

In the Command Center of the *Star Cross*, Admiral Kurt Vickers watched the main viewscreen, which was focused on the light carrier, as four Lance fighters left the flight bay to patrol in front of the fleet. The light carrier had twenty fighters in its bay, plus ten small Scorpion bombers.

"CSP has been launched," Lieutenant Lena Brooks reported, as four friendly green icons appeared on her sensor screen. The twenty-eight-year-old woman let out a quiet breath.

Vickers could tell Lena was hoping they would remain undetected by her rapid breathing. She wasn't the only worried one in the Command Center.

Lena focused her hazel eyes upon the admiral, awaiting further orders. She trusted him to bring them through the coming ordeal.

"Current status?" asked Vickers in a steady voice, turning to his XO and commander of the battlecruiser, Captain Andrew Randson.

The captain checked several data screens before answering the admiral. "Long-range sensors indicate no unusual movement from the enemy ships. I don't think they detected our hyperjumps." Randson let out a deep, ragged breath.

He seemed to be feeling the tension running through the Command Center. Everyone's nerves were on edge. The first part of the mission was a success. They had jumped into the Sol System without the enemy becoming aware of the small battle fleet.

Admiral Vickers nodded, as his gaze returned to the main tactical screen, now displaying information from the long-distance scans. He felt a tremendous weight of responsibility upon his shoulders, knowing his next few decisions could well determine the future of the human race. His fleet was the last fleet Earth still possessed; all the others had been destroyed by a vicious and unknown enemy.

The Command Center crew waited his further orders in silence. Everyone wanted to know what had happened here in their home star system, and if their friends and families were still alive. Kurt knew they had good reasons to be concerned.

Two weeks back a mysterious and hostile alien fleet had appeared out of hyperspace and annihilated the two human fleets permanently stationed around Earth for protection. The majority of the ships had been destroyed before their shields could be raised or a single weapon fired. Only a few had managed to fight back and then only briefly. This wasn't surprising, as no aliens had been detected by any of Earth's long-range exploration ships, and no one had been expecting an attack. So the ships had been at a low level of alert. Many of the crewmembers had even been on leave down on Earth.

The *Star Cross* and her fleet had been in the Newton System, practicing maneuvers and testing the new particle beam weapons the battlecruiser and the light cruisers had been equipped with. The Newton System held a thriving human colony of nearly eight million inhabitants, plus a large orbital station designed for deep-space exploration and minor ship repair. The colony had a number of large scientific outposts, since ships sent on exploratory missions were required to report to Newton before being allowed to return to Earth. Newton was also the only true Earth-type planet to be discovered so far in the humans' explorations. Humans could survive on other planets, but none could compare to Earth or Newton.

A heavily damaged light cruiser had limped into the Newton System and reported the shocking news of the attack on Earth. The ship's commander, Captain Owens, had barely escaped and had lost over half of his crew in the brief battle above the planet. The report of the attack had shaken the Newton colony, and, after conferring with the colony's governor, it had been decided that Admiral Vickers would return to the Solar System. His mission was to determine the current condition of Earth and the number of alien ships still present.

"What now?" Captain Randson asked, as he stepped closer to the admiral. Upon the tactical screen, a large number of red threat icons were visible. "Twenty alien ships are in orbit above Earth. Four of them are approximately the same size as the *Star Cross*, and the rest seem to be similar to our own light cruisers."

Vickers nodded. "From the reports we received from the captain of the light cruiser, the alien ships are heavily armed. I don't want to risk an engagement with them at this time if we can avoid it. We have the Newton colony to think about. Our fleet is their only means of protection."

"The enemy ships are still above Earth," Randson pointed out. "They may not even know about Newton."

"We can't afford ship losses," Kurt replied with a heavy sigh. "Governor Spalding specifically requested that we return to Newton rather than risk involvement in a major combat operation."

"You don't have to answer to Spalding," responded Randson, raising his eyebrow. "Fleet Command and the president are on Earth."

"I'm not sure about that," Kurt said. "If Earth has been conquered, then Governor Spalding's next in line for the presidency. There are no other high ranking members of the government off Earth."

Randson was silent for a moment, as he seemed to consider that. "So what do you want to do?"

"We need more information." Kurt had spent hours with Captain Owens, going over the tactical data recorded during his light cruiser's brief battle above Earth. It had been painful to watch as Earth's proud space fleet had been all but annihilated.

"Our new particle beam weapons should give us an advantage," Randson carefully pointed out. "None of the ships we had over Earth were equipped with them. I'm very concerned about what the aliens may have done to our people."

Kurt didn't like entering such an unknown situation while the Solar System was so quiet. The Moon and Mars both held sizable human colonies. The total silence was eerie and frightening as to the possible cause that ceased all communications. Normally the radio frequencies were full of transmissions and messages. "Can we detect any transmissions from Earth, the Moon, or from Mars?"

"No, and all the scientific outposts are also silent. Not a peep coming from the asteroids or the moons of Jupiter and Saturn," Randson replied with growing concern in his eyes. "It's just too damn quiet! I can't believe they've all been wiped out."

Kurt could only imagine how Randson felt. His wife and twelve-year-old daughter were on Earth, just outside of Houston. So was Kurt's sister and her family.

"We could send in a couple destroyers," Randson suggested, "to check on some of the outposts."

"Not yet," replied Kurt, shaking his head, as he thought about the absence of signals. "They might be detected. Right now, our biggest tactical advantage is that the aliens don't know we're here. Let's keep it that way for a little while longer."

"Sir," Lieutenant Brooks said, her eyes alight with fear. "The long-range sensors are picking up elevated radiation levels from Earth." Lena worked at her console fervently. "I'm trying to get better readings."

Captain Randson stepped over and studied the data, the frown on his face deepening. He shook his head, and his breathing quickened. "A few nuclear weapons have definitely been dropped on the surface," he stated, drawing in a sharp breath. "The level isn't dangerous, but it's four times higher than normal." He gazed at the admiral, his expression deeply concerned. "I'm not sure we can afford to wait. What if they drop more bombs?"

"The bombs may have been dropped in the original attack," Kurt said evenly, struggling to stay calm.

He knew, if the radiation-level readings were correct, that millions of people could be dead on the planet. He felt anger growing inside him at such an enemy who would nuke a planet from orbit. This said a lot about the temperament of the aliens they faced. While Kurt had never gotten married and his parents were deceased, he worried about his sister, Denise, and her six-year-old son, Bryan. Denise's family lived in Houston because her husband, Alex, had a systems analyst job with an up-and-coming company there.

"What are your orders?" Randson asked.

The indications of nukes being used on the planet might also explain the communications silence, if everyone was afraid of drawing the aliens' attention.

Admiral Vickers studied the tactical screen for a few more moments, while he decided on the best course of action. The enemy ships couldn't be allowed to continue to orbit the planet. They had to be driven off before they nuked Earth again. The presence of an elevated radiation level changed things considerably. Vickers was afraid to even guess how many people had already died. He wondered if the aliens had landed ground troops. In the back of Kurt's mind, he could hear Governor Spalding saying to not risk his fleet. He had a hard decision to make, and it wouldn't be easy.

"It looks as if the shipyard is relatively intact," Kurt said, looking at the large green icon on the tactical screen. Earth's only shipyard orbited forty thousand kilometers above the planet.

"It is, sir," Lieutenant Brooks said, nodding her brunette head as she studied one of her data screens. "My scanners are showing only minor damage to the shipyard, and its power systems still seem to be operating."

"I wonder why they spared the shipyard?" asked Captain Randson with a questioning look upon his face. "You would think it would've been one of their first targets."

"Unless they want it for themselves," Kurt responded, thinking about the two thousand men and women who operated the station. He wondered if they were still alive or had been killed by boarders. So many unknowns faced them.

"The first alien race we encounter and they're the ones to find us," Randson said, as his eyes narrowed. "Why did they attack us in the first place?"

The higher officers in Earth's space fleet had always expected to eventually encounter an alien race with the planet's exploration ships ranging deeper and deeper into unexplored space. First-contact protocols had even been set up with linguists and other specialists assigned to each exploration mission, just in case another exploring spacecraft from an alien civilization was encountered.

"We may never know," replied Kurt brusquely. "Lieutenant Brooks, are you detecting anything else on the long-range sensors?"

"No," responded Brooks, shaking her head.

"What about communications?"

"Nothing," replied Randson. "No radio or video broadcasts of any type have been picked up from Earth, the Moon, or Mars. Everything's silent."

"I've got additional information on the radiation in Earth's atmosphere," Lieutenant Brooks added, her eyes showing growing worry. "It originates from twenty-two different sources where major cities are located on the planet."

The silence in the Command Center was profound, as everyone realized the magnitude of the calamity that had struck Earth.

Randson's eyes widened in anger. His gaze shifted back to the admiral. "We need to get into Earth orbit!"

"Get Captain Watkins on the *Vindication*," ordered Kurt, folding his arms across his chest, as he thought about his options. He knew he didn't really have any but one. The knowledge that some of Earth's cities had been nuked was the deciding factor. He didn't think Governor Spalding would react negatively to Kurt's decision, once the governor learned of this.

"Captain Watkins is on the comm," Ensign Brenda Pierce, the communications officer, reported.

"Henry, we need to drive away those alien ships. From our scans, it's obvious that Earth has suffered a nuclear bombardment. We can't afford to allow them to bomb the planet again."

"I was afraid of that," his longtime friend replied. "Our scanners are showing the same thing. What do you have in mind? We're outnumbered by nearly two to one."

"I'll jump in first with the light cruisers. We've spotted what looks like four enemy capital ships. We'll try to take them out with the new particle beam weapons. Once we're engaged, you and the destroyers will jump in. Launch your bombers and have them target the smaller ships with their Hydra missiles. Hopefully we'll have enough surprise on our side to carry this out."

"It's risky," Henry replied after a moment's pause. "But I don't see where we have any other choices. We'll only have one shot at this."

"Get your bombers ready," Kurt ordered decisively. "We make the jump in twenty minutes."

Lieutenant Brooks stepped over and handed Kurt a list of the nuked cities. He noted with relief that Houston wasn't on the list. However, Chicago; Washington, DC; Rome; Cairo; Moscow; and numerous other cities scattered around Earth were. He felt his heart grow cold as he looked over the list. If this was correct, well over forty million casualties could have resulted from the orbital attack. His eyes shifted to the tactical screen and the twenty red threat icons. How could an enemy be so callous as to nuke defenseless civilians?

The tension and anxiety in the Command Center had increased considerably as the time for the attack neared. All the ships in the fleet were at Condition One with their crews at their battlestations. This would be the first time any member of Admiral Vickers's fleet had actually gone into combat. They had trained for it and even participated in war games against other Earth fleets, but never in the history of the fleet had a weapon been fired against another ship.

"Ready to jump," reported Captain Randson, as he listened to the readiness reports from various ships over the short-range comms. His eyes focused on the admiral, still studying the large tactical screen on the front wall of the Command Center.

Kurt nodded. There was no point in waiting. Pressing the fleetwide button on his command console, he announced, "All ships, initiate jump in sixty seconds. All ships to fire upon targets as soon as you exit hyperspace. Don't wait on orders from the flag to engage. The element of surprise is essential if we want to win this battle. Good luck and good hunting."

Captain Randson activated a counter on his console. "Helm, prepare for hyperspace insertion." Randson buckled himself in his chair in preparation for combat maneuvers.

The hyperspace jump would only last a few seconds. Kurt, like everyone else, wondered what they would find when they reached Earth.

"Tactical, ready the main particle beam cannon," ordered Kurt, noting the increased activity in the command crew as they prepared for combat. "Lock on the enemy's nearest capital ship and fire as soon as you have a confirmed firing solution." The cannon could only be fired once every forty seconds due to heat buildup. They needed every shot to count.

"Weapons are ready," reported Lieutenant Evelyn Mays from Tactical.

The counter on Captain Randson's console reached zero. "Jump!" ordered Randson, his hands gripping the armrests on his command chair.

High Profiteer Creed of the Gothan Empire stood in the Command Center of the Profiteer ship *Ascendant Destruction*. He was bipedal and slightly taller than a human, with light blue skin and coarse white hair. His face, while humanoid, had larger-than-normal eyes. The last few days had been quiet, while he awaited the return of the rest of his ships, plus the others he had sent for: a large fleet of detainee ships and a number of heavy cargo ships.

The Gothan Empire, with planet Marsten as its capital, was a loose federation of 118 star systems that routinely raided many of the civilized races of the galaxy. It was a dangerous living, but the huge rewards from the bounty collected more than offset the danger.

"We'll make huge profits from this planet," gloated Second Profiteer Lantz, as he gazed at the main viewscreen on the front wall of the Command Center, depicting the blue-white planet beneath them. "Their people will sell well in the slave markets on Kubitz."

"Their world is rich in many things that will bring good profits on the black markets," added Creed, recalling his last trip to the bustling black market world. "Gold, platinum, jewels, and even some of their art will add much to our coffers."

Hundreds of alien races could be found on the planet Kubitz, either selling or buying, some of it openly and some done in the back rooms of the pleasure houses. It was also a very dangerous place for someone unfamiliar with the workings of the black market system. People were known to vanish quite routinely, and the local authorities always seemed to look the other way.

"We were fortunate to find this world in this backwater system," Lantz said. "Few ships have ventured into this area where the stars are so far apart."

"We can thank the Kreel for that," Creed said. "Several of their cargo ships have reported unknown ships detected by their satellite marker buoys in a number of systems they have claimed. It wasn't difficult for the computers on Marsten to correlate the data and extrapolate the most likely location of those ships' home world."

Lantz nodded in agreement.

Though it hadn't been quite that simple, as the computers had given them an area of space nearly thirty light-years across, which had contained quite a few stars, even in this sparse region. The Profiteer fleet had searched for two weeks before finally pinning down the system they sought.

"It is well that we found this system when we did," Lantz said with greed showing in his eyes. "They had a sizable fleet and, in a few more years, would have been too powerful to overwhelm without major losses. They still remain hesitant to obey our demands, even after we destroyed their cities. More examples might need to be made."

Before Creed could reply, warning klaxons sounded, and red lights flashed in the Command Center. His eyes instantly went to the sensor operator. "What's with the alarms?" he demanded.

"We have ships exiting hyperspace," reported Third Profiteer Bixt, as red threat icons appeared on the sensor screen before him. Then, after a moment, he looked at First Profiteer Creed with astonishment on his face. "They're human!"

"We didn't get them all," muttered Lantz.

Admiral Vickers felt the familiar gut-wrenching sensation as the *Star Cross* dropped from hyperspace within close proximity to its intended target. The tactical screen quickly updated, showing the alien ships in orbit around Earth.

"Energy shield is coming online," reported Captain Randson.

"Target lock!" called out Lieutenant Evelyn Mays, as green lights flashed on her console. "Firing particle beam cannon." She reached forward and pressed several buttons, activating the deadly weapon. Beside her, two ensigns entered targeting information for the ship's heavy KEW batteries and prepared to fire the ship's missiles.

From the *Star Cross*, a deep blue beam flashed across space, smashing into the targeted enemy battlecruiser. Its defensive energy screen was operating at a low level, which failed to stop the beam. A massive explosion tore into the cruiser, leaving a gaping hole fifteen meters across in its hull and blasting a huge fragment off into space. The ship seemed to stagger, as valuable systems inside were compromised and ceased to function. Several secondary explosions rattled the ship, sending waves of fire through shattered interior compartments and corridors.

From the bow of the *Star Cross*, the two heavy KEW cannons fired, sending a pair of large armor-piercing rounds at 10 percent the speed of light toward the reeling enemy cruiser. The rounds impacted the alien ship, tearing completely through it, setting off additional explosions. The energy generated was like twin nuclear explosions. With a brilliant flash, the battlecruiser blew, sending debris in all directions.

"Enemy battlecruiser is down!" Lieutenant Brooks reported with elation, as the red threat icon swelled up on her sensor screen and then vanished.

"We caught them before they could raise their shields!" uttered Captain Randson, his eyes shining with a wolfish glint. "We surprised them, just like they did when they attacked Earth."

"Switch to secondary target," ordered Kurt, as he intently watched the tactical screen, seeing what success his other ships were having. They had to hit the enemy quick and hard if they were to have any hope of victory.

"The *Hampton* has downed a second enemy battlecruiser," reported Brooks, as she saw another red icon vanish from her screen.

"*Vindication* is jumping in!" added Captain Randson, seeing more green icons appear on the tactical screen. "We caught them flatfooted!"

First Profiteer Creed picked himself up from the deck, looking around the Command Center in anger. "What's happening!" he demanded, as his gaze shifted to the ship's tactical screen. He could see numerous red threat icons appearing nearby. They were appearing almost on top of his fleet!

"It's a human fleet, and they're attacking," reported Second Profiteer Lantz breathlessly. "We've already lost the *Warriors Pride* and the *Addax*. The enemy is using a powerful particle beam weapon against us and kinetics."

"Particle beams and kinetics!" roared Creed in disbelief, his eyes growing wide.

He knew that, for most warships, particle beams were impractical—as they required a tremendous amount of energy and needed a long cool-down time between firings. Most Gothan ships were armed with ion cannons, energy projectors, and missiles, which were cheap and efficient. Kinetics were a thing of the past and had been given up to be replaced by more modern weapons. No one used kinetics anymore!

"One of the new arrivals is a carrier of some kind," Third Profiteer Bixt warned. "It's launching smaller warships toward us."

"We've lost four of our escorts," said Lantz, watching the ships drop off the tactical screen. He groaned and murmured, "My profits ... the pleasure houses ..." Then he reported, "All our ships have their shields up and are returning fire, but I fear we've already lost too many. The *Glimmer Fire* is reporting heavy damage, and they're asking permission to withdraw."

The *Glimmer Fire* was their only other remaining battlecruiser besides the *Ascendant Destruction*. Creed looked at the viewscreen, which showed numerous explosions in space. He could even see the flash of a few beam weapons. "Order all ships to jump!" he grated out, knowing that he had no other choice but to withdraw or risk being destroyed.

They were in this for profits, not to lose expensive warships! He would return to Kubitz and come back with a much more powerful fleet. This planet was too rich to allow a single human fleet to keep him from it. The humans could have the planet for now, but, in time, he and his much larger force would retake it. He would also have to intercept the detainee and cargo ships on their way here and have them return to the Kubitz System.

"We've taken out two more of their light units," Captain Randson added, watching as a pair of red icons fell off the tactical screen.

Andrew Randson breathed a little easier. At this rate, they would win the battle, and then, as soon as possible, he intended to take a shuttle to Houston and evacuate his family. He knew others would be doing the same thing.

"Destroyer *Brant* is down," Lieutenant Brooks reported grimly, as the friendly green icon representing the small destroyer vanished from the sensor screen.

Kurt winced at that news. It was the first ship under his command he had ever lost.

"Enemy ships are showing an energy spike," Lieutenant Brooks informed them, per one of her sensors. "They're activating their hyperdrives."

Kurt switched his gaze to a large viewscreen just in time to see one of the two remaining enemy battlecruisers jump away. On the tactical screen, other red threat icons also vanished.

"Their last battlecruiser is too damaged to jump," Brooks reported, as the enemy ship turned toward them with its weapons firing. "They're attacking!"

Kurt felt the *Star Cross* shudder slightly as an energy beam struck the ship's screen.

"Some type of ion beam is hitting us," Lieutenant Brooks reported, looking at the data on one of her sensor screens.

"The shield is holding at 84 percent," Captain Randson said.

"Particle beam is recharged," Lieutenant Mays stated, as she targeted the alien battlecruiser. "Firing!"

The deep blue particle beam smashed into the *Glimmer Fire*, flashing right through its weakened defensive energy screen. A huge hole was blasted in its bow, and the ship seemed to lose all power. Two heavy KEW rounds from the human's bow cannons plowed into the Profiteer ship, traveling nearly its entire length, and then the vessel detonated in a blaze of light as too many vital systems were compromised.

"All enemy ships have either jumped or been destroyed," reported Lieutenant Brooks, breathing a sigh of relief. "We have control of Earth orbital space."

Kurt nodded, allowing himself to relax. This battle had gone far better than expected. "Get me Captain Watkins. I'll have the *Vindication* check out the shipyard. We may need their Marines to secure it." Kurt turned his attention back toward one of the viewscreens, which showed Earth.

"Now let's try to contact someone down on the surface and see just what the hell is going on!"

Chapter Two

Denise Hunter looked up at the star-studded night sky with renewed hope, after hearing the recent horror stories on the few news broadcasts they had been able to get. For two weeks the world had been held in the tight grip of their alien conquerors. At first the governments of the world had refused to cooperate and had paid a terrible price in the loss of a number of cities. Denise knew that, in the North American Union, both Chicago and Washington, DC, had been struck. Hundreds of thousands of people suffered from radiation sickness. The total number of dead from the attacks remained unknown but was believed to be in the millions.

Over the last few minutes she had seen brilliant flashes of light, briefly lighting up the night sky in a furious frenzy. She knew she watched an ongoing battle being fought in space. The only ships Earth still possessed that could rally such a fight was her brother's fleet, which had been at Newton on maneuvers.

"Please let it be Kurt, and please keep him safe." She spoke softly, as the flashes died away. The last few weeks had been terrifying, and she was ready for the nightmare to end.

"Is it Uncle Kurt?" asked Bryan in his childish voice, looking up at the flashes.

At six years old, he didn't understand the recent events or what the bright flashes in the night sky were.

"They're pretty," he said with a big smile.

"They've stopped," Alex said, standing just behind his son. Glancing about the neighborhood, he could see a lot of people outside, looking up toward space and speaking excitedly.

"Are the pretty lights coming back?" Bryan asked his father.

"I don't know," responded Alex, putting his hand protectively on Bryan's shoulder, squeezing gently, and gazing at Denise.

"Alex!" yelled Claude, one of their nearby neighbors. "The TV's on, and the president's making an announcement."

"Let's go inside," Alex said, reaching out and taking Denise's hand. "Maybe we can find out what just happened."

Since the attack, the TV had only been on sporadically. The government of the North American Union had been strangely silent, perhaps afraid the aliens would discover where they were hiding.

Bryan ran to the kitchen. "I'm getting a drink first."

"I'm glad to hear the president's still alive," Denise said, as they entered their house in a secluded residential development just east of Houston.

There had been no formal word as to what had happened to the president and others in the government once reports had reached Denise that Washington, DC, had been destroyed. The nuclear blasts and the ensuing fallout had supposedly killed millions. She had heard unconfirmed rumors that the government had gone underground, and was in hiding. The brief reports issued over the TV had instructed everyone to stay indoors and to not leave their homes unless absolutely necessary. At least the power had remained on, and several local radio stations had stayed on the air, informing people where to go for food and emergency services.

"If the president announces the aliens have left," suggested Denise with hope in her eyes, "maybe that had been Kurt's fleet in orbit, and he drove off the invaders." She couldn't imagine her brother not returning, once he learned what had happened to Earth.

"We'll see," Alex said noncommittally, as he turned on the TV and sat down with Denise next to him on the couch. "Don't get your hopes up yet. We don't know if the aliens attacked Newton as well. Those flashes of lights could have even been two different alien fleets battling it out for control of Earth."

The TV came on, and the emergency broadcast emblem appeared with words scrolling across the screen, stating that the president would be making an announcement shortly.

"Do you want some coffee?" asked Denise, looking at her husband. They were fortunate that they had a well-stocked pantry. Alex was always teasing her for having so much food in the house. Denise disliked spending time at the supermarket, so, when she did go, she bought in volume. That way she wouldn't have to return anytime soon.

"Later," Alex said, squeezing Denise's hand. "Let's see what the president has to say."

"Is the TV coming on?" Bryan asked, his eyes growing wide, walking slowly with his drink in hand. "I want to watch cartoons!"

"Maybe later," Denise answered with a smile. "We have some of your favorite shows recorded, and, if you eat a good supper, we can watch one later."

"The one about the horse," announced Bryan, sitting down with his parents. "I like that one."

"Sure," Denise promised, as the emergency broadcast emblem suddenly vanished, and the president appeared on the screen. "Now be quiet, so Mommy and Daddy can hear the TV for a moment. Can you do that for me?"

Bryan nodded his head enthusiastically.

"People of the North American Union," President Mayfield began in a steady voice, "I come to you tonight with important news. Two weeks ago the answer to whether we are alone in the universe was answered. In a very decisive and aggressive manner. Alien ships appeared in our orbital space and launched an unprovoked attack against our orbiting spacecraft. Most of our ships were quickly destroyed, and only a few managed to escape." The president paused, as if making sure of his words.

"As we learned from one of our fleet's survivors, the aliens are called Profiteers. They're a race who raids planets, and strips them of their wealth and anything else of significant value. Once they secured the space around our planet, they issued demands, instructing us to gather up gold, platinum, jewels, and other valuables at specific sites to be picked up. When we refused to do so, they nuked a number of cities around the planet. In our own country, Chicago and Washington, DC, were lost. Civilian casualties from those two attacks are expected to reach ten to twelve million."

"So many people," Denise said, shaking her head. "It's difficult to imagine the horror of what it must be like living close to either one of those cities."

"And that's just in our country," Alex said with a heavy sigh. "Claude said he heard that Rome and Cairo were also nuked."

The president continued. "There have been unconfirmed rumors that a number of humans were taken away on some of the alien ships. As of this time, we have been unable to substantiate those reports."

"I hope that's not true—the aliens abducting people," continued Denise.

"The president said it wasn't confirmed," Alex reminded her. "Those rumors have been circulating for several days."

"Fortunately not all of our space fleet was destroyed in the original battle," President Mayfield continued. "A large task group was at Newton, undergoing special maneuvers. The light cruiser *Johnas* was heavily damaged in the battle above Earth but managed to escape into hyperspace, and so Captain Owens informed Admiral Kurt Vickers about what had transpired. Admiral Vickers returned to Earth a short time ago and destroyed part of the Profiteer fleet in Earth orbit, forcing the rest to withdraw."

"It *was* Kurt!" Denise said, her face lighting up. She leaned forward, closer to the TV, wanting to hear every word. "I knew it!"

"But how long will the aliens stay away?" questioned Alex, raising an eyebrow. "We don't know how big a fleet they might have."

"Is Uncle Kurt coming to see us?" asked Bryan.

Denise smiled. She knew how much Bryan liked his uncle. Uncle Kurt always brought him special gifts whenever he visited.

"We don't know," answered Denise. She hoped her older brother would find some way to send a message. "Be quiet and listen to the TV."

"I will shortly be contacting other world leaders to determine our future path of action during this time of uncertainty," Mayfield continued, his eyes looking directly into the camera. "I am ordering everyone to report to their jobs as normal tomorrow. We need to get the stores open and our economy running again. I am also ordering the military to ensure no looting or price gouging occurs during this emergency. People caught doing either will be severely prosecuted."

"We better fill up the vehicles with gas and stock up on groceries," uttered Alex, looking over at Denise for a long and thoughtful moment. "I'll also see about getting a portable generator for power. If the aliens come back, who knows what might happen."

"We should talk to Kurt," Denise replied. She was certain that her brother would be contacting her shortly.

"We will," Alex promised, as his gaze returned to the TV. "I'm sure he will better understand what's going on."

"Our world has suffered a great disaster in this attack and many lives have been lost," President Mayfield continued. His face took on a very serious and determined look. "As president of the North American Union, I promise to do everything in my power to protect our people and keep our planet safe. In the morning when you get up, take comfort in the fact that our space fleet is in orbit around Earth, ready to defend us if necessary. It may take a while, but our lives will return to normal, but we will never forget those who died such a violent death. I just want to ask each and every one of you to do your part to ensure that happens. As soon as we know more, I will give another address. Thank you for your time."

The TV switched to a message stating that normal programming would resume at 6:00 a.m.

"I guess that's all they're going to say," Alex said, leaning back on the sofa, deep in thought.

"So you think the aliens will come back?" asked Denise, putting her arm around Bryan and pulling him close.

"Let me go!" Bryan said, squirming away. "I want to go play."

"Go play in your room," suggested Denise, allowing their son to get up. "I'll check on you shortly."

"Then can we watch the horse movie?" asked Bryan, his eyes lighting up.

"Yes," Denise answered with a patient smile. "After supper we'll all come in here and watch the horses."

In a secret underground bunker deep beneath a mountain in southern Canada, President Mayfield looked around at his Cabinet. Not all the members had made it out of Washington, DC.

Mayfield had barely won the last election in a heated battle against his opponent. There had been a lot of mud-slinging, and it had left a bad taste within the political scene. Several new campaign laws had been passed to ensure that such activity didn't occur again. Mayfield sincerely hoped there would be future elections. It would indicate this threat from the Profiteers had been eliminated.

Since the USA, Canada, and Mexico had eliminated their borders and established the North American Union, no elected president had faced a threat such as the one Mayfield faced today. Some important decisions needed to be made, and some of them would be very difficult. He knew what they were about to do would probably anger several of his Cabinet members.

"What's the status of Admiral Vickers's fleet?" asked Mayfield, looking expectantly toward Fleet Admiral Tomalson.

"He has his battlecruiser, a light carrier, four light cruisers, and now five destroyers. One destroyer was lost in the brief battle fought in Earth orbit," replied Fleet Admiral Tomalson, glancing down at a sheet of paper on the conference table before him.

Tomalson was an older man, graying around the temples, verging on retirement, when he had been offered the esteemed Cabinet post.

"There are also a few destroyers based at Newton which he didn't bring."

"Can he keep these Profiteers from attacking Earth again?" asked Secretary of State Anne Roselin.

She had barely escaped Washington before the first nuke fell.

Fleet Admiral Tomalson let out a deep breath and looked around the small group of men and women. "No," he said with a deep sigh. "He caught them by surprise, and the new particle beam cannons were quite effective. His task force got several kills before the Profiteers could fully raise their shields. The admiral and I have a strong suspicion they'll be back and with a much larger fleet. When they do, Admiral Vickers will not be able to keep them from attacking Earth."

"But it's his job," grunted out Secretary of Labor Marlen Stroud. "That's why we allocated the funds to build the fleet."

A lot of heated arguments had occurred between Cabinet members about spending so much for a fleet of warships that might never be needed. Finally several other countries, including the European Union, had agreed to help foot the bill. Several ships with European personnel on board had been a part of the two fleets destroyed in Earth orbit.

"If we order him to stay and defend the planet, he will," replied Fleet Admiral Tomalson. "But to do so will be the end of his fleet and of any hope to free our planet in the future."

The room was silent, as everyone digested what Tomalson had just said. No one liked the implications.

"Then what do we do?" asked General Braid, the secretary of defense. "If we order our ground military units to fight, the Profiteers will just bomb them from orbit. The few units that tried to resist the original attack were annihilated by missile strikes. The same goes for any jet fighters we launch."

"We send Admiral Vickers back to Newton with as many people as we can possibly evacuate," answered Tomalson, leaning forward, his voice sounding determined. "We relocate off planet as many scientists, technicians, scholars, teachers, physicians, and whoever else we determine might be useful in the war effort. Perhaps, if given the necessary time to build a bigger fleet and more particle beam cannons, the admiral's fleet can return and drive the Profiteers from Earth permanently."

"What!" uttered Stroud, standing up and waving his fist at the fleet admiral. "We can't allow them to leave Earth orbit. They have to fight. It's their duty!"

"Then they will die, and where does that leave us?" asked Tomalson, his eyes narrowing sharply. "With no fleet, we will be powerless against these Profiteers."

"I agree with the fleet admiral," commented General Braid after a moment. "I understand the military situation, and now isn't the time to fight. We can't ask Admiral Vickers to sacrifice his fleet in a hopeless battle that leaves us defenseless before the aliens. Vickers's fleet is a valuable asset and must be preserved."

"But the Profiteers might not return," protested Stroud, looking around at the others for support. "Just having our fleet in orbit might be enough to keep them away."

"We managed to intercept a lot of their communications, while they were in Earth orbit," Secretary of Homeland Security Raul Gutierrez said. "They were boasting to each other about all the credits they would make from looting our world. They will be back, and they'll bring others with them. We're too big a prize for them to give up on."

"What else do we know about these Profiteers?" asked Mayfield, looking intently at the secretary of homeland security. The president had been briefed by Raul already, but he wanted the entire Cabinet to hear what the man had to say.

"They come from what they call the Gothan Empire," responded Raul, taking a deep breath. "We determined from the communication intercepts that it's a loose federation of nearly 120 star systems that routinely raid many of the civilized races of the galaxy."

"One hundred and twenty star systems," uttered Anne Roselin, shaking her head in amazement. "Just a few weeks ago we were wondering if we were alone in the galaxy."

"That question's been answered," commented Mayfield dryly. "What else do we know about them, Raul?"

"They do only a limited amount of raiding against the more civilized worlds," continued Raul. "They don't want to encourage any reprisals from the more powerful star systems. However, they are constantly seeking out new worlds in what they consider unexplored space. We just happened to be the latest one they found."

"What do they want?" asked Secretary of Energy Max Sallow.

"Rare minerals, jewels, platinum, art, and, strangely enough, gold," Raul replied.

"Gold!" echoed Secretary of the Treasury Dwight Michaels. "Why gold? The platinum they are asking for is more valuable, and our Moon is overflowing with it. Plus other lesser-known minerals are even more valuable, like black opals from Australia, red diamonds from Brazil, the bixbite from Utah."

"As hard as it is to believe, the galaxy at large uses a form of money called *credits*, and it's based on the value of gold," Raul said, his dark eyes focusing on Dwight.

"Reports confirm several thousand people being abducted and taken to some of the ships, which left immediately after the original attack," Mayfield said, looking at Raul with raised eyebrows. "Any idea as to why they took those people?" He had tried to downplay those rumors in his broadcast so as not to alarm the civilian population.

"Yes," Raul answered, not looking too happy about what he was getting ready to say. "Evidently there is a market for slaves on many of the worlds in the galaxy, including some of the more civilized ones. The slaves are used for simple household jobs and others for more dangerous work. It's a very lucrative market."

"Slaves!" retorted Stroud with a deep frown. "Are you certain of that?"

"Yes," Raul replied with a slight nod of his head. "In one of the star systems of the Gothan Empire is a planet called Kubitz, where the slaves are sold. The planet also operates a huge black market. Supposedly nearly anything you can imagine is for sale on this world."

A moment of silence prevailed. President Mayfield studied his trusted group of advisors. He knew that several of them would like to see Admiral Vickers's fleet stay in orbit and defend the planet. However, to do so might doom Earth to be plundered for generations by these Profiteers. Mayfield couldn't allow this, not if there was another option. This was one of those difficult decisions that had to be made and would be highly unpopular, even with some of his Cabinet.

"We need to look at what sites we can make secure from enemy detection," he announced. "We need to have elite military units ready to attack targets of opportunity once the Profiteers return."

"You're sending away the fleet," croaked Marlen Stroud, his face turning livid. "You can't do that! I can't believe you would leave our planet defenseless."

"We have no choice," Mayfield answered in a firm voice. "That fleet's the only hope we have for a future."

"Our remaining fleet has to be preserved," Tomalson said with General Braid nodding his head in agreement.

Stroud leaned back in his chair with his shoulders drooping. He looked at the president, then sighed heavily. When his gaze fell on Fleet Admiral Tomalson and General Braid, he just shrugged.

"Fleet Admiral Tomalson, make immediate arrangements to get key people off Earth," ordered President Mayfield. "Get me a report as soon as possible of everything Admiral Vickers might need to make his job easier. Now let's discuss what other measures to take before these Profiteers return."

"Newton only has eight million people," muttered Stroud, shaking his head. "What can eight million people do against a star empire?"

"Give us hope," Mayfield answered without hesitation. "They can give our entire world hope for a future."

Stroud slowly shook his head in dismay.

Denise had just put Bryan to bed and returned to the kitchen to prepare coffee for her and Alex. Something about the smell of hot coffee helped her to relax.

"Is he asleep?" asked Alex, walking up behind Denise and putting his arms around her. They had been married for eight years, and it had been the best time of his life.

"Finally," Denise said, wriggling from Alex's arms so she could pour both of them a cup of coffee. "He's so excited about the possibility of Kurt coming to see him."

"Your brother might not be able to," replied Alex, reaching for his cup and taking a cautious sip. "Maybe he can't leave his ship with the crisis we're currently in."

"I know." Denise sighed, holding her cup with both hands, allowing it to cool. "This entire situation with these aliens scares me. I don't know what we'll do if they come back."

"Claude said some people were taken in a suburb on the eastern side of the city," Alex informed her. "He claims a handful of small ships came down, and the aliens rounded up several hundred people, taking those people with them."

"I'm sure that's just a rumor. Why would they be here in Houston?" Denise replied with a slight shiver. "Why would they want any of our people? The president said it was just a rumor."

"Supposedly a lot of people in this suburb work at the space complex. They took men, women, and even children. I also don't think the president's telling us everything. The rumor about the aliens abducting people really worries me."

Before Denise could say anything else, her cell rang. Phone service had been erratic the past few weeks since the alien attack, and she looked at her phone in surprise. She reached over to the counter and picked it up.

"Hello?" she said hesitantly. Then her face brightened as she recognized the voice. "It's Kurt!" She listened for nearly a minute without saying anything, her face taking on a very intense look. "Are you sure? When? What can we take? Just a minute, let me tell Alex." She looked over at Alex with a concerned and troubled expression on her face.

"Kurt says we need to evacuate."

"Evacuate!" uttered Alex, looking confused. "Where to?"

"Newton," replied Denise in a soft voice. "He says the aliens will be back, and, when they come, his fleet will probably have to withdraw. He's in the process of making arrangements to evacuate the families of the crews in his fleet as well as some others."

Alex looked stunned as he considered this. "How soon?"

"In the next day or two."

It didn't take Alex long to decide. "Tell him we'll be ready."

If Kurt didn't feel they would be safe on Earth, then it implied that things were a lot worse than they had been led to believe. It also sounded as if Kurt felt the aliens would be in control of the planet for quite some time once they returned.

Denise spent another few minutes speaking to Kurt and then turned off her phone, laying it on the kitchen counter. "We can take some clothes and a few other essentials," she told Alex. "He says to pack light, as we can get what we'll need at Newton."

Alex let out a deep breath. He looked around the kitchen. "What will happen to all we're leaving behind? Yeah, our house is modest, but it's nearly paid for. And our jobs. Good, well-paying jobs. But you and Bryan, your safety concerns me the most. ... And we should stay together as a family."

He stroked Denise's hair. "We'll tell Bryan that we're going on vacation," Alex said, pursing his lips. "I suspect he'll be excited at the idea of traveling in space and flying to another planet."

"What about your parents?"

Alex looked at Denise and then spoke. "Mom and Dad have a cabin up in the mountains. I'll call them and suggest they go there. It's in a pretty isolated area, so they should be safe. They're friends with several neighbors up there, so they won't be completely alone."

Denise looked over at one of the kitchen walls covered with family photos. "It will be hard to leave so many memories behind, but I'll pack in the morning. Kurt said he would send a shuttle to pick us up the day after tomorrow."

She wondered what pictures she should take and what life would be like on the new world. When she woke up this morning, going into space never entered her mind; now they were preparing to leave everything behind and go to Newton. She just hoped they were making the right decision. However, she trusted her brother, and, if he said they needed to leave, then that was what they would do.

Chapter Three

Admiral Kurt Vickers stood in Earth's shipyard next to Fleet Admiral Tomalson. In the main construction bay, the new 1,200-meter-long heavy battlecarrier *Kepler* was covered with framework. Flashes from numerous welders constantly lit up the bay, as frantic workers attempted to finish welding the last few plates of hull armor on the massive ship. Every available worker was inside and outside this one vessel, bringing online as many systems as possible. The main cargo hatches stood open with a constant flow of material and supplies passing through. Officers and construction supervisors could be heard shouting orders and instructions to the hundreds of people in the bay.

"Is she flight-ready?" asked Kurt, turning to the older fleet admiral. The *Kepler* by herself could almost double the firepower of his fleet.

"She will be in seventy-two hours," Tomalson answered with a nod. "We're fortunate that the shipyard crew was left unharmed. From what Colonel Hayworth told me, the Profiteers were interested in having the *Kepler* completed for their own use. In the two weeks the aliens were here, they kept a small security force on the shipyard and kept the crew working on that ship."

"What happened to that security force?" asked Kurt, wondering if some of them had been captured. They could be a treasure trove of valuable information.

"There were twenty of them altogether," Tomalson replied, his eyes narrowing sharply. "Twelve of them were killed when the station crew realized your fleet had returned and was attacking the Profiteer ships. The other eight, while banged up pretty good, are in the brig, awaiting questioning."

"What about the *Kepler*?"

"She's going with you when you leave," the fleet admiral answered. "Still needs a lot of inside cosmetic work, but most of her weapons, the sublight drive, and the hyperdrive are operational. We'll fill the cargo holds and her two flight bays with most of what's needed to finish her. In addition, we're loading two large cargo ships with missiles and other munitions your fleet might need."

"What about her energy shield?" Kurt asked. Even from here, he could see a lot of the small antennae like emitters that powered the shield were missing.

"Not operational," Tomalson admitted with a grimace. "Take the *Kepler* back to Newton. The station there can finish the ship. Most of the shipyard's crew will be transferring to Newton as well to give you a trained force of ship-construction people. We're also in the process of bringing the rest of the *Kepler*'s crew up from Earth. Only about half of them have been trained and have any actual space experience."

"Newbies," grumbled Kurt with a sigh. They would have to learn quickly if they were to fight a war.

"There are also two light cruisers in the other bays," Tomalson continued. "The *Dallas* and the *Birmingham* were being updated with new sensors and particle cannons when the attack commenced. The majority of their crews were on leave, and we're in the process of recalling them. Colonel Hayworth feels he can have both cruisers ready in four more days."

"The *Kepler* and the two light cruisers will greatly enhance the fleet," Kurt said, looking over at the older admiral. "What about the bombers and the fighters?"

"Done," responded Tomalson, with a half-hearted smile. "Only problem is that most of them are still in their assembly crates, and the pilots need a lot of training."

"What about the fighters and bombers based on this shipyard?" Kurt knew there were two fighter squadrons and one bomber squadron permanently assigned to the station.

"They'll be going with you also. We'll cram them into the *Vindication*'s bay. Captain Watkins won't be able to launch anything until they're unloaded. Of course that will give you a group of well-trained pilots for those three squadrons."

"They can help train the newbies," responded Kurt, thinking about how to get the new pilots up to speed as rapidly as possible.

"We'll also be sending the fighter and bomber construction facilities along with you. We can have everything disassembled in two weeks and loaded aboard four cargo ships."

"Where will we put them?" asked Kurt, recalling how the station above Newton was set up. It was large, but there wasn't much room to add anything else, let alone new construction facilities.

"We'll have to enlarge Newton Station," Tomalson answered. "We already have a team of engineers designing a new addition. We'll add a new construction bay, a large manufacturing assembly area, and a new flight bay for fighters and bombers. There were some discussions about disassembling part of this station and shipping it to Newton. It would be the quickest and easiest way to get what we need. We're just not sure we'll have the time to do it."

"We would have to dedicate a lot of cargo ships to move everything," Kurt said, as he looked around the massive bay.

"We have two heavy tugs, equipped with hyperdrives, which could drag the sections along with them," Tomalson responded.

It was one of the options they had been discussing and the easiest. All they would have to do was basically carve up the shipyard into manageable pieces and allow the tugs to haul them through hyperspace to Newton. Once at Newton, the sections could be reassembled. They would need to decide on the tug idea in the next day or two.

After discussing a few other items, Kurt and Tomalson left the construction bay and took a turbolift to the station's Command Center. Going inside, they saw Colonel Hayworth, who was in charge of ship construction, speaking animatedly to several junior officers.

"Is there a problem?" asked Tomalson. He could tell Hayworth was highly excited about something.

"I just learned we may have another ship we can recover," responded Hayworth, turning from the two officers, who quickly went back to their posts. "Lieutenant Haley informed me that the light carrier *Dante* has been located and may be salvageable."

"Where is she?" Kurt asked with interest. If they could save her, it would augment his force even more, allowing him to launch a powerful contingent of fighters and bombers. The Dante had been crewed by fleet personnel from the UK.

"On the far side of the planet," Hayworth answered. "We should have a video feed coming in shortly. I've dispatched a fleet tug to the area to see if it's practical to bring the ship to the shipyard."

Tomalson nodded. For the last twenty-four hours, they had been checking all the wrecks in orbit to see if anything could be repaired or salvaged. Most of the ships had been blown apart. Only a few had been found with the hulls relatively intact but were so heavily damaged from internal explosions that even boarding them had been considered too hazardous.

"Video feed is coming in," reported Ensign Paul Simmons from Communications. "I'm putting it up on the main viewscreen."

Everyone looked toward the screen as it flickered to life, and then an image of the battered light carrier appeared. The ship had been hit by some heavy weapons fire, as the hull was badly compromised in several areas.

"The tug captain is reporting no indications of power from the ship," Simmons added. "He's also reporting several airlocks are open."

"Do you think the aliens removed the crew?" asked Kurt, looking intently at the viewscreen. The main airlock hatch stood wide open. He had been briefed earlier about the possible abductions.

"Possibly," Tomalson responded with a heavy frown. "From reports we've received across the planet, we know the Profiteers took several thousand people. They may have taken this crew as well."

"Where to?"

"We believe they'll be sold as slaves on a world called Kubitz," Tomalson answered. "We picked up a lot of their ship communications and managed to decipher their language pretty quickly. The Profiteers didn't seem too concerned about attempting to encrypt what they were saying."

This greatly concerned Kurt. The last time he had checked, Captain Randson hadn't been able to locate his wife and daughter. Plus there were rumors that the aliens had abducted people from the vicinity where Randson's home was.

"Passenger liners are preparing to depart," reported Lieutenant Vargas.

Another screen came to life, displaying four small space liners and two much larger superliners. The small liners could carry five hundred people each while the superliners could hold 2,200.

"The destroyers *Titan* and *Phobos* will be escorting them from Earth and back to Newton," Kurt said.

The plans were for the ships to stay long enough to unload and then return to pick up more evacuees. Also two more small liners and one more superliner were in transit from Newton with a destroyer escort. Denise, Alex, and Bryan were scheduled to ride on one of those. Kurt would feel better once his sister and her family were safely off Earth. He had sensed the fear in her voice when he had spoken to her.

"The cargo ships are still being loaded with supplies and should be ready shortly for their first trip to Newton," Tomalson added, as he watched the liners grow smaller on the screen.

The two destroyers join up with them, and Kurt knew they would shortly be activating their hyperspace drives. A number of cargo ships were located on a dozen small spaceports across the planet. They were rapidly being loaded with surplus supplies and other items that Newton might need, once all trade with Earth was cut off. Other cargo ships would be sent to Mars and the moons of Jupiter and Saturn.

"How much time do you think we have?" asked Colonel Hayworth, as the ships suddenly vanished from the viewscreen, making their jumps into hyperspace.

"Ships have successfully jumped," confirmed Lieutenant Haley. She had a relieved look on her face.

"It's hard to tell," Tomalson replied, "since we're uncertain where their planet is."

Kurt studied the viewscreen to see the tug move in closer to the *Dante*. He knew the tug would latch onto the ship with magnetic grapples and then bring the ship back to the shipyard to be further evaluated.

"The analysts I've spoken to," Tomalson added, "feel pretty certain that the Profiteers will regroup at their home world and then return with a larger and better armed fleet."

"I wonder how much bigger?" Kurt said with a frown.

He didn't want his ships to be caught in orbit like the Profiteers had done to the Earth fleets to begin with. The only difference was, his ships were keeping their energy screens up at low power as a precautionary measure and were staying at a higher level of alert. It wouldn't be so easy to catch his fleet unprepared, especially now that they knew what was coming.

"We'll know more when we finish interrogating the prisoners," Tomalson answered. "That will start later today."

Kurt nodded. He needed to get back to the *Star Cross* and arrange for more munitions, particularly missiles, to be transferred to all his ships. They hadn't fired any during the brief battle, but that didn't mean they wouldn't be needed later.

Entering the Command Center of the *Star Cross*, Kurt saw Captain Randson sitting in his command chair with a look of deep concern on his face.

"Still no luck contacting Emily?"

"No," Andrew answered grimly. "I did manage to reach Emily's parents, and they haven't heard from her either."

"Here are the latest status reports, as requested, sir," Lieutenant Mays said, handing Kurt a small computer pad. "It lists the current ammunition levels, plus supplies for all the ships in the fleet."

Kurt nodded. "Make sure we requisition everything we might need for a long deployment."

"Already working on it, sir," Mays replied, as she turned and went back to her console.

"There have been rumors that these Profiteers abducted some people in the Houston area," Andrew continued with a hint of fear showing in his eyes. "Do you think it's possible that Emily and Alexis were taken?"

"Fleet Admiral Tomalson is still working on getting more information about any missing humans," responded Kurt, knowing how concerned Andrew must be. "If these aliens did take Emily and Alexis, I promise you that I'll do everything in my power to get them back."

"Sir, the tug is approaching with the *Dante*," reported Lieutenant Lena Brooks.

"Put it up on the screen."

The *Dante* appeared with the tug's magnetic grapples holding the ship.

"She's been hit hard," pointed out Andrew. "It looks as if Engineering is open to space, as well as the starboard munitions bunker. From the size of the hole, I would guess there was a major explosion. See how the hull is peeled back, as if an explosion occurred inside the ship?"

Kurt nodded in agreement. The six-hundred-meter-long light carrier had been badly damaged. They wouldn't know if the ship could be repaired until the shipyard personnel took a closer look. However, before that could happen, some technicians would have to board it to ensure it was safe to bring into the shipyard.

"We can't stay at a high level of alert continuously," Kurt said, looking over at Andrew. Ever since their arrival, the fleet had been at Condition Two. "Have the *Vindication* and the light cruisers *Alton*, *Blair*, and *Sydney* stay at Condition Two with energy shields at 50 percent. The rest of the fleet will go to Condition

Three, so the crews can get some rest. After twelve hours, we'll switch, and the carrier and the three cruisers can go to Condition Three while the rest of us take their place at Condition Two."

"What about the destroyers?" Randson asked.

Kurt nodded. With the one that had been destroyed and the two that had just left with the passenger liners for Newton, that left three more, still here orbiting Earth.

"We'll pull them in close to the shipyard, in case they're needed to help defend it," replied Kurt, rubbing his brow with his right hand as he thought over what still needed to be done. "We'll need the three to escort more passenger liners and cargo ships to Newton. We may have to send just one destroyer with each convoy."

"How long will we continue evacuating people from Earth?"

"Until the Profiteers come back," responded Kurt evenly. They had a tremendous job ahead of them and probably not enough time to get it done.

Ever since they had driven the enemy from Earth orbit, Mars, the asteroid mining settlements, and the colonies on the moons of Jupiter and Saturn had been screaming for evacuation. The colonists on the Moon were already further securing their underground cities. Though Kurt didn't know what good it would do them. If the Profiteers wanted to destroy any of the settlements or colonies in the system, one well-placed missile would do the job.

"Admiral, what is Fleet Admiral Tomalson going to do? Is he returning to Newton with us?"

"I don't know," answered Kurt with a sigh. "We haven't discussed that yet."

"What will we do when the Profiteers do return? Will we fight or jump straight out?" Andrew asked.

Kurt knew Andrew was trying his best not to worry about his wife and daughter.

"We'll leave," answered Kurt somberly. "We can't afford to take any more losses to the fleet. If we get the *Kepler* back to

Newton and finished, and the *Dante* repaired, we'll have a pretty solid fleet. Two more light cruisers in the shipyard were undergoing updates when the Profiteers attacked. We can add both of them to the fleet in another four days."

"Don't forget the *Johnas*," added Randson. "She's in the repair bay at Newton now." He faced Kurt. "We're putting together a pretty powerful task force."

"I know Captain Owens will be glad to get his ship back."

"Admiral, we have several cargo ships coming up from Earth," Ensign Pierce reported. "They're asking where you want them."

"Put them in orbit at ten thousand kilometers above the planet," Kurt ordered. "We'll have one of the light cruisers move over to cover them, until the convoy is ready to depart."

"And when will that be?" asked Randson.

"I want a convoy leaving every seventy-two hours," Kurt replied. "We need to get those ships to Newton and unload them, so they can return. We'll send one destroyer along with each convoy." It was a two-day trip to Newton with one day to unload, check ship systems, and then return. That would be five days for a complete turnaround.

Looking at the main viewscreen, he could see several shuttles docking with the *Dante*. The shuttles would carry suited-up technicians to check the light carrier. Leaning back in his command chair, Kurt knew a lot of work needed to be done in the next few days, if the human race wanted to stand any chance at all of prevailing against the Profiteers.

In the underground presidential bunker in Canada, an argument ensued.

"Why are my people being denied access to the ships going to Newton?" demanded Stroud with a dark scowl on his face. "No one I've suggested has been approved."

"I'm sure it's only a misunderstanding," answered Anne Roselin, attempting to placate the angry secretary of labor.

"No, it's not," Fleet Admiral Tomalson said in a loud and commanding voice. "No one you've suggested will benefit the Newton colony or the war effort against these Profiteers." Tomalson decided to put Stroud in his place once and for all. He had never cared for the obnoxious man and didn't understand why President Mayfield had appointed him to the Cabinet. "All your people have been either big donors to your political campaigns or rich people who don't know anything else but having others wait on them hand and foot. I will not allow any such people on one of the evacuation ships."

Stroud stood up, shaking a fist at Tomalson. "You have no right!" he bellowed. "I will have you removed from office. I demand your immediate resignation!"

Tomalson looked at Stroud and then did the unthinkable. He burst out laughing. "You and whose army? I control the fleet crews, and every one of those men and women are fiercely loyal. Everyone going aloft has their background thoroughly checked. Anyone not well qualified and not approved by my people will not be leaving Earth."

"That's easy enough for you to say," growled Stroud, looking around at the others for support. "Your ass won't be here when the aliens return. We will!"

"I'm afraid you're mistaken," President Mayfield said in a calm voice. "Fleet Admiral Tomalson will remain behind on Earth and will turn full control of the fleet over to Admiral Vickers. I also helped Fleet Admiral Tomalson set up the vetting process for those traveling to Newton. Only our best and brightest will be offered positions on the liners and cargo ships."

"Why aren't you going?" asked Roselin, looking with confusion at Tomalson. "Why remain on Earth when you can possibly be safe on Newton?"

"I'm too old," Tomalson replied. "I would serve no useful purpose on Newton. Admiral Vickers is younger and a very good strategist. Upon his departure, he will be promoted to fleet admiral."

President Mayfield added, "I've spoken to the leaders of the European Union, plus the Russian Collective and the Chinese Conglomerate. They all do some trading with Newton, and both the European Union and the Russian Collective have agreed to send additional supplies and people to the colony."

"Why would they do that? Stroud demanded, confused. "My people can't go, but the Europeans and the Russians can?"

The European Union along with Australia and Japan had placed colonies on Mars, while the Russian Collective had taken the moons of Jupiter and the Chinese Conglomerate the moons of Saturn. Only the North American Union had elected to colonize a planet outside the Solar System.

"They realize that, if they ever want access to their colonies again, it will be up to Admiral Vickers and the people of Newton to free the Solar System from the Profiteers," Mayfield responded. "They're also sending additional supplies to all their colonies and evacuating some of the smaller ones that might not survive, if they're cut off too long."

"What about that special help we asked for?" Fleet Admiral Tomalson asked.

"They all agreed to your plan to significantly improve Newton's ability to defend itself and to help Earth," Mayfield replied. "The Chinese Conglomerate balked at first, but I finally made them understand why they should cooperate. Their donation will be going into orbit within the week."

"What are the two of you talking about?" demanded Stroud. "Sounds as if some deals have been made without the full knowledge and approval of the Cabinet."

"It's necessary that these particular arrangements remain classified for the time being," Mayfield responded without hesitation. "I will reveal to the entire Cabinet what we're doing when the time is right."

"I don't like this," mumbled Stroud.

"Neither do I," agreed Max Sallow, Secretary of Energy. "What you're proposing may be illegal, according to the Constitution of the North American Union."

"We may be facing a major crisis, but we have a Constitution for a reason, and we should abide by it," Attorney General Maureen Roberts said with some concern in her voice.

"I realize that, Maureen," Mayfield replied. "But this is an international emergency, and, as president of the NAU, I have broad and liberal powers during such times. That is also clearly spelled out in our Constitution. I can assure you that what I'm doing is in the best interest of our planet."

"What about in the best interest of the North American Union?" demanded Stroud. "My business associates are deeply concerned about the present situation. Their profit margins are way down and, in some instances, showing negative returns on investments."

Ignoring Stroud, Mayfield gazed at his Cabinet members, most of whom he had known for years. "In a few weeks I will fully brief the Cabinet."

-

Stroud sat down, not pleased with all he had heard. There had to be some way he could get his people on one of those evacuating ships. He had promised his wife that the two of them would shortly go to Newton, where he would have a very big say in the governing of the colony. They had already packed up many of their more expensive belongings and chosen several servants to accompany them.

-

Two days later Fleet Admiral Tomalson, as well as Secretary of Defense General Braid, met Admiral Vickers aboard a large cargo ship docked at Earth's shipyard. Four heavily armed Marines guarded the hatch they were approaching.

"What's the firepower for?" asked Kurt, as the Marines allowed them to enter. He wondered what could be so valuable on this cargo ship to require such extreme measures. He had also passed another full squad of Marines in the outside corridor of the shipyard.

"We finished interrogating our prisoners," replied Tomalson, gesturing for Kurt to follow him and the general.

"Most refused to talk, but a few, with the right encouragement, gave up a lot of information."

"So what are we up against?" They had stopped at another locked hatch.

"It's bad," answered General Braid, shaking his head. "The name *Profiteers* means exactly as it sounds. This particular race, who attacked us, is from the planet Marsten in the Golite System. For a lack of a better word, it serves as the capital for this Gothan Empire of Profiteers."

Tomalson nodded. "One of our captives believes that their High Profiteer will return to either Marsten or Kubitz and hire a group of mercenaries to destroy our fleet," Tomalson said. "From what we've been able to gather from our interrogations, some Profiteers become mercenaries and hire themselves out to the highest bidder or, in our case, for a very lucrative payment."

"A payment that will be made in gold, platinum, and jewels primarily," added General Braid, as he keyed in a code on a door pad. Several locks could be heard disengaging, and the hatch swung open.

All three of the men stepped inside, and Kurt froze as he looked around in amazement. "You have got to be kidding me." The room was full of pallets of gold bars all secured to the floor. Kurt walked over to the nearest stack and gazed in awe at the wealth it represented. "Where … ?" He stepped closer and touched one of the bars. He let out a deep breath; this was the stuff that dreams were made of. "Why?" he asked, turning around to face the two older officers.

"When you return to Newton, you will have a new mission," explained Tomalson. "From what our prisoners have told us, almost anything anyone may want is available for sale on the planet Kubitz. It has a massive interplanetary black market and the largest slave market in our section of the galaxy."

"The people who were taken from Earth," Kurt began, as his mind worked, "could they be there?"

"Probably," General Braid answered. "From what our prisoners said, the captives will be trained for three or four months on the planet Kubitz to increase their worth in the slave auction. They will be sold there—to people and representatives from planets near and far—as household servants, general laborers, and even to brothels."

"You're going to Kubitz with the *Star Cross* and buy our people back," Tomalson said.

"That won't be easy to accomplish," Kurt said, his eyes narrowing. "We don't speak their language, understand their culture, have knowledge of the planet … Hard to plan for our safety and the captives' protection with such disadvantages."

"We will not allow our people to be sold into slavery," Tomalson said in a very determined voice.

"I agree. I'm thinking strategy out loud here," Kurt replied with a nod. "But once the Profiteers return, won't they just send more humans to Kubitz to be sold as slaves?"

"Most likely," Braid responded. "But going to Kubitz to buy back our people is only a cover. From what our prisoners say, it's quite common for representatives from other worlds to show up at Kubitz to buy back their people who have been taken captive. It seems as if the Profiteer race as a whole hijacks cargo ships and passenger liners from some of the more civilized worlds on a pretty routine basis."

"Why do these civilized worlds tolerate this pirate activity?" asked Kurt, with a deep frown. "Why don't they put an end to these Profiteers?"

"Too costly," Tomalson explained. "The commercial price of dealing with the Profiteers is far less than fighting a war with them. The Gothan Empire is careful not to overstep their raiding, lest they give the civilized worlds a sufficient reason to retaliate."

"So what other reason is there for me to travel to Kubitz?" Kurt asked, still eyeing the shiny bars stacked everywhere. He knew he was looking at billions of dollars in gold.

"To procure an orbital defensive weapons system," Tomalson said, his eyes focusing sharply on Kurt. "Most of the civilized worlds have such systems, as well as Marsten and

Kubitz. It keeps their worlds safe from attacks or makes such attacks so costly as to render them impractical. We want one."

"Just one?" Kurt asked.

"Yes. Put it around Newton," answered Tomalson. "Once Newton is secure you can begin to concentrate on making it too expensive for these Profiteers to remain in the Solar System. We want you to take a page from their book. Turn your fleet into raiders, and take their ships and convoys leaving our Earth. If we can get the Profiteers to withdraw, perhaps we can eventually install such a defense system around Earth also."

"So why would they sell us something that cuts into their profits? And what's to stop them from destroying my fleet when we fly into their den and selling me and my crew as slaves? Do you really think the Profiteers will allow us to walk away, once we've paid the ransom for our people? Plus, how do we know we can trust anything those prisoners told you? I need to see a map of Kubitz, if that's even possible. Otherwise how are we going to find our way safely around that foreign planet that we didn't even know existed two weeks ago?" asked Kurt, seeing a number of serious holes in the general's and fleet admiral's plan. What they were asking sounded nearly impossible.

"With this," General Braid said. He opened another door, and the three men stepped inside. Two more heavily armed Marines stood next to the wall, keeping a close watch on the third individual in the room.

Kurt came to a stop, as he stared open mouthed at his first alien. He was humanlike in that he had two feet, coarse white hair on his head, but with larger eyes, and his skin was a light blue color. He sat tall in the chair, which make Kurt think he'd be taller than most humans when standing

"This is Grantz," General Braid said, gesturing toward the alien.

The alien looked toward the three men and placed both his hands on the table he sat behind. On the table were two bars of gold. He reached out and rubbed his hands over the gold and smiled. "So you want to know about Kubitz?" he asked in a guttural-sounding voice.

"That's our agreement," responded General Braid. "Two gold bars now and two more when the mission is complete."

Grantz looked down at the gold on the table, his hands still touching it. Kurt could almost see the greed in the Profiteer's eyes at the thought of what that much gold could buy.

"Four when the mission is complete, and I promise not to betray you to my people. I will act as a member of your ship's company, until we agree that I have met my contract."

"Contract?" asked Kurt, looking even more confused. Had they actually bribed one of the aliens to betray his own people?

"Yes," muttered Fleet Admiral Tomalson unhappily. "There will be a signed contract by all parties. We will have a copy, and Grantz will have a copy. From what I understand, if he violates the contract, and we file a complaint on Kubitz with a Controller, he will be banned from doing any Profiteering for the rest of his life."

"It is our way," Grantz explained.

Kurt nodded; he wondered how he would explain this latest addition to his human crew. He felt a headache coming on, as he realized that his life had suddenly become even more complicated.

Chapter Four

High Profiteer Creed gazed in aggravation at the main viewscreen, which showed a massive cylinder-shaped ship with a flaring bow and a flared rear area that housed the warship's powerful engines. The ship belonged to the Dacroni, a mercenary clan from the heavy-gravity world of Dacron Four. The ship was 1,100 hundred meters in length and 220 meters in diameter, except for the two flared sections that added another 100 meters in width at the fore and aft of the ship. It was covered with energy projectors and hatches, which hid hypermissile tubes. The imposing vessel was a battleship—one of the most powerful ships in the Gothan Empire.

"Clan Leader Jarls will be aboard shortly," Second Profiteer Lantz reported with a scowl on his face. "To hire this Dacroni clan will cost a fortune!"

Creed knew Lantz didn't like doing business with mercenaries; it was always very expensive. Creed agreed on both accounts.

"Fortunately we have the credits, due to what we took from the human world," responded Creed, dismissing Lantz's comment. "We lost a number of valuable ships and control of Earth. We must rectify that situation immediately. We'll hire this Dacroni clan to clear the space in the humans' system and to remain there on guard duty for ninety days. During that time, we will plunder enough riches off the planet to enrich every member of our crews. We also have some debts on Kubitz that need to be paid off, before we're branded as unwanted."

"The humans we brought back to sell should satisfy those debts," Lantz grunted out.

The credits they had borrowed on Kubitz had updated several of their warships, including the *Ascendant Destruction*, and the charges had been outrageous. However, the shipyards above Kubitz were the best in the empire.

"Yes," High Profiteer Creed responded with a slight nod of his head. "The humans should bring a good price, particularly the females. The pleasure houses will buy many of them. But we also need to replace the warships and crews we lost, and that'll be a heavy cost." Creed knew it would take a major portion of the gold, platinum, and jewels they had taken from Earth to bring his fleet up to full strength and hire the mercenaries.

"Three battlecruisers and six escorts," groaned Lantz.

Yes, Creed was also concerned about the costs, not just to replace the ships. The families of the lost crews would have to be paid their share of the bounty brought back, plus sign-on bonuses were necessary for the replacement crews to override their fear of death. In all it would be very expensive but necessary.

"A drop in the bucket if we can spend ninety days gleaning all the treasures on Earth." Creed spoke with a light now in his large eyes, strongly suspecting they had only touched a smidgen of the gold and other treasures available on that planet. "We can pay for a new fleet, larger and far more powerful than our current one, and still have a huge reserve of credits for future expenditures. We'll never have to worry about the Kubitz Controllers again."

"Our cargo ships and slave detainee ships are in orbit, waiting further orders," Third Profiteer Bixt reported from his sensor console.

The ships had arrived a few days ago, before Creed and his fleet's return to the planet. On the ship's main sensor screen, hundreds of icons were visible, representing the massive amount of vessels in orbit around the planet Kubitz. Some were other raiders, like the *Ascendant Destruction*, while some were passenger ships and cargo vessels.

"We need to repair our battle damage and then return to the human system," Creed announced. The holds of several of his ships were packed with gold, and he was anxious to return for more. That precious yellow metal meant financial freedom for his fleet.

"Clan Leader Jarls has come aboard," reported Third Profiteer Lukon from Communications.

"Excellent," Creed said, pleased that the Dacroni mercenary leader had accepted Creed's invitation to meet. "Have him escorted to the main briefing room on the command deck."

"He'll be expensive," reiterated Lantz, shaking his head. "Hiring these mercenaries will cut into the profits from this trip."

"But they're the best," Creed answered. Fortunately they had taken more than one thousand gold bars from several underground vaults on the human planet. He took a deep fortifying breath, as he strolled purposely from the Command Center to meet Clan Leader Jarls.

A few moments later Jarls was escorted into the briefing room. His humanoid form—with his bulky legs, torso, and arms—were the result of living on a heavy-gravity world, and his powerful muscles were evident in his every step. His face was similar to a human's but rounder and chunkier. Even his neck seemed to be shorter and thicker, with his head almost resting on his torso.

"Greetings, Clan Leader Jarls." High Profiteer Creed gestured for the Dacronian to have a seat.

Jarls's eyes lit up seeing the four bars of gold stacked prominently on the conference table directly in front of him. Creed probably thought the presence of the yellow gold bars would serve as a distraction during their meeting, to get every advantage possible.

"Greetings, High Profiteer Creed," Jarls replied, his eyes never leaving the gold. "I have heard that you need assistance in dealing with a rebellious alien race you've discovered."

"Yes," replied Creed.

The Dacronians had a reputation for garnering these contracts, even though their fees were exorbitant. Jarls knew of Creed's need for his powerful Draconian ships. Rumors of what had happened to Creed's fleet were already flying around Marsten and Kubitz.

"We've discovered a rich world to plunder in one of the backwater regions of unexplored space," began Creed, keeping his voice calm. "We thought we had eliminated their primitive space fleet, but another fleet we knew nothing about jumped in. My fleet was unprepared for such an unexpected attack, and we lost a number of ships before we could raise our shields."

"I don't believe they're quite as primitive as you suggest, if they could take out some of your ships," Jarls replied with a crafty look in his eyes. "I heard what happened to your fleet in the human system."

He had done his research prior to coming over to the *Ascendant Destruction*. His people had bribed several crewmembers of the Marsten ships in order to get them to reveal what had happened. The humans did to High Profiteer Creed exactly what Jarls would have done to them. A mercenary fleet would never have let their guard down, like Creed had.

Creed remained silent.

"Particle weapons and KEW batteries," Jarls said in a matter-of-fact voice. "Hyperdrives and energy shields. I don't know if I would call them primitive."

"But KEW weapons," protested Creed, shaking his head. "No one uses them anymore!"

"Perhaps not," replied Jarls, reaching out and touching one of the tantalizing gold bars. He ran his fingers across the metal thinking about what he could buy with several of these. "But a ship without an energy shield can easily be destroyed by the type of KEW batteries the humans used. They're a very effective weapon in the right situation, as I'm sure you recently learned. They're also extremely inexpensive to operate."

Jarls picked up one of the gold bars and knew from its weight that it was real and worth about 1.2 million credits. Credits were the universal currency used throughout the known galaxy. A fully armed battlecruiser cost around ten to twelve million credits. A battleship, like the ones he possessed, would cost around fifteen to twenty million.

"I would like to hire your battleships to remove the threat of the human warships and to ensure that the human system stays under my control for at least ninety days," Creed said.

"You wish us to remove a fleet that will undoubtedly be expecting an attack," Jarls began, as he added up the cost in his head. "After the human fleet has been destroyed or driven off, we then need to hold the system for an additional ninety days, while you strip the human planet of its wealth."

"Yes," Creed said in a low voice.

"One hundred million credits up front and 10 percent of what you remove from the planet in those ninety days," Jarls said, as he picked up a second gold bar with his other hand.

"One hundred million credits and 10 percent!" roared Creed, standing up in anger. "That's ridiculous. I could buy my own battleships for that price!"

"Not with the well-trained crews I have," Jarls answered, nonplussed by Creed's reaction. "In ninety days, you can strip this human world of several billion credits, if this gold is an example of what's available on that planet. I can give you ninety days of guaranteed safety to remove whatever you want from the planet, with the option to renew for another ninety days for an additional 20 percent."

Creed sat back down and thought over Jarls's proposal. "You guarantee my ships' safety?"

"Yes," Jarls replied. "Your ships will not be attacked while my fleet is in the system."

"I will agree to it with one modification. I want one of your battleships to accompany any cargo ships or detainee ships I send back to Marsten or Kubitz. I will provide my own warships as well, to help protect these convoys, but one of your battleships must go along to ensure their safety."

Jarls gazed at Creed thoughtfully. It sounded as if this human world might be very rich in gold and perhaps other valuables. His 10 percent could be a very sizable payoff. "I agree," he said after a moment. "I will have you a signed contract, notarized by one of the Kubitz Controllers, within twenty-two hours."

"How soon before you can get to Earth?"

"I will be taking twenty battleships," Jarls answered. "I have twelve here and will need to send for eight more. I should be able to leave within five days."

"Very well," replied Creed.

The Kubitz government kept Controllers on each world of the Gothan Empire to maintain records of all contracts signed. Any violation of a contract could easily result in a clan's lifetime banishment from participating in raiding activities. Even an entire planet could suffer penalties. Normally a planet would be given the choice of paying a hefty fine or refraining from raids for a specific time period of a few days to several years. It was one reason why contracts were almost never violated. The Dacronians would honor their contract to ensure that their stellar reputation remained intact.

"Once you receive the signed contract, I will expect the one hundred million credits to be deposited in my account on Kubitz within twenty-two hours."

"It will be done," replied Creed, standing up. "As a symbol of my appreciation, these gold bars are a gift for your personal account."

For the first time, Jarls allowed himself to smile. This might be a very profitable venture, indeed, with High Profiteer Creed making this gesture. "Prepare your ships," Jarls said, rising and picking up the four gold bars. "With my protection, you're about to become very rich."

Creed didn't reply, as Clan Leader Jarls left the room, carrying the gold.

Since the bars to Jarls were a personal gift, there would never be any record of this transaction. It also ensured that the clan leader would do everything in his power to keep Creed's ships safe. Now Creed needed to return to the Command Center and make the necessary final arrangements to get his ships repaired and to gather the fleet he planned to retake Earth with.

When he was done, there would be no gold, platinum, jewels, or major works of art left on the human planet. Then, for years to come, humans could be taken and sold in the Kubitz slave markets. There were enough human and humanoid races to make the Earth humans a very desirable commodity, particularly in the sex trade. He suspected that human females would be in high demand on Kubitz and the other worlds of the Gothan Empire.

-

For two weeks the evacuation had continued at a steady pace. On the surface of Earth, massive rescue efforts were underway in the devastated cities hit by the nukes. Hospitals were full of hundreds of thousands of people suffering from radiation sickness, with more coming in every day. The early death toll from the Profiteer bombardment had already climbed to over forty-two million worldwide. Doctors and specialists were predicting another two to six million would die in the next year from radiation poisoning and other immediate side effects. In the long term, a drastic increase in cancer deaths were expected over the next few decades.

-

"Rescue efforts are continuing in the Chicago and the Washington, DC, areas," President Mayfield informed the other Cabinet members. "In DC we're retrieving some of the valuable historical documents stored there. The radiation levels are still high, and our people can only work in some of the hotter areas for a few hours."

"I've read the reports, describing the near panic of people who live in close proximity to the two stricken cities and how martial law has been declared in the surrounding areas to ensure public safety. What are we doing to limit the spread of the radiation?" asked Secretary of the Treasury Dwight Michaels.

"We're using cargo planes filled with a special chemical," General Braid said. "We're also spraying another agent to reduce the radiation in areas with high rad counts. We're enforcing a mandatory evacuation of everyone living within twenty miles of Chicago and Washington, some of the most heavily populated areas in the country."

"How many people are we talking about?" asked Michaels.

"We're evacuating slightly over three million people," Braid replied. "We're moving them through triage centers and testing them for radiation. Those that test high are detained and placed in hospitals for treatment. We've mobilized both the National Guard and the Reserve to help with the evacuations."

"Hospitals in the immediate vicinity of both cities are already filled to capacity," added Raul Gutierrez of Homeland Security. "We're using military transport helicopters to aid in moving the overflow to other facilities. The civilian medical helicopters didn't have the lifting capacity."

"We're doing everything we can to help the affected areas," President Mayfield informed them. "Leaders in other areas of the world, where cities were hit, are doing their best to alleviate the suffering and contain the radiation."

"What do we do when these Profiteers return?" demanded Stroud with a stormy look. "Are we going to resist? It seems as if we are just going to turn the planet back over to the Profiteers when they show up again. Some of my business associates have already expressed their concerns, in a not-very-polite manner."

"We're setting up special operation units to be used as we see fit to take out targets of opportunity," General Braid answered. "Also a half dozen secure command and control centers will be responsible for military activities in their areas."

"What about the Europeans, Russians, and the Chinese?" asked Max Sallow. "All three possess sizable militaries."

"They're setting up quick-reaction forces also," answered General Braid. "We don't dare offer heavy resistance with major forces. The Profiteers would just nuke them from orbit, and we don't want to encourage that."

"So, for the most part, we just cooperate with them," muttered Stroud, his eyes narrowing. "None of that would be necessary if the fleet would stay and fight, instead of fleeing to Newton. I'm already losing some of my financial backers."

"As we've discussed before, Admiral Vickers's fleet would be wiped out, and then we would have no hope of ever being free of these Profiteers," President Mayfield said, frowning at Stroud. "The course of action we've chosen offers the best opportunity for our world to be free in the future."

"I still think the fleet should stay," grumbled Stroud, shaking his head in denial.

"How's the evacuation going?" asked Secretary of Education Connie Saxon.

"As well as can be expected," replied Mayfield, letting out a deep breath. "The Russian Collective is using eight cargo ships and two passenger liners to shuttle people and supplies to Newton. The Chinese Conglomerate has another twelve cargo ships and three passenger liners doing the same."

"Who's picking these foreign people?" demanded Stroud. "The North American Union established the Newton colony, and I don't like the idea of the Russians and the Chinese sending people there. How can they be sending people when my recommendations are immediately rejected by Fleet Admiral Tomalson's people?"

"No one is allowed to go to Newton without our approval," Tomalson informed Stroud, as well as the others. "The Russians and Chinese are both submitting lists of proposed evacuees to our shipyard personnel. They've been given some strict guidelines as to who we will accept and those that we will not. So far there have been no problems."

"Until the Profiteers show up again," muttered Stroud. "And my people remain on Earth."

"How much longer can we expect Admiral Vickers to remain in orbit?" asked Maureen Roberts.

Everyone on the Cabinet knew, when the fleet left, that either the Profiteers had returned or were about to. Several looked frightened, probably thinking about what that would mean for the North American Union and the rest of the world.

"It's difficult to say," Fleet Admiral Tomalson responded. His eyes looked tired, as if he had been getting very little sleep, with so much planning and work to be done in a very short time frame. "I would guess two more weeks at the outside—three if we're lucky—but I'm not planning on it."

"What about the Moon, Mars, and the other colonies in the Solar System?" asked Dwight Michaels. "Are they being evacuated?"

"Some are," answered President Mayfield. "The Profiteers never went anywhere else in the Solar System other than here at Earth."

"Why?" asked Stroud. "Why us and not them?"

"All the money is here," responded Michaels. "These Profiteers are after gold, platinum, jewels, and anything else that can be turned into a quick profit. The other colonies are dependent upon Earth to some extent for supplies and support. Only the Moon and Mars are close to being self-sufficient."

"Most of the smaller mining operations are to be evacuated to the larger colonies," Mayfield added. "The Europeans are shipping as many supplies to Mars as possible. The Russians and the Chinese are doing the same thing with the moons of Jupiter and Saturn, in the hope that their colonies will be spared."

"We all have bases on the Moon," Fleet Admiral Tomalson continued. "Most of those are evacuated or being reduced to skeleton crews, until this crisis is over. A few of the larger underground cities are being heavily supplied, and the people who don't come down to Earth will move into them."

"If it's ever over," mumbled Stroud, with an angry glint in his eyes. "My office is receiving thousands of calls each hour, demanding to know what our government will do to protect the people. What do I tell them?"

Mayfield leaned back and crossed his arms over his chest, as he contemplated Stroud's question. It was a legitimate one. Every government office was swamped by incoming calls, demanding to know what the government would do. The North American Union didn't have a big enough fleet to defend the whole Earth.

If the NAU still had their original ships of the fleet, then things might be different. However, they didn't. They had Admiral Vickers's task group, and the NAU couldn't afford to risk it in a battle they couldn't win. Most of the other major powers had concentrated their explorations to inside the Solar System so had never built warships. The NAU had signed agreements with all of them that the NAU fleets would protect Earth in case of an attack or invasion. The NAU had also accepted crews for several ships from contributing countries that had helped to pay for the protective fleets.

The same thing with military forces. The air force would be shot down from the sky, even with their modern attack jets. Ground units would just be bombed out of existence from the enemies in orbit. The NAU and other countries would keep some forces hidden and ready for when the opportunity presented itself to strike a telling blow against the enemy, for everyone expected the Profiteers to return in far greater force than before. So, for an unknown amount of time, the humans of Earth would have to live as a conquered people.

The path of least resistance to the Profiteers would ensure that most of the people on the planet survived. There was also a reasonable chance that the rural areas would see little change in their daily lives, as the Profiteers were bound to concentrate their activities in the metropolitan areas where most of the planet's riches were located.

"When the Profiteers return, I'll make an announcement, explaining what must be done," Mayfield said, leaning forward and placing his hands on the large wooden conference table. The wood felt cool to the touch. "We'll tell our people that the enemy has returned and to cooperate with them. There will be no armed resistance, and all our efforts will be aimed at preserving this Union and our people."

General Braid explained further. "Our Special Forces units will only be sent into action if the Profiteers are intent on killing," General Braid said, his face taking on a deadly look. "If we lose citizens, then all holds are off. We'll engage the Profiteers at every opportunity, regardless of the risk."

"How will the Union function under the conditions the Profiteers will bring?" asked Connie Saxon. "Parents may not be willing to send their children to our schools, fearing for their safety."

"Those are questions that will have to be answered when the time comes," Mayfield responded with a deep sigh.

He knew they were facing tough and trying times ahead. He just prayed they were doing the right thing. They had a plan in place that might mean there was, indeed, a light at the end of the tunnel. However, the tunnel might be unbelievably long.

Chapter Five

President Mayfield looked across the conference table at his Cabinet. It had been decided the Cabinet members would be split up and sent to three secure locations to ensure that succession to the presidency remained intact.

"Has anyone seen the secretary of labor the last few days?" asked Connie Saxon.

"No," replied Max Sallow. "I heard a rumor that he took a flight to Hong Kong to meet with some of his business associates."

Mayfield turned toward General Braid with a questioning look.

"He wants off the planet," the general answered, shaking his head. "I'm sure he's trying to make a deal to board one of the Chinese vessels going to Newton."

Mayfield looked over at Anne Roselin. "Contact the Chinese Conglomerate and remind them that only qualified people are to be allowed on their cargo ships and passenger liners. Secretary of Labor Stroud is not to be allowed to board one of their ships."

"I'll contact MaLin Chung," Anne replied with a nod of her head. "He has no respect for Secretary of Labor Stroud and will see to it that he doesn't have access to one of the Chinese ships."

"Past problems?" asked Connie Saxon curiously.

"Yes," Anne answered with a confirming nod. "They had some dealings that went bad, and MaLin lost a considerable sum of money. There is no love lost between the two."

With a sigh and a shake of his head, Mayfield addressed Fleet Admiral Tomalson. "What's the situation in orbit?"

"The *Kepler* and the *Dante* have left for Newton," Tomalson replied. "The two light cruisers in the repair bays have been updated and have joined Admiral Vickers's fleet in orbit. We're in the process of dismantling part of the shipyard to send as well."

"The entire shipyard?" asked Dwight Michaels with a stunned look in his eyes. "We spent billions building the damn thing!"

"We don't have the time to dismantle the entire shipyard," Tomalson explained with a deep sigh. "We have two heavy tugs taking the construction bay and a manufacturing section to Newton."

"How soon before the Profiteers return?" asked Connie Saxon.

"We're expecting then any day now," the fleet admiral replied. "We're actually surprised they haven't shown up already."

"What will the fleet do if some our evacuee ships are still in Earth orbit?"

Fleet Admiral Tomalson looked over at Connie and then replied. "They have orders to stay in orbit until all the cargo ships and passenger liners have safely entered hyperspace. As soon as the last ship is away, Admiral Vickers will break orbit and head for Newton."

The room became quiet, as the Cabinet thought over those cryptic words. They all knew that, once Admiral Vickers was gone, their world would be at the mercy of the Profiteers.

-

"Fleet tug *Juno* is ready to enter hyperspace," reported Ensign Brenda Pierce from Communications.

"She's taking the main manufacturing section of the shipyard," added Captain Randson, as he peered intently at the main viewscreen, which was focused on the tug and its precious cargo.

Kurt nodded. The fleet tug *Poseidon* had left the day before with the large construction bay. Kurt just hoped the *Poseidon* made it safely to Newton. She was in a convoy consisting of two destroyers, three passenger liners, and seven cargo ships. However, due to the mass of the construction bay, the tug's hyperspace engine would be tasked to the max.

"Unidentified contact!" called out Lieutenant Lena Brooks. "Range is four million kilometers. We're being scanned!"

"Order the *Juno* to enter hyperspace now!" ordered Kurt, sensing this might be the return of the Profiteers. "Get me an ID on that contact."

"Ship is 1,100 hundred meters in length and 220 meters in diameter," Brooks promptly reported. She turned toward the admiral with a look of deep concern on her face. "She's not one of ours."

"All ships go to Condition One," ordered Kurt, taking a deep breath. "Bring all weapons systems online." Then, turning toward Ensign Pierce, he said, "Instruct all ships currently in orbit that they have ten minutes to make their jump into hyperspace and head for Newton. Contact any ship on the surface ready to launch and tell them to do so immediately, or they will be left behind." Looking around, Kurt could see the Command Center come alive with intense activity as the crew prepared for battle. He nodded in satisfaction at their professionalism.

"Colonel Hayworth says it will take him twenty minutes to get the last of his construction people aboard the *Newton Princess*," reported Ensign Pierce.

"Tell him to hurry," instructed Kurt, shifting his gaze to one of the viewscreens, which showed the partially disassembled shipyard. He could see a large passenger liner still docked. They needed those construction people off the station, plus the fleet personnel still on board.

"Shields are at 97 percent, and weapons are ready to fire," reported Lieutenant Mays.

Kurt switched the comm channel so he could speak to Captain Watkins on the *Vindication*. "Henry, bring in the fighters you have out on CSP. We'll be leaving as soon as the evacuating civilians are safely away."

"Leaving like this leaves a sour taste in my mouth," Henry replied tonelessly. "We don't know what the Profiteers will do to Earth."

"We have a plan," Kurt answered. He had spoken briefly to President Mayfield and Fleet Admiral Tomalson, offering a suggestion to make things go easier on Earth when the Profiteers returned, at least initially. "We'll be coming back again someday. I promise."

"I know it's what we have to do," Watkins answered somberly. "It's just hard to actually do it."

-

A number of minutes passed as the red threat icon sat on the tactical screen not moving. With satisfaction, Kurt saw his fleet forming up around the *Star Cross* in a loose globe formation with the battlecruiser and the light carrier in the center.

"*Juno* is jumping into hyperspace," Lieutenant Brooks reported, as the green icon representing the fleet tug suddenly vanished from the sensor screen.

"We have two passenger liners and six cargo ships launching from Earth," reported Captain Randson.

Kurt had overheard him talking to the launch controllers at the spaceports on the ground, continually stressing to them the importance of getting those ships up.

"Numerous contacts!" cried out Lieutenant Brooks in near panic, as alarms sounded on her sensor console. "Nineteen more hostiles have exited hyperspace in combat range!"

"What about the civilian ships in orbit?" demanded Kurt.

They would be sitting ducks for the weapons of these large ships. Their captive, Grantz, had indicated High Profiteer Creed would probably hire a group of mercenaries to retake Earth. They would most likely come in battleships, which could easily destroy the Earth ships.

"They've all jumped out," Brooks answered, as the last civilian ship vanished into hyperspace.

"What about the *Newton Princess*?"

"She has undocked from the shipyard and is accelerating away, toward open space," reported Captain Randson, as he kept his eyes glued to the viewscreen showing the fleeing passenger liner. "Colonel Hayworth reports they got everyone from the shipyard on board."

Moments later, the green icon representing the large passenger liner vanished from the tactical display, as the ship jumped into hyperspace.

"Enemy vessels are closing," reported Lieutenant Brooks.

The *Star Cross* shook slightly, and Kurt knew they were under fire from the unknown ships. This pretty much confirmed they were dealing with Profiteers or Profiteer mercenaries.

"All ships return fire," Kurt ordered firmly. On the tactical screen, he could see a number of green icons crawling slowly upward from the surface of Earth. These were the passenger liners and cargo ships that Captain Randson had been trying to get into space. Suddenly one of the icons swelled up and vanished. "What just happened?"

"The Profiteers are targeting the passenger liners and cargo ships," reported Lieutenant Brooks in a horrified voice. Even as she spoke, another green icon vanished from her sensor screen.

"Those ships don't have any weapons or energy shields," Andrew said in anger. "They'll be picked off before they can make orbit. Why the hell are they targeting unarmed ships?"

"Order them to land!" commanded Kurt, his eyes glinting in anger.

The remaining cargo ships and passenger liners had no chance to make orbit. Their only hope was to return to ground. The Profiteers had demonstrated once more how merciless they were toward civilians. Kurt wasn't sure, but those two downed ships had probably held several thousand people.

Clan Leader Jarls grinned in mirthless satisfaction as his ship blasted the civilian ships trying to escape the planet. On one of the viewscreens, he watched as an energy projector drilled a glowing hole in the hull of a fleeing human vessel. Moments later the ship vanished in a bright explosion, obliterating it.

"The other human vessels are turning back and are apparently attempting to land," reported Salas, his second in command. "Should we destroy them?"

"No," Jarls answered. "Let them land. They might contain some valuable cargo. Concentrate our fire on the human warships. Either destroy or drive them from orbit."

In space, the fire between the two fleets rapidly intensified. The Dacroni mercenary ships were using ion beams, energy weapons, and hypermissiles to strike at the human warships. The humans, in turn, were firing back with their particle beam cannons, laser turrets, KEW batteries, and heavy ship missiles. Space was full of exploding munitions and crisscrossed with various beams of energy.

The human destroyer *Titan* was suddenly bracketed by the fire of four Dacroni battleships. Her energy shield flared brightly and then wavered. A pair of hypermissiles flashed through the compromised screen, impacting the stern of the ship. Two small glowing suns appeared as the ship was turned into glowing plasma.

"The destroyer *Titan* is down," reported Lieutenant Brooks in a pained voice.

"Admiral, the light cruiser *Sydney* is reporting moderate damage," Captain Randson added. "We need to get out of here. We're facing too much firepower, and our own weapons don't seem to be causing significant damage."

Kurt nodded. "All ships, accelerate along vector south eighteen degrees, coordinates seven by fourteen. Full sublight. We'll enter hyperspace as soon as we're clear of the enemy ships."

The human fleet promptly accelerated from the Dacroni battleships in an outward trajectory toward Earth's Moon. Moments later, the fleet entered the safety of hyperspace and vanished from all Dacroni sensors.

"Human ships have jumped into hyperspace," reported Second Officer Salas. "We destroyed one of their light units and damaged several of their heavier vessels in the brief exchange."

"And our own ships?" demanded Jarls. Any damage to be repaired he fully intended High Profiteer Creed to pay for.

"The *Marsuth* is reporting light damage from a particle beam strike," reported Salas. "It's repairable, and the ship should be fully operational within the hour."

Jarls nodded, satisfied. The humans hadn't put up much of a fight. This concerned him, as he had thought his fleet would have to engage in a pitched battle in orbit for possession of the planet. Now they would have to be vigilant in case the human ships returned. "Contact High Profiteer Creed and inform him the planet is ours. Tell him the fighting was heavy, and several of our ships suffered damage."

Jarls had no problem in exaggerating the truth in order to glean more credits for his fleet. From the amount of gold that Creed had paid for protection by the clan's battleships, Jarls was certain the High Profiteer could easily afford this additional charge. It was all in the course of doing business.

-

After going into orbit around Earth, High Profiteer Creed gazed at the main viewscreen displaying the blue-white world. The planet was once more under his firm control, and his fleet of cargo ships and the detainee ships would be arriving shortly.

"Clan Leader Jarls is demanding five million credits to cover the damage to his ships suffered in their brief battle with the Earth ships," growled Second Profiteer Lantz. "I am leery of his claim, as our own sensors are not showing that any of his vessels suffered serious damage except the *Marsuth*."

Creed looked over at Third Profiteer Bixt on Sensors. "How serious is the damage to the *Marsuth*?"

"There is a two-meter hole in her hull close to Engineering," Bixt replied. "It should be easily repairable by the ship's crew."

"Lukon, contact Clan Leader Jarls and inform him that we will set aside five hundred thousand credits for his ship repairs."

"That might anger him," warned Lantz, his large eyes growing wider.

"I doubt it," Creed replied. "He stands to make sufficient profit off our deal. He won't risk it over this slight squabble. I suspect he'll agree to our offer."

A few moments later Creed's prediction proved true, as Clan Leader Jarls accepted the offer with little protest.

"Put us in orbit above what the humans call New York City. Our other ships are to take up geostationary orbits above other major population centers." Creed intended to leave no doubt in the humans' minds what he intended. If they refused to cooperate, he would use his fleet's energy weapons to take out selected targets in the cities.

It would be much easier if he forced the humans to gather their planet's riches for him. Once the detainee ships arrived, those crews would begin loading up humans to be sold in the slave auctions on Kubitz. The first batch he had taken there had been very well received, particularly the women. Once their initial training was complete, they would be sold, and a select group of the women would be sent to the planetary pleasure houses. With the rich variety in the human form, he strongly suspected these women would be in high demand. He could already taste the profits he would receive from selling so many human slaves on Kubitz. He would have to be careful not to overload the market and risk driving down the prices.

"We're receiving a message from the surface," reported Third Profiteer Lukon from Communications. "The humans are offering a payment of gold and other metals, if we don't destroy any more of their cities."

Second Profiteer Lantz looked over at High Profiteer Creed with a greedy glint in his eyes at the mention of gold.

Creed was silent for a moment, as he considered the humans' offer. "Ask them where this gold is, and we will send a cargo ship to collect it. Warn them that any attempt at subterfuge will have disastrous consequences for their world. Tell them that their planet now belongs to us."

"They've agreed," reported Fleet Admiral Tomalson, as he listened to the message just delivered by one of the communications officers for the underground facility. "They're sending a ship to the Atlanta airport."

"Are we doing the right thing?" asked Secretary of the Treasury Dwight Michaels.

"If it will save our cities," President Mayfield replied in a tired voice.

They had watched from their secure underground location as the Profiteers had returned to the system and briefly engaged Admiral Vickers's fleet. In anguish, they had witnessed the destruction of two cargo ships and a passenger liner attempting to reach orbit and then enter the safety of hyperspace. Fifteen hundred people had died on the overly crowded passenger liner.

"They'll want more," pointed out General Braid. "This will only whet their appetite."

"We have hidden a number of stashes of gold and other metals they have shown an interest in," Dwight Michaels said, his eyes revealing deep concern. "We can dole them out over an extended period."

"A very lengthy period," President Mayfield added. "We need to buy as much time as we can and hope Admiral Vickers can return someday and drive these Profiteers permanently from our world."

The Profiteer cargo ship *Calpis* landed directly in front of the Atlanta airport's international terminal. The six-hundred-meter vessel settled easily on the concrete, and, after a few moments, a large hatch opened, and a ramp descended to touch the pavement. Twenty Profiteers, dressed in dark gray body armor and heavily armed, walked down the ramp and stood waiting expectantly.

Inside the control tower, personnel sent word to the waiting armored trucks to proceed, while a number of military officers watched to ensure that everything was filmed and documented.

Two armored trucks came around the terminal and drove up to the waiting Profiteers.

Captain Nathan Aldrich rode in the passenger seat of one of the trucks, and, when they came to a stop, he opened the door and stepped out. Taking a deep breath, he walked over to the Profiteer who seemed to be in charge of the group standing on the tarmac.

"I have a delivery for you," Nathan said, trying to sound calm. He gazed at the Profiteer, noting the differences between him and normal humans. The alien's skin had a light blue tinge with coarse white hair on his head. His face, while humanoid, had bigger eyes. The Profiteer was a little taller than Nathan's six foot two inches.

"Show me!" demanded the Profiteer, his eyes focusing intently on the nearest vehicle. "If there is not gold in your transport vehicle, your world will be severely punished!"

"The gold is in the trucks," Nathan replied. He didn't care for the Profiteer's tone but knew there was nothing he could do about it, at least not this time.

Nathan turned and strode to the truck, unlocking the doors and swinging them open. Inside were forty bars of gold. "Here's your gold. There's more in the other truck as well."

The Profiteer gazed at the gold with greed in his eyes. Stepping inside he reached out and touched one of the bars. "How many bars?"

"Forty in each truck," Nathan responded. This gold was like a ransom payment, and it pained Nathan to see the Profiteers take it.

The Profiteer stepped outside the truck and removed a small communications device from the thick black belt he wore. He spoke into it for a few moments and then turned to face Nathan. "Your payment has been accepted. Your cities will remain unharmed for now. Our High Profiteer will be contacting your leaders shortly to arrange for the next tribute."

"Next tribute?" Nathan said, feigning confusion. They had actually expected this response.

"Yes," the Profiteer responded with a sneer. "As long as payments are made, your cities will not be destroyed. If you fail to make a payment on time, the repercussions will be immediate."

"I will pass on the message to our government," Nathan answered. His hand strayed to the 45-caliber Colt pistol in its holster. Then taking a deep breath, he moved his hand away. Now was not the time to kill one of the invaders.

The Profiteer then motioned to the others standing behind him, and several went back up the ramp and returned shortly with two antigravity sleds. It took them only a few minutes to load the eighty bars of gold and secure it inside the cargo ship. Once the bars were loaded, all the Profiteers boarded again; the ramp lifted off the runway, and the cargo hatch slammed shut. Moments later the enemy ship was in the air and soon vanished from sight.

"I guess that's done," commented one of the drivers of the armored trucks, who had stepped out to watch the alien ship take off. "Damn shame we had to give them all that gold."

"It's better than losing a city," Nathan replied brusquely. He needed to get back to the control tower and make his report. He was still a little shaken at being so close to an actual alien.

-

"Eighty bars of pure gold!" gloated Second Profiteer Lantz.

Creed agreed the amount of gold offered would, indeed, add considerably to the treasure he expected to take from the planet. He strongly suspected Lantz would spend much of his take in the pleasure houses on Kubitz. "Don't forget we have to take Clan Leader Jarls's share out first."

The glint faded from Lantz's eyes at this reminder. "We need to send our people to the planet, searching for more plunder. The sooner we can depart this planet, the better, as far as I'm concerned. The Dacroni mercenaries will try to pry from us every credit they can."

"Our detainee ships will be arriving shortly," Creed said, staring at one of the large viewscreens on the front wall of the Command Center. "Once they're here, we'll begin collecting humans to be sent to the slave pens on Kubitz. At the same time we'll search their world for more gold, platinum, and other valuables."

"What about their offer to pay us to leave their cities untouched?"

Creed allowed a greedy smile to cross his face. His large eyes turned toward Second Profiteer Lantz. "Eighty gold bars per human month. That will be the price to leave their larger cities alone and not plunder them."

Lantz frowned. "Tempting, but there's bound to be a lot of gold and other valuables in those cities."

"At some point in time they will no longer be able to pay," High Profiteer Creed replied. "When that day comes, we'll move into the larger cities and take what we want!"

-

"They've agreed," reported Fleet Admiral Tomalson to the gathered Cabinet members. "In exchange for eighty bars of gold per month, they'll stay out of all major cities with a population in excess of one million."

"How long can we make that payment?" asked President Mayfield. "Eighty bars of gold sounds like a lot."

"Almost indefinitely," Secretary of the Treasury Dwight Michaels replied. "We have some major hidden reserves of both gold and platinum, from which we can make the payments. I don't believe these Profiteers have the faintest idea what our gold reserves are."

"Let's keep it that way," ordered Mayfield. He then turned toward Fleet Admiral Tomalson. "Is there any way we can contact the mercenary ships in orbit and perhaps make a deal with them to turn on the Profiteers?"

"No," replied Tomalson, shaking his head. "From what we learned in interrogating our Profiteer captives on the shipyard, the Profiteers and the mercenaries will have a signed contract on file on Kubitz, and the Controllers will ensure the contract is fulfilled. Any attempt by the mercenaries to violate that contract will have serious consequences. From what I understand, it's very seldom, if ever, that a contract is not fulfilled."

President Mayfield took a long, deep breath. "Then it will be up to Admiral Vickers to drive these Profiteers from Earth. General Braid, what's the status of our military forces?"

"Sent home," Braid answered simply with a haunted look in his eyes. "We felt, for their own safety, it best to temporarily disband most of the units. The rest of the world is following our lead. Our naval vessels are putting into port, and their crews have been placed on extended leave."

"What about our Special Forces?"

"Hidden," replied Braid, a wolfish glint appearing in his eyes. "We have 12,000 highly trained troops we can call upon, if needed."

President Mayfield nodded. With the Profiteers and the mercenaries in orbit above the Earth, the humans could do little but seem as unthreatening as possible. It galled him that they had to act so powerless against these aliens. The North American Union and the rest of the world had been conquered once more, without even a shot fired on the planet in protest. Mayfield just hoped they had made the right decision.

Chapter Six

Admiral Kurt Vickers let out a long sigh of relief as the fleet tug *Poseidon* dropped from hyperspace ten million kilometers from Newton. That only left the fleet tug *Juno*, and he expected it to put in an appearance the next day. "They made it!" He had greatly feared the size of the bays would wreak havoc with the tugs' large hyperspace drives. As it was, they were forced to travel much slower in hyperspace than normal.

"Damn good thing," said Captain Randson, as he watched the main viewscreen, where the distant tug and the large construction bay she had brought with her were displayed.

Lieutenant Lena Brooks checked her sensors and then turned toward the admiral to report. "Detecting twelve ships with the *Poseidon.*"

"That's all of them," Randson said with a nod.

"Get them into Newton's orbit," ordered Kurt, as he leaned back in his command chair. He was anxious to get the large construction bay attached to Newton Station, so they could complete the *Kepler*. Once the heavy carrier was finished, the fleet would be considerably more powerful, and he could begin thinking about the mission to Kubitz.

"I have Colonel Hayworth on the comm," reported Ensign Pierce. "His crew is aboard Newton Station and is ready to attach the construction bay. He says he can have it operational in five to six days."

Captain Randson looked over at Kurt meaningfully and nodded. "That's good news. We need to get the *Kepler* finished as soon as possible."

"Inform Colonel Hayworth to use whatever resources he needs to get it done," Kurt replied.

He knew that Andrew was anxious to head to Kubitz to rescue his wife and daughter. From what they had learned from their Profiteer prisoner, that was where Andrew's family and the other abductees would be taken to be sold. Kurt had clear orders from President Mayfield to rescue those people and procure a new defensive weapons system from the arms dealers on that planet.

Kurt spent a few minutes studying the tactical screen with its friendly green icons. He had the *Star Cross*, the light carrier *Vindication*, seven light cruisers, and eight destroyers to defend the system with. Soon he could add the *Kepler*. He also had the light carrier *Dante*, but it needed major repairs. It would be several months before the light carrier was fit for duty.

"Put us into an orbit close to Newton Station," ordered Kurt. "I want to monitor the attaching of the construction bay, as well as the manufacturing section that the *Juno* is bringing."

The helm officer adjusted the course of the large battlecruiser, and, on the main viewscreen, Newton Station grew larger. It didn't take Ensign Styles long to place the *Star Cross* twenty kilometers from the station, where they could observe the work.

"Have a full crew here in the Command Center to monitor everything," ordered Kurt, looking over at Randson. "We can't afford for anything to go wrong."

"How soon before we can launch the rescue mission?" Captain Randson asked in a low voice.

Kurt understood why Andrew looked so exhausted and hesitated briefly before answering. "Colonel Hayworth says he can have the *Kepler* fully operational in three weeks. Once the ship's done, we'll set out."

"Three more weeks," repeated Andrew, letting out a deep sigh. "I just hope we get there in time."

"We'll find them," promised Kurt. He knew how he would feel if it was his sister's family who had been taken. He wouldn't allow humans to be slaves anywhere in the galaxy. And, if he had to tear apart the galaxy to do so, he would find every last human taken.

Kurt was asleep in his quarters, when the comm unit next to his bed chimed. Rolling over, he pressed the receive button. "Yes?" he said, still half asleep.

"We have a problem developing on Newton," Captain Randson announced over the comm, his voice concerned. "It seems that Secretary of Labor Marlen Stroud arrived on a Chinese cargo ship and showed up on Newton, at the governor's office, demanding that the governor step down. Stroud's saying that, since he's the highest-ranking Cabinet member not trapped on Earth, and since Newton is a colony of the North American Union, the governorship falls to him."

Kurt came instantly awake. "Bullshit! Tell Governor Spalding to place that idiot under arrest immediately. Then find out what ship he arrived on to see if anyone else came to Newton without being screened. Send a platoon of Marines if necessary."

"He is a member of the Cabinet," Andrew reminded Kurt in an uncertain voice.

"I don't care who he is," replied Kurt, as he rolled from bed and reached for his clothes. "We were careful to ensure that no one like Stroud could come to Newton, just so nothing like this could happen. All Stroud cares about is power and money—something he no longer has, since the Profiteers have retaken Earth. He and his entourage took the place of much-needed individuals, who we can no longer evacuate. I have direct orders from President Mayfield and Fleet Admiral Tomalson to keep the current government of Newton intact, as well as my control of the fleet. I have a written copy of those orders in the safe here in my quarters. Do you need to see them?"

"No, sir," Andrew hastily replied. "I just wanted you to be aware there might be consequences for our actions."

"Arrest the son of a bitch," ordered Kurt. "I'll be in the Command Center shortly but get word to Governor Spalding. I want the responsible Chinese parties arrested." He disconnected the comm with a slap of his hand.

Marlen Stroud sat in Governor Spalding's office waiting for the governor to return. Marlen had demanded that the governor immediately resign and turn over Newton to him. Leaning back in the governor's plush chair, Marlen allowed himself to smile. It had cost him a fortune to procure passage on a Chinese cargo ship bound for Newton. He had made arrangements for his wife, several of their better servants, and a few powerful supporters to accompany him. Their quarters had been quite spartan, but at least they were off Earth and now could lead a normal life. He would keep the fleet at Newton to ensure his security.

As soon as Spalding returned with the resignation he was writing, Marlen would go on all the comm channels to inform the citizens of Newton that he was their new leader, and they would not be taking part in the war against the Profiteers. He would also be relieving Admiral Vickers of his command and replacing him with someone more tolerable.

Marlen stood up and stepped over to the large window, which overlooked the capital city. The city held slightly over six hundred thousand residents. While small by Earth standards, it still possessed many of the comforts he was seeking. His wife was already searching for a new home suitable for their needs. He was fairly certain that, if they left the Profiteers alone, Newton wouldn't see them. Marlen could build a good and comfortable life here, living in luxury and fully in control of the planet.

The sound of the door opening behind him drew his attention. With a wide smile, he turned around, expecting to see Governor Spalding, holding his resignation in his hand. Instead, two heavily armed Marines stood there with grim looks upon their faces.

"Marlen Stroud, you are under arrest for subversion and treason."

Stroud's face turned pale at hearing those words. "What do you mean? Is this some joke?"

"No, it's no joke. You came to Newton illegally, with no screening, even though ordered by the government of the North American Union. Your authority isn't recognized here, and yet you demanded that the Newton government be turned over to you without due process."

"I'm a Cabinet member," snarled Stroud, growing angry. "That's all the authority I need!" How dare these Marines threaten him. There must be some misunderstanding. He would see to it that they were cleaning latrines before the day was over.

"We are aware of who you are," the Marine sergeant replied in an uncompromising voice. His right hand touched the pistol in the holster at his waist. "Are you coming peacefully, or do we need to use force?"

Marlen gazed at the Marine sergeant, his blood pressure boiling, but seeing the hard and cold look in the sergeant's eyes took away any thoughts of resisting. These men weren't to be trifled with. "I'll go with you," he grated out. "But this isn't over. You don't realize who you're messing with."

"We do know," replied the sergeant. "But this is Newton, not Earth. You have no power or authority here."

The two Marines led the angry Cabinet member from the governor's office and down the hall to a waiting elevator. They had orders to take him to a small residence on the outskirts of the city and to keep him there under house arrest. His wife, their servants, and his supporters had already been rounded up and were unhappily waiting for him.

–

Governor Spalding stepped back into his office and sat down in the chair behind his desk. He hoped they had done the right thing. If President Mayfield and the other Cabinet members were dead, then Stroud was next in line for the presidency. It that were true, then Stroud had every right to demand control of the government. However, as far as they knew, President Mayfield was still alive, along with the other Cabinet members. Until they knew otherwise, Stroud would be kept under twenty-four-hour lockdown and surveillance. Spalding just hoped nothing had happened to the president, or they could find themselves in a sticky situation.

–

"It's done," Captain Randson reported, as he stepped from Communications, where he had been in constant touch with the senior Marine officer at the governor's mansion down on Newton, who had been responsible for sending the Marines to arrest Stroud. "You have one very upset Cabinet member on your hands now."

Kurt nodded and let out a deep sigh. Marlen Stroud was the least of his worries. He had to get the Newton System prepared for war, as well as get the fleet ready for what was ahead. "Schedule a meeting with Colonel Hayworth and the commanding officer of Newton Station, Captain Simms."

"What are you planning?"

"I want all our ships equipped with particle beam cannons, including the destroyers," Kurt explained. "I also want to discuss the possibility of arming the station. The shipyard above Earth wasn't armed, as the fleet was supposed to protect it. I don't want to make that same mistake here."

Andrew nodded, as he thought over what Kurt wanted. "Once we get the construction bay and the manufacturing section attached to the station, we'll have a lot of hull space to work with. Hell, we could make Newton Station more heavily armed than a battlecruiser."

"Exactly," Kurt replied. He also needed to get in touch with his sister. He had made arrangements for a modest home to be made available for them. Her family had made it safely to Newton and should be settled in by now.

-

Several hours later Kurt arrived on Newton Station. He was escorted to a small conference room where Captain Simms, the commanding officer of Newton Station, and Colonel Hayworth, the commanding office of Earth's shipyard, were waiting.

"Admiral," said Colonel Hayworth, standing up and saluting.

"It's good to have you aboard, sir," Captain Simms said, also standing and saluting.

Kurt returned the salutes and gestured for the two men to sit back down. "Captain Simms, how many exploration ships do we currently have out?" Exploration ships left and returned to Newton Station on a regular basis. All were required to report in on a strict schedule.

"Four, sir," Simms answered. "The *Himalaya*, *Carlsbad*, *Trinity*, and *Surveyor Three* are all currently away. Only the *Surveyor Two* is still here. The *Carlsbad* should be back within the week and the others three to four weeks from now." The *Surveyor One* had been the first survey ship and had been retired years earlier.

Kurt nodded. That was about what he had expected. The ships were required to send hyperspace message drones once per week, reporting on their current status. All exploration vessels were expected to return to Newton eight weeks after departure. Currently the exploration ships were surveying every star within fifty light-years of the Newton System. Their primary mission was to seek out potential habitable planets. They were also doing mineral surveys in asteroid fields and upon small moons. The ships were lightly armed and had strict instructions to return to Newton if they turned up anything that could be considered a danger. Each ship also had a First Contact team on board, just in case they stumbled across an alien vessel.

"Colonel Hayworth, how soon can you have the construction bay and the manufacturing facility up and running?"

"Five to six days on the construction bay and another eight to ten on the manufacturing section," Hayworth answered. "Captain Simms and I have been discussing it, and we'll have to make some modifications to Newton Station so the new configuration will be stable."

"It shouldn't be too difficult," Simms added. "We always planned on expanding the station, so we have the structural supports in place."

"Finish the *Kepler* as soon as possible," Kurt ordered. "We'll need her firepower, plus the fighters and bombers she can launch."

"It won't take long to finish her," Hayworth replied, as he looked down at the notes he had brought to the meeting. "We need to finish installing the energy shield emitters and do some cosmetic work inside. We also need to assemble the fighters and bombers assigned to the ship."

"Speaking of fighters and bombers, can we build a flight bay on the station to handle several squadrons of each?"

Simms looked over at Hayworth before replying. "It'll have to be a complete build. We have nothing in the plans for such a flight bay."

"I have plans that I brought with me," Hayworth said, as he thought over what would be involved. "We can make most of the necessary parts in the manufacturing section. I'm guessing we'll need at least eight to twelve weeks, once we start on actual construction."

"Can the *Dante* be put in the station's repair bay, or is the damage too severe?"

Simms thumbed through a couple pages of information on the table in front of him. He picked up one sheet and studied it. "We can do it," he said after a moment. "Not sure of the time it'll take, as some of this damage is quite extensive."

"Let's get on it," Kurt ordered. "Once we're done with the *Dante* and *Kepler*, have particle beam weapons installed on all our ships that currently don't have them."

"I was expecting that," Hayworth said. "Should we arm the station as well?"

"Yes," Kurt replied, pleased that Hayworth had guessed his next question. "Weapons plus an energy shield."

"That's a lot of work," Simms said, his eyes narrowing. "Fortunately, with the people that Colonel Hayworth brought, we should be able to do it." Simms took out a calculator and ran some numbers. "Four to six months to complete everything. Does that sound about right to you?" asked the captain, looking over at Hayworth.

"Sounds doable," Hayworth responded. "Our people will be putting in a lot of hours."

"Recruit and train more if needed," ordered Kurt. "Also, when the ships are being updated, don't hesitate to use their crews to help with the work. We're at war, and the security of Newton is paramount."

Hayworth grinned. "Would love to order about the crews. We'll get it done, sir."

Kurt spent another hour speaking in greater detail to the two men about the things he wanted. When the meeting was over, he felt satisfied that a number of important issues had been resolved. Now he wanted to go to Newton and speak with Governor Spalding, plus visit his sister, Denise.

Denise was busy cooking when her cell phone rang.

"I'll get it!" yelled Bryan, as he ran through the house toward her phone, lying on the kitchen counter.

The six-year-old had been hyperactive ever since they arrived on Newton. Denise put down her knife and the potato she had been peeling.

Pressing the green flashing light on the cell phone, Bryan said, "Hello?" He listened for a moment, and then his eyes lit up. "Uncle Kurt, is it really you? When are you coming to visit? Our new house is really neat, and it's close to my new school."

"Let me have the phone, dear," said Denise, pleased that Kurt had finally called. She knew he had been tremendously busy the last few days.

Bryan handed her the phone with a big excited smile. "He says he's coming over!"

"Hello, big brother," Denise said. "Bryan says you're coming over?" She listened for a moment, nodding to herself. "The house is fine. It's nearly as big as the one we left in Houston. Alex is out checking on a potential job. One of the local companies has a need for a systems analyst."

"Let me talk some more!" begged Bryan with his eyes open wide. "I want to tell Uncle Kurt about our spaceship ride."

"Why don't you come over for supper? I'll have it ready around seven." She listened to Kurt's reply, and a soft smile covered her face. "I'll see you then, and Bryan can't wait to tell you about our trip on the passenger liner."

Denise pressed the end button on her cell phone and looked down at her son. "Uncle Kurt's coming for supper, and you can tell him then all about your ride on the spaceship."

"I can't wait," Bryan said, his face lighting up with excitement. "I'll color him a picture of the spaceship." With that comment, Bryan turned and rushed off toward his room.

Denise picked up the knife and the potato again. She would have to cook a little more for supper than usual. It would do her brother good to have a home-cooked meal for a change.

-

"What was the final total of refugees we managed to evacuate?" asked Kurt, looking across the desk at Governor Spalding. He had stopped by the governor's office to cover some of the events that had occurred at Earth and to discuss the potential problem having Marlen Stroud on Newton might mean.

"One hundred and twelve thousand," Spalding replied, as he checked some information on the computer screen on his desk. "Most of them families, with at least one member being someone who can greatly benefit Newton. We have teachers, engineers, doctors, nurses, scientists, and even some farming specialists."

"We tried to be very careful in our screening of potential colonists," Kurt answered. He just wished they had caught Stroud before he managed to board the Chinese ship. That Cabinet member would be an ongoing migraine for Kurt and Spalding.

"We arrested the Chinese crewmembers who brought Stroud and his entourage to Newton," Spalding said with a heavy sigh. "He brought along several household servants and six other influential people, who have been involved in his past political and business dealings."

This was the first Kurt had heard how many others were involved. "What did you do with them?"

"Same as Stroud. They're under house arrest for the time being, until we can figure out what use, if any, they can be."

Kurt leaned back in his chair and shook his head. "Stroud is bound to stir up trouble. We can't keep him isolated forever."

"This might help," said Spalding, taking a thick envelope and a small metal box from the right-hand top drawer of his desk. "President Mayfield sent this on one of the first passenger liners carrying evacuees."

"What is it?" asked Kurt, curious. He hadn't been aware that the president had any special orders for Governor Spalding.

"One moment," Spalding said. "I need a few witnesses for this." The governor reached forward on his desk and pressed a button. "Send them in."

The door opened, and General Mclusky—in command of ground forces on Newton—plus Colonel Hayworth, and several representatives of the civilian government came in with Spalding's secretary.

"What's going on?" Kurt asked in confusion. He was surprised at Hayworth's presence, as Kurt had only left him a few hours previously.

"Admiral Kurt Vickers, will you please stand," said Governor Spalding in a formal voice.

Kurt did so, not understanding why.

Spalding opened the envelope and took out a letter with the presidential seal of office. "By orders of President Mayfield of the North American Union, you are hereby promoted to the rank of fleet admiral."

"But Admiral Tomalson is fleet admiral," protested Kurt, bewildered.

"Not any longer," answered Governor Spalding. "He has no fleet to command and is retired from combat. He has resigned his active commission but will continue to advise President Mayfield, as long as his services are needed." Spalding opened up the small metal box and removed two shiny five-pointed gold stars. Stepping around the desk, he pinned them to the new fleet admiral's shoulders. "Congratulations, Fleet Admiral Vickers," he said with a broad smile. "I believe the rank of fleet admiral is on a par with a Cabinet member, during peace or war. That should help us to deal with Stroud, if he becomes a bigger problem."

The other men and women in the room stepped forward, shaking Kurt's hand and offering their congratulations. Spalding then had each of them sign the Presidential Declaration and had his secretary, who stood by to notarize it.

"We'll put this in a safe, in case it's ever needed," Spalding said in satisfaction. He dismissed the others and then gestured for Kurt to sit down. "I believe we have some other issues to cover. I understand from President Mayfield that you will shortly be going on a rescue mission to this Gothan Empire."

"Not until I'm satisfied Newton is adequately protected," Kurt replied as he sat back down. "That's one reason I want the *Kepler* and *Dante* finished and repaired. With those two ships and the rest of the fleet, Newton should be safe from attack."

"How will you find your way around this Gothan Empire or even find the abductees you're searching for?"

"I have a Profiteer on board the *Star Cross*," Kurt replied. "His name is Grantz, and he has agreed to be our guide."

"A Profiteer!" exploded Spalding, his eyes bulging. "How can you afford to trust him after what they did to Earth?"

"It's quite simple," answered Kurt with a conniving smile. "We bought his loyalty. He has signed a contract to act as a faithful member of my crew. The contract will be registered with a Controller, once we reach Kubitz. Due to their culture, Grantz wouldn't dare violate the contract, because of the severe repercussions he would receive. It would effectively ruin his life to betray us in any way."

Governor Spalding shook his head worriedly. "I just hope you know what you're doing."

"So do I," replied Kurt with a deep sigh.

-

Denise had just finished setting the table when she heard a knock at the front door.

"I'll get it!" yelled Bryan, as he shot toward the door like a bullet. Opening the door, he let out a happy whoop. "It's Uncle Kurt!"

Denise set down the last plate and headed toward the door, as a smiling Alex met her in the hallway.

"Your brother's here."

Reaching the door, they found Bryan dragging Kurt into the house with a determined look on his face. "I drew a spaceship, and I want to show it to you. It's just like the one that brought us here."

"You can show him the spaceship in a moment," Alex said, reaching out and shaking Kurt's now free hand. "It's good to see you, Kurt."

Denise stepped forward and gave Kurt a big sisterly hug. "I missed you, big brother."

"I'm glad to see you're all safe and settled in," Kurt said, as they walked down the hallway to the living room.

"I heard about Captain Randson's family," Denise said with a distressed look in her eyes. "It's just horrible."

"There were several thousand people taken off Earth," Kurt replied.

"You're going to go get them, aren't you?" asked Denise. "I know you won't allow humans to be held captives by these alien Profiteers."

"We're going to try," Kurt admitted. "But not for a while. We have some other things to take care of first."

"I hope you get them all back," commented Denise.

"How's the job hunt?" Kurt asked Alex, wanting to change the conversation.

"Good," Alex responded. "I had an interview at a computer service company today, and I think they'll offer me the job."

"That's great, honey!" Denise was pleased to hear this. "Once Bryan is settled in school, I'll also look for employment." Denise had an accounting degree and had been working at a law firm on Earth.

"Can I take Uncle Kurt to see my spaceship now?" asked Bryan, growing impatient.

"Yes," Denise said with a smile. "He's very happy to see you, *Uncle Kurt.*" She added in a whisper, "And he's adjusting well to the move. Better than me and Alex." She patted Bryan on the shoulder. "Go show Uncle Kurt your spaceship, and then it'll be time to eat."

"We're having fried chicken," Bryan announced. "Mom says it's your favorite."

Kurt laughed. "Let's go see this spaceship."

As Denise watched Bryan lead Kurt toward his room, she turned toward Alex. "I'm glad Kurt came over. It's good to see him."

"Yes, it is," replied Alex, taking Denise's hand. "He's a good man, and Bryan thinks the world of him."

Denise stood up. "Come help me put the food on the table? I don't know how long Kurt can stay, and I want to make the most of it." As Denise and Alex headed into the kitchen, she couldn't help but smile to herself. Facing Alex, she said, "You know, for the first time since the aliens attacked Earth, I feel completely safe. We have nothing to fear here."

"I hope so," Alex said. "You sure fixed a lot of chicken," he commented, as he set the large platter in the center of the table.

"You've never seen my brother eat fried chicken," Denise said with a grin. "He can really put it away. And, … for the rest of the evening, let's not talk about events on Earth or the Profiteers. This night will be about family. I know in my heart that Kurt will enjoy that. Okay with you, honey?"

"Sure," responded Alex, knowing how important this was to his wife. "I think we can manage that."

Chapter Seven

High Profiteer Creed gazed in satisfaction at the gold, platinum, and other rare metals piled high in the large hold of the cargo ship *Diadem*, still in Earth's orbit. At a quick guess, he estimated easily eight hundred million credits were in the hold. This was just the tip of what he expected to take from Earth.

"A good beginning," commented Clan Leader Jarls. He stepped over to a large crate, brimming full of different colored precious stones. He picked up several diamonds and rubies, and gazed critically at them, probably estimating their value. "These will bring a good price at the gem markets on Kubitz."

"The first two shiploads of humans leave tomorrow," Creed said, wishing Jarls would keep his hands out of the gems crate. Creed wouldn't put it past the Dacroni to slip one or two into his pockets.

"I have seen the women of this world," Jarls said, turning around to face Creed, still holding several dark red rubies in his hand. He held them up to the light, gazing at their radiant color. "They will do well in the slave markets on Kubitz. There will be a high demand for them in the pleasure houses. I suspect many humanoid races will be highly interested in procuring them."

"They have other uses besides the pleasure houses," pointed out Creed, watching the clan leader closely. "Household servants, taking care of children, and basic labor to name a few. Races other than humanoids will be highly interested in acquiring them for a number of uses both domestic and in their general labor force."

"Nevertheless, when I return to Kubitz, I may go to one of their pleasure houses to sample these human women myself," responded Jarls, as he turned and dropped the rubies back into the crate. "As for labor uses, this is not a heavy-gravity world. They will be useless in the mines and other heavy industries."

"One of your battleships will escort the two detainee ships and this cargo ship back to Kubitz," Creed continued. He knew the humans would bring a good price; they weren't the first group he had delivered to the slave markets. "I will be sending one of my battlecruisers and two light escorts along as well."

"Very well," Jarls replied. "After all, you're paying for my services." With that comment, Jarls exited the cargo hold.

"We should keep an eye on him," suggested Second Profiteer Lantz, who had been standing back, watching the other two. "He will do everything he can to increase his take from this venture. It wouldn't surprise me if one or two diamonds are missing from that crate."

"He will abide by our contract," growled Creed, agreeing in part with Lantz's statement. He walked over and looked down at the crate of precious stones. There was no way to tell if one or two were missing. "We just need to ensure that none of his mercenaries go to the surface. As long as we control all access to the planet's riches, we have nothing to fear."

"What about the human fleet that left this system?" Lantz asked. "What of it?"

"They have a small colony world a number of light-years from here," High Profiteer Creed replied. "From what we have been able to learn, it's not a very rich world, not worth the credits it would take to conquer it. As long as their ships stay away from Earth, we'll not interfere."

"And Clan Leader Jarls will see to that," said Lantz, nodding his head as his large eyes looked across the cargo hold. "That is why we signed a contract with the Dacroni."

Creed smiled a greedy grin. "He will, and, while he makes sure the Earth ships stay away, we'll continue to strip the planet of all its wealth. Our latest estimates indicate the potential for ten to twelve billion in credits, just from the gold and other precious metals."

"And the humans themselves," Lantz added. "Once they are sold on Kubitz, I plan to, at the least, visit several of the more esteemed pleasure houses too. Maybe I'll see Jarls."

"Next week the humans will make their next payment of eighty gold bars," Creed announced. He walked over to the two pallets that contained the tribute the humans had already paid. He picked up one, testing its weight. He turned it over in his hand, gazing at the alluring yellow color of the gold. "We could buy a new Profiteer fleet with each one of these pallets."

"We could become the largest and most powerful Profiteer fleet in the empire," said Lantz, as he thought about the ramifications. "With several fleets out raiding, we could become the richest Profiteers on Marsten."

"*Marsten!*" gloated Creed, his large eyes glinting. "We'll become the richest and most feared Profiteers in the empire!"

Down on the surface in the secret underground command bunker deep beneath the Canadian Rockies—the Rocky Mountains in southern Canada—President Mayfield looked at Fleet Admiral Tomalson. "I wish we knew what was happening on Newton."

"None of the Profiteer ships or the ships of their mercenaries have left the system," Tomalson responded. "We still have some surveillance data coming in via our stealthed military satellites." Even though Tomalson had retired from active duty he was serving as the president's advisor and would retain the rank of fleet admiral while on the Cabinet or until Fleet Admiral Vickers returned.

"No one's died anywhere on the planet yet due to this latest appearance of the Profiteers," General Braid added. "We're keeping a close but clandestine watch on all their activities. They've been active across the planet, landing their shuttles in nearly every country. So far no incidents."

"They've been content to strip the gold and jewelry from the shelves of our smaller cities," Raul Gutierrez reported. "We've sent word for our people to stay indoors anytime a Profiteer shuttle lands. They're to offer no resistance."

"What happens when these Profiteers realize how much gold and jewelry is owned by our civilians?" asked Mayfield with a deep and worried frown on his face. "What happens when they go door to door, taking our citizens' personal wealth? A hell of a lot of guns are out there. Someone will shoot one of the Profiteers, and then all hell will break lose."

Everyone in the room was quiet at that thought. There had been numerous attempts to pass laws to restrict gun ownership, but all had failed. The average North American Union household had at least one firearm, with the majority being shotguns or hunting rifles. Also a disturbing amount of large caliber semiautomatic assault rifles were in the hands of a lot of people who knew how to use them.

"We could offer more gold," suggested Raul, shifting uncomfortably in his chair. "Perhaps we can buy off the Profiteers, if there is, indeed, a shooting."

"It'll happen," General Braid predicted in a grim voice. "The question is, how will the Profiteers react?"

"They could bomb a city as an example," Tomalson said somberly. "I don't think they're that concerned about human life. We learned that when they first arrived and nuked our cities."

Mayfield looked around the room. Most of the chairs that normally held Cabinet members were empty. The vice president and the rest of the Cabinet had been dispersed to several other secure underground bunkers to ensure the government would continue to function in the event the presidential bunker was bombed.

"We'll continue to tell our citizens to cooperate," Mayfield said, letting out a deep breath. He leaned back in his chair and looked at General Braid. "Have our Special Forces keep a close eye on any of the Profiteers down here. Our men are to take no action, just observe."

"I'll make the arrangements," Braid replied. "It'll be difficult, as the Profiteers are landing their shuttles everywhere. We may not have people in position to get there quickly enough. We may need to use some reserve units in some of the smaller cities."

"Do the best you can," Mayfield ordered. He knew they couldn't move any military aircraft, as the Profiteers would probably shoot them down. The aliens had already restricted air travel to only a few flights per day. "This situation will get a lot worse before it gets any better. Speaking of a situation getting worse, has anyone seen or heard from the secretary of labor?"

"It's not good news," answered Raul, opening a folder and pulling out a sheet of paper. "It looks as if he bribed his way on board a Chinese cargo ship bound for Newton."

"Crap," muttered Fleet Admiral Tomalson, his eyes widening in concern. "That could cause some problems."

"If Governor Spalding and Fleet Admiral Vickers acted quickly enough," Mayfield responded. "Marlen Stroud's welcome to Newton will not have been what he desired."

"I hope they can contain him," Tomalson said in an aggravated voice. "I just can't believe he managed to get off the planet."

"Money," General Braid responded. "I suspect he paid a huge amount to get to Newton."

"Mr. President," Raul continued, as he shuffled through several papers. "I hate to bring this up, but I'm getting reports that the Profiteers have been rounding up people and taking them into orbit in their shuttles."

"There are several large ships up there," Tomalson pointed out. "They may be transport ships to house their captives."

"To sell on Kubitz," added General Braid with a forlorn look. "They're selling our people into slavery!"

"Fleet Admiral Vickers has his orders in that regard too," said Mayfield, trying to keep his own anger in check.

He hated the thought of more humans being taken by the Profiteers. It would make Vickers's job even harder. However, Mayfield could do nothing, other than use the military. If he did that, he would risk devastating reprisals from the Profiteers. The area around Washington, DC, and Chicago still bore witness to the dangers of angering the orbiting aliens.

-

Captain Nathan Aldrich gazed intently at the school across the street. A Profiteer shuttle sat in the large parking lot with a number of the aliens standing guard outside. In the last several hours, he had watched as a large number of humans had been taken inside the school's gymnasium.

"They're taking them up to their ships," Corporal Lasher said in anger. "We can't let them do this!"

"What if they're eating them?" Private Malone said in a shaky voice.

"They're not eating them," snapped Aldrich, glaring at Malone. There had been rumors of every kind in recent days.

"I don't know," Malone continued dubiously. "I saw several movies in the past where aliens came down to Earth and took people away to be eaten."

"Maybe we'll send you to them," Corporal Lasher responded. "That will give them a bellyache."

"That's enough," Aldrich said, shaking his head. These aliens had everyone on edge. "I don't see what we can do about the civilians."

He had six other Marines with him, and they had been following the Profiteers as they moved through the small town. The aliens had stripped all the valuables from the town's two jewelry stores and then proceeded to round up twenty humans.

"We can take them out," suggested Lasher. "They're not expecting an attack. We can take them out and free the captives."

"Then what?" asked Aldrich evenly. "The Profiteers might nuke the town. That would result in the deaths of thousands. Is that what you want?"

Lasher shook his head and let out a deep breath. "No."

Aldrich heard what sounded like frightened voices, and, looking back around the wall he and his men stood behind, he saw the captives being led from the gymnasium to the waiting shuttle. He wanted more than anything to order his squad to attack, to free the men and women. Several of the women were crying and sobbing hysterically. A few of the men looked like they wanted to fight back, but the heavily armed Profiteers were having none of that. Aldrich saw that most of the twenty were young, probably in their early to mid-twenties. Most of the women were quite good looking. Aldrich could feel his heart pounding, and he was taking deeper breaths. His grip tightened on his assault rifle.

"What's happening?" asked Corporal Lasher intently.

"They're moving the prisoners," Aldrich answered. He ducked back behind the wall, when one of the Profiteers looked in his direction. "Let's move and report in. Headquarters needs to know the aliens are rounding up humans."

As they pulled back and went down several deserted side streets to where they had left their vehicle, Aldrich felt as if he had failed in his mission. The duty of the military was to protect civilians, not observe them being herded into shuttles as if they were animals. Someday the word would be passed down for them to fight back; he hoped that day would come soon.

Aboard the *Ascendant Destruction*, First Profiteer Creed watched in deep satisfaction as the last shuttle full of humans docked to one of the detainee ships to unload its cargo. He had given strict orders that only young and healthy humans were to be sent to the slave markets on Kubitz. He wanted prime merchandise to be presented, so the prices could be driven up. He fully expected to receive anywhere from ten to fifteen thousand credits from each sale. That would make this load worth over twenty million credits! Enough money to buy several first-line battleships, if he wanted. If he did that, and hired the necessary crews, he would never have to hire mercenaries again.

The first bunch of captives had been taken to Kubitz for training and should be nearly ready for the slave auctions. He wished he could be at Kubitz for the sales, but that was impossible, so he had hired a dependable handler to take care of selling the humans. It would cost him a commission on each sale, but the profits would easily cover it.

It didn't take long for the shuttle to unload its cargo, and then both detainee ships and the cargo ship formed up with the Dacroni battleship, the Profiteer battlecruiser, and the two light escorts going along for protection. While Creed wasn't worried about the humans attempting to intercept the small convoy, it wasn't totally unheard of for other Profiteers to ambush another competitor's ships to take its riches. Creed was making sure that didn't happen.

"All ships are ready to depart," reported Third Profiteer Lukon from Communications. "Clan Leader Jarls is waiting for your permission to send them on their way."

"He wants to see that cargo deposited in the holding accounts on Kubitz," growled Second Profiteer Lantz.

"It's in the contract," Creed reminded his second in command. "There will be plenty for all of us before this is over. Earth will make us very rich."

Creed gazed at the tactical screen for several moments at the seven green icons representing the waiting convoy. Once word of this convoy reaching Kubitz got out, everyone would know he had made a major find. Others might possibly even come looking for Earth. Just another reason why he had replaced his lost ships and hired Clan Leader Jarls. There would be no trespassing on his new territory.

"Inform Clan Leader Jarls that the convoy may leave," he ordered.

Moments later, the convoy vanished into hyperspace. Creed allowed himself to smile; his first booty from Earth was safely away. It would take the convoy twelve to fourteen days to reach the open star cluster where the Gothan Empire and Kubitz were located. Once the ships were unloaded, they would immediately return. This was only the beginning of many such convoys.

-

Jarls watched in satisfaction as the convoy left. He had already been paid one hundred million credits for his fleet's services, and, once the convoy reached Kubitz, an additional eighty million would be paid to him as his share. This would be the easiest money he had ever made. Already he was making plans to double the size of his clan's fleet. He might even buy a large estate back on Dacron Four. He was interested in a prominent estate set back in a large mountain range there. This contract would give him the credits to buy it and more. Jarls folded his massive arms across his powerful chest. He was already planning on pushing High Profiteer Creed to extend the contract for an additional ninety days.

In Youngstown, Ohio, Corporal Donald Mercer watched angrily as six heavily armed aliens escorted twelve humans into a small fenced-in enclosure within one of the city's public parks. From what the corporal could see, at least fifty people were already inside the enclosure, sitting on the grass. They looked frightened and were talking to each other in low voices. Corporal Mercer knew he had strict orders not to interfere with the Profiteers, but his sister and her husband were two of the people the aliens were now putting inside the enclosure.

"What are we going to do?" asked Private Patricia Hatterson, standing next to him.

Donald motioned for his squad to move out of sight into an alley. "I can't let them take my sister," he said, knowing he was about to disobey orders. He looked at the other eight men and women who were with him. "I can't ask you to do the same."

"We're with you," Hatterson said without hesitation. "If it were a member of my family who the aliens had, I would do everything in my power to get them back."

"No alien shuttle on the ground," another private pointed out. "When it returns, it will probably take the people they've rounded up. So, whatever we do, it needs to be soon."

"My sister has a three-year-old son, who's staying at my parents," Donald said in a quiet voice. "I don't want him raised without his mom and dad. If we do this, we have to take out all the aliens and hide the bodies."

Hatterson moved to the edge of the alley and raised her rifle, gazing through its scope at the aliens around the enclosure. "I count fourteen of them," she said, as she stepped back farther into the alley. "They're all heavily armed and wearing some type of light body armor."

"We have armor-piercing rounds," commented another private. "They should penetrate the body armor."

"We'll have the element of surprise," one of the other privates pointed out. "We can do this."

"Very well," Donald said, reaching another decision. He felt his heart beating faster, knowing what he was about to commit his squad to. "We'll spread out around the perimeter of the park. Everyone pick out a target, and, at my signal, you'll open fire. Once the first alien goes down, we have to take out the rest quickly, before they can signal their shuttle or one of their spaceships in orbit."

"A lot of cover in the park," Hatterson said. "Between the trees and the statues, we should be able to get pretty close without detection."

It took a few minutes, but the nine determined soldiers quietly made their way to the boundaries of the park, and then used the tall trees and park statues to gradually move into firing range. The Profiteers seemed more interested in looking at their captives and making comments to each other, as they pointed out various humans.

Donald reached the position he sought behind a pair of large trees, which concealed him from the Profiteers. He waited a few more minutes, until he was satisfied the rest of his squad had reached their firing positions. He took a deep steadying breath, knowing what he was about to do could result in his court-martial and end his military career.

Raising his rifle, Donald took careful aim as he looked through his scope, until it was centered on the chest of the nearest Profiteer. As soon as his shot was fired, the others would follow suit. Donald took a deep breath and slowly squeezed the trigger. A loud shot rang out, and he saw his target stumble back with a startled look on his face. His light blue skin color suddenly turned white, as he looked down at the spreading red stain on his chest; then he fell to the ground.

Other soldiers were firing now, and more of the aliens were taken out. From the enclosure, panicked screams could be heard, as the captured humans dove for cover. However, now the aliens were firing back. Bright blue beams of energy lashed out from the Profiteers' weapons.

Donald heard a loud scream over to his right and saw one of his soldiers stumble from behind a tree with a smoldering hole in his chest. The soldier looked over at Donald with a frightened look on his face and then collapsed to the ground, not moving. An energy beam struck one of the trees near Donald, blowing a large smoking hole in the trunk. He winced and then resumed firing at the aliens. They needed to end this quickly; he would mourn the dead later.

For another minute, the firing was intense. The Profiteers were exposed with little cover, while the soldiers were behind the trees and statues. The sound of heavy weapons fire filled the air, along with the high-pitched humming sound made by the aliens' energy weapons.

Private Hatterson was under heavy fire from a Profiteer, who was kneeling and firing energy burst after energy burst toward her position. Taking careful aim, Donald fired two rounds into the alien's chest, dropping him to the ground. Then the firing died down and came to a stop. It suddenly became very quiet.

Stepping from behind the trees, Donald jogged toward the park's interior enclosure, his assault rifle held at the ready in case any of the aliens had survived the attack. Other soldiers appeared, quickly approaching the enclosure.

Private Hatterson stopped at a Profiteer sitting on the ground, holding his shoulder. The alien looked up at her with a scowl on his face. Without a moment's hesitation, she pulled the 9mm pistol from her holster and put a bullet in the alien's head. "No prisoners," she said firmly. "Not after what they did to Chicago and Washington, DC."

Donald nodded. He agreed with her sentiment. "Let's set these people free and get them away from the park. Then we'll come back and hide the bodies." Looking around he saw that three of his soldiers were missing. It didn't take long to confirm they had been killed in the brief battle.

Several of his squad quickly opened the gate to the enclosure and ushered out the people. A few had to be helped, as they had been wounded too.

"Donald!" his sister screamed, as she saw who had rescued them. She rushed up, giving him a quick hug, and then stepped back. "Where did you come from?"

"Don't worry about that for now," he replied, as he looked at his sister and brother-in-law. "Get to Mom and Dad's, and stay there."

"Is there anything we can do to help?" his brother-in-law asked.

"Just get these people as a far away as possible," Donald said.

After a few minutes, his sister and her husband were far down the street, leading away the other freed human captives. Satisfied they were out of danger, Donald turned. It was time to remove the dead bodies of the aliens and to hide what had happened here.

Donald heard a vehicle engine and saw Private Hatterson drive up in a pickup truck.

"Where did you find the keys to that?" he asked.

"I hot-wired it," she said with a grin. "Something I learned as a kid."

"Let's get these bodies loaded up, and we'll hide them where the other aliens won't find them," Donald ordered. He wondered briefly what type of life Hatterson had had before joining the military, if she knew how to hot-wire a vehicle. He was afraid to even ask.

"We can't hide all the evidence of a battle being fought here," one of the other privates pointed out. "The Profiteers' energy weapons left burn marks and spent shell casings are everywhere."

"We'll police the area as well as we can," answered Donald, knowing the private was right. "Maybe we can cause just enough doubt so they won't be certain what happened here."

"Will you report to command what we did?"

Donald let out a deep breath. "Yes, I think I have to, just in case there are repercussions." It was just starting to set in that three of his soldiers had died in the battle. He had been in command and he was responsible for their deaths.

An hour later the park was clear. All that remained was an empty enclosure and a few smoldering trees were Profiteer energy weapons had struck.

-

Several hours passed and two Profiteer shuttles landed in the large parking area next to the park. Twenty heavily armed profiteers swarmed out and moved carefully to the enclosure. For twenty minutes, they searched, looking at the burn marks and finding a few spent shell casings that the human soldiers had overlooked. They also found several telling areas of blood on the ground. They took a few samples and then returned to their shuttles, which promptly lifted off.

An hour later the park suddenly exploded, as a powerful ion beam impacted the ground. Other beams flashed down from space, destroying parked vehicles, buildings, and even blasting deep holes in the city's streets. For ten minutes, the deadly onslaught continued before finally coming to a stop. When it ended, a ten-block area around the park had been devastated. Bellowing fires raged everywhere, and smoke rose to blot out the sun.

-

In orbit, First Profiteer Creed looked at a large viewscreen, which showed the devastation his ion beams had wrought. He had promised the humans he wouldn't nuke any of their larger cities, as long as they paid the monthly tribute. However, he had never said anything about not using other weapons.

"That should teach them a lesson," Creed said, his ruthless gaze watching as the smoke from his attack covered the stricken city.

"For now," Second Profiteer Lantz agreed. "However, there'll probably be more incidents."

"Then they'll pay the penalty each time," Creed said, feeling no remorse at what he had done. "We own this world now, not them."

General Braid stepped into President Mayfield's office with a grim look on his face. "There's been an incident in Youngstown, Ohio."

Mayfield knew from the tone of the general's voice that the news wasn't good. "What's happened?"

"A young corporal and his soldiers attacked a compound where the Profiteers were holding people for transport to their ships," Braid began. "Evidently two of the captives were his sister and brother-in-law. He killed the fourteen Profiteers holding them and freed the prisoners. When the Profiteers learned what had happened, they used some type of energy beam to level about ten city blocks. Casualties are estimated to be around two to three thousand."

President Mayfield closed his eyes and shook his head. "This was bound to happen," he said, pained at the loss of so many civilian lives.

"At least they didn't destroy the entire city," Braid said. "They could have, if they wanted to."

"What will you do about the corporal?"

"He's turned himself in and accepted responsibility for his actions."

"His sister," said Mayfield, thinking about the corporal's actions. He wondered what he would have done in the same situation. "Hold the corporal for a few days and then let him go. I suspect this won't be the last incident."

General Braid nodded and replied grimly, "No, it won't."

After the general left, President Mayfield moaned and thought over what had happened. It would be many long months before newly promoted Fleet Admiral Vickers could do anything, possibly even years. Mayfield dreaded thinking about what could happen to the people of Earth between now and the time Vickers returned. Mayfield greatly feared that many more people would die before this was over.

Chapter Eight

Fleet Admiral Vickers gazed at the large viewscreen on the front wall of the Command Center. A blue-white globe floated there with deep blue oceans and a scattering of white clouds. Newton was a beautiful world, holding a little over eight million people. He hoped it would still be unharmed when he returned from the Gothan Empire.

Leaning back in his command chair, he thought briefly about the conversation he had had with Profiteer Grantz several weeks before.

Kurt and Captain Randson had sat down in a secure briefing room with the Profiteer. On the table was a small bar of gold that Kurt had brought along to ensure that Grantz was cooperative.

"More gold," Grantz said with a slight hint of greed in his voice. "What is it you want this time? I have already agreed to act as one of your crew, until such a time as my contract has been fulfilled."

"Your contract is pretty simple," Kurt said, as he ran his right hand over the bar of gold, which sat on the table directly in front of him. "What I want to discuss are what we humans call *bonuses*."

"Bonuses?" Grantz asked with a confused look in his large eyes. "What do you propose?"

"For you to act as more than just a member of this crew," Kurt said carefully. "For you to do everything in your power to ensure our mission is a success. If it is, you will leave this ship a very rich man."

Grantz seemed to consider what Kurt had just said. His large eyes strayed to the bar of gold on the table. "If I agree, I want the guards on my quarters removed."

"Demonstrate your willingness to do as I ask first," countered Kurt.

Grantz leaned back and ran his right hand through the coarse white hair that covered his head. "Very well," he said. "As we approach the star cluster that contains the Gothan Empire, your fleet needs to be on guard. Word of what High Profiteer Creed discovered will have spread through the empire by now. Others will seek your world and attempt to intercept any convoys inbound toward the cluster."

"You would rob from your own people?" Captain Randson gasped, his eyes widening at this concept.

"Some of the smaller Profiteer fleets would," responded Grantz, shrugging his shoulders. "It's just how things are done. The larger fleets will recognize Creed's claim to your world and will not interfere."

"We need to emerge from hyperspace before we enter the cluster," Andrew said, responding to Grantz's words. "We'll also have to drop out of hyperspace several more times once we're in the cluster, as the star density will preclude us from jumping straight to Kubitz."

"Is there any place in the cluster that will be safer than others?" asked Kurt, looking at Grantz.

His eyes were still focused on the bar of gold.

"No," replied Grantz, shaking his head. "The smaller fleets, when not out on raiding missions, normally patrol the cluster, seeking small unescorted ships or convoys."

"We can hold our dropout times to a minimum," suggested Andrew. "Compute our next hyperspace jump and leave as quickly as possible."

"How long will it take to compute the jumps?"

"Twenty to thirty minutes at the most."

"What type of weapons will these ships be armed with?" asked Kurt. He had hoped to reach Kubitz without being involved in a battle, particularly with the *Newton Princess* and the *Lansing* along. Both ships were lightly armed and were being equipped with rudimentary energy shields.

"Same as High Profiteer Creed's ships," Grantz answered promptly. "Ion beams, energy projectors, and hypermissiles for the most part."

"What's a hypermissile?" asked Andrew.

"It has a miniature hyperspace drive which can be activated once it exits the firing tube. The missile will enter hyperspace and won't stop until it strikes its target. Either an energy shield or a ship's hull. If it strikes nothing after a given amount of time, the missile will drop from hyperspace and self-destruct."

"What about other weapons?" asked Andrew. "Do any of the other worlds in the Gothan Empire use different weapons than these?"

"Direct energy cannons," Grantz said uneasily. "They're more expensive and take a very powerful energy source. For that reason they're mostly found on mercenary ships, particularly those used by the Dacroni."

"What happens when we reach Kubitz?" asked Kurt. He wanted as much information as possible about what they were getting into.

Grantz's brow furrowed as he thought over the question. "Kubitz maintains a large fleet of what you would call police craft. They patrol out to the sixth planet and will intercept any ship that enters the quarantine zone without permission. They have a large fleet of powerfully equipped battleships at Kubitz, which they can call upon if necessary."

"So we can't jump in close to Kubitz?" asked Andrew.

"No. Ships are not allowed to jump inside the orbit of the sixth planet. Most ships exit hyperspace between the orbits of the sixth and seventh planet near the Controller space station."

"What's the Controller space station?" asked Kurt. Grantz was telling them a lot of information he hadn't mentioned before.

"I was going to tell you once we neared the Kubitz System," Grantz answered. "All inbound ships must register with the station before proceeding to the inner system. A fee will be assessed for each ship. Ships can stay out near the station to conduct their business or, for a higher fee, can proceed into orbit over Kubitz. The space above the planet will be packed with ships from all over the galaxy."

Kurt nodded, satisfied with the answers Grantz had given. "I'll have the guards removed from the door of your quarters.

You're free to roam the ship but stay out of restricted areas." Kurt paused for a moment and then slid the small bar of gold across the table to Grantz, who quickly picked it up. "It's yours, plus more where that came from, if you continue to show your value to this mission. And that means no withholding of information."

Grantz nodded, as he gazed down at the bar of yellow gold in his hand. He hefted it, and a broad smile spread across his face. "With me to advise you, I promise that your mission will be a success."

"See that it is," Kurt responded, as he and Andrew turned and left the room.

"Ready for departure," reported Captain Randson bringing Kurt's attention back to the present. "The *Newton Princess*, the cargo ship *Lansing*, and the light cruisers *Sydney* and *Dallas* are in formation."

Kurt nodded. The *Newton Princess* was a large passenger liner, which could bring back any captive humans they could free. Also a handpicked First Contact team from the exploration cruisers was on board. The *Lansing* carried some very valuable cargo—a portion of the gold brought from Earth. The remaining portion, a good part of the gold, platinum, and other precious metals and stones, was in a new secure hidden vault on Newton, under heavy guard. The *Lansing* would also be used to bring back any weapons they managed to procure.

"Break orbit and proceed outward at 10 percent sublight," ordered Kurt, leaning back in his command chair, anxious to get this mission started.

On another of the screens, he could see Newton Station. It was much larger than it had been in the past. The construction bay and manufacturing section taken from the shipyard above Earth had been added. In addition, work had already commenced on the large flight bay that would eventually house the station's fighters and bombers.

"Rear Admiral Wilson is wishing us the best of luck," reported Ensign Brenda Pierce from Communications.

Wilson had been promoted to rear admiral and would be in charge of the fleet while Kurt was gone. He had formerly commanded one of the fleet's battlecruisers but had been on leave on Earth when the Profiteers had originally attacked. Kurt had been relieved to have someone with Wilson's experience available to step into the rear admiral position. The *Kepler* would serve as Wilson's flagship.

"Put the *Kepler* on the main viewscreen," ordered Kurt.

Instantly the 1,200-meter-long battlecarrier appeared. The *Kepler* had a crew of 1,400 and held 80 Scorpion bombers and 120 Lance fighters in her large twin flight bays.

"Damn, that's a big ship," commented Andrew, as he looked appreciatively at the battlecarrier.

"Big enough so the Profiteers will regret ever coming to the Newton System, if and when they show up," Kurt said. He could see several small groups of Lance fighters flying in formation around the ship as part of its normal CSP.

In the distance, he could see the smaller carriers, the *Dante* and the *Vindication.*

One of the reasons he had waited so long to leave for the Profiteer's Gothan Empire was to allow for the *Kepler* to be finished and the repairs to the *Dante* to be done. The crews on the station had worked around the clock to finish everything, which was a lot considering all that had to be done to the small carrier *Dante.* They had accomplished a miracle in repairing it so quickly.

"The system should be safe until we return."

"With our kidnapped people," Andrew said in a firm and determined voice.

Kurt knew it had been difficult for Andrew these last few weeks, not knowing what had happened to his wife and daughter.

"We'll find Emily and Alexis," promised Kurt. His XO had been greatly concerned about his missing family. "We'll bring them all back."

"Do you trust Grantz?" asked Andrew, raising his eyebrow. "All of this depends on the Profiteer to guide us, once we reach the Gothan Empire."

"He'll do what's in his contract," Kurt answered. He had dwelled on this considerably. "Plus he's anxious to receive the gold we've promised him."

"An entire culture based on greed and thievery," muttered Andrew, shaking his head. "This Gothan Empire is like something out of Earth's past."

"The Barbary pirates," suggested Kurt. "They raided from North Africa for several centuries until most nations paid them a tribute to allow their ships to pass by unmolested. Two small wars were fought between the United States and the pirates, which finally ended their threat to American shippers. This Gothan Empire seems to be the modern-day Barbary pirates but on a much larger scale."

As he spoke, the *Star Cross* and her fleet broke orbit, and accelerated away from the planet. On the viewscreens, the planet Newton, the *Kepler*, and Newton Station rapidly dwindled.

"Hyperdrive is charged," reported Ensign Charles Styles from the Helm. "Course is laid in."

"All ships report ready to enter hyperspace," added Ensign Pierce.

Kurt took a deep breath. He looked longingly at Newton, now nearly two hundred thousand kilometers away. He had told his sister good-bye the night before and had even spoken to Bryan for a few minutes, promising to bring the six-year-old something from this new adventure.

"Take the fleet into hyperspace," he ordered. It was time to go to the Gothan Empire.

-

Ten days later, Kurt and Captain Randson sat down once more in a secure briefing room with Profiteer Grantz.

"What kind of defenses does Kubitz have?" asked Kurt. He felt uneasy about taking his ships in close to the planet considering how many unknown ships would be in orbit.

"The most powerful in the galaxy," boasted Grantz, his eyes lighting up. "A full-scale orbital defense system, with battleships, and planet-based defensive and offensive weapons. I once heard High Profiteer Creed say that Kubitz by itself could hold off any one of the major galactic powers."

"Is there any reason they would attack us or allow other Profiteers to try to take our ships?"

"No, the Controllers won't permit it," Grantz said in a serious tone. "Once you arrive at the outer Controller station and have declared your intent to trade, no attacks against competitors are allowed. Your ships fall under the protection of the Kubitz government. Of course no ships are allowed to discharge a weapon or fire a missile once the fee has been paid."

"What happens if someone does?" asked Andrew.

"I saw it once a number of years ago," Grantz admitted, as his large eyes narrowed, recalling the incident. "Two of the smaller rival Profiteer fleets were having a dispute over a cargo ship that both claimed. One ship fired on another, and, before anyone else could respond, the Kubitz defense grid activated. The offending ship was blown from space, and the breaching Profiteer fleet eventually had all its ships confiscated. There hasn't been an incident since."

"Any other surprises you haven't mentioned?" asked Kurt.

"No," Grantz answered.

"Very well, you can go," Kurt said. He watched as Grantz stood up and left the room.

"What do you think?" asked Andrew. "Can we trust him?"

"I think so," answered Kurt, thinking about what the Profiteer had said. "The gold and our contract filed with the Controllers will see to that."

Two days later, the *Star Cross* and her small fleet dropped from hyperspace into a small star system just short of the Gothan star cluster.

"Report!" ordered Fleet Admiral Vickers, as he gazed anxiously at the tactical display and the viewscreens. The screens quickly cleared, showing a scattering of unfamiliar stars.

"Sensors are clear in our immediate area," answered Lieutenant Brooks. She pressed several icons on her computer screen. "Beginning long-range scans."

"Keep the fleet at Condition One, until we're ready to jump," Kurt ordered. "Ensign Pierce, contact the *Newton Princess* and inform Captain Mertz that he can send the shuttle with the First Contact team." The First Contact team had requested to sit down with Grantz to discuss in more detail what would be occurring at Kubitz and also to learn more about the Controllers. They had already met with Grantz several times in the past before the fleet had left Newton, as well as talked to him numerous times over the ship's comm.

A few moments later, Lieutenant Brooks turned toward the admiral. "Shuttle has departed the *Newton Princess*. It should be docking in seven to eight minutes. Long-range scans are showing no unknown contacts."

Kurt breathed a sigh of relief. "Take the fleet to Condition Two until further notice."

"We are fortunate no Profiteers were waiting for us," commented Grantz, who had been called to the Command Center for this dropout from hyperspace. "I suspect there are numerous small fleets on this side of the cluster, hoping to locate one of High Profiteer Creed's cargo ships."

"Surely he will have a powerful escort with any ships he sends back?" said Captain Randson.

"He should," answered Grantz. "That's one of the reasons he hired the Dacroni mercenaries. Their battleships will make for a dangerous escort to any small Profiteer fleet looking for a quick profit."

"Shuttle is docking," Captain Randson reported. "It will be returning to the *Newton Princess* shortly. We should be able to reenter hyperspace in twelve to fifteen minutes."

The minutes slowly passed. On one of the viewscreens, the shuttle that had brought over the First Contact team returned to the *Newton Princess* and entered its small flight bay.

"Contacts!" Lieutenant Brooks suddenly called out. "Twelve million kilometers. Detecting scans!"

"They just dropped from hyperspace," uttered Captain Randson, as he looked at the tactical display, now displaying the unknown ships. "They're way outside of weapons range."

"They'll locate us shortly," warned Grantz, while he studied the red threat icons on the tactical screen and the data displayed. "It looks like a small Profiteer fleet. Their biggest ship will be an escort cruiser."

"Four ships all around six hundred meters in length," confirmed Lieutenant Brooks, as she checked the information from the sensor scans.

"Prepare for combat," ordered Kurt, leaning forward in his command chair. He had hoped to leave this system without detection.

Alarms sounded, and red lights flashed as the Command Center came alive with intense activity while the crew prepared for possible battle.

"They've detected us," warned Lieutenant Brooks. "I'm reading active sensor scans. The four contacts have turned in our direction and are accelerating on an intercept course."

"Jump coordinates are locked in, and the hyperdrive is fully charged," reported Ensign Styles. "We can enter hyperspace at any time."

"All ships reporting ready to jump," added Ensign Pierce from Communications.

"Take us into hyperspace," ordered Kurt. At least this would be one battle they could avoid.

"Entering hyperspace," confirmed Ensign Styles, as he activated the ship's hyperdrive.

Kurt felt a momentary wrenching sensation, and then the red threat icons on the tactical screen vanished. His fleet was safe for now, but they would have to drop from hyperspace twice more before they reached their destination.

—

Kurt sat in his quarters behind his desk. They would shortly be dropping from hyperspace again, and he wanted to catch up on a little paperwork before that happened. He was tempted to go to the briefing room, where the First Contact team was locked away with Grantz. He allowed himself to smile briefly. The very concept of a culture based on profits and thievery was almost unbelievable, at least in modern times. The Gothan Empire, to put it in simple terms, was nothing more than a collection of pirates.

Looking down at the reports on his desk, he let out a deep sigh. Fuel usage, consumables usage, status of spare parts—the lists went on and on. He allowed his gaze to shift to a picture of his sister and her family on the right side of his desk. Denise and Alex had their arms around each other's waists, and Bryan stood slightly in front, holding a small replica of the *Star Cross* in his hands. All three had smiles on their faces.

Kurt reached out and picked up the photo. Family was very important to him; sometimes he regretted not finding someone special and settling down. However, his career had always prevented that. He had hoped someday to command one of the large exploration cruisers but had been given the *Star Cross* instead. Now here he was, farther from Earth and Newton than any human exploration ship had ever gone, on a mission bound to encounter numerous and different alien cultures.

"Hyperspace dropout in twenty minutes," Captain Randson said over the ship's comm system.

Letting out a deep sigh, Kurt replaced the picture. It was time to return to the Command Center. He knew that Andrew was anxious to reach Kubitz and see if they could find Emily and Alexis.

—

Sitting down in his command chair, Kurt read the counter on the tactical display, which showed two minutes until dropout.

To his right stood Grantz, who had been summoned to the Command Center. Lieutenant Tenner, the lead officer for the First Contact team, had come also.

"Take us to Condition One," ordered Kurt. "Contact the *Sydney* and *Dallas* and inform them to go to Condition One as well." Traveling together in hyperspace allowed for short-range communications.

"Dropout!" called out Ensign Styles.

The last few seconds quickly passed, and then the *Star Cross* dropped from hyperspace.

Kurt took a deep breath, as he felt the familiar wrenching sensation. Then he intently watched the viewscreens come on and the tactical screen update.

"All systems functioning normally," reported Captain Randson.

"Energy shield is up, and all weapons are online," added Lieutenant Mays.

"No contacts on the short-range sensors," reported Lieutenant Brooks, as her hands moved quickly over her computer screen, lightly touching different icons.

"Get our next jump calculated," ordered Kurt. "All ships will stay at Condition One."

"*Lansing* is reporting a fluctuation in their hyperdrive power retainment system," reported Ensign Pierce. "Their chief engineer says it will take about twenty minutes to check it. He advises that we don't jump until they've completed their diagnostics."

"Understood," answered Kurt. "Tell them to get it done as quickly as possible."

On a main viewscreen appeared the *Lansing*, among the largest and more modern cargo ships in the fleet. That was one of the reasons the ship had been chosen to accompany the fleet on this mission.

"It's dangerous to remain here too long," warned Grantz. "This part of the empire is heavily traveled by Profiteer ships."

The minutes passed slowly by, as they waited for the *Lansing* to finish their diagnostics, so they could determine if it was safe to jump into hyperspace. The tension in the Command Center mounted as every extra minute spent in this system risked the chance of detection. Suddenly warning alarms sounded, and a red light flashed above the sensor console.

"Unknown contacts emerging from hyperspace," reported Lieutenant Brooks nervously. "Distance is two million kilometers."

"Put them on a viewscreen," ordered Kurt, leaning forward in his command chair.

"Tellurites," muttered Grantz unhappily, as he saw the ships and identified the markings. "They operate a midsize fleet."

"Who are Tellurites?" asked Lieutenant Tenner.

"One of the smaller worlds in the empire," Grantz informed him. "They operate a number of small fleets, similar to this one, which routinely prey on inbound cargo ships."

"Give me a ship count and type," Kurt ordered from Sensors, as he listened to Grantz.

"Eight escort cruisers and one battlecruiser," reported Lieutenant Brooks. "They have turned and are moving toward us at a high rate of acceleration."

"How long until the *Lansing* has completed its diagnostics?"

"Five more minutes," Captain Randson reported, his eyes focusing on the admiral. "We could attempt to jump and hope the problem with the hyperdrive system on the *Lansing* is only a computer glitch."

"No," Kurt answered, shaking his head. "We can't afford to lose the cargo ship. It has the gold on board that we'll need to complete our mission on Kubitz." Kurt thought over his options. "The fleet will jump as soon as the *Lansing* has completed her diagnostics and confirmed there are no problems."

"The Tellurites will attack as soon as they're in range," warned Grantz, his large eyes narrowing sharply. "They will show your crews no mercy. They want the cargo ship and possibly your passenger ship as well."

Kurt activated the ship-to-ship comm frequency. "All ships, stand by for combat operations. *Newton Princess* and *Lansing*, you're to stay behind the *Star Cross* and our two light cruisers. We'll give you covering fire, until we're ready to jump."

"What if the Tellurites don't fire?" asked Andrew, looking over at Grantz. "They may want to negotiate first."

"No!" Grantz said emphatically, shaking his head. "They won't negotiate. They won't leave any witnesses to their attack."

Kurt gazed at the tactical screen and the rapidly approaching ships. "Grantz, contact those ships and tell them to stop their approach, or we'll fire on them."

"It won't do any good," Grantz said with a frown, as he walked over to the communications console.

Ensign Pierce changed to the frequency Grantz indicated, and sat there listening, while he warned the inbound ships in the Profiteer language. It only took a moment for a reply to come back.

"They're demanding you drop your shields and power down your weapons," Grantz reported grimly. "They say, if you do, that they'll only search your ships, take whatever valuables they may find, and then allow you to go on your way."

"Fat chance of that," muttered Captain Randson.

"They can't be trusted," reiterated Grantz, his large eyes gazing intently at Kurt. "You should fire on them first."

"They're nearly in weapons range," warned Lieutenant Brooks with a look of concern.

"Stand by to fire," ordered Kurt, reaching a decision. He could feel his pulse race. "Both light cruisers and the *Star Cross* will target the battlecruiser with our particle beam cannons. Ignore their lighter units for now."

"Good decision," commented Grantz, folding his arms across his chest and gazing expectantly at the viewscreens.

Andrew focused on Kurt. "That might let their lighter units get in some hits."

"True," Kurt replied. "But, if we can take out their battlecruiser, the lighter units may turn back."

"Do we fire first?" asked Andrew, looking unsure. Then, in a quieter voice, he added, "What if Grantz lied to us about what the Tellurites said?"

"I didn't lie," Grantz said, overhearing Andrew's comment. "I signed the contract. You can trust me."

Kurt gestured toward the tactical screen and the rapidly approaching Profiteers. "Does that look like a peaceful formation?"

Andrew shook his head and went to stand behind the tactical station, in case he was needed.

"Weapons are ready to fire," reported Lieutenant Mays, as she spoke to her tactical officers. "Targeting the battlecruiser with our particle beam cannon."

Kurt toggled on the ship-to-ship communications. "Lock particle beams on target and prepare to fire."

"Combat range," Lieutenant Brooks said, her face whiter than normal.

"Fire!" ordered Kurt, his eyes focused sharply on the tactical display.

"Firing," reported Lieutenant Mays from Tactical.

From the bow of the *Star Cross*, a dark blue particle beam flashed forth to strike the energy shield of the inbound Tellurite battlecruiser. From the *Dallas* and the *Sydney* additional beams lashed out, striking the alien ship. The enemy's screen flared brightly, and then one of the beams penetrated, striking the bow section of the vessel. A brilliant explosion erupted when the beam struck the hull, and debris began drifting away from the ship. The ship's energy screen seemed to flicker, and another particle beam penetrated it, blasting a huge glowing gash in the side of the now partially disabled Tellurite battlecruiser.

The two light cruisers turned broadside and opened fire with their laser turrets and railguns, pounding the weakening shield with their fire. Then the screen failed completely, and the weapons fire from the two light cruisers tore open compartment after compartment rapidly disabling the battlecruiser.

"Launch a Hydra missile," ordered Kurt between clenched teeth. "Let's finish her off." He wanted this battle over with as quickly as possible before any of his ships could be damaged. With their fleet so far from Newton, there would be no way to implement major repairs.

From the *Star Cross* a small Hydra missile launched from one of the ship's missile tubes. The missile contained a ten-kiloton warhead, which smashed into the Tellurite battlecruiser. The ship vanished in a brilliant flash of light, as a small sun appeared in its location.

"Your missiles travel too slowly," commented Grantz, shaking his head in disapproval. "If the defensive batteries on the battlecruiser were still functioning, they would have easily intercepted it."

"Tellurite battlecruiser is down," confirmed Lieutenant Brooks, the color returning to her face.

The *Star Cross* shuddered slightly as an energy beam from one of the inbound escort cruisers struck the ship's shield.

"Grantz, contact whoever is in charge over there and tell them, if they don't withdraw immediately, we'll destroy their other ships."

Grantz quickly stepped back over to the communications console and sent the message.

"The Tellurites are breaking off," Lieutenant Brooks reported.

On the tactical screen, the inbound Tellurite ships came to a stop and then reversed course.

"They agreed," Grantz said with a grin. "They apologized for the attack and said it was a misunderstanding. They didn't like losing their battlecruiser."

"Why would they apologize?" asked Andrew with a frown.

"So you won't file a complaint with the Controllers at Kubitz," Grantz explained. "In a failed attack, and, if it can be proven the Tellurites were guilty, they are required to pay for any damages they may have caused."

Andrew shook his head in disgust. "That's one hell of a legal system you have."

Grantz shrugged his shoulders. "It works and keeps the peace between the worlds of the empire."

"The *Lansing* reports the diagnostic scan is complete, and they did find a small malfunction with the energy system," Ensign Pierce reported. "The fault has been corrected, and they're ready to jump."

"Let's get out of here, before someone else shows up," Kurt ordered. "We have one more jump, and then we'll make the final one to take us to the Kubitz System."

"Finally," Andrew said, his eyes focusing on the admiral.

"We're nearly there," Kurt said, knowing what Andrew was thinking. "A few more hours and we'll reach Kubitz." Kurt just hoped that all the abductees were still there and hadn't already been sold at one of the slave auctions. Grantz had confided to Kurt that, in all likelihood, the auction hadn't been held yet, but that time was growing short.

As the *Star Cross* and her fleet jumped into hyperspace, Kurt wondered what was ahead of them. They were in an unknown section of the galaxy depending on an alien, whose people had nuked Earth, to guide them. So many things could go wrong that he was afraid to even think about them. Kurt's eyes shifted over to Grantz, who was leaving Command Center with Lieutenant Tenner. If the conniving Profiteer had lied to them, it was doubtful any of them would ever see home again.

Chapter Nine

"Emergence in five minutes," reported Captain Randson, as he waited anxiously for dropout.

"We will be detected immediately," Grantz informed Fleet Admiral Vickers. He stood next to the admiral, observing the activity in the busy Command Center. "The entire Kubitz System is covered by a series of hyperspace detection satellites."

"We'll inform them that we're here to make some military purchases and to check out the slave markets," spoke up Lieutenant Marvin Tenner. He and the other members of the First Contact team had spent a lot of time speaking with Profiteer Grantz about the Kubitz System and what they could expect when they arrived.

"Fleet is at Condition Two," added Captain Randson, impatient for them to arrive at their destination.

"All ships will come to a dead stop once we emerge," ordered Kurt over the ship-to-ship comm. "We will make no overtly hostile moves. Once we have established communication with the Controller station, Profiteer Grantz will explain to them why we're here." Kurt, Grantz, and Lieutenant Tenner had devised a plan that should allow them to go to Kubitz. Kurt just hoped everything worked out. It made him nervous being so dependent on the Profiteer and the information he had provided them.

"It will be necessary for me to go to the station and pay the fees, so your ships can stay in the system and be under protection of the Kubitz defense forces," Grantz reminded the admiral.

"Lieutenant Tenner and I will be going with you," Kurt informed Grantz. He wondered why the Profiteer was so insistent about them not accompanying him. Was there something on the station he didn't want Kurt to find out?

"Emergence," called out Ensign Styles.

Kurt felt the *Star Cross* drop back into normal space. He grew tense waiting for the screens to clear. Grantz had made it clear that the fleet should leave their energy shields down and their weapons at minimal power.

"Contacts!" called out Lieutenant Brooks, as her short-range sensors detected numerous power sources. "I'm picking up a large number of ships and one truly massive structure."

"That would be the Controller station," commented Grantz, as he looked over at the admiral. "They should be hailing us shortly."

"We're being challenged," Ensign Pierce reported, as a demanding voice came over her comm console.

"I'm detecting a squadron of six small warships accelerating toward us," added Lieutenant Brooks. "Ships are two hundred meters in length and heavily armed."

"Kubitz police ships," Grantz informed Kurt. "I better explain to them why we're here and make arrangements for us to go to the station."

"Do so," Kurt ordered, unhappy that Grantz seemed to be the one in charge of the situation. Kurt needed to find some way to correct that.

Grantz stepped to Communications and quickly established contact with the station. He spoke quickly in the Profiteer language and, at one point, seemed to become aggravated, as if he were arguing with whomever he was speaking with. He relayed a few more terse sentences and, at last, appeared satisfied and cut the comm channel.

"It's done," he said. "We may approach the station, and we're to stop at fifty thousand kilometers. From there we're to take a shuttle to the station and pay our fees."

"What were you arguing about?" asked Captain Randson, his eyes focused intently on Grantz. He didn't trust the Profiteer.

The Profiteer laughed and slowly shook his head. "They weren't happy to see a group of unknown and obviously heavily armed ships appear unannounced. They were demanding a fee nearly three times normal. I managed to talk them down to the normal fee, explaining that you would spend a large number of credits on Kubitz. Unfortunately I also had to offer a small bribe."

"A bribe!" blurted out Andrew, his eyes bulging. "Why a bribe?"

"Everyone skims from the top," Grantz explained evenly. "The bribes aren't large, and the Controllers are aware of them."

"Ensign Styles, take us to fifty thousand kilometers from the station," Kurt ordered with a frown covering his face.

It concerned him that they were already paying bribes. Grantz had casually mentioned this to Kurt earlier, but he had dismissed it as Grantz merely trying to get his hands on more gold. They were about to enter a culture they knew very little about.

As the small fleet moved slowly toward the assigned coordinates, the long-range sensors showed the rest of the system. Kurt stared in awe at the sight of the Controller station on the viewscreen, easily forty kilometers in length and ten in width. On its surface were a number of what looked like small habitable domes, one to two kilometers in diameter. Around the station were over four hundred ships of various types in orbit, a count validated by the ship's sensors. Most of them anywhere from ten to seventy thousand kilometers out.

One other thing the sensors reported was that the station was very heavily armed with ion cannons, energy projectors, and what appeared to be hundreds of hyperspace missile tubes. In near orbit of the station were twenty squadrons of the small police ships. Also hundreds of shuttles were traveling back and forth between the ships in the outer orbits and the station.

"Busy place," commented Captain Randson.

Kurt nodded, as the viewscreens put up images of different ships of every size and configuration. Some nearly boggled the mind.

"It's one of the biggest trading centers in the galaxy," bragged Grantz. "Many ships come to Kubitz, because they can buy things here not available anywhere else in the galaxy."

"And each has to pay a fee just to enter the system," muttered Captain Randson, shaking his head in disbelief.

After a few more minutes, Ensign Styles turned toward the admiral. "We're in position, sir."

"Very well," Kurt said, "let's board the shuttle and get over to the station."

"Are you sure you don't want an armed escort?" Andrew asked. "We have some Marines I can assign. We don't know how safe it will be over there."

"It might be wise, Admiral," added Lieutenant Mays. "I can arrange for a security team."

"No weapons," said Grantz, shaking his head. "They're strictly forbidden on the Controller station. You have nothing to worry about. No violence of any kind is allowed."

"I'm sure we'll be safe," Kurt said, drawing in a deep breath. "Let's get going." He looked around the Command Center as they left, seeing the concerned looks on the faces of his crew. They were just as worried as he was about their current situation.

Kurt watched nervously as the small shuttle neared the massive station. He wondered how many years it had taken to build this monstrosity. It made Newton Station seem insignificant. Kurt sighed and looked over at Grantz, who sat near the pilot, giving him instructions for landing. The Profiteer was in constant communication with the station, as he passed on their directives.

The shuttle entered a large airlock and shuddered slightly.

"What was that?" asked Kurt, seeing the startled look on the pilot's face.

"Atmospheric retention field," Grantz answered simply. "It's a weak energy shield that prevents the air inside the landing bay from escaping."

Brilliant lights illuminated the inside of the massive bay. Hundreds of shuttles were either docked or sitting on landing platforms. Very few shuttles were identical, and hundreds of beings moved about.

"We're to land on Platform 218," Grantz informed the pilot. "It's over there." Grantz pointed to a landing area where lights blinked.

The pilot carefully followed the Profiteer's instructions and set down the shuttle with scarcely a jar. "We're down, sir," the pilot reported. "Atmosphere outside registers as near Earth normal."

"Let's go," Grantz said, standing up. He paused, and looked at Kurt and the lieutenant. "There will be an armed reception committee, as this is your first time here. Once the fees have been paid, the armed escort will leave us."

"This should be interesting," Lieutenant Tenner said, as he stood up.

Kurt nodded his head in agreement and, bending over, picked up a case, which contained two small gold bars, then looked over at Grantz. "Lead the way."

Grantz walked to the back of the shuttle and waited until Lieutenant Tenner pressed the two buttons to open the airlock. With a whoosh the hatch slid open, and a metal ramp extended until it touched the platform.

When they stepped out, Kurt paused and breathed the air. Grantz had assured him that it was safe. Kurt detected several smells, which he couldn't identify, but nothing seemed off. As they walked down the ramp, four armed aliens walked up—vaguely humanoid with large muscular arms and legs and a squat chest.

"They're from Lylan Six," Grantz explained. "It's a high-gravity world where many of the system's police forces come from. They're very strong, and you don't want to get into a fight with one."

The one in front stopped and barked a question at Grantz. The Profiteer answered quickly, pointing at Kurt and Lieutenant Tenner. Then turning, the humanoid motioned for them to follow.

"They will escort us to one of the Controllers," Grantz explained. "This shouldn't take long."

"Keep your eyes open," suggested Lieutenant Tenner, looking around with intense curiosity. "We need to learn as much about their culture as possible, particular how these Controllers act."

Kurt nodded; he trusted the lieutenant to help guide him through this, if it became necessary. They were in a situation neither had ever expected to be in. Lieutenant Tenner had been trained, but Kurt doubted that the lieutenant's training had ever taken into account a situation quite like this.

As they walked through the station, Kurt couldn't help notice all the different alien species. What really surprised him was that most of them were humanoid and a few actually resembled humans. Kurt asked Grantz about that.

"It's a mystery," the Profiteer said after a moment. "Most of the races in this section of the galaxy are humanoid. It makes trading and dealing with the various races much simpler. There are a few alien races not of humanoid stock, and some of them do show up here from time to time."

Kurt nodded; this explained the interest in the slave trade, particularly if so many races were humanoid. It didn't take much longer, and their escorts stopped, motioning for them to enter a door. Going inside, Kurt was surprised to find a small and efficient-looking office. Several desks were there, behind which sat the Controllers—easily seven feet tall and humanoid. Their heads were slightly larger than normal, completely bald, with eyes of a normal size, though their lips were a little slimmer. Their bodies were lean, and their hands had six long digits. They were also a little pale, as if they very seldom saw any sunlight.

Several chairs of different sizes sat in front of the desks, and one of the Controllers motioned for them to come over and sit down. The Controller looked at Kurt and asked a question.

Kurt shook his head, not understanding what the Controller was saying, and looked over at Grantz.

Grantz said a few words to the Controller who frowned, shaking his head.

Grantz spoke again, and once more the Controller didn't seem to agree with what the Profiteer was saying.

"What's wrong?" asked Kurt, wondering if there was a problem.

"Nothing," replied Grantz dejectedly.

The Controller stood and walked over to a cabinet and took out two small gold chains with a tiny egg-shaped object attached. Returning, he handed one to Kurt and the other to Lieutenant Tenner.

"Put them around your necks," Grantz said a little gruffly. "You'll feel a brief moment of dizziness."

"What are these things?" asked Kurt. What had Grantz gotten them into?

"Put them on. You won't be harmed," Grantz promised.

Kurt put the small chain around his neck and suddenly felt very dizzy and weak. He shook his head and looked over at Lieutenant Tenner. From his expression, he felt the same.

"Can you understand me know?" asked the Controller in perfectly good English.

"Yes," Kurt replied, stunned. "How is that possible?"

"The egg-shaped device is a universal translator," replied Grantz, looking crestfallen. "It allows all races to communicate with each other. To me, you're speaking my language. To you, it will sound as if we're speaking your language."

Kurt instantly understood why Grantz was so disgruntled. They would no longer have to depend on him to communicate with the Controllers and others they might meet. Suddenly the entire situation had been changed.

"Why have you come to Kubitz?" asked the Controller, getting down to business.

"We wish to purchase some humans who were taken from our world to be sold at the slave markets on Kubitz," Kurt answered promptly.

"A common-enough request," the Controller answered, as he entered information on a nearby computer. "What is your world called, and what are its coordinates?"

"Earth," replied Kurt. He looked over at Grantz. "I'm not sure of the coordinates you may need. Our system of references may be different than yours."

"I know them," Grantz volunteered, as he gave the necessary information to the Controller.

The Controller entered the information into his computer console and then turned back to Kurt. "The humans you refer to are to be sold at the primary Kubitz servant auction in two weeks. They will be sold by the group representing High Profiteer Creed of planet Marsten. Preliminary estimates are that they will bring an exceptional price. They will be very expensive for you to purchase."

"Is there someone on Kubitz we can contact about buying the entire group?" asked Kurt. He didn't want any humans to be sold into slavery.

The Controller hesitated for a moment and then pressed an icon on his computer screen. A small disk popped out. "This will explain who you need to contact. I assume Profiteer Grantz is acting as your guide and advisor in this?"

"Yes," Kurt answered. He took out the contract Grantz had signed from his pocket and handed it to the Controller.

The Controller examined it for a moment. He then passed a wand over it, scanning the information into his computer. "The contract is valid and has been recorded." He then passed the contract back to Kurt. "Will your ships be traveling to Kubitz?"

"Yes," Kurt replied evenly. "I understand a fee is involved in that."

"Yes," the Controller replied. He checked his computer once more and then looked over at Kurt. "The fee for all five of your ships will be 220,000 credits."

Kurt opened the small case he had brought and placed one of the gold bars on the Controller's desk. When he did, he noticed the Controller's eyes widen.

The Controller ran another device over the gold bar and then nodded in satisfaction. "This bar is worth 320,000 credits. I assume you want the extra credited to your account?"

Kurt nodded and then spent the next few minutes answering more questions and setting up the account. Just as they prepared to leave, Kurt paused and asked the Controller if he could purchase more of the universal translators. In the end, he ended up depositing the other bar of gold as well and left the Controller's office with ten more of the valuable devices.

"This is why you didn't want us coming to the station," said Kurt, looking accusingly at Grantz, as they walked down a large corridor. Numerous other humanoids were also in the corridor, hurrying to wherever.

"Yes," admitted Grantz reluctantly, letting out a deep breath. "I had hoped it would gain me more gold, if I were your only source of communication."

"These translators will be highly useful," Lieutenant Tenner said, touching the one hanging from his neck. "I would like to give several of them to my team, so they can better study what's going on in this system. We should now be able to understand their broadcasts and any messages the *Star Cross* intercepts."

"We can do that," Kurt replied, as they exited a hatch and stepped into the landing bay. "Have your team gather as much information as possible."

Grantz led them to where the shuttle was parked, and, in a short time, they were back on board the *Star Cross*.

"Set course for Kubitz," Kurt ordered, as he stepped into the Command Center. "It's time to get our people back."

The *Star Cross* and her small fleet slid into orbit ten thousand kilometers above Kubitz. The planet was slightly larger than Earth but of less density. The gravity was nearly Earth normal, but its day was only twenty-two hours' long.

"What the hell happened to the planet?" asked Captain Randson, gazing at Kubitz on the main viewscreens. The plant's atmosphere looked to be heavily polluted with plumes of brown and gray.

"Heavy industry," replied Grantz, shifting his eyes to the viewscreen. "The main sections of the cities have environmental domes over them to protect them from the acid rain and other extreme weather that occurs from time to time. One area on the planet is under strict and very expensive weather control, where crops and food animals are raised."

"What now?" asked Kurt, glancing over at the Profiteer. He had already discussed some of this with Grantz earlier, but he wanted to go over it again.

"We go on the planet," Grantz began. "We'll need to deposit some gold at the Controller exchange office at the spaceport. They'll give us a computer card we can use for purchases. We can also rent a vehicle to take us around."

"What about armed escorts?" asked Andrew, expecting Grantz to say no once again. From what Grantz had been saying, the planet was a particularly dangerous place with a lot of unscrupulous humanoids taking advantage of the unwary. Andrew also knew that, somewhere down on the planet, were his wife and daughter.

"I would highly recommend it," answered Grantz, looking over at Captain Randson. "The planet has a police force called Enforcers. They normally stay out of sight, unless a problem arises. Once word spreads that you deposited a significant amount of gold, some curious people may want to see just who you are. Most of the client races who visit Kubitz have an armed escort to ensure their safety."

"Get a squad of Marines ready," Kurt ordered. "Armed with pistols only."

"We may have a problem," muttered Grantz, looking with concern at a large cylinder-shaped ship on one of the viewscreens. Several other smaller ships were around it. "That's a Dacroni battleship with a Profiteer battlecruiser and several other ships. If I had to guess, they just arrived from Earth."

"You said the Kubitz government would ensure there are no problems," said Kurt, as he studied the ships and wondered if they could be a threat to his fleet.

"There won't be while we're in orbit," Grantz answered uneasily. "But, down on the surface, it will be a different matter altogether. They may try to find out what we're doing here."

Kurt looked over at Andrew; Kurt really needed the captain to stay on the *Star Cross* and keep an eye on things. But then again, how could he order the captain not to go to Kubitz to find his wife and daughter?

"Lieutenant Mays, you have command. If there are any problems, contact me immediately."

"Yes, sir," replied the tactical officer, as she got up and took the command chair.

Kurt had handed out several of the small universal translators to the command crew—Lieutenant Mays, Lieutenant Brooks, and Ensign Pierce at Communications.

"If things go south, don't try to rescue us," ordered Kurt. "Just get the hell out of here and report back to Newton. Tell Rear Admiral Wilson what happened."

As Kurt left the Command Center, he just hoped they all made it back safely. They were about to step foot on an alien world where hundreds of different species conducted business. From what Grantz had told them, it was a dangerous place where deals for almost anything, both legal and illegal, could be made for the right price. Grantz had also mentioned that it wasn't too unusual for people to vanish and never be heard from again.

It didn't take them long to take a shuttle and fly to one of the many spaceports on Kubitz, but the one they were landing at was the closest to where the slave auction would be held. As soon as they arrived, Kurt, Captain Randson, Lieutenant Tenner, Grantz, and their six Marine escorts left the shuttle. A pilot and two other Marines stayed on board.

"This is a gloomy place," commented Andrew, as they walked toward the large building that Grantz had indicated contained the Controller facilities. Around them vehicles flew by and even a few work robots were in view. Vehicles pulling heavily loaded trailers headed toward waiting shuttles and ships.

"Pollution," replied Grantz, as he led them around several humanoids, arguing about how to load a trailer with a number of large and differently shaped crates. "Years and years of it."

Kurt looked up, and he could barely see the sun. Kubitz was the fourth planet out from its primary, and he was amazed at how much of the sunlight was blotted out. He knew sadly that Earth, in some ways, might someday resemble Kubitz if more wasn't done to stop pollution. Several efforts to curb greenhouse gases and end the use of fossil fuels were well underway, or they had been until the Profiteers had attacked.

Grantz led them into the large building, and shortly they were in a room with another Controller and two Lylan Enforcers. Their Marine escort had been asked to remain outside, which had made Sergeant Jones protest. Grantz had explained that armed escorts were not allowed inside the actual offices of the Controllers on Kubitz. With a frown, Sergeant Jones had relented. Two of the Marines left their weapons outside to allow them to carry inside the office a small crate they had brought along.

Kurt couldn't help but notice the heavy weapons the two Enforcers were armed with. Each had some sort of rifle that obviously shot some type of energy beam, plus a large pistol attached to the wide belt at their waist. Kurt decided to ask Grantz about the weapons later.

"How may I help you?" asked the Controller, looking curiously at the group before him.

"We wish to make a deposit to do business on Kubitz," Kurt explained without preamble. He was a little surprised to see that this Controller also had the same pale skin as the ones he had seen on the outer station.

"How large a deposit?" asked the Controller in a bored voice.

Kurt gestured to the Marines, who were carrying the small crate between them. They sat it on the Controller's desk, causing it to creak from the weight, and then Kurt slowly opened the lid.

The Controller's eyes grew wide when he saw the bars of gold. "Where did you say you were from?" he asked, rising to his feet and taking one of the bars from the crate.

"Earth," Kurt answered.

The Controller scanned the gold bar, using the same type of device as the Controller at the space station had. He gestured for one of the Enforcers to step forward and instructed him to get a cart to move the gold. The Enforcer quickly left and shortly returned with a small heavily built cart that the Controller slowly placed the bars of gold on, as he carefully scanned each one.

"I make it twenty-four million credits," he said, as he scanned the last one. "You're aware that High Profiteer Creed has claimed Earth and its wealth as his?"

"Yes," Grantz replied. "However, while these humans are originally from Earth, they reside on a small colony world called Newton. This gold was removed from Earth before High Profiteer Creed officially made his claim."

"That's no concern of mine," answered the Controller dismissively. "The gold is in your possession, and that's good enough by the laws Kubitz applies to such things. How would you like this credited to your account? Do you want some of it in actual credit notes?"

"Yes," Grantz quickly answered. "We would like two hundred thousand in credit notes, and the rest deposited into our account. We have already set up an account on the station."

"So I see," answered the Controller, as he checked his computer.

He quickly entered some information on his screen and then walked over to a door made of a heavy shiny metal with a DNA lock. The Controller placed his hand upon the sensor and spoke a short sentence. With several loud clicks, the door swung open. Stepping inside, he soon returned, carrying several small bundles of credit notes.

Taking his time, he slowly counted out the credits. He also handed Kurt a small computer disk with a record of their account and which could be used to withdraw whatever funds were needed.

"If I can be of any further assistance, don't hesitate to stop by," the Controller said when they were finished.

"We will," responded Kurt, as they turned and left the office. Once they were outside and no longer in hearing distance of the Enforcers, Kurt turned toward Grantz. "Why did you insist on so much cash?"

"Bribes," answered Grantz with a conniving grin. "People seem to talk a little better, if their palms are well greased."

"What now?" asked Lieutenant Tenner.

"We find a suitable vehicle and then go search for the individual responsible for auctioning off your people," Grantz answered. "We already know that it's a group which represents Marsten's interests." He took out the small disk the Controller on the station had given them. "From the information on this disk we at least know where to start."

"So how do we find out who we need to contact?" asked Andrew, looking over at Grantz, growing impatient.

"This is Kubitz, and everything is for sale for the right amount of credits, particularly information."

"It makes sense, considering how their culture is based," commented Lieutenant Tenner, nodding at Grantz. "I've examined the disk, and it tells exactly where our people are held, as well as the Marstens holding them. They will not agree to see us unless we go through a few channels. It's just their way of doing business."

Kurt let out a deep sigh, looking around the spaceport, he could see dozens of shuttles landing and taking off. Even a few larger spacecraft were evident. He paused for a moment, thinking about all the diverse technology visible to him. They had a lot more gold on the cargo ship under heavy guard. He wondered just what all was available for purchase here. One of his directives from President Mayfield and Fleet Admiral Tomalson was to secure a defense system for Newton. Before they left the Kubitz System, Kurt was determined to see what other weapons systems might be available. If Grantz had told them the truth, everything was for sale here for the right price, including military weapons of every type. There was a chance Kurt might find something useful to use against the Profiteers orbiting Earth.

Up in orbit, the Dacroni battleship *Rellal*, along with a Profiteer battlecruiser, two escorts, a cargo ship, and two detainee ships had witnessed the arrival of the human vessels.

"Humans from Earth," Dalet said, the battleship's second in command.

"An interesting development," responded Second Clan Leader Castel. "The same battlecruiser was present when we retook the Earth System from the humans."

"What's it doing here?" asked Dalet, his eyes showing concern. "How did they learn of Kubitz?"

"Spending gold," answered the communications operator. "One of our clan on the Controller station says they paid their system fee with gold bars, and they had a Profiteer with them."

"They must have captured him when they drove High Profiteer Creed from the system," said Castel, thinking about the possible ramifications of this.

"They have a cargo ship," pointed out Dalet, gesturing to it on a viewscreen. "How much gold can they have?"

"Clan Leader Jarls needs to be informed of this," commented Castel, as he weighed his options. "It's evident the humans moved some of their gold off Earth between the time High Profiteer Creed was driven away and when we returned. We have no way of knowing just how much."

"What are your orders?"

"Send two clan groups to the surface to keep a close eye on the humans. Make sure they're heavily armed. Find out who they're talking to and how much gold they have. If at all possible, I would like one of the humans seized and brought back to the *Rellal*."

"I will pass on the orders," replied Dalet.

Castel watched as Dalet hastened away to carry out his instructions. Turning his eyes toward the orbiting human ships, Castel focused his attention on the large cargo vessel. He wondered if they could place a tracking device on it. They couldn't attack the ship while in the Kubitz System, but, once it left, those rules no longer applied. While he might not be able to get the gold from the humans—after all they were obviously here to trade—Castel would reclaim what the humans bought with their gold, as well as the cargo ship itself.

Chapter Ten

Emily Randson and her twelve-year-old daughter, Alexis, were in their spartan quarters in the large squat building currently home to all the captive humans. Each day she was expected to help serve meals to the different aliens who stopped by the large dining hall to eat. Fortunately most of the aliens were humanoid, and even a few seemed as if they could have come from Earth. Around her neck, she wore a medallion with a number engraved upon it. This was her identification number. She knew the aliens coming to eat were prospective buyers and how well she served them could well decide if she was chosen as a household servant or sent to do other more demeaning work. She had heard rumors that some of the younger women were being trained to work in the pleasure houses. She shuddered, thinking what they must be going through.

"Mother, do you think we'll ever go home?" asked Alexis, as she put on the dark gray outfit that designated her as kitchen staff.

Emily sighed and, standing up, walked over and hugged her daughter. "I don't know," she replied, wishing things were different. "We're a long way from home, and no one back on Earth knows where the Profiteers took us."

The last few months had been horrible. The trip from Earth in the crowded Profiteer ship had been heart-wrenching. They had no privacy and very little food and water. She knew a few people had died on the trip.

"So we may never see Dad again?" Alexis asked, her eyes turning cloudy. "I want to go home. I don't like it here!"

"Don't say *never*," Emily said, wiping a tear from her daughter's cheek. "If your father finds out what happened to us, he'll never give up trying to find us."

"He could be dead," said Alexis in an uncertain voice. "The aliens killed all the starships in orbit. If Dad and the *Star Cross* were to come back to Earth, wouldn't they do the same to him?"

"He's smart enough to stay away," Emily said. "Admiral Vickers won't risk the *Star Cross*, and he won't be caught by surprise like our other ships. Remember, the *Star Cross* is a very powerful warship."

"I hope Admiral Vickers kills them all!" said Alexis heatedly. "These aliens are evil!"

"They're just different," answered Emily. "Some we've met have been very polite."

"Not the Profiteers," replied Alexis, shaking her head. "They're mean!"

Emily sighed, wishing her daughter wasn't going through this ordeal. She knew the odds of Andrew ever finding them was pretty close to zero. Her only hope was to find a humanoid buyer who would give her and Alexis a decent home. Right now her main priority had to be finding Alexis a safe environment to grow up in, even if she had to do things that she once considered unthinkable.

A bell chimed three times, indicating it was time for them to report for their shift in the dining hall. Alexis helped wash the dishes and keep the large kitchen clean. It was hard work for a child who was so young. Emily knew she only had a few days left before the first auctions began. She had to find the right buyer for her and Alexis shortly. She felt disgusted about what she was considering, but she had to think of Alexis first.

"Come, dear. Let's go to the dining hall," she said in a soft voice. "Our shift starts shortly."

Alexis nodded and followed her mother out the door.

-

Kurt and Andrew were in what, on Earth, would be considered a bar. Loud music played; scantily clad humanoid women danced on a stage, and alcohol was being consumed in large quantities by the people inside. Kurt had decided not to look at them as aliens or humanoids but as people, since many of them resembled regular humans.

Kurt kept his eyes on Grantz, who was speaking to a very human-looking man near the stage. Both were drinking heavily and laughing, as they watched the dancers. Occasionally Grantz would point to the table where Kurt and Andrew sat. Grantz had asked to talk to the man privately as he was an old acquaintance and very wary of strangers.

"Did you notice that nearly everyone in here is armed?" commented Andrew uneasily, as he looked around the establishment.

"Yeah," Kurt replied with a nod. He and Andrew were carrying 9mm pistols.

Their Marine escorts and Lieutenant Tenner waited outside, as armed bodyguards were not allowed inside the bar. What also concerned Kurt was the complete absence of any Enforcers. Since leaving the spaceport, he hadn't seen even one. Grantz had commented that they were always around, just out of sight.

"They're coming over here," Andrew said suddenly.

Kurt watched as Grantz and the man he had been talking to made their way toward them. For the first time Kurt noticed the man was armed with what looked like two very large pistols in holsters hanging from a large black belt. They came to a stop, and the human gazed speculatively at Kurt.

"I'm Avery Dolman. Your friend here says you want access to the Marsten servant training facility here on Kubitz." The man spoke in a quiet voice, folding his arms across his chest.

"Yes," Kurt answered. "We have some business to conduct there." Kurt noticed how cold the man's eyes looked. This was a man not to be trifled with.

Dolman was silent for a long moment and then spoke. "According to Grantz, the humans who are inside belong to your race. I should let you know that an additional two thousand were brought down in the last few days from the orbiting detainee ships."

"That's four thousand people," Andrew said, stunned that so many had been brought to Kubitz so quickly. It would press the *Newton Princess* to take on so many.

"We want to make an offer for the entire group," Kurt said evenly, staring into Dolman's eyes.

"You must have a lot of credits," Dolman said casually. "It'll cost you in the neighborhood of forty million credits to buy the freedom of so many. Are you certain you wouldn't rather pick out just a few? I understand some of the women are quite beautiful."

"We want all of them," Kurt said, holding his anger in check. "Can you help us?"

"Ten percent," the man answered with a smug look on his face. "For ten percent I can get you into the local facility and arrange for you to meet the right people."

"One hundred thousand credits," growled Grantz with a threatening look on his face. "For that you'll provide security to ensure we get to the facility and back to the spaceport, or we find someone else."

"Six percent," countered Dolman. "A Dacroni battleship is in orbit. They may send people down to ensure you stay away from the servant training facility. One hundred thousand credits will not buy you adequate protection." He unfolded his arms, and his hands touched his pistols. "Six percent and I will provide sufficient security to ensure you and your people remain safe."

"Six percent is too high," Grantz pointed out, shaking his head. "You can make a tidy profit from this. Two hundred thousand credits and, if you refuse to accept our offer, we'll look for someone else."

"Four percent and it's a contract," Dolman said after a moment of thought. "We may have to go against the Dacroni, and they're not easy to kill."

Grantz looked questionably at Kurt.

"For 250,000 credits, it's a deal," said Kurt firmly; he didn't want any more haggling.

Dolman grinned. "Have your people ready in an hour. I have a few messages to send. I'll want 50 percent before we leave for the facility and the rest when we reach the spaceport."

"Just make sure you keep up your end of the agreement," warned Kurt firmly.

"I always do," answered Dolman, as he walked off.

Kurt looked over at Grantz, who sat down across from him, holding a large glass containing an amber-colored liquid. "What, no contract? Can we trust him?"

"As well as you can trust anyone on Kubitz," Grantz said with a laugh, then taking a long swig of his drink. "He'll do as asked." Grantz took out a small recording device from his pocket. "I'll send a copy of this recording to one of the Controller stations to make it official."

"Won't he get upset about that?" asked Andrew, gazing at the small recorder.

Grantz laughed again, shaking his head. "No. I strongly suspect he did the same thing." He tipped his glass and drank the last of the amber liquid. "This is good stuff." He looked at Kurt and Andrew. "When this is over, I'll take you to the pleasure houses. I promise you've never seen anything on Earth like what we have here."

"No thanks," answered Kurt, shaking his head. "I think Captain Randson and I will both pass on that offer."

Grantz grinned. "Your loss." Waving his hand, the Profiteer ordered another drink.

An hour later Dolman pulled alongside the bar in two very large vehicles that resembled old military trucks. Both were fully armored with a small turret on top.

"Are those legal?" asked Lieutenant Tenner, as he examined the vehicles. "I thought large weapons were illegal on Kubitz."

"No," Grantz answered, as he gestured for the others to follow him. "However, it's not uncommon for vehicles like these to transport large amounts of credits or important clients. The Enforcers will look the other way, unless the turrets are fired. If they are, the Enforcers will take everyone into custody. Normally only large fines have to be paid, if you can show the weapons were used in self-defense."

Dolman stepped from the lead vehicle and walked over to Kurt and the others. "I've made arrangements for you to eat a meal in the dining hall at the training facility," he informed them. "There is the matter of payment before we're on our way."

Kurt handed over the metallic computer card, which Dolman inserted into a small device he held. He pressed several buttons and then gestured toward Kurt. "It needs your thumbprint to complete the transaction."

Grantz took the device and checked the amount deposited to Dolman's account. "Everything looks all right." He handed the device to Kurt and indicated where to place his thumb. Then, after Kurt had approved the transaction, Grantz removed the computer card and handed the device back to Dolman; the card he returned to Kurt.

"Let's be on our way," Dolman said. At a signal from him, the back of the large trucks opened. "Half of you in one truck and the rest in the other."

Kurt saw several heavily armed men inside each vehicle. After quickly dividing the Marines, he climbed into one, followed by Andrew, Grantz, and three Marines, including Sergeant Jones. Lieutenant Tenner and the remaining three Marines took the other vehicle. The men inside looked coldly at Kurt and the others, and didn't say anything.

"Pretty primitive vehicles," commented Andrew, as the vehicles pulled out and headed down the street. "I expected something more advanced."

"Practical," Kurt replied. "I suspect that really advanced technology is held to a minimum."

"Only where weapons are concerned," one of the armed men said. "Heavy energy weapons could seriously damage the city, so their use is restricted. These old transport vehicles are very dependable and sturdy enough to withstand most attacks we might face." He rapped his knuckles against the armor on the wall. He then settled back, as if he had lost interest in talking.

"We should be safe," commented Sergeant Jones. "The armor on these vehicles seems adequate."

Grantz didn't say anything; he just sat there and smiled, as if he was enjoying a private joke.

For nearly thirty minutes, the vehicles moved through the city until they finally came to a stop. The backs of the vehicles opened, and the men climbed out.

Kurt looked at the large structure before them. It covered several city blocks and was about ten stories high.

"Your people are here," Dolman said, joining them. "I have made arrangements for four of you to go inside. Your armed escorts will have to remain here with the trucks."

As Kurt turned to go, Dolman stopped him. "I almost forgot to mention that there will be a fee to get inside."

"How big a fee?" demanded Kurt.

"It's negotiable," Dolman said with a grin. "Everything on Kubitz is negotiable."

"I'll handle it," Grantz said. "Let's get inside. I don't like being out in the open like this with a Dacroni battleship in orbit."

Kurt agreed.

"Also the sky is clouding up. We don't want to get caught outside if it begins to rain."

"Why is that?" asked Andrew, looking up and noticing the dark clouds.

"Acid rain," answered Grantz. "Some storms are bad enough the raindrops will eat away your skin. Normally an alarm will sound, just before the rain falls, sending everyone to cover."

Andrew shook his head in disbelief. "Just what type of world is this?"

"The best!" said Grantz with a grin. His eyes widened. "I still say again that you should try the pleasure houses while you're here. There are none comparable in the rest of the galaxy."

"Let's get inside," Andrew said, ignoring Grantz. "I need to find my wife and daughter."

At least the Marines and Dolman's people would have the armor of the trucks to protect them. "Lead the way," Kurt said, looking at the Profiteer.

Emily was four hours into her shift and in the kitchen, full of tantalizing smells, picking up a food order. She saw the despairing looks on many of the human faces around her. Most had given up hope and felt they had no future. They were also not allowed to eat any of the food they prepared. Their own fare was quite bland by comparison.

A number of overseers in the kitchen ensured the food was prepared properly. Punishment for not doing one's job was quick and quite painful. Emily was glad to see that Alexis and several other young teenagers were busy keeping the dishes washed and stacked and seemed to be staying caught up. It was warm in the kitchen, and the work wasn't easy.

"The auction is in two more weeks," commented one of the other servers. Karen Calvin was also doing her best to find a decent buyer for her and her young son. "Have you found anyone yet?"

"No," Emily replied with a heavy sigh. "I think, for the most part, they're interested in the younger women and the single men."

"Those two weeks will pass by quickly," commented Karen, but looking worried all the same. "What if they split us apart from our children?"

Emily didn't reply; this was her fear also. She couldn't have Alexis taken from her. Picking up the tray with her food order, she exited the kitchen. Stepping out into the large dining hall, she noticed it was nearly full. Her eyes traveled over the several hundred potential buyers, until her gaze fell on the back of one who seemed strangely familiar. Looking across the table from him, she gasped recognizing Admiral Vickers. Her heart stopped, and she dropped her tray, which made a loud clanging noise when it hit the floor. At that moment, the other man turned around, and Emily felt as if she were about to faint. It was Andrew! Her pulse raced, and she could barely breathe.

"Pick up that tray and clean up that mess," growled one of the Overseers, who had come over to see what the commotion was. "Get that food order replaced quickly and don't be so clumsy. Sometimes I despair of ever making you humans into a decent servant."

"Yes, sir," Emily said, bending down and quickly doing as she was told. There was no doubt in her mind that Andrew and Admiral Vickers had both seen and recognized her. Picking up the tray, she hurried back to the kitchen. She couldn't wait to tell the others.

"I heard a tray drop," said Karen, coming over to Emily. She stopped and gazed worriedly at Emily's face. "Why are you so pale? Did an Overseer strike you?"

"No," replied Emily, struggling to keep her voice low. "Andrew and Admiral Vickers are both out there."

"What!" exclaimed Karen, her eyes widening in shock and hope. "Are you sure? How could they have found us?"

"I don't know," answered Emily, her heart racing. "But I can tell you one thing. They won't leave until they've rescued all of us. She grabbed Karen and hugged her, not caring who saw. "We're going home!"

"That was Emily," said Andrew, his eyes wide with hope. "They're here!"

"Stay seated," cautioned Kurt, not wanting to draw any undue attention their way.

"Your mate," commented Grantz in understanding. "She is here?"

"My wife," Andrew answered. "What do we have to do to get her free? I'm not leaving here without her and Alexis."

Grantz was silent for a moment. "I wouldn't recommend making an offer on just one human. It will only drive the price up on the others. Your best price will come from making an offer for all of them."

"Who do we need to talk too?"

"We wait," answered Grantz. "Dolman has made arrangements. They will come to us."

"It is best we do as Grantz suggests," commented Lieutenant Tenner. "We have a plan, and, if it works, we can free all the hostages."

"I hope they hurry," Andrew said, looking in the direction of the kitchen, hoping to see Emily again. "I want to see my wife and daughter!"

-

Up in orbit Second Clan Leader Castel listened to the latest report from the surface.

"It's confirmed," reported Dalet. "The humans are at the Marsten training center." Marsten maintained a large training center on Kubitz to handle the slaves they brought to sale.

"Surely they don't want to buy back their fellow humans?" Castel asked in confusion. "It would cost over forty million credits."

Dalet motioned toward the large human cargo ship in orbit. "They may have more gold than we originally believed."

Castel was silent as he thought over Dalet's words. "What if, during the weeks High Profiteer Creed was away from Earth, they sent the biggest part of their gold to their colony planet to keep it safe?"

"It will greatly aggravate the High Profiteer," predicted Dalet. "We could arrange for a Dacroni battle group to go to this colony and take the gold."

"We will leave that decision up to Clan Leader Jarls," Castel replied. He didn't have the authority to make such a decision. "He will be highly interested in what we've learned. In the meantime, we'll wait and see if they actually have enough gold to buy back all the humans who have been taken from their world. I still want one of the visiting humans captured and brought to me. Perhaps then we can learn just how much gold they have."

-

Kurt and the others had finished their meal when several men in colorful attire walked up to their table.

"I am Alvit Meer, and this is Baltwer Janetks," the taller one said. "We understand you're interested in procuring some of these humans?"

"Yes," Grantz said. "I'm serving in an advisory position for these negotiations."

"Just how many would you be interested in?" Alvit asked, his eyes focusing on Grantz.

"All of them," Grantz replied evenly. "Every single one!"

Alvit's eyes widened considerably at this announcement. "That would involve a very large sum of credits. Do you have a Controller computer card showing how many credits are in your account?"

Kurt handed over the card, and Alvit handed it to Baltwer, who ran it through a handheld scanner. "Not quite enough," he announced.

"We can get more," Kurt replied. "Is there somewhere we can go in private to discuss this?"

Alvit looked at Baltwer, who nodded. "Come with us. There's a suitable office nearby."

Kurt and the others stood up. Glancing at the door to the kitchen where he had seen Emily before, he saw her standing there, watching with hope in her eyes. He gave her a quick smile and a casual thumbs-up signal and then turned to follow Alvit. If things went as he hoped, Andrew would shortly be reunited with his family.

Emily was in her quarters, sitting on the bed, her hands lying in her lap. It was all she could do not to stand up and pace nervously. She hadn't told Alexis about her father being here. She didn't want to get her daughter's hopes up, if he couldn't find a way to free them. However, she knew that he would move heaven and earth to do just that. She and Karen had quickly spread the word to the other adults in the kitchen that Admiral Vickers was on Kubitz. The spirits of everyone suddenly skyrocketed, as they realized that, just maybe, they were about to be rescued, and their trying ordeal might be coming to an end.

"What's going on, Mother?" asked Alexis, noticing her mother's odd behavior. "All the adults in the kitchen were acting strangely. A few were even smiling and laughing. I haven't heard that in a long time."

Before Emily could reply, there was a knock on the door. Her heart nearly stopped, as she could think of no reason for someone to be coming to her quarters at this time. Standing up, she walked hesitantly to the door, praying that she would know the person standing on the other side. Grasping the handle, she slowly opened it.

"Hello," said Andrew with a big smile, as he stepped forward and took his wife in his arms.

"Daddy!" screamed Alexis, as she saw who held her mother. She ran over and grabbed her father in a tight hug, never wanting to let go. "Is it really you?"

"Yes, sweetheart, it's me."

"How?" asked Emily, freeing herself from Andrew with tears running down her face. "How did you find us?"

"We captured a Profiteer," Andrew explained. "He told us everything."

"Are we going home?" asked Alexis, still holding on to her father.

"We're going to Newton," answered Andrew, bending down and looking his daughter in the eyes. "We'll build a new home there."

"The Profiteers still have control of Earth then?" asked Emily wiping the tears from her eyes.

"Yes," Andrew answered grimly. "For now they do, but, if Admiral Vickers has his way, someday we'll free Earth."

"Are we supposed to go with you now?" asked Emily. She didn't know if she could bear being away from Andrew after all that had happened.

"Yes," he replied, taking Emily's hand. "I've made arrangements for you and Alexis to leave now. The rest of our people will be transported to the spaceport over the next few days and taken up to the *Newton Princess*. It'll be a little crowded, but we'll manage."

"They'll free all of us?" asked Emily, her eyes widening.

"For a price," Andrew answered. "We paid forty-five million credits to free everyone and arrange for transport to the passenger liner."

"Where did you get forty-five million credits?" asked Emily.

"That's a long story," Andrew replied. "Now get your stuff and let's go. I want you and Alexis safely on board the *Star Cross*."

Emily looked around the room that had been her and Alexis's home for the last three months. "There's nothing here that I want," she said somberly She took her daughter's hand and looked directly into the eyes of her waiting husband. "Take us home."

Andrew nodded as they exited the room, closing the door behind them.

Admiral Vickers and the others waited at the ground level. They would shortly be returning to the *Star Cross* to discuss more matters. Andrew felt a vast relief and joy in knowing his family was safe. Admiral Vickers had delivered on his promise, and Andrew would never forget that.

Chapter Eleven

Kurt watched anxiously as the first shuttles docked with the *Newton Princess*. Each shuttle contained fifty humans who had been held captive in the Profiteers' training center. In all 4,206 people needed to be moved. Most were adults, but nearly three hundred were children. Kurt had seen the working conditions his people had been subjected to; while not extremely harsh, it had been a very poor environment for kids.

"I can't believe it worked," Andrew said, as he gazed at a viewscreen, showing a shuttle docking with the passenger liner.

"Money talks here," Kurt said, agreeing with Andrew. It had been expensive, but buying their people back, keeping them from potential slavery, was worth every cent spent.

"There will be more."

"I know." Kurt sighed. "Lieutenant Tenner and two of his First Contact team will be staying. We've leased a small building complex to serve as an embassy of sorts. The Kubitz government even guarantees the buildings and the small area around it will be secure. Armed Enforcers will be at all gates to the property. Of course the price is ten million credits per year."

"Three people doesn't sound like a lot," answered Andrew, frowning, looking over at Kurt. "Emily says she overheard some of the Profiteers talking, and they claim that tens of thousands of humans will be brought to Kubitz. I don't know if Lieutenant Tenner and a couple of others can handle what might be coming at them."

"If we let them get here," Kurt answered.

He recalled what Fleet Admiral Tomalson had suggested. Use the fleet like the pirates did theirs and ambush the Profiteer ships before they could reach the Gothan Empire and Kubitz. After what he had seen and understood could be bought on this godforsaken planet, there was no doubt in his mind that he would do just that.

"You mean, locate their convoys and take our people back before they reach here?" asked Andrew, his forehead creasing in a frown as he thought that concept over. "We don't have the technology to locate a ship in hyperspace. Once a ship jumps, we have no idea where it's going."

"The technology might be available here on Kubitz," Kurt replied. Earth may not have developed the technology yet, but it didn't mean that others might not have. Also, when they had first jumped into the system, Grantz had mentioned that Kubitz had a way to locate ships when they exited hyperspace.

"What does Lieutenant Tenner think about staying here on Kubitz?" It was something Andrew wouldn't consider. From what he had seen of the planet, it was a madhouse and extremely dangerous.

"He volunteered," answered Kurt promptly. "We have eight other specialists—besides the First Contact team—who will be staying, so we can get everything organized and set up. I'm also leaving twenty Marines to act as a security detail with Sergeant Jones in charge. I don't fully trust the Kubitz government to hold up their end of the agreement as far as security goes. It wouldn't take much to buy a few officials and get them to look the other way."

"I assume we'll leave some gold behind to ensure Lieutenant Tenner has the credits available to procure the release of future human captives."

"More than that," Kurt replied. "I'm leaving the light cruiser *Dallas* behind. If things get too hot, Lieutenant Tenner and his people can always evacuate to the cruiser and even return to Newton if necessary. I've been speaking to Grantz, and nearly every government in the galaxy that has had contact with the Gothan Empire has a compound on the planet to do business when necessary. They also keep at least one ship in permanent orbit to ensure the safety of their people. It costs a fee, but it will be worth it. It seems as if no one actually trusts the Kubitz government fully, though Grantz claims there has never been a major incident, due to the penalties that would be levied by the Controllers."

"These damn Controllers," muttered Andrew, his eyes showing a contemptuous glint. "They seem to control all the money. I wish we knew more about them."

"Perhaps Lieutenant Tenner can learn more. I intend to rotate the *Dallas* and the *Sydney*. When the *Sydney* returns, they'll bring more embassy staff. I'm also returning to the surface this afternoon. You recall that one of our other orders was to procure a defense system for Newton. Grantz is in the process of contacting the right people for us to speak to. Lieutenant Tenner has set up a conference room in our new embassy, and we'll be meeting there."

Andrew groaned and shook his head. "Why do I think this will be very expensive?"

"That's why we have the *Lansing*," answered Kurt, glancing up at a viewscreen that showed the cargo ship.

They monitored every ship in the fleet twenty-four hours a day to ensure no unscheduled visitors appeared from the surface. A viewscreen displayed each ship, plus the tactical screen was closely watched. In addition, at least one of the three warships was kept at Condition Two at all times.

He knew the Kubitz government had no idea how much gold was on the cargo ship. It was one reason why he had moved an additional fifteen Marines from the *Star Cross* to support the twenty already assigned to the ship. He would also move the battlecruiser a little closer to the *Lansing*, just as a precaution. The gold on that ship was the key to protecting Newton and perhaps someday freeing Earth.

"How's Emily and Alexis doing?" Both had been brought aboard the *Star Cross* and were staying in Andrew's quarters.

"Great! From what I understand, the food they were fed was quite bland in taste and nearly the same every day. I took Emily and Alexis to the mess hall and let them order whatever they wanted. The cooks even managed to whip up some spaghetti for Alexis. They're back in my quarters, resting."

"If they need anything else, let me know," Kurt said, and he meant it. He knew how he would feel if this was his sister and nephew they were talking about. He was just glad they were both safe on Newton.

"You rescued them," Andrew answered with a smile. "That's enough for me. Alexis is still a little shaken up from her ordeal, and Dr. Willis has indicated that she should be back to normal in a few weeks. He's planning on checking on her and Emily regularly."

"I'm glad to hear that," Kurt replied. He could well imagine how frightened Alexis had been by all this. What child wouldn't have? It still angered him immensely at the sheer audacity of the Profiteers in abducting children. He wished there was some way he could make them suffer for their actions.

"Admiral, several shuttles have left the Dacroni battleship in the last hour," reported Lieutenant Brooks with some concern in her youthful voice. "All landed at the same spaceport our people are being taken to."

Andrew looked over at Kurt with concern in his eyes. "Do you think there'll be a problem?"

"I don't know," answered Kurt. "I hired Dolman for extra security for our people. He promised everything would go smoothly."

"Dolman makes me feel uneasy," commented Andrew, his eyes narrowing sharply. "He's a damn shyster!"

Kurt laughed. "The man's working the Kubitz black-market system to make a living. He runs a very large security and information-gathering business. He has connections all over the planet and even a few on other worlds of the Gothan Empire. We could find him very useful in the future."

"Dolman and Grantz," muttered Randson, shaking his head in disbelief. "What are we coming to?"

"The galaxy's not as we believed," answered Kurt, his voice taking a serious tone. "It's full of intelligent space-going races. While many of the more advanced ones are reportedly peaceful, some are like the Profiteers who aren't. We have to adapt, or we're done for."

"You're right," Andrew said, as he looked down at a console, which showed the ship's current status. "I just wish things were different."

"We all do," Kurt replied, as his gaze shifted to a screen showing Kubitz.

Kurt stepped from the shuttle and looked over at the man in charge of his Marine escort, Sergeant Jones.

"Grantz made arrangements for a couple vehicles to pick us up," the sergeant said, as he eyed the vicinity of the landed shuttle for signs of anything suspicious. He was responsible for the admiral's safety, and he took his job very seriously. He would also be staying behind to command the security detachment at the embassy compound.

"What do you think of Grantz?" asked Kurt, curious to hear the sergeant's opinion.

Jones smiled. "He's one hell of a poker player. I've never met someone who can bluff like he can."

"Cleaned me out," commented Private Lucy Dulcet. "I thought he was bluffing, and he laid down a full house. Made my two pair meaningless."

"I won't gamble with him," Corporal Evans said loudly. "He's a crook, and I wouldn't put it past him to be cheating."

"No," responded Private Dulcet, shaking her head. "He doesn't have to cheat, and, besides, you're a lousy poker player."

Corporal Evans glared at Dulcet, but, before he could make a retort, two vehicles pulled up.

"Here are our rides," spoke up Jones, carefully scrutinizing the vehicles.

These were two of the more modern vehicles that ran on hydrogen as a power source. They were very quiet and, according to Grantz, highly economical. The hydrogen-powered vehicles were something the Kubitz government initiated to help curb the rampant pollution. Looking across the city, Kurt could see a thick gray haze and recognized it as heavy smog. About 40 percent of the city was covered by a large habitation dome; the poorer areas were left outside. Grantz had told him, at times, it was too dangerous to go outside the protective city dome without a breathing mask. Kurt knew, in the past, that some of the cities in China had done the same thing. Those days were long gone, but industrial smog was still a problem in some of the underdeveloped areas of Earth.

Five Marines and the sergeant accompanied Kurt. Two Marines and Sergeant Jones got in the vehicle with him, and the remaining three Marines were in the other one. Kurt had purchased twenty more of the translation devices, so the Marines could understand what was said around them. He also planned on each member of the embassy staff having one.

The driver was a humanoid with a very white complexion; his eyes were set wider on his head than normal, and the hair on his head was limited to a very narrow strip down the center.

"Profiteer Grantz has directed that I take you and your people to the complex of buildings you have leased in the dome," the driver said nonchalantly.

"Yes," Kurt replied. "I have a meeting scheduled there shortly."

The driver nodded, and the vehicle started moving. Kurt was amazed at how quiet it was. Even the air in the vehicle had none of the foul smells associated with the spaceport and the smog.

"The air smells better in here," Sergeant Jones commented.

"Yes," the driver responded. "All these new hydrogen-powered vehicles have an air-filtration system installed that cleans out the impurities. The vehicles also injects clean air back outside."

-

As they drove through the outskirts of the capital, Kurt looked at the busy and crowded streets. There were vehicles of every type imaginable. Hydrogen-powered vehicles, several different electric-powered cars, and even a few of the old-style combustion engine varieties. Many people walked, and the sidewalks were as crowded as the ones in New York City. It was obvious from the condition of the older vehicles that the poorer citizens were dependent on them. There was some public transportation. Huge lumbering vehicles resembling buses rumbled up and down the streets. Kurt wasn't sure how they were powered.

On the crowded sidewalks, human species from dozens of different planets were evident. They were garbed in colorful to dull-looking outfits. Even from the inside of the vehicle, he could see people haggling and money passing from hand to hand. The numerous shops had advertisements in the windows, just like the stores back on Earth. One thing that Kurt found disturbing was the number of guns people wore on their hips.

They had just turned down a less crowded street and were nearing one of the large entrances to the dome when the driver slowed down and stopped.

"What is it?" asked Kurt, leaning forward and looking ahead. He couldn't see anything other than more stopped vehicles.

"Must be an accident," the driver replied, as he gazed up ahead to see what was holding up traffic. "They happen quite regularly."

Kurt's response was cut off when an explosion rocked their vehicle. He was flung hard against the door and had the breath knocked out of him.

"We're under attack!" yelled Sergeant Jones, as he struggled to free his 9mm pistol. "That was an explosive round!"

Several more explosions rang out, shaking the vehicle, with the last knocking it on its side. Kurt could smell something burning and was fearful the vehicle was on fire. He coughed several times from the black smoke slowly filling up the interior. Looking up front, he saw the driver was unconscious.

"We need to abandon this vehicle," Kurt said, struggling to sit up. They were sitting ducks inside and helpless to defend themselves. They needed a better tactical location.

One of the other Marines stood up, managed to fling open the door, and crawled free. A shot rang out, and the young Marine slid back into the vehicle with a startled look on his face. Kurt felt ill seeing the bullet hole between his eyes and the red blood running down his face.

"Stay down," ordered Sergeant Jones, as he activated his comm gear to speak to the Marines in the vehicle behind them. "Corporal Evans, what's your status?"

"We're outside the vehicle, but we're pinned down. A couple snipers are on the roof of the tall building on the right side of the street. They're out of range of our pistols. I wish we had our assault rifles."

"Just a moment," Jones said. He turned to the other Marine, who reached under his shirt and pulled out the long barrel of a weapon. Jones rolled over the dead Marine and removed several gun parts from his clothing as well. Looking at Kurt guiltily, he took a few items from his uniform also. "I know we were told pistols only, but I didn't trust the situation down here. There are just too many guns."

"Corporal Evans, I'll take out the snipers. When I do, get your butts over here to help cover the admiral." Jones quickly assembled the weapon and loaded a large diameter clip into it, slamming it home.

"We're ready," Evans answered back.

"I'll stand to take out the snipers," said Jones, drawing in a deep breath, looking at the admiral and the other Marine. "As soon as I do, we need to exit this vehicle. They attacked us for some reason." He looked at Kurt with concern. "They may be after you, Admiral."

"Get it done," Kurt ordered, wondering where the Enforcers were. They had to have heard all the gunfire and explosions.

Jones took another deep breath, and then suddenly rose up and fired two explosive shells at the tall building just to the right of the turned-over vehicle. Several figures with long-barreled weapons stood on top of it. The building was about ten stories high, and two explosions, much more powerful than a grenade, suddenly rocked its roof. Debris fell, hitting the street among the screaming people still trying to find cover. A body made a loud thump as it hit the sidewalk from where one of the snipers had been blown off the building.

"Got 'em!" Jones said, as he searched for more targets. "At least I think I did." He looked down at the admiral. "Let's go." With that the sergeant pulled himself out and slid off the vehicle. Kurt and the other Marine quickly followed.

"Over here, sir," yelled Corporal Evans.

Kurt turned toward the voice and found the corporal, his two Marines, and their vehicle's driver standing behind a large truck. Kurt hurried over to the corporal, pulling his pistol from its holster. He flipped off the safety and, glancing down, quickly chambered a round.

"How many more are there?" asked Sergeant Jones, as he assessed the situation.

"Not sure," Evans answered. He peered around the truck and then ducked back as several light blue energy beams impacted the street near him.

"At least four or five more," he said breathlessly. "The two snipers on the roof were armed with projectile weapons and the explosive rounds they used to immobilize your vehicle. The rest are armed with some type of energy weapons."

"Where are those damn Enforcers?" muttered Private Dulcet. She was holding her pistol with both hands, occasionally peeking around the corner of the truck for a target.

"Can your comm unit reach the shuttle?" asked Kurt, realizing they were in a bad situation. The pilot and two more Marines were still there.

"No," answered Jones, shaking his head. "Too many buildings, plus all the local comm channels block our communications after a short distance. We're on our own."

Kurt was about to say something else when a number of small canisters fell around them, and gray smoke poured forth.

"Gas!" screamed Private Dulcet, as she glanced at Sergeant Jones with a terror-stricken look on her face and then collapsed.

Before Kurt could say anything, he felt dizzy, and then blackness clamped down on his senses.

Kurt opened his eyes to the sound of strange voices. He lay on the sidewalk still behind the large truck. His head was throbbing, and everything seemed to be spinning.

"Are you all right?" a woman asked. She was wearing a brightly colored blouse and very tight pants.

"Just dizzy and my head is pounding," Kurt said, as he struggled to sit up. With his right hand, he rubbed his forehead. "What happened?"

"The Enforcers are still checking into that," the woman said. "I'm Keera Jelk, and I work at one of the medical centers here on Kubitz."

"You look human," Kurt said, as he more closely studied the young woman. She seemed to be in her late twenties with dark hair and a fair complexion.

"I am," she said with a laugh. "Approximately 44 percent of the humanoid races come from the same genetic stock as you do. How that happened is open to speculation. Many say some type of Supreme Being did it, and others claim a very advanced race in the distant past seeded many worlds with the same or similar species. Many others—such as the Enforcers, the Profiteers, and even the Dacroni—are closely related."

"What about the Controllers?"

"Them too," admitted Keera with a grimace.

"How are the people who were with me?"

"Fine," Keera answered, as she glanced where a few other medical personnel were treating the other humans. "You were struck with some type of knockout gas. Probably V-14, which is one of the more common ones used in hits."

"Hits?" mumbled Kurt, as he stood up and swayed slightly on his feet. "Are those very common?" He was anxious to check on the rest of his people.

"In this part of the city, yes," replied Keera, her voice sounding aggravated. "Inside the dome very seldom. You should have been traveling with a larger security force. Out here, the Enforcers never seem to show up in time, at least not until someone has died."

Kurt could hear Sergeant Jones's voice, and he didn't sound pleased.

The sergeant was talking heatedly to one of the Lylan Enforcers, gesturing toward his Marines. With an angry look on his face, he turned and walked over to Kurt. "Private Dulcet is missing," he announced grimly. "The Enforcers have found no signs of her or of the snipers we blew off the building."

"Who did the snipers look like to you?"

"Dacroni mercenaries!" stated Jones emphatically. "They were very muscular and had on dark gray battle armor, just as Grantz described."

"One of your people is missing?" asked Keera with concern in her voice. She looked around but saw no sign of the missing human.

"It looks that way," replied Kurt, growing concerned. How the hell was he going to find his missing Marine on this planet? If she was still even on the planet.

"They may be holding her for ransom," suggested Keera, shifting her attention back to Kurt. "If they are, they'll be contacting you shortly to arrange for an exchange. It happens pretty regularly here."

"The driver of the other vehicle has arranged for additional transportation," reported Sergeant Jones, his eyes looking nervously at the curious crowd that had gathered.

"I have some questions," a large Lylan Enforcer said, walking up to Kurt. "That tall building was damaged by explosives, which are illegal in the city, and the owner is demanding payment."

"It wasn't us," answered Kurt, seeing that Sergeant Jones's weapon was strangely absent. "It must have been the people who attacked us."

The Enforcer took out a computer tablet and entered some information. "We found no bodies are any signs of blood. If anyone was injured in this incident, they did a good job of cleaning it up. From speaking to Sergeant Jones, he indicated that one of your security people is missing. If you can provide a description, it will be downloaded to the tablets of the other Enforcers, and, if she is spotted, you will be notified."

Kurt nodded; he didn't know what else he could do. He needed to talk to Grantz or Dolman. Between him and Sergeant Jones, they managed to give the Enforcer the information he requested.

"There is also the matter of a fine," the Enforcer continued. "Fighting in the city streets and the damage that occurred is illegal. The owner of the building is demanding restitution."

"We didn't initiate the fight," Kurt said firmly.

"Doesn't matter," answered the Enforcer. "You were part of what happened, and, as the only party still here, you are liable for the damages."

Before Kurt could say anything else, Keera put her hand on his arm.

"These people have been subjected to V-14 gas, which is also against Kubitz law. I would ask that the fine be reduced, due to extenuating circumstances."

The Enforcer eyed Keera for a moment and then nodded his head. "Twenty thousand credits," he announced. He entered some information on his computer pad and then handed it to Kurt. "I need your thumbprint, plus your Controller computer card, to make payment."

Kurt pressed his thumb against the tablet and handed the Enforcer the card. Moments later the Enforcer returned it and walked off.

"Thanks," Kurt said, turning to Keera. "Could I talk you into coming to our embassy? I have some questions I'd like to ask about what goes on here on Kubitz. The more I'm here, the more confused I get."

"The hellhole of the galaxy," Keera replied with a grin. "My shift is over, so I have the time. It will cost you though."

Here it comes, thought Kurt. She'll demand money for treating me and answering questions. Was everyone on this barbaric planet the same?

"A nice meal would be greatly appreciated," she said in a pleasant voice.

Kurt tried not to show his surprise. "I think that can be arranged."

A few minutes later, they were on their way to the embassy in new and better-armored vehicles. Kurt guessed, from the armed guards who were in the vehicles with them, that Dolman had made the arrangements. Kurt wondered how much this would cost. Once at the embassy he would contact the *Star Cross* and inform Captain Randson of what happened. Somehow or another he had to find Private Dulcet. He wasn't leaving her in the hands of her captors.

Chapter Twelve

Kurt watched with interest as they pulled up to the new embassy compound. It contained one large building and half a dozen smaller ones. It was surrounded by a five-meter wall with two guarded entrances. One of the things they had discussed doing was modifying several of the satellite buildings into dormitory like structures to house any humans who were brought to Kubitz to be sold in the slave auctions. Kurt still found it revolting to think that, even on civilized worlds, people could be sold into slavery. However, from what Grantz had patiently explained, most of the jobs were for some type of household servant.

"How long have you been on Kubitz?" asked Kurt, looking over at Keera, sitting next to him in the vehicle.

"Six years," she responded. "My brother came here to do business, and we ended up staying. I had just passed my final medical exam and was offered quite a lucrative contract to stay on here in one of the larger medical centers."

Before Kurt could say anything else, the vehicles came to a stop, and he was surprised to see both Grantz and Dolman standing at the entrance to the main building. He wanted to talk to them about finding his missing Marine.

"Avery Dolman," muttered Keera unhappily, gazing at the man. "How did you fall in with him?"

"Profiteer Grantz introduced us," Kurt answered, as they left the vehicle. "Is there a problem?" He wondered how she knew Dolman.

"Not really," responded Keera, shrugging her shoulders. "Just watch him. He runs a large protection agency and is rumored to be heavily involved in the black market. Make sure anything you do with him is under contract with every detail spelled out."

"Thanks for the advice," Kurt said, as they walked up the steps where Dolman and Grantz waited.

"I'm glad to see you're all right," Grantz said. "I was concerned when I heard your vehicles had been hit."

"I'm sure you were," answered Kurt, knowing Grantz was probably more worried about his next payment of gold.

"The Dacroni from the battleship in orbit hit you," Dolman said evenly. His gaze shifted to Keera and then back to Kurt. "They sent down two groups of mercenaries with orders to kidnap one of your people. They seem to be highly interested in what's in that cargo ship that's staying close to your battlecruiser."

"How do you know all that?" demanded Kurt. The Enforcers hadn't indicated any connection with the orbiting Dacroni ship.

"Let's just say, I have my sources," Dolman replied noncommittally.

"Where's Private Dulcet now?" asked Kurt, growing deeply concerned, since it seemed this was more than a mere kidnapping for ransom. "Is there any way we can rescue her?"

"Two Dacroni shuttles left the spaceport shortly after the attack," Dolman answered. "From my source, Private Dulcet was on one of the shuttles. Once she's on their battleship that will put her effectively beyond our reach."

Kurt wasn't pleased with this news. From what he had been told, it would be tantamount to suicide to attempt to launch an attack against the Dacroni battleship. The Kubitz defense grid would activate and take out all the attacking ships.

"How do we get her back?"

"You don't," Grantz said, his eyes shifting suspiciously to Keera. "Who is this woman with you?"

"She's a doctor who helped us after the attack," Kurt answered, his mind still on private Dulcet. "I asked her to come to the embassy for a meal to show my gratitude for her assistance. Is there any type of deal we can make with the Dacroni?"

Dolman frowned and slowly shook his head. "I doubt it. I'll make some inquiries and see what's out there. If I were you, I wouldn't get my hopes up of ever seeing Private Dulcet again."

Several hours passed, and Kurt met with a number of people in the business of selling weapons on Kubitz. A Controller was also at the table, in case his services were needed. Neither Grantz nor Dolman had been allowed to attend this particularly meeting, as Kurt didn't really want them to know what he was up to. He had brought along Lieutenant Tenner, so he could become more familiar with how things were done on Kubitz. It would probably be a learning experience for both of them.

"I understand you want to procure some high-tech weapon systems," said Lomatz, who was the chief negotiator for one of the military weapons firms that worked directly for the Kubitz government. Lomatz looked nearly human, except his eyes had a yellow tint to them.

Kurt nodded. Most of the people in the room were from Kubitz. "Yes, we're interested in procuring a defense grid to put around our planet."

Lomatz frowned and called up some information on a small computer tablet he had with him. "I understand your home world has been taken by Profiteer Creed, and he has hired some Dacroni mercenaries to help maintain control of the planet. As long as the Dacroni battleships are in orbit, it will be impossible to emplace a defense system."

"We also have a colony world," explained Lieutenant Tenner. "The defense grid is to ensure the safety of that world."

"A wise choice," one of the other humanoids said, nodding his head in understanding. "Just what type of system are you interested in?"

"Something that would discourage an attack, such as what Profiteer Creed launched against Earth," Kurt answered evenly. "I have been told, if we can destroy or damage enough Profiteer ships, they will pull back rather than risk a loss to their profits."

"That is true in most cases," Lomatz responded, his eyes narrowing.

Lomatz had brought three others with him, and they quickly huddled together and talked animatedly to one another. One of them took out another tablet. Finally the four seemed satisfied, and Lomatz turned toward Kurt.

"Six orbiting defense platforms, twenty-four satellites armed with standard energy weapons, and one control center to coordinate everything."

"How much?" Lieutenant Tenner asked, his eyes focusing on Lomatz.

Lomatz looked over at one of his associates who answered, "Eighty-two million credits."

"And this would ensure that Profiteers such as Creed would leave us alone?" asked Kurt. It made him uneasy having to depend on these humanoids to plan the defense of Newton.

"Yes," one of the others answered. "These weapons systems are capable of inflicting just enough damage on an attacking fleet to make profits impossible. In most cases just the presence of the defense system will deter aggression. Most of the systems in the Gothan Empire, plus a number of others outside the empire, have this type of system."

Kurt leaned back and folded his arms across his chest. Newton was Earth's only hope of eventual freedom. "Are there more powerful weapon systems available for planetary defense?" He suspected that, while it might be true that this type of system would deter most attacks, he wanted something that would discourage even a full-size battlefleet from attacking Newton.

The humanoids seemed surprised by the question.

"Yes, there are more powerful systems," Lomatz answered carefully. "However they're extremely expensive, and most planetary governments can't afford them. The type of system I'm speaking of is widely used in some of the more enlightened systems that don't want to depend on a warfleet for protection."

"What type of system would it take to destroy an attacking fleet such as the one Profiteer Creed has at his disposal?"

"Destroy it completely?" asked the humanoid holding the tablet. "You're talking about a system that would cost several hundred million credits. It would involve no less than twelve Class Two Orbital Defense Platforms, forty-eight satellites with dual firing energy weapons, a Class Two Command and Control Center, and six Planetary Defense Centers with top-of-the-line direct-energy cannons that can hit anything in orbit."

"We'll take it," Kurt answered without hesitation.

"What!" uttered Lomatz, looking stunned. "We rarely sell those systems because of their price. Do you have that many credits?"

"I can have that much in my account within twenty-two hours."

The four humanoids talked again. This time it took much longer. Finally they turned back to Kurt.

"We can have the system ready for delivery in sixty days," Lomatz answered. "We'll use one of our special cargo fleets to deliver the system and two of our construction ships to install it. We'll also guarantee the safety of your planet from the time we arrive until the time the system is activated."

"Very well," replied Kurt, surprised at how quickly they could have it ready. Then he leaned forward and looked intently at the four. "We also want to purchase a large supply of hypermissiles."

"Hypermissiles are one of the standard weapons most species in the galaxy employ," one of the humanoids answered, leaning back and focusing his attention on Kurt. "The basic missile costs twenty thousand credits each. How many are you interested in and what type of warheads do you want on them?"

"One thousand," Kurt answered without hesitation. "What are the options for the warheads?"

"For twenty thousand credits the missile comes with a standard ten-kiloton explosive warhead. For fifty thousand credits the warhead detonates in the fifty-kiloton range," Lomatz answered.

"Do you have anything more powerful?"

Lomatz looked at his associates a little uneasily. "There are the antimatter warheads which detonate in the fifty-megaton range. Those warheads, once they have been sold, are not allowed back inside the Kubitz System or the Gothan Empire. We have special detection equipment that constantly scans the system, and any ship entering Kubitz space will be annihilated if it contains such weapons. Other inhabited worlds in the empire are similarly equipped and follow the same policy. They are two hundred thousand credits each."

"Let's change our order slightly," Kurt said. "I want one hundred antimatter warheads and two hundred of the fifty-kiloton and the rest in the standard ten-kiloton range."

"What about the defense system?" asked the humanoid with the tablet. "The system comes equipped with the standard hypermissile warhead. Do you want some of the stronger missiles for it as well?

"Yes," Kurt answered. "Twenty percent of the hypermissiles are to be in the fifty-kiloton range and the rest can be of the standard ten-kiloton warheads.

"Fifty million additional credits."

"Done," responded Kurt without hesitation.

"What about ships?" one of the others ventured. "We sell warships as well. We have the largest orbital shipyards in this section of the galaxy. We can provide you with a standard model or one built to your specifications."

Kurt looked over at Lieutenant Tenner. This wasn't something he had even considered. Was it possible he could actually buy a fleet or have one built? "How much does a battleship cost, like the ones the Dacroni possess?"

"Those are special vessels and very heavily armed," Lomatz answered. "They were built specifically for the Dacroni. Normal battleships equipped with ion cannons, energy projectors, and hypermissiles will run about fifteen to twenty million credits each. A battlecruiser similarly armed will run about twelve to fifteen million. All of this is, of course, dependent upon what options you want included."

Kurt could scarcely believe what he was hearing.

"If we purchased the standard model, how soon could you have a battlecruiser or battleship completed?"

"Sixty to eighty days," one of the other humanoids answered promptly. "We keep a supply of the hulls on hand already completed. We just need to add what weapons and options you want. Most of these are modules that just need to be slid into place. We can also adjust the crew quarters and other areas inside to fit whatever design scheme you prefer. We can do an entire fleet rather quickly."

"If we order some vessels, can it be done in secret?" asked Lieutenant Tenner.

"Yes," Lomatz replied. "It can be written into the contract, and no one, not even the work crews, will know where the ships are heading. I should inform you of one other important piece of data. It is against the laws of the Gothan Empire for any ship built at Kubitz to be used against any world of the empire. If that were to occur, then you would be at war with all 118 worlds. This will be explained in great detail in the contract."

"What about outside the empire?" asked Kurt carefully. "Could I attack the Profiteer fleet in orbit around Earth with a fleet purchased here at Kubitz?"

"The rule does not apply outside the cluster," answered Lomatz, his eyes unwavering.

Kurt knew this was a big decision. It would also be necessary to come up with the crews. However, how could he not jump at the opportunity to buy a warfleet? It might be the solution to freeing Earth from Profiteer Creed's grasp. "Give me a day or two to consult with some of my people on the ships. If we do decide to buy some warships, can I send some of my own construction engineers to help with modifications to the interiors?"

"That's perfectly fine," responded Lomatz, nodding his head. "Most worlds that purchase vessels do send engineers so the interiors can be built to specifications they are more comfortable with. Do you want to complete the contract for the hyperspace missiles and the Class Two defense system today?"

"Yes," Kurt answered.

-

For the next hour, they hammered out the exact details for delivery of the hypermissiles and the defense grid. They would take immediate delivery of one hundred of the missiles and would load them aboard the *Lansing*. The rest would be delivered when the defense grid was brought to Newton. It ended with Kurt pressing his thumb against the computer pad the Controller had brought.

"You have twenty-two hours to have the credits deposited in either your account at the spaceport or the one at the station," the Controller said. "Failure to do so will result in forfeiture of all credits currently in your accounts."

"The credits will be in our account in the morning," responded Lieutenant Tenner.

As the meeting broke up, Kurt glanced at his watch; nearly three hours had passed. It was past time for him to meet Keera for the meal he had promised her. For the first time in quite a while, he was actually looking forward to something.

-

"Second Clan Leader Castel gazed at a large viewscreen, showing the human cargo ship so tantalizing close.

"We've finished interrogating the captive human female," Dalet reported. "It took time, but, in the end, we got what we wanted or at least most of it."

Castel turned his attention to his second in command. "Is there more gold on that cargo ship?"

"Yes," Dalet answered. "Unfortunately her mind collapsed from the use of the mind probe before we could learn how much. We know they came to Kubitz to buy back their people and to learn as much as they could about the Gothan Empire. She admitted that the gold on the cargo ship was taken off Earth during the time High Profiteer Creed was absent."

"Why did the machine fail to get us all the information we wanted?"

"When pressed for how much gold had been removed from Earth, her thought pattern disintegrated due to the high setting we were using on the mind probe. Her answers now are mostly gibberish."

Castel sighed and shook his head. He knew, in time, her mind might return to normal or her thought patterns might never reestablish. It was dangerous to use the mind probe. The machine was banned on most worlds, including Kubitz. "Imprint some basic memories and sell her to the Brollen Pleasure House. She's good-looking enough to bring a fair sum, and they'll stay quiet about the transaction."

"It will be done," Dalet replied. "What will we do about the cargo ship?"

"We take it!" Castel answered with greed in his eyes. "Put a hyperspace tracer on the ship. When they leave the Kubitz System, we'll follow and take the ship when they exit hyperspace."

"That battlecruiser is equipped with particle beams that can penetrate our shields," warned Dalet.

"Yes, that's a problem," admitted Castel, as he thought up a plan. "We'll have High Profiteer Creed's battlecruiser and two escort cruisers come along as well. We'll let them take the first hit from the particle beam cannon, and then, while it's recharging, we'll move in and take out the battlecruiser. Use our energy projectors to take out the cargo ship's hyperdrive, so it can't escape. Once the battle is over, we'll dock and remove whatever gold is still on the ship. I suspect it will be quite a lot. They won't be comfortable with leaving all of it here on Kubitz."

"They've set up a diplomatic compound," Dalet pointed out. "They'll need credits to operate it."

"We'll let High Profiteer Creed worry about that," responded Castel dismissively. "Our interest is in that cargo ship and what it might be carrying."

-

"I'll be leaving shortly," Kurt said, as he looked across the table at Keera.

She had done her hair and put on a little makeup since he had seen her last. They were in the small cafeteria on the bottom floor of the main building of the compound. One of the cooks from the *Star Cross* had come down to show the locals, who had been hired how to run the place, the type of food the human staff would want.

"I'm sorry to hear that," Keera replied, as she took a bite of the chicken on her plate. "This meat is quite tasty. What's it called?"

"Fried chicken," answered Kurt, smiling. "It's very popular on our home world and our colony on Newton."

"You're embarking on a dangerous path," Keera said after a moment.

"What do you mean?"

"I saw the Kubitz arms people leaving," she explained with a grimace. "Lomatz only deals in big weapon orders."

"It'll be expensive to protect what remains of my people," Kurt answered.

"That may be true," Keera said, as she stirred her mashed potatoes and gravy with her fork. "But the Profiteers will know that you have credits to spend when they learn what you've purchased. They'll be curious where the gold came from and may pay a visit to your colony. I'm sure the word is already out on the streets."

"It's supposed to be a secret," answered Kurt, leaning back, curious about what this young doctor had to say. "It's in the contract I signed with the Controller and Lomatz."

"Perhaps," Keera said, as she took a curious bite of the potatoes. Her eyes widened, and she smiled. "These potatoes are very good, particularly with the gravy. We have similar foods, but every culture puts its own spin on them."

"You don't think the Controller and Lomatz will keep our purchases a secret?"

"Oh, they'll try," Keera said, shrugging her shoulders. "But on Kubitz, nothing stays a secret for long. There are spies everywhere, and enough credits can buy any information that's supposed to be secret. Once the Profiteers learn of your purchases, they may decide to strike your colony to see what riches it has before your weapons can be delivered."

"I considered that," Kurt admitted. He was enjoying Keera's company. "If they do, we'll be ready."

"I hope so," Keera said in a softer voice. "I would hate to see anything else happen to you or your people."

Later that evening, Kurt sat down with Lieutenant Tenner. "I intend to leave as soon as possible. Is there anything else that you might need?"

"I'm sure there are a hundred things," Tenner responded with a partial smile. "We have the *Dallas* in orbit, and, if she can't provide what we need, we'll just add it to the list."

"I'm leaving 120 million credits in the embassy account," Kurt said. It had taken some time to determine just how much Tenner might need. "We'll change out the light cruisers every month or two, depending on what happens at Earth. Each time a new ship arrives, they'll be accompanied by a passenger liner, in case you have had to buy the freedom of any more of our people."

"What about the warships?" Tenner asked, his eyes narrowing. "We need to tell Lomatz what you want. I still can't believe that warships are for sale, as Lomatz indicated."

"I was surprised also," admitted Kurt. "It was something I wasn't expecting. Right now I'm leaning toward four battleships and ten battlecruisers. The problem will be finding the crews to operate them."

"Earth," Tenner answered simply. "There are bound to be some fleet people still on the planet, and others who could be easily trained. If you can find a way to sneak into the system and get down to the surface, I'm sure you can probably contact Fleet Admiral Tomalson and explain what your needs are."

"It's a thought," Kurt answered, as he considered Tenner's suggestion. He would think about it on the return trip. "I'll meet with Lomatz again tomorrow. I spoke to Dolman earlier, and he confirmed that a hyperspace detection system surrounds the

Kubitz System, so they can detect inbound ships before they arrive. I want such a system for Newton. It might also be useful in tracking Profiteer ships leaving Earth."

"I'll make the arrangements for a meeting early in the morning," Tenner answered with a nod.

"I'm still greatly concerned about Private Dulcet," Kurt added with a deep frown. "I know that Dolman feels she's probably dead, but you keep Grantz searching for her."

"I will," Tenner promised with a nod. "I'll push Grantz to find her."

"As far as Dolman goes, use him and his sources as needed, just watch the amount of credits he demands for his services," Kurt said.

Tenner allowed himself to smile and nodded. "I suspect there'll be a lot of bargaining between me and Avery Dolman."

Kurt hesitated for a moment and then spoke. "The young doctor I was with earlier tonight, I think it would be wise to offer her a contract to care for the embassy staff."

"I thought you might suggest something like that. I'll have a simple contract drawn up for her to sign."

Kurt nodded. He didn't know why, but he had a feeling he would be seeing the young doctor many more times in the future.

Captain Randson was in his quarters with his wife and daughter. It had been a huge relief to finally rescue them. Alexis was still having a hard time sleeping and had woken up several times, screaming.

"What's Newton like?" asked Alexis, looking at her father.

"It's a beautiful world," Andrew replied with a loving smile. "You'll enjoy living there. In some ways it's much like Earth, only cleaner. There's no pollution. Everything's pretty modern, and they have some very good schools."

"So we won't be living in a tent or out in the wild?"

"No," answered Andrew with a laugh. "There are over eight million people on Newton with over six hundred thousand living in the capital. We'll find a nice house to live in, and everything will be back to normal."

"What if the Profiteers come to Newton? I don't want to come back to Kubitz. They were going to sell us to the highest bidder!"

Andrew reached out and put his arms protectively around his daughter. "I can promise you that will never happen. We have a large fleet around the planet, and we won't be taken by surprise, like the fleets protecting Earth were. We even have the heavy battlecarrier *Kepler* finished. That ship, by itself, is quite capable of protecting Newton."

"We're safe now, honey," Emily said, sitting down next to Andrew and Alexis. "Your father will see that the Profiteers never bother us again."

Andrew nodded. Once the new defense system arrived, Newton would be secure from any conceivable attack. The only problem was that the new system was still a few months away from being installed. After all the credits they had just spent on Kubitz, the word had to be out that the Earth humans still had a large quantity of gold and possibly other valuable assets. In all probability an attack on Newton would happen before the defenses arrived. He wouldn't share this fear with his family, as he didn't want them to worry. He would do the worrying for them.

Fleet Admiral Vickers was watching the Dacroni battleship on the main viewscreen, when Captain Randson returned to the Command Center. He had finished the arrangements for the battleships and battlecruisers, and had deposited sufficient gold with the spaceport Controllers to cover the costs, as well as to operate the embassy. He had also spent another twenty million credits on some special hyperspace detection buoys. He had bought twenty of them, and each one could detect a ship in hyperspace for a distance of five light-years.

"We're ready to leave," Kurt announced, upon seeing Randson. He knew that Andrew had been with his family.

"All ships are in formation," reported Lieutenant Brooks, as she checked her short-range sensors.

"We've been cleared by Kubitz Orbital Control to leave," added Ensign Pierce. "We can't enter hyperspace until we've cleared the orbit of the sixth planet."

Kurt nodded. Turning to Andrew, he gave an order. "Take us out at 60 percent sublight."

Moments later he watched the viewscreens, as they pulled away from Kubitz. His thoughts turned to Keera, and he wondered when he would see her again. He had found the young doctor to be quite intriguing and enjoyable to be with.

On the Dacroni battleship *Rellal*, Second Clan Leader Castel looked on, while the human ships broke orbit and accelerated away from the planet. We'll follow them shortly," he informed Dalet. "Let them clear the orbit of the fifth planet, and then we'll leave Kubitz. Is the hyperspace tracer working?"

"Yes," Dalet answered. "We managed to successfully place two of them on the outer hull of the cargo ship."

Castel nodded. If things worked out as he hoped, that human cargo ship would bring vast riches to the clan. Clan Leader Jarls would be very satisfied when he heard what Castel had done. Once the humans entered hyperspace, he would follow and set up an ambush. He strongly suspected that, once they were away from the Gothan Empire, the humans' fears of an attack would lessen. That would be when Castel would strike. He would eliminate this small human threat and take the cargo ship. Leaning back in his command chair, Castel was confident of his success. The humans were such fools to think they could travel all the way to the Gothan Empire and not suffer the consequences for their rashness. He would shortly show them the error of their thinking.

Chapter Thirteen

Kurt had left the Command Center to take a tour of the ship. They had just completed their second hyperspace dropout after leaving the Gothan Empire, and he was breathing easier. They had made it out of the star cluster without encountering any other ships. One thing he did want to do, when they made it back to Newton, was see if they could adopt the science behind the hyperspace buoys, so they could use a similar detection system on the *Star Cross*. Of course Kurt wasn't certain the science was even decipherable.

Stepping into the med bay, he saw Dr. Willis sitting at a desk with a bored look on his face. Willis was an older man, graying at the temples, and very qualified to handle all the requirements of a ship's doctor.

"Admiral," Willis said, standing up when he saw Kurt at the hatch. "What brings you down this way?"

"Sit back down," Kurt said, walking over and taking the other chair in front of the doctor's desk. "I'm just making a quick tour of the ship before we jump back into hyperspace. How are things here in med bay?"

"Too damn quiet," Willis said with a satisfied grin. "Only one patient today and he was complaining about a bellyache. Gave him some antacid medication and sent him to his quarters."

"We'll be at Newton in eight more days," Kurt said.

He would be relieved to get back, as it would allow him to know the planet was still safe. He was fully confident that Rear Admiral Wilson could handle any Profiteers who might come his way, particularly with the *Kepler* at his disposal.

"I'll be glad," Willis replied. He opened a folder and pointed at some notes he had written down. "I've been making a tentative list of all the different humanoid and alien species that we encountered in the Kubitz System."

"How?" Kurt asked surprised. "Where did you get that information?"

"Your friend, Avery Dolman," Willis answered. "I got Lieutenant Tenner to pay him a nice little sum for this information. He sent a lot of medical files that describe the differences between the various humanoid species on Kubitz. Even a few files on some of the alien ones."

"That's one thing I didn't see," Kurt commented. "In the time I was on the planet, everyone I saw was human or at least humanoid to some extent. I wonder where the alien species were?"

"In another one of the domed cities that specializes in serving them," Willis answered. "I asked the same question and was told that many of them require specific atmospheric environments in order to survive. I guess the Kubitz government built a special city, just to take care of their needs, so they could trade with them."

"While I was on Kubitz, I met a doctor. Her name is Keera Jelk. She said she studied at some advanced institute that specializes in the different humanoid species plus a few of the major alien ones. I should have arranged for you to meet her."

"Maybe next time," Willis said with a nod. "I would be interested in speaking with someone with that type of experience."

Kurt's conversation with Willis was cut short when the ship suddenly shook violently, and the Condition One alarms began sounding.

"What the hell?" uttered Willis with his eyes widening. "Was that an explosion?"

"Admiral Vickers, report to the Command Center." The anxious voice of Captain Randson came over the ship's general comm system. "We have a Dacroni battleship closing on our position."

"Looks as if you're about to get busy, doc," Kurt said, as he reached across Willis's desk and pressed the comm button. "Captain, jump the fleet back into hyperspace. No need for us to fight that battleship."

"Can't," Randson replied. "They took out the hyperdrive on the *Lansing* with the first shot. The crew is evaluating the damage to see how severe it is."

"I'm on my way," Kurt answered, as he turned and rushed from the med bay. The news about the *Lansing* was disconcerting. The ship only had a weak defensive shield and a few railgun batteries for defense. The ship also had a crew of seventy, plus twenty Marines.

It only took Kurt a couple of minutes to reach the Command Center. During that time he felt the *Star Cross* shake severely on more than one occasion. Bursting into the Command Center, he hurried over to his command chair. "Status!"

"We have a Dacroni battleship, a Profiteer battlecruiser, and two support cruisers closing on our position," reported Captain Randson, standing behind the tactical station. "We're currently under fire from the battlecruiser and the two support vessels."

"Damage?"

"Only minor," Randson answered. "Our energy screen was up and has deflected most of the energy directed toward us."

"The *Sydney*?"

"Covering the *Lansing* and the *Newton Princess*."

Kurt knew instantly what he had to do. Activating the ship-to-ship comm, he contacted the captains of the *Newton Princess* and the *Sydney*. "Both of you jump into hyperspace and go to Newton."

"We can help, Admiral," protested Captain Danforth from the *Sydney*.

"I know you can, but there are more than four thousand civilians on the *Newton Princess*. Their survival is now your number one priority. I want both your ships gone immediately and don't stop until you reach Newton. If I don't make it back, tell Rear Admiral Wilson that he's in command."

"Yes, Admiral," Captain Danforth answered. "We'll do as ordered. Good luck."

Moments later, both vessels vanished from the tactical screen, as they jumped into hyperspace.

"*Sydney* and the *Newton Princess* have jumped," confirmed Lieutenant Brooks.

The ship shook violently once again, and several warning alarms sounded on the damage control console.

"I'm tired of that Profiteer battlecruiser using us for target practice," Kurt said, his eyes taking on a dangerous glint. "Target it with our particle beam cannon. Follow it up with four rounds each from our two forward KEW batteries."

"Target locked," reported Lieutenant Mays from Tactical.

"Fire!" ordered Kurt, his eyes focused intently on the main viewscreen, which showed the nine-hundred-meter-long enemy battlecruiser rapidly closing range with the *Star Cross*.

A dark blue particle beam flashed from the *Star Cross*, tearing through the energy shield of the Profiteer battlecruiser. The beam struck the bow of the vessel, causing a powerful explosion and hurling debris from the ship. Secondary explosions blew out other hull sections.

"Their shield is down!" called out Lieutenant Brooks, as her sensors detected the sudden collapse of the Profiteer's defensive energy shield. "The particle beam must have hit something vital inside the ship."

"Take them out," Captain Randson ordered the tactical officer. "Fire the forward KEW batteries."

The *Star Cross* shook slightly as her bow KEW batteries fired four projectiles at nearly 10 percent of the speed of light at the enemy ship. The projectiles slammed into the main part of the Profiteer warship, setting off massive explosions and hurling more debris into space. The battlecruiser seemed to stagger and began to drift, as additional secondary explosions tore through the vessel.

"Helm, turn us ninety degrees starboard, flank speed!" ordered Captain Randson. "All laser batteries and defensive railgun turrets to target the Profiteer battlecruiser on completion of the turn."

The *Star Cross* quickly turned, and her laser turrets fired ruby-red beams of energy at the heavily damaged Profiteer battlecruiser. Explosions erupted across the hull as the defensive railgun turrets fired their smaller rounds at the enemy ship. Suddenly a bright fireball appeared in the heart of the battlecruiser, and it blew apart.

"Profiteer battlecruiser is down," reported Lieutenant Brooks in a shaken voice.

"The two support cruisers are still closing, and the Dacroni battleship is making toward the *Lansing*," called out Captain Randson, his eyes focused on the tactical screen. "I think they intend to board her."

"How long until the *Lansing* can repair her hyperdrive?" demanded Kurt. "Helm, set a course for the *Lansing*, put us between it and the Dacroni battleship."

"Admiral, we don't have the firepower to take on a Dacroni battleship," warned Captain Randson. "Their shields are too powerful, and their ion beam can penetrate our energy screen, if they keep it focused on us long enough."

"I have Captain Blair on the comm," reported Ensign Pierce.

"Captain Blair, how long until you can have your hyperdrive operational?" Kurt asked, as the viewscreen shifted suddenly to show the Dacroni battleship. "You also need to deploy your Marines. We believe the Dacroni battleship is sending a boarding party."

"We can't," answered Blair in an even voice. "Engineering has been destroyed, and it's open to space. "It'll be hours before we can even get a crew in there. We have sporadic sublight but even that will probably be gone shortly. I've already deployed the Marines to the main airlocks."

Kurt swore silently to himself as he weighed his options. "Prepare for us to dock with you to remove your crew."

"No, Admiral," Blair said calmly. "It's too late for us. I've already ordered several self-destruct charges to be set. They're wired to a detonator I'm holding in my hand. When the Dacroni battleship docks, I intend to set them off."

For several long seconds Kurt remained silent, as he tried to think of a way to save the *Lansing*.

"He's doing the right thing," Captain Randson said somberly, listening to the conversation over the command channel. "There's no other option." His face was pale, knowing what was soon to happen.

Kurt closed his eyes and shook his head; yet he knew Andrew was right. "It's been an honor serving with you, Captain Blair," Kurt said in a calm and respectful voice. "Your sacrifice will be remembered."

"Just drive those bastards from Earth someday!" Blair replied.

"I will," promised Kurt, feeling a lump in the back of his throat.

"Signing off," Blair announced. "I have a few other things that need to be taken care of before that Dacroni battleship docks with us."

The comm went silent, and Kurt leaned back in his command chair. Then, taking a deep breath, he looked over at Captain Randson. "Take us into hyperspace and set course for Newton."

"Yes, Admiral," Randson said, as he quickly passed on the order.

Moments later Kurt felt the *Star Cross* accelerate and then the wrenching sensation as the ship entered hyperspace. They were safe now, but it pained him immensely knowing they had left behind the *Lansing* and her crew.

Second Clan Leader Castel grinned in satisfaction as the human battlecruiser fled the battle, leaving the cargo ship unprotected.

"The human battlecruiser has jumped into hyperspace," Dalet reported. "The cargo ship is ours!"

"The cowards!" roared Castel, as he gazed at the now nearly empty tactical screen. A cloud of debris expanded from the destroyed Profiteer battlecruiser. An unfortunate loss, but one that could be made up for quite easily by the gold he expected to find on the human cargo ship.

"They're still attempting to use their sublight drive to elude us," reported Dalet.

On the tactical screen, the human vessel changed course and put more distance between it and the *Rellal*.

"Use one of our energy beams to disable it permanently," ordered Castel. "Without its hyperdrive the human vessel is worthless to us anyway."

From the *Rellal* a slim white energy beam flashed toward the cargo ship, drilling through the hull and destroying the faltering sublight drive. The cargo ship instantly began to drift.

-

"Sublight drive is down," reported Ensign Brickman, as his navigation panel died.

"Then that's it," Captain Blair said in the suddenly quiet Command Center. "Once the Dacroni have locked their ship to ours, I'll set off the self-destructs."

No one replied, as the small command crew were lost in their own private thoughts, knowing their lives were about to end.

A few minutes passed, and then the ship shuddered slightly, and a loud clanging noise was heard echoing down the now empty corridors.

"They've docked," one of the crew said quietly.

In the distance they could hear heavy weapons fire as the *Lansing*'s Marines engaged the boarding Dacroni mercenaries.

"I wish we all could have seen Earth one more time," Captain Blair said, as he pressed the flashing red button on the detonator he held in his right hand.

-

Instantly the ship's nuclear reactor overloaded and exploded. Torrents of energy were released, annihilating bulkheads, walls, and equipment. A second explosion near the bow destroyed the hypermissiles the ship had been carrying. Several of the warheads had been taken apart and detonators emplaced, arming the warheads. It was a slipshod affair but effective.

The warheads detonated simultaneously, and a brilliant fireball formed in the hold, blowing out the walls and engulfing the Dacroni battleship. With its shield down, it was helpless to protect itself from the raging destruction. Three seconds after the warheads detonated, the Dacroni battleship exploded, as its engineering compartment was breached, and then its fusion reactor became unstable. A massive fireball formed where the two ships had been, and, for a moment, it seemed as if a new sun had formed.

In the two Profiteer escort cruisers, the crews recorded the total destruction of the human cargo ship and the Dacroni battleship. The recordings of the entire battle would be delivered to High Profiteer Creed. If the Dacroni were shown to have acted recklessly, and, as a result, the Profiteer battlecruiser had been destroyed by their negligence, then there would be compensation expected from the mercenaries.

After another few minutes of observations, the two escort cruisers jumped into hyperspace and set course for Earth. Behind them, a glowing debris cloud marked the death of the three ships. In another few days, there would be no obvious evidence that a battle had ever been fought in this small discreet star system.

-

Kurt sat in his quarters, morose in thought. The loss of the *Lansing* had stunned him and had been so unexpected. He made an after-action report, listing his own observations as a reference for future combat missions against both the Profiteers and the Dacroni. The problem had been the Dacroni battleship; if the *Star Cross* had only been fighting the Profiteer battlecruiser and its two escorts, Kurt would have been willing to stay and slug it out.

It was also upsetting that their first group of purchased hypermissiles had been lost. Those would have been useful in the defense of Newton, if the planet were attacked. Now he would have to do without them, until he could make arrangements for more. Credits wouldn't be a problem, as he had ordered a transfer of much of the gold from the *Lansing* to the underground vault beneath the compound they had leased on Kubitz. The vault was under constant guard by the Marines he had left behind. The Marine presence should raise no eyebrows in that neighborhood. Not even Dolman or Grantz knew of the underground vault or what was hidden there. Kurt had gone to great lengths to ensure that.

He was anxious to return to Newton. He wanted to see his sister and her family. He wondered if he should mention Keera to Denise. His younger sister had been hassling him for years to get out and date more often. However, Kurt had been too career-oriented and had never taken her advice seriously.

Leaning back in his chair, he let out a deep sigh. Captain Randson was in his quarters, explaining to his wife and daughter what had just happened. The brief battle had probably frightened them. After the ordeal they had already been through, it was a shame they had to suffer another so quickly. Andrew and several other Command Center officers would also be working on after-action reports. When combined, they would help them to develop a more effective strategy to use in the future.

Closing his eyes, Kurt thought about what still lay ahead of them. One of the things he needed to arrange was to slip several stealth shuttles into the home system and attempt to contact Fleet Admiral Tomalson. The old admiral would be pleased to hear that Kurt had managed to procure a defense system for Newton. However, what Kurt really wanted the fleet admiral informed about were the new warships coming from Kubitz and possibly getting together crews for them from Earth. Kurt had never imagined that even first-line battleships and battlecruisers could be bought for the right amount of credits. The entire economic system of the Gothan Empire was screwy as hell.

With the new warships and the right crews, he just might be able to drive the Profiteers and the Dacroni mercenaries from the Solar System. However, that was months in the future. For now he would have to take it one step at a time. The first step was to get safely back to Newton.

Chapter Fourteen

Captain Nathan Aldrich's anger grew as the Profiteer shuttle lifted off and headed back into space. He had just made another gold "tribute" delivery, and the Profiteers had casually informed him that, from now on, the amount of gold necessary to protect Earth cities had doubled. They had sneered when Aldrich protested, indicating that the next payment had better not be missed.

"The president won't like this," commented Corporal Lasher, as he raised his assault rifle and followed the vanishing shuttle. "I wish I could shoot down that shuttle." He lowered his rifle and looked over at Nathan.

"It's not our call," Nathan answered, as he climbed back into the now empty truck. They had delivered eighty gold bars as this month's payment.

Lasher climbed in next to him and nodded. "I guess what worries me is just how much gold we have stockpiled. I heard that some of the Profiteers are now going door to door, demanding that everyone turn over their jewelry. They even cut off one man's finger for refusing to give up his wedding ring."

"The situation's getting worse," admitted Nathan, as he started the truck and drove off the airport runway. "It's only a matter of time before things get out of hand. Some civilian will shoot one of the Profiteers, and then all hell will break lose."

Lasher patted his rifle. "I'm ready," he said. "My rifle and I are itching to kick some Profiteer butt."

"If they don't kick yours first," replied Nathan, as he shifted gears.

They were in a difficult situation. Any attempt at resistance would result in bombardment from the orbiting spaceships. It had already happened a few times, such as the incident in Youngstown. Each time the Profiteers had retaliated by blasting the offending city with energy beams. Nathan greatly feared that, before this was over, a lot of people would die.

High Profiteer Creed watched the viewscreen in the Command Center of his battlecruiser the *Ascendant Destruction*. The returning shuttle was prominently displayed.

"More gold tribute," gloated Second Profiteer Lantz. "Eighty gold bars to add to what we've already collected."

"Yes," muttered Creed, although not pleased with the way things had been going. "We're not finding near enough gold and other valuables on Earth as we did before."

"You think they've hidden it?"

"Some of it," answered Creed, gesturing toward the returning shuttle. "Where else would they be getting the gold they're paying for tribute?"

"It's true that our raiding parties aren't finding as much as we had expected," admitted Lantz. "We could send down even more Profiteers. We've found a surprising amount of gold and jewels among the civilian population."

"I have considered that. However, there is another answer," Creed said, pointing to the tactical screen, showing the two escorts that had recently arrived. "According to Second Profiteer Trilt, the humans have set up a compound on Kubitz and have been spending large quantities of credits. The credits had to have come from the sale of gold."

"Gold they took from Earth," Lantz said in dawning realization. "Our gold! What did the humans buy on Kubitz? How did they even know where to go?"

"Weapons obviously," Creed answered simply. "We know they wanted hypermissiles and who knows what else. I'll be sending a ship soon to Kubitz to see what information they can find. As to how they knew about Kubitz, the answer is easy. Third Profiteer Grantz was on board the humans' orbiting shipyard and is missing. There are reports he has signed a contract to act as a liaison for the humans. He was spotted with them and Avery Dolman on Kubitz."

"I know Grantz," muttered Lantz, shaking his head in disgruntlement. "He'll do anything for enough credits. As far as Dolman goes, he has his hands in everything legal and illegal on the planet. He wouldn't be involved with the humans, unless the potential existed for him to make a tidy sum of credits."

"We must learn more of what the humans are doing on Kubitz," announced Creed with a sharp frown. "I have some contacts in the Controller station. Perhaps they can find out for us just how much gold the humans exchanged for credits."

"Once it's in the Controllers' hands, we can't get to it," said Lantz despondently.

Creed gazed at the viewscreens for another few moments before reaching a decision. "We need more gold and other precious metals. Send a message to the South African government that we expect the delivery of one hundred gold bars and ten thousand carats of diamonds in one week. If they fail to deliver, then they'll lose a city."

"What about the tribute they pay for us to leave their cities alone?" asked Lantz.

"We make the rules, not them!" retorted Creed. "Also contact Clan Leader Jarls. We need to discuss the battlecruiser I lost due to the recklessness of the Dacroni on the *Rellal*. The cost of that ship will be coming from the mercenaries' take."

Lantz shook his head. "He won't agree to that, but I'll inform him of the meeting."

President Mayfield sat behind his desk, listening to General Braid describe the latest tribute payment. "They're doubling the tribute we pay them every month?"

"Yes," responded the general. "That's what Captain Aldrich reported. The Profiteers made the demand when he delivered the gold earlier today."

"More bad news," added Raul Gutierrez, pointing to a sheet of paper in front of him. "The South Africans are reporting that they just received a message from High Profiteer Creed demanding the payment of one hundred bars of gold and ten thousand carats of diamonds."

"This is what we were afraid of," said Fleet Admiral Tomalson with a frown. "With what we sent off world and what we've hidden, they're not finding what they want. We cleaned out all the major gold depositories."

"Their demands will only increase," warned Raul, his eyes focusing on the president. "What will we do when it's our turn?"

"We have sufficient gold reserves to keep our cities safe a bit longer," replied President Mayfield. He leaned back, closed his eyes, and then opened them. "We have to hope that Fleet Admiral Vickers will be successful in his mission and can somehow force the Profiteers to leave Earth."

"As soon as he intercepts the alien convoys leaving for the Gothan Empire, it could make a difference," Tomalson pointed out. "If we can take out some of their ships, they may decide it's not worth the time and money to strip Earth of its wealth."

"Everything they do is based on profit," Raul said. "If we can make Earth unprofitable, such as Fleet Admiral Vickers inflicting heavy damage on their convoys, it could very well cause them to reconsider occupying our planet."

"Why is gold so valuable?" asked President Mayfield with a curious look in his eyes. "You would think it could be easily mined on asteroids and other worlds, and would be plentiful."

"From our communication intercepts we've learned part of the answer," Raul replied. "On most worlds, gold is found too deep to make mining practical. It's also highly valued for jewelry and several other industrial uses due to its malleability. It seems to be a little bit rarer that what one would expect. Here on Earth much of the gold we've found has been from very shallow deposits. From what we understand, this is a very uncommon occurrence and doesn't happen on too many worlds."

The door to the office opened, and a Marine lieutenant stepped in. "Mr. President, the South Africans have responded to the Profiteers."

"What did they say?" Mayfield asked, his attention shifting to the lieutenant.

The South African government had been one of the more reluctant governments to support the monthly tribute payments to the Profiteers. In recent years the South Africans had moved more to a socialist government, and corruption in the higher levels was a major problem. Much of the wealth the country once possessed had disappeared.

The lieutenant looked worried, and then he replied, "They told the Profiteers to go to hell!"

"Crap," muttered General Braid, not liking the sound of that. "The Profiteers won't tolerate that attitude. What are the South Africans thinking?"

"Place our forces on alert," ordered President Mayfield with a deep sigh.

They had numerous hidden assets that could be called into play, if needed. Missiles, jet fighters, and even a few submarines hiding out in the depths of the oceans. What had thus far held in check the North American Union was the fear of massive civilian casualties if armed conflict broke out.

The phone on the president's desk rang, drawing his attention. Picking it up, Mayfield listened for a moment and then turned toward the others. "We're needed in the situation room. The South Africans have activated their military and are putting jet fighters in the air."

"They're crazy," said General Braid. "Jet fighters can't do anything against orbiting spaceships."

"Tell the South Africans that," replied Raul, as he stood up.

"This will get ugly quick," warned Fleet Admiral Tomalson, looking over at President Mayfield. "We don't want to get dragged into their fight, if we can help it."

"I agree," answered Mayfield. "This thing could spread rapidly, if other nations decide to join the South Africans. We may get dragged in whether we want to or not."

A few moments later, they entered the situation room, where a number of military officers were monitoring a group of large computer screens.

"Status," demanded General Braid.

"The South Africans have nearly forty jet fighters in the air, and they're calling all their reserve units to active duty," reported defensive coordinator Colonel Stidham. "They've just issued an ultimatum to the Profiteers, stating than any shuttles entering South African airspace will be shot down."

"The fools!" uttered Fleet Admiral Tomalson. "All they're doing is inviting the Profiteers to nuke their cities."

"Their leaders have all the gold and diamonds in the country hidden in their private vaults on those massive estates they've built over the years," Raul answered. "They don't want to give any of it up."

"They're as bad as the Profiteers," muttered General Braid. "Their greed will cost a lot of people their lives."

"We have South African jet fighters on the screen," reported Colonel Stidham, pointing to one of the larger viewscreens, which fed the image from an orbiting military satellite.

Everyone looked to see the silhouettes of a number of South African jet fighters rising into the air. No doubt it wouldn't be long before the Profiteers responded to this provocation.

Lieutenant Evan Scottsdale flew his F-72 Falcon at thirty thousand feet. Below him, he could easily see the Kimberley diamond mine. From this altitude, he could see the massive pit that had yielded some of the world's largest diamonds.

"We have contacts descending from orbit," reported Captain Mason Belonn. "Home plate has identified them as Profiteer shuttles."

"Go weapons hot," ordered Major Jeffrys. "We're to engage any targets that enter our patrol zone."

"Confirmed," replied Lieutenant Scottsdale. He wished they were patrolling closer to Durban, where his wife and two-year-old son were. He felt anxious, wondering how their weapons would fare against the inbound shuttles.

Suddenly a bright light appeared on the horizon, and the Falcon was struck by massive turbulence.

"What the hell was that!" yelled Captain Belonn over the squadron comm channel.

"A nuke," replied Major Jeffrys, sounding stunned. "It's over the city of Kimberley."

Lieutenant Scottsdale fought to maintain control of his fighter and, in a few seconds, had it back in stable flight. Looking toward the horizon, he could see a terrifying orange-red mushroom cloud rising.

"We have Profiteer shuttles entering our engagement zone," reported Major Jeffrys in a shaken voice. "All fighters engage!"

Lieutenant Scottsdale checked his sensor screen and saw a shuttle rapidly closing on his fighter. The new sensor screens were far better than the old-fashioned radar or lidar ones. He pushed forward the throttle lever, and the Falcon quickly accelerated toward the approaching shuttle. Looking through his cockpit window, Evan could see a silvery object heading toward him. A loud, steady tone suddenly rang out, as his targeting system locked on the inbound Profiteer shuttle. Without hesitation, he pressed the missile-firing button twice, and a pair of Hellcat Two missiles blasted from the wings of his fighter. His gaze followed them; they were flying straight and true. Then two bright detonations occurred as his missiles struck the shuttle, obscuring it.

"I have two confirmed hits," he reported over his comm.

Glancing at his sensor screen, he saw with consternation that his target remained, rapidly closing with his fighter. It must be protected by an energy shield, he realized. In near panic he dove his fighter to escape his pursuer. Glancing around, he could see bright beams of white light crisscrossing the sky. Occasionally one of the beams would hit a Falcon, blowing it apart. Over his comm, he could hear the panicked voices of the other pilots in his squadron, as they were ruthlessly shot down.

"All Falcons, this is Major Jeffrys. Our weapons are ineffective. Break off and return to base. I have a confirmed report from home plate that Pretoria and Port Elizabeth have also been nuked."

"What about Durban?" demanded Lieutenant Scottsdale.

His comm remained silent, and, looking around, he couldn't see any of the other fighters in his squadron. Taking a deep breath, he dove toward the surface and then, pulling up at the last minute, set a course for Durban. He could land at the military airport there. He would grab some transportation, pick up his family, and head into the countryside, avoiding the bigger cities.

Time passed rapidly, and Evan pushed his fighter to get to Durban as quickly as possible. Comm traffic was gone, except for the constant static. Several times he had attempted to contact military traffic controllers but had received no response. Pulling up the nose on his fighter, he gained altitude. He was close enough now that he should be able to see the city in the distance, once he was high enough. As his fighter climbed, he gazed intently toward where Durban should be. A cold chill ran down his back as a rising mushroom cloud became visible. "They're gone," he said, stunned. It looked as if the nuke had gone off over the bay. With a sinking feeling in the pit of his stomach, he knew his family couldn't have survived.

His fighter suddenly shook violently, and warning alarms sounded. Glancing at his sensor screen, he saw a Profiteer shuttle rapidly approaching from the rear. He didn't even try to dodge as an energy beam tore through his aircraft, blowing it apart.

"What are the latest reports?" asked President Mayfield. They had another satellite view on one of the large viewscreens in the situation room, and it showed what appeared to be six nuclear detonations in South Africa. Mayfield felt as if a cold hand had just squeezed his heart.

"Johannesburg, Pretoria, Port Elizabeth, Kimberley, Durban, and Bloemfontein have been nuked," reported Colonel Stidham. "We also have unconfirmed reports that all of South Africa's jet fighters have been shot down."

"What type of fighter did they have?" asked President Mayfield.

"F-72 Falcons," replied Colonel Stidham.

"Not as modern as our jet fighters but still a pretty good weapons platform," remarked General Braid.

"What else are the Profiteers doing?"

Colonel Stidham shook his head in disbelief, looking down at a message one of his communication officers had just handed him. "They've reissued their demand for one hundred gold bars and ten thousand carats of diamonds."

"Any response from the South Africans?" asked President Mayfield, shifting his gaze to the colonel.

"From Cape Town," replied Colonel Stidham. "The provincial governor has agreed to the demand."

"What other choice did he have?" said Raul, shaking his head. He looked up at the viewscreen. "Those six nukes will cause millions of casualties. A big part of South Africa will be uninhabitable for years. The nuke that went off in the bay near Durban will spread an ungodly amount of radiation. We can only hope that most of it goes into the ocean."

"We'll offer them what aid we can," President Mayfield said. "Though I don't know what the Profiteers will allow. If we can't move any domestic aircraft, the South Africans may be on their own."

"The Profiteers don't seem to be making demands of anyone else," commented General Braid.

"They don't have to," President Mayfield answered grimly. "After what they just did to the South Africans, no one will dare deny their demands."

"Do you think they chose South Africa, knowing how they would respond?" asked Raul, looking over at President Mayfield and General Braid.

"It wouldn't surprise me," answered Braid. "They probably wanted to set an example for the rest of us."

Raul looked back at the viewscreen. Six areas in South Africa were now covered in dense smoke and raging fires. "That's one hell of an example. Just what sort of people are we dealing with?"

"They look at us as property," replied President Mayfield forlornly. "If we don't do as they ask, they'll kill us all."

Everyone was silent, as they thought that over. They were in a dire situation that was about to get much worse.

-

First Profiteer Creed nodded with satisfaction, as he was told the South Africans had capitulated. "We'll have the gold and diamonds within the week."

"A good plan," commented Second Profiteer Lantz. "There are numerous small countries on this planet. We can make the same or similar demands to each one."

"Over time," Creed said with a nod. "For now, this little example should suffice. I strongly suspect our collections of gold and other valuables will greatly increase."

"Jarls's shuttle has arrived," reported Third Profiteer Bixt.

"Have him meet me in my quarters," responded Creed. "I have much to discuss with the Dacroni clan leader."

-

High Profiteer Creed entered his quarters to find Jarls waiting for him.

"I watched your attack upon this world," Jarls said. "Are you not concerned about the riches you may have destroyed with the nukes?"

"There are hundreds of such cities on this planet," Creed said dismissively. "This was a lesson in humility. Next time I make a demand, they'll make haste to meet it."

"Perhaps," Jarls said, as he sat down. His large frame and weight made the chair creak. "What is it that you want? It's nearing time for us to discuss if you want to hire my fleet for the additional ninety days."

"I have more than that to discuss," Creed replied. "Because of the recklessness of one of your clan, I lost a valuable battlecruiser."

"Ah, yes," Jarls said with a slight nod. "I also lost a battleship. The *Rellal* was quite a valuable possession. I expect to be compensated for it. Battleships are not cheap."

"Compensated for it!" sputtered Creed, his eyes growing wide in anger. "I should be compensated."

"The ships were destroyed by the humans," Jarls pointed out. "Humans who should have never been in the Gothan Empire, let alone Kubitz. One of your own Profiteers led them there."

Creed was silent for a moment. "The First Profiteers of my two escort ships report that the humans on Kubitz have set up a diplomatic mission of a sort. It's also rumored that they used a large quantity of gold, which they changed into credits, to buy possible weapons systems."

Jarls's eyes narrowed. "What type?"

"Hypermissiles for one," Creed answered. He wondered if he would have been better off not mentioning this. Jarls could demand an increase in his compensation for protecting the Profiteer fleet and keeping Earth under control.

"Hypermissiles are of no concern to me," Jarls responded. "My ships' energy shields can handle them."

Creed studied the facial expression on the Dacroni mercenary. Jarls was a hard one to read. "I want to attack the human colony on Newton."

Jarls looked long and hard at Creed. "Why?"

"Gold and other valuables," Creed responded. "I have reason to believe that a large amount was removed from Earth and transferred to their colony world. Their trip to Kubitz seems to confirm that."

"Their remaining fleet is at Newton," Jarls pointed out. "It's likely they will not flee if we attack the colony, as it's their only other world besides Earth. They'll fight to the last ship. Their particle beam weapons will be a problem. To attack Newton will cost me some of my battleships."

"You will be compensated," promised Creed. He could see the look in Jarls's eyes as he thought over how much he would require. "I'll give you 20 percent of any gold or other valuables we find on the colony world."

"Fifty percent," Jarls countered with a crafty look in his eyes. "Fifty percent and you pay to replace ships I lose."

"Thirty-five percent and you pay for your ship loses." Creed held his breath, waiting to see if Jarls would accept his offer.

"Forty percent and I'll cover my own losses," Jarls responded. "That's my final offer."

Creed hesitated. It was a steep offer, but he wasn't sure he could take the colony world without Jarls's battleships. "Agreed."

"How soon before we move on Newton?"

"A few weeks," Creed answered. "I need to summon more of my ships and make some preparations. I don't believe, between the two of us, we'll have much trouble with the human fleet. All they have is the one battlecruiser, and, once it's been eliminated, the rest won't matter."

"Let's hope you're right," Jarls said with a slight frown. "Remember, this human battlecruiser and the ships with it just destroyed one of my battleships and one of your battlecruisers. This might not be as easy as you believe."

Creed wasn't too concerned. He knew, with the forces at his command, he could easily overwhelm the remaining human ships. What interested him the most was how much gold had been taken to the human colony. He strongly suspected this was why they weren't finding as much as they had the first time on Earth. Well, that was about to change. He would go to Newton and get his gold. It was his right as a Profiteer!

Chapter Fifteen

Kurt was at his sister's home, enjoying some time playing with his nephew and telling Denise and Alex about their experiences on Kubitz.

"It sounds like a crazy mixed-up world," commented Alex, shaking his head. "I just don't see how a system like theirs can work. It seems as if it would fall into anarchy, and then there would be chaos."

"It's the Controllers," Kurt answered. Bryan had gone to his room to draw a picture of a spaceship. "They keep everything in check through the system of contracts they have set up. They also control all the credits."

"So these credit things are what they use for money?" asked Denise, coming to sit down on the sofa next to her brother.

"Yes, and their entire system is backed by gold and other precious metals, which the Controllers also have control of. Their credits are worth much more than the North American Union currency we're used to. On Kubitz everything is for sale, but there's a stiff penalty for failing to honor a contract."

Denise was silent for a moment and then looked at Kurt with a mischievous smile. "Let's hear more about this woman doctor you met. She's actually human?"

Kurt shifted uncomfortably on the sofa. He never should have mentioned Keera to Denise. "Yes, she's human. A lot of the different civilized races in the galaxy are."

"So after this attack where they kidnapped Private Dulcet, she was the first person you saw?"

"Yes," Kurt answered. "We had all been gassed, and she seemed to know what to do. I invited her to come to the diplomatic compound for a meal to show my appreciation for what she did."

"You don't normally invite women out to eat," Denise said, cocking her eyebrow. "The last one I remember was Carolyn Donner back in high school."

"Did you ever find out what happened to Private Dulcet?" asked Alex.

"No," Kurt answered with a deep and frustrated sigh. "Avery Dolman is making some inquiries, but he didn't sound very hopeful. Grantz is also searching for her."

"You said they have actual brothels on Kubitz?" asked Denise.

"Yes," Kurt answered. "Brothels and pleasure houses."

"Aren't they the same?" asked Alex, looking confused.

"They're similar," Kurt said. "According to Grantz, the brothels are full of women from various worlds who have been bought by the companies. The pleasure houses have women and various pleasure-stimulating drugs and specialized entertainment. As I said before, nearly everything imaginable can be bought on Kubitz for the right price."

"I don't think I even want to know what some of those things are," said Denise, her face flushing slightly.

"Did any of your crew go to these brothels or pleasure houses?" asked Alex.

"No," replied Kurt, shaking his head. "The only person I know who did was Grantz, and, from what I understand, he's a regular customer."

"I still can't believe you hired that Profiteer to work for you," Denise said unhappily. "How can you trust him?"

"I don't," answered Kurt. "However, I trust the contract he signed."

"Uncle Kurt, I have the spaceship!" Bryan yelled, as he ran from his room into the living area, holding a piece of colored paper. "I drew the *Star Cross*, because it's the most powerful ship there is."

"Come show me," Kurt said, grinning. He really enjoyed spending time with his nephew, and, as long as Bryan was around, Denise wouldn't ask any more questions about Keera.

The next day Kurt sat in Governor Spalding's office, per the governor's request to brief him on the mission to Kubitz and what Kurt's next plans were.

"We've gotten all the refugees pretty well situated," Spalding began, as he shuffled several papers on his desk. "We're building additional housing and increasing our infrastructure to ensure they're able to live normal lives here on Newton. The people you rescued from Kubitz have been taken to our hospitals for evaluation. From what I heard, a number of them went through some very trying experiences."

"They survived," answered Kurt, thinking about Captain Randson's wife and daughter.

"There'll be more," Spalding said sadly. "I suspect every passenger liner we send to Kubitz will return with people kidnapped from Earth."

"What about Marlen Stroud?" asked Kurt, making sure the former head of the department of labor wasn't becoming a bigger threat. Stroud made Kurt feel uneasy, as the man was only interested in power and not the well-being of the people.

Spalding let out a deep sigh. "When we finally checked into all who had come from Earth on the passenger and cargo ships, we were surprised to find seventy-eight people came to Newton illegally. Most of them have few or no talents we can use."

"What did you do with them?"

Governor Spalding grinned. "We have a small fishing village on the other side of the planet. We sent all of them there, including Stroud. They're being taught how to fish."

"I bet that went over well," Kurt said. He couldn't imagine Stroud willingly getting his hands dirty.

"We gave them a choice," Spalding answered simply. "We'll provide them basic housing and living supplies. If they want something more, they have to work for it. Most of them are doing some fishing, though I understand Stroud is still claiming to be the legitimate head of the government and is threatening to have me hung someday."

"I'd keep a close watch on him," warned Kurt. "Stroud is not one to be taken lightly."

"I have some security people in place, keeping an eye on things," Spalding assured Kurt. "I receive regular reports about what's going on at the village. Now what I really wanted to talk to you about is, what are your next plans?"

Kurt nodded. "As you know, we managed to secure a very powerful defense grid for Newton. Once it's in place, I don't think we'll need to be overly concerned about an attack. We should have delivery in two to three months."

"That will be a huge relief for everyone on Newton," Spalding said. "I understand some of the hypermissiles you purchased were destroyed. I'm sorry about the *Lansing*."

"It was unfortunate," Kurt admitted, still angry about the loss. "Captain Blair was a brave man, as was his crew."

"I never got to meet the captain," Spalding said with sadness in his eyes. "I wonder how many more good people we'll lose before this is over?"

"There will be others," Kurt admitted somberly. "We also made arrangements to purchase additional warships."

"Warships!" exclaimed Governor Spalding, his eyes widening in disbelief.

"Yes, ten battlecruisers and four battleships," Kurt answered with a satisfied smile. "Once they're delivered, we'll have a fleet fully capable of resisting any possible invasion force."

"When are you sending more ships back to Kubitz? Is there anything else there we might be interested in?"

"Everything you can imagine is for sale on Kubitz for the right price. Another cargo ship along with the light cruiser *Sydney* is going there immediately. I want those hypermissiles, as they're so much better than the missiles we use. I'm also sending more of the First Contact teams, additional Marines, and a few specialists to delve more into technology we might be interested in."

Spalding steepled his fingers with a thoughtful look in his eyes. "I have a few recommendations for people to help round out Lieutenant Tenner's staff. I know some well-qualified people who can make this embassy run smoother."

"That would be helpful," Kurt replied. The governor would know more about the people needed to run a compound like the embassy on Kubitz.

Spalding's eyes narrowed. "Where will you get the crews for these new ships? Doesn't it take several years to train fleet personnel?"

"We have a few available in the people we brought from Earth," Kurt replied. "Plus a few extra on the shipyard. We should also see if we can recruit anyone here on Newton, but the ones I really need are still on Earth."

"What are you proposing?" asked Spalding, looking inquisitively at Kurt.

"I currently have two long-range shuttles in the shipyard with a special composite hull overlay. We'll do everything we can to make the shuttles undetectable to the Profiteers and the Dacroni mercenaries. I intend to land those shuttles on Earth, make contact with either President Mayfield or Fleet Admiral Tomalson, and arrange to get the people we need off the planet."

"To the best of my knowledge shuttles are too small for a hyperdrive system," commented Spalding, a frown in place.

"They are," admitted Kurt. "I'll send the light carrier *Vindication* to the inner edges of the Kuiper Belt. From there the shuttles can use their sublight drives to reach Earth."

"I assume the *Vindication* will have other escorts?"

"Two destroyers," Kurt answered. "I don't want to take too many ships from Newton, until the defense grid is in place."

"Do you think they'll attack us before the grid gets here?"

"I think so," Kurt answered. This was something he had given great thought to. "Once High Profiteer Creed finds out we've been to Kubitz and used gold to exchange for credits, he'll surmise a lot of gold must have been removed from Earth. As greedy as these Profiteers are, he'll come here looking for it."

"What will we do?" asked Governor Spalding, his worry evident in his voice. "We can't lose Newton."

"We won't," Kurt promised with a wolfish smile. "I'll have a few surprises waiting for the High Profiteer. We're not like Earth. They weren't expecting an attack. We are, and that will make the difference."

"I hope you're right," Spalding said uneasily. "You're the fleet admiral, and the safety of the planet is in your hands. Let me know if you need anything. Make sure you keep General Mclusky informed. You may also want to discuss with him what weapons can be purchased on Kubitz that would help with his ground defense forces."

"I'll do that," Kurt answered. "I have a meeting scheduled with the general for later this afternoon."

For the next hour, Kurt described to the governor their experiences on Kubitz and what his future plans were. Spalding asked a lot of questions, and, in the end, they both felt they had a very productive meeting.

Newton Station had gone through a lot of changes since Kurt had left for Kubitz. Captain Simms and Colonel Hayworth had been working their crews like mad to update the station and prepare it for a possible Profiteer attack.

Kurt stood in the large construction bay, brought from Earth, gazing at the exploration ship *Trinity*. Four of the five large exploration ships had been out exploring, and all had been recalled. Each ship was the same size as the *Star Cross*. Unlike the *Star Cross*, they were only lightly armed. The ships had been designed for exploration and not for war. Work crews were crawling all over the hull of the *Trinity*, removing hull plates with cutting torches, while other dock workers installed additional equipment.

"How far along are we?" Kurt asked. The exploration cruisers were built to the same hull design as the *Star Cross*, with some interior changes to allow for research labs and other facilities needed for deep-space exploration.

"We've been working on the *Trinity* for four weeks," answered Captain Simms. "We had to gut some of the interior and reroute a lot of power systems."

"Two more weeks and she'll be done," added Colonel Hayworth, as he observed the work crews with a critical eye. "We have crews working around the clock. When we're done, she'll be as heavily armed as the *Star Cross* with a fully functional military-grade energy shield."

"Are you making the necessary changes to the *Trinity*'s missile tubes to accommodate the hypermissiles?" Kurt was keenly interested, as the hypermissiles would be a great asset to the fleet.

"Yes," Colonel Hayworth replied. "The hypermissiles are smaller than our missiles, and it's not that big of a modification to redesign the tubes for them."

Kurt nodded, as a number of workers maneuvered large crates through one of the ship's cargo hatches. Raw materials were brought up from Newton and then used in the manufacturing facility they had brought from Earth to produce the hull armor and other essential parts for the Trinity.

"Do we have everything we need to convert the exploration cruisers to warships?" Kurt asked. He knew they had brought a lot of weapons material from Earth and that some could be made in the shipyard construction facilities.

"We can convert three without a problem," replied Captain Simms. His face took on a frown, and then he continued. "However, the last two will take longer, as we'll need to build some of the more intricate parts for their larger particle beam cannons. We can do one cruiser every six or seven weeks, depending on any bottlenecks we might encounter."

"We had to spend a full day just removing a quarantine containment facility from the *Trinity*," Hayworth said, shaking his head in exasperation. "Why they thought they might need something with two-foot titanium walls is beyond me. Just what were they planning on putting in there?"

"They're scientists and explorers," commented Simms. "Maybe they thought they could bring back a dinosaur."

"I understand the problems," Kurt responded. He was surprised they could convert three of them so quickly. Three more battlecruisers, all armed with particle beam cannons, would greatly enhance his fleet.

"What about the crews?" asked Colonel Hayworth. "The personnel on the exploration ships are good, but they're not trained for combat. Captain Anniston mentioned that to me the other day. We have a few on the station who were on leave from some of the ships destroyed in Earth orbit, though most were down on Earth with their families,"

"A few more came with the refugees," added Captain Simms.

"I think I can find the necessary crew personnel we'll need," Kurt answered. He knew Captain Cheryl Anniston, and she was a strong-minded captain. He was fully confident she could command the *Trinity*, if he could find a few key people to assist her in combat operations.

"The two shuttles are nearly complete," Captain Simms added, as he led Kurt toward the station's large repair bay.

"We've done everything we can to make them undetectable to Profiteer or Dacroni scans," Colonel Hayworth commented. "If they can make it to Earth, they should be able to land safely."

"How many passengers can each accommodate?"

"Twenty," Hayworth answered. "That's in addition to the five-person crew, plus a six-person security team on each shuttle."

"I wish we could have used larger shuttles," Kurt said, as they entered the repair bay where the two shuttles were. They had been painted black, and all insignias removed. The shuttles vaguely resembled the old space shuttles but with cleaner lines and a slimmer look.

"We can have two more shuttles ready within the week," suggested Colonel Hayworth. "I spoke to Captain Watkins, and he says he can accommodate two more, if he crowds his flight bay."

"Henry would say that," replied Kurt. "I'll contact him and suggest he leave ten of his Lance fighters behind. "So far we've seen no indication the Profiteers or the Dacroni use any type of fighters or bombers, other than their ships' shuttles."

"That would make room for four shuttles," stated Hayworth, looking inquiringly at Kurt.

"Go ahead and do the other two shuttles," Kurt ordered after a moment of thought. "We need to bring back as many crewmembers and potential crewmembers as we can on this first trip, particularly since we're converting the exploration cruisers to warships."

"We'll get it done," promised Colonel Hayworth.

"How is the arming of the station going?" Kurt looked over at Captain Simms, waiting for his response.

"Slowly," confessed Simms dolefully. "We're working around the construction we're doing, including the new flight bay. So far we've installed two particle beam cannons and six laser turrets. We've also managed to put in place about 40 percent of the energy shield emitters."

Kurt turned toward the two commanding officers. "Don't bother with the missile tubes for now. Concentrate on the laser turrets and the particle beam cannons. We could be looking at a possible Profiteer attack in the next few weeks."

The two men's faces paled upon hearing that announcement.

"We'll do everything we can," promised Colonel Hayworth. "Give us two weeks, and I can have at least six more of the laser turrets done and another particle beam cannon."

"What about the energy shield?" Kurt knew the shield was essential for the survival of the station.

Hayworth let out a deep breath of resignation. "That'll be a problem. The energy shield is set to extend one hundred meters from the hull. At the moment, the new flight bay is in the way. Once we have the outer hull armor in place, we can install the emitters, but not before."

Kurt nodded, knowing they were talking about an engineering problem. "See what you can come up with. I would hate to see the Profiteers plant a hypermissile in the station."

The two men shared a worried look and nodded their understanding. "I'll convene a meeting of our station engineering staff and see if they can come up with a solution," Hayworth said.

"We have some very smart and resourceful engineers," added Simms. "They'll figure something out."

"Very well," Kurt answered. "The mission to Earth will be launched as soon as you have the next two shuttles finished."

"We'll have them ready as soon as possible, Admiral," promised Captain Simms.

-

Fleet Admiral Kurt Vickers stepped inside the Command Center of the *Star Cross*. Part of the crew was on leave, with Rear Admiral Wilson and the *Kepler* responsible for the fleet and the defense of Newton, until Kurt said otherwise. He had spent a busy couple days visiting with his sister, meeting with Governor Spalding, General Mclusky, Colonel Hayworth, and Captain Simms. Kurt was satisfied that everything possible was being done to get Newton ready for a potential attack.

"Status?" he asked, looking over at Lieutenant Evelyn Mays, who had been responsible for the ship while he and Captain Randson had been down on Newton. Andrew was busy looking for a place for his wife and daughter and hoped to find a home close to Kurt's sister.

"The destroyers *Starburst* and *Kline* are currently emplacing the hyperspace detection buoys," the tactical officer replied, as she stood up and vacated the command chair. "They should be finished sometime tomorrow with the first set."

Kurt nodded and sat down in the command chair. The two destroyers were placing eight of the expensive buoys in open space far outside the Newton System. Each buoy could detect a ship in hyperspace for a distance of five light-years. Even then that would only give them about a ten- to fifteen-minute warning before a ship could reach Newton. It would be just enough time to bring the fleet to Condition One and prepare for an attack.

Looking at the one of the main viewscreens, he could see the heavy battlecarrier *Kepler*. Even as he watched, four small Lance fighters launched from one of the ship's two flight bays and moved to take over the CSP for the four fighters inbound from their patrol.

"Everything's been quiet, sir," Lieutenant Mays reported. She then walked over to her tactical station and sat down.

"Sir, I have Captain Watkins on the comm," reported Ensign Pierce.

Kurt pressed the receive button on the comm station on his command console. "How are things, Henry?"

"About as expected," Captain Watkins replied. "I understand you had an interesting time on Kubitz. Sometime you'll have to tell me all about it. Sorry to hear about Private Dulcet and the *Lansing*."

"We haven't given up on Dulcet yet," replied Kurt. "We're still hoping we can work out something for her safe return." Kurt knew in his heart that wasn't likely. From what Grantz and Dolman had indicated, she was most likely dead. It greatly upset Kurt to know that she had probably been tortured. Grantz had indicated that was one of the methods the Dacroni used to extract information from captives.

"I was glad to hear that Captain Randson found his wife and daughter. I know it was a big relief to him. So, when do I set out for Earth?"

"Sometime in the next seven days," Kurt answered. "I'm having Colonel Hayworth convert two more shuttles to be used in ferrying passengers from Earth to the *Newton Princess*."

"That'll crowd my flight bay," said Henry, sounding concerned. "But I think we can manage."

"Leave a squadron of your Lance fighters at Newton Station," suggested Kurt. "I don't think you'll need them, and that will free up the necessary space in your flight bay."

Henry was silent for a long moment before replying. "I hate leaving the fighters behind, but it would solve the space problem. Who are you sending to contact President Mayfield?"

Kurt looked where Captain Randson normally sat. Kurt knew that Andrew was the only one he would trust with the job and who was familiar with what they had learned on Kubitz— information that might prove useful to President Mayfield and the North American Union.

"Captain Randson," Kurt answered. "On a light cruiser. Once he's contacted the president, he'll be returning immediately."

"We'll get it done," promised Henry in a solemn voice. "I know how important these trained crew personnel will be."

Kurt let out a deep breath. Shifting his gaze to the other viewscreens, he could see Newton, Newton Station, and the stars. One viewscreen had a faint yellow star in its center. He knew without asking Lieutenant Mays that this was Earth's sun. He wondered what was occurring on the home planet. No doubt that life under Profiteer rule would be harsh and uncompromising. Kurt was determined to remove that threat. And soon.

Chapter Sixteen

On Kubitz, Grantz walked down one of the busy streets under the central city dome, in one of the more profitable districts, lined with pleasure houses and brothels. His pockets were full of credits, and he had a big satisfied grin on his face. The deal he had worked out with the humans was highly profitable, and his quarters at the compound were more than satisfactory. He had just finished eating and had gorged himself on his favorite foods, foods he normally stayed away from, due to their extreme price.

Sliding his right hand into his pants pocket, he felt the large wad of credits tucked safely inside. The street he walked along was closed to vehicles and on both sides were tall brightly colored buildings with flashing lights and advertisements. Loud music could be heard coming from several establishments, and the aromas of tantalizing foods drifted in the air. Happy voices and laughter from partygoers was everywhere. The street was full of people, nearly all of them human or at least humanoid.

Tonight he was heading to the Brollen Pleasure House. One of Dolman's contacts had casually mentioned that a human woman from Earth was working there. She was rumored to be very beautiful and in high demand. In such high demand that it had been necessary to book his appointment through the pleasure house four days in advance. Normally one could just show up and take part in any type of pleasure one might want to indulge in, and Grantz had a good imagination.

Reaching the pleasure house, Grantz looked up at the multicolored building. It advertised human women from different worlds and even a few nonhuman. Almost every type of drug or physical pleasure could be purchased for the right price. Opulent foods, drinks, entertainment, and, of course, women were available upon request. A substantial cover fee was due at the entrance just to get inside. The Brollen Pleasure House was one of the classier ones in the district and only served the best of everything.

Grantz was in no hurry, it was still a good hour before his scheduled appointment. Strolling to the entrance, he handed over a one-hundred-credit note and was allowed admittance. Several heavily armed guards were at the doors and also attendants who collected the credits. He did have to leave his pistol at the entrance and would pick it up on his way out. No weapons of any type were permitted inside the pleasure houses or the brothels.

Stepping inside, he took a deep breath and grinned as he checked everything out. Scantily clad women walked around, visiting with different patrons. The lower section entailed four levels of the pleasure house, offering eating establishments and bars with every type of alcoholic or nonalcoholic drink one could ask for. Also several groups of musicians played, and some customers were even dancing. It wasn't unusual for a visitor to dance and talk to a number of the women before making his selection. Once made, the two would go to the upper floors to consummate their transaction.

"Ah, Grantz!" yelled a familiar voice from a nearby alcove.

Grantz turned and saw a fellow Profiteer from the planet Marsten, sitting at a private table. He motioned for Grantz to come over.

Walking to the table, Grantz took a seat and nodded at his fellow Profiteer. "Albetz, it's been a while."

"Nearly a year," replied Albetz, motioning for a server to bring over two drinks. As she turned to leave, Albetz reached out and slapped her on the rear, causing her to squeal. "I love this place!"

"I thought you were settling down on Marsten," Grantz said. At one time, Albetz had served a short stint with High Profiteer Creed.

Albetz frowned and then smiled. "I thought so too, but what can I say? I ran short of credits, and I went back to Profiteering."

Grantz took a deep drink and allowed himself to grin. His beverage was strong, and it burned going down. Albetz's story was quite common. It was easy to retire off a Profiteer's earnings. The only problem being how easily it was to spend the accumulated credits from Profiteering and then finding oneself broke again.

"I understand you're working with these Earth humans," Albetz said in a quieter voice. "Rumor has it that they have a lot of gold."

"It pays well," Grantz admitted casually. "As for gold, who knows? Rumors are just that, rumors."

"An Earth woman is supposedly working here at this pleasure house," Albetz added, his eyes narrowing slightly. "Is that why you're here tonight?"

Grantz became more cautious. "Who did you say you're working for?"

"I didn't," answered Albetz, taking a sip of his drink. "As one Profiteer to another, I would watch my back. I think they're observing this woman very closely." With that Albetz laid enough credits on the table to pay for the drinks and stood up. "I'll be on my way. Perhaps someday we can work together again." Albetz walked off and entered one of the noisier bars, where loud music played.

Leaning back, Grantz slowly sipped his drink, wondering just what he had gotten himself into. It bothered him to be sitting at a table unarmed, if trouble was brewing.

Finishing off his drink, Grantz stood up and spent the next half hour wandering around the lower levels. He was careful to mix in with large groups of people and kept a wary eye out to see if he was being followed. If this human was Private Dulcet, and if he could bring her back to the human compound, he could net himself a nice bonus. He hadn't mentioned to Lieutenant Tenner where he was going, as the lieutenant might have sent some of the compound's human Marines to attempt to rescue Private Dulcet. That would have been a disaster and would have brought the Enforcers down on the embassy compound. Grantz liked his job too much to risk that.

Nearly time for his appointment, he climbed the wide stairs to the fifth floor where several attendants waited. He presented his confirmation pass for his appointment and was allowed to proceed. He felt a cold chill run down his back, knowing just how defenseless he was. Even a knife in his possession now would feel comforting.

Grantz took a high-speed turbolift to one of the midrange floors and exited, walking down a short well-lit hallway, lined with different colored doors. Thick, soft carpet covered the floor, which absorbed the sound of his footsteps. After a moment he found himself standing before the door indicated on his confirmation card. Taking a deep breath, he knocked and then waited expectantly.

The door swung open, and a beautiful brunette stood there. She was dressed in a skimpy dark red outfit that accented her figure and left very little to the imagination.

"Hello," she said demurely. "You must be Profiteer Grantz."

"Yes," Grantz replied, as he stepped into the room.

The woman closed the door and then locked it securely.

He knew that was misleading, as her handlers would have code passes to the door and could have it open in an instant, if necessary. He also strongly suspected the room was under surveillance. Looking at the young woman, Grantz instantly recognized her. This was, indeed, Private Lucy Dulcet.

Lucy walked over to a table with several bottles of colored liquid in them and proceeded to pour two drinks. Grantz noticed that she poured his drink from one bottle and hers out of a different one. No doubt his drink would be a strong alcoholic beverage and hers nonalcoholic. This was a standard trick used to get the patrons to spend more credits.

Walking over to Grantz, she handed him a drink and then, stepping back, took a small sip of hers. She smiled and posed. "Do you like what you see?"

"Yes," Grantz admitted. "What's your name?" He strongly suspected from her actions that she had been mind-probed and a new personality implanted. The use of a mind probe was highly illegal on Kubitz. He had also played poker with her several times on the Star Cross, and her lack of recognition seemed to confirm the use of the probe.

Lucy seemed confused for a moment and then smiled. "That's not important." She took another sip of her drink and then set it down on the small table. Turning back to Grantz, she reached up behind her neck and unfastened her garment, which fell to the floor.

Grantz felt his heart pound, seeing the beautiful nude human woman before him. With a heavy sigh, he reached into his pocket and pressed a small device hidden inside the wad of credits. It instantly sent out a jamming signal, causing any nearby surveillance devices to malfunction. Reaching into his other pocket, he took out a small plastic tube and pointed it at Lucy, pressing the button on the end causing it to eject a clear, odorless gas. The human woman paused and look confused. The gas was a memory inhibitor and highly illegal. It also served to weaken a person's will, making them highly subjectable to suggestions or orders.

Taking one last long look at Lucy's nude body, Grantz instructed her to get dressed. It only took her only a few moments to follow his orders, and then she stood with an innocent and questioning look on her face.

"Take my arm and we'll leave this room and go to the bottom level. You're to laugh and act like we're having a great time."

"We are having a great time," Lucy responded, as the suggestion took hold. She smiled and took hold of Grantz's arm.

Going to the door, Grantz opened it, and the two of them were soon walking down the corridor toward the turbolift. He knew, at any moment, security people would respond to see why the surveillance system on this floor had suddenly quit working.

Reaching the door to the turbolift, he pressed the button and waited. It quickly arrived, and, as soon as the door slid open, he took the small jammer from his pocket, pressed a button on its side and dropped it into a large planter against the wall. He knew that, in thirty seconds, the jammer would disintegrate, giving off a horrendous volume of thick and heavy smoke, which should trigger the pleasure house's fire alarms.

Entering the turbolift with a smiling and laughing Lucy hanging on his arm, he pressed the button for the fifth floor. Now he just needed to get by the awaiting attendants.

They were nearly to the bottom when alarms sounded and a voice came over the speaker in the turbolift.

"Due to a safety issue we are asking all guests to go to the bottom four entertainment levels. There is no reason to be alarmed, and you are not in danger. This is a precautionary measure only. To show our gratitude for your patronage, all drinks will be free for the next hour."

Grantz allowed himself to grin. A huge stampede of patrons would be escaping the upper levels. With any luck he would make it safely past the attendants.

Exiting the turbolift, he saw his supposition was correct. Dozens of guests ran down the stairways and were hurriedly exited the other turbolifts. The attendants had a flustered look on their faces, as they were rapidly overwhelmed. Trying not to draw attention, Grantz led Lucy past the attendants and down the wide staircase to the already crowded bottom level. The loud music was overwhelmed by the aggravated and concerned voices of hundreds of patrons. Many made their way to the bars to take advantage of the free drink offer.

Grantz slowly maneuvered Lucy close to the main doors and waited. He didn't have long to wait as a loud explosion suddenly rang out in the street in front of the entrance. Instantly the guards and the attendants rushed forward to see what the commotion was. Using the distraction, Grantz hurriedly led Lucy out the doors and turned down the street, walking at a fast pace. They hadn't gone more than forty meters when a man walked up to Grantz and casually handed him a weapon to replace the one he had left at the pleasure house.

"A vehicle's waiting at the end of the street," the man said, as he turned and vanished into the crowd.

Grantz placed the weapon in the holster at his waist and continued on down the street.

"That's far enough," a familiar voice said.

Grantz froze and, turning around, saw Albetz standing there with a large-barreled pistol pointed in his direction. "I thought you wanted to work together someday."

"I tried to warn you," Albetz said, shaking his head sadly. "You should have listened. We would have made a great team."

A shot rang out, and Grantz stepped back in surprise, as Albetz's head exploded in a shower of blood. People screamed and ran from the sudden commotion. Looking where the shot had come from, Grantz saw Avery Dolman step from a nearby doorway, holstering his weapon.

"You were followed," Avery explained. "Now let's get to the vehicle and leave before the Enforcers arrive."

Grantz nodded, taking one last look at Albetz, face-down in the street. Unfortunately this type of death was quite common for a Profiteer.

Captain Randson breathed a sigh of relief as the light cruiser *Johnas* dropped from hyperspace at the inner edge of the Kuiper Belt. They were just outside the orbit of Pluto, where numerous comets and icy remnants from the birth of the Solar System orbited.

"I have the *Vindication* and the destroyers *Deimos* and *Sultan* on the short-range sensors," reported Ensign Greenfield. Then a moment later he added, "The *Newton Princess* has just arrived. The two destroyers are taking up defensive positions around the passenger liner."

Captain Owens nodded. The last time he had been in the Solar System was when the Profiteers had appeared and wiped out the orbiting fleets. It was a nightmare he would never forget.

His ship had been heavily damaged and nearly half of his crew killed. He had barely made it to Newton to warn Admiral Vickers about the invaders.

"How long before the long-range scans can detect the Profiteer and Dacroni ships?"

"Just a few more minutes," the sensor operator replied. "We're really way out on the edge of the Solar System."

"I don't think they'll detect us this far out," Captain Randson said, as his eyes shifted to the tactical screen. At the moment it only showed five green icons, which represented their small fleet.

"*Vindication* is launching their CSP," added the sensor operator.

On the tactical screen, four small green icons—Lance fighters—left the light carrier and began their patrol around the fleet one thousand kilometers out.

"Why don't you think so?" asked Captain Owens, looking over at Captain Randson. "As advanced as the Profiteers and the Dacroni are, surely they have sensors as good as what our ships do."

Randson shrugged his shoulders. "They're only interested in what's going on around Earth. I doubt if they're even looking for ships this far out."

Andrew's words were soon proven correct, and, an hour later, he transferred over to one of the waiting stealth shuttles on the *Vindication*. As he prepared to board the shuttle, Captain Henry Watkins put in an appearance.

The older man looked at Captain Randson and then spoke. "Andrew, be careful. We don't know what to expect on Earth. With the changes the shipyard people made to the shuttle, it should get you safely down to the surface."

"We'll be careful," Andrew promised. He had known Watkins for many years. "I'll only be on Earth for a few days. Kurt wants me to meet with the president and Fleet Admiral

Tomalson. Once I've made my request, we'll be on our way back."

"We'll be waiting," Watkins replied.

A few moments later the shuttle exited the flight bay and accelerated toward Earth. The flight would take nearly eighteen hours, and all they could do was hope the shuttle was, indeed, undetectable.

An ensign woke Andrew to let him know they were nearing the orbit of the Earth's moon. From the sound of the ship's sublight drive, he could tell they had slowed down considerably. Getting up, he made his way to the cockpit, where the crew was busily managing their approach to Earth.

"Captain Randson," acknowledged Lieutenant Macy Hiat, who was the shuttle's commander and chief pilot. "We're just passing the orbit of the Moon, and we have a lot of Profiteer and Dacroni ships on the sensors. Also a large number of shuttles traveling back and forth between them and Earth."

"Any sign they've detected us?"

"No," replied Lieutenant Hiat, shaking her head. "We'll drop in over northern Canada. Even so, we'll pass within a few hundred kilometers of several of the orbiting ships."

"Just take it slow and easy," suggested Randson as he looked at the shuttle's small sensor screen. It was full of red threat icons. "They won't be expecting us, so we should be able to slip in between them without a problem."

"I hope so," Hiat said, as she reached forward and adjusted several controls on the complicated panel before her. She looked at her copilot. "Let's do this."

Andrew sat down in a heavily padded chair behind Hiat. He looked out the viewports, seeing Earth rapidly growing larger. The large blue-white globe made him feel momentarily homesick. He had been raised in the Houston area and had even married Emily in one of the local churches. He wondered idly what had happened to their home in the quiet suburb they had once lived in.

"We'll have to slow down considerably to reduce the turbulence in the atmosphere," Hiat said, as she put her hands on the flight controls. "We don't want to look like a meteorite flashing through the sky when we enter Earth's atmosphere."

Andrew nodded. He knew they were approaching the critical moments of the flight. There was no way to know for certain if the protective covering on the shuttle would shield them from the sensors on the Profiteer and Dacroni ships.

A few moments later, they passed between two orbiting vessels. One was a Profiteer escort cruiser, and the other was a massive Dacroni battleship. Everyone in the cockpit held their breath, but there were no reactions from the two ships. Moments later the shuttle began to vibrate, as it hit the upper edges of the atmosphere.

"They didn't detect us," Andrew said with relief. Now would come the even more dangerous part of descending through the Earth's atmosphere.

"I'll do some gentle S curves to bleed off our acceleration to a more acceptable level," Hiat said, as she watched the speed indicator. "If we heat up the atmosphere too much with our passing, we'll be very easy to spot."

Andrew nodded and leaned back in his chair. He felt tense, knowing that, at any second, an energy beam could strike the shuttle, incinerating it. However, the minutes passed by, and nothing happened. The Earth's surface gradually neared. Andrew could hear the air buffeting the shuttle as Lieutenant Hiat steadily slowed the small vessel.

"I'm setting down in a forested area, where we can hide the shuttle. I assume you have a method to contact someone in the government?"

"Yes," Andrew replied. He had a small transmitter that Kurt had given him with Fleet Admiral Tomalson's emergency contact codes. They were about to see if they would work.

The next day in the underground bunker, President Mayfield was reading the latest intelligence reports. Since the fiasco in

South Africa, the Profiteers had made two other demands for increases in gold and other valuable metals. Both times the demands had been met under protest by the targeted countries.

"I don't like this," General Braid said with a scowl. "Not only are we giving them the monthly tribute we agreed upon, but now they're making additional demands."

"It gets worse," Raul Gutierrez said, pointing to a message he had just received. "They're demanding Australia turn over one thousand bars of gold in two days."

"One thousand!" blurted Mayfield, his eyes bulging. "I don't think they have one thousand, not after what we sent to Newton. They were one of the countries that contributed heavily."

"They may have it in reserve," suggested Raul. "After all, Australia is one of the main producers of the yellow metal. Surely they didn't send it all to Newton."

"This could be a problem," General Braid said.

Mayfield quieted for a moment and then shifted his eyes to the Secretary of Homeland Security. "Raul, see if we can find out if Australia can make the payment. If not, we may have to help them."

"Yes, Mr. President," Raul answered, as he made a quick note.

The door to Mayfield's office opened, and Fleet Admiral Tomalson stepped in. He had a huge grin on his face. "I have someone I want all of you to meet." Gesturing behind him, he led another man into the room.

Mayfield looked at the newcomer curiously. He looked to be in his early thirties with dark hair and a deep tan.

"This is Captain Andrew Randson, Fleet Admiral Vickers's executive officer on the *Star Cross*," Tomalson said.

Mayfield's eyes grew wider, as he stared at the captain. "How did you get to Earth? Did you bring a message from Fleet Admiral Vickers?"

"I came on a stealth shuttle," Captain Randson replied. "I have some information for you, as well as a request." He quickly outlined what Fleet Admiral Vickers needed and the reasons why.

"You have got to be kidding me," Mayfield said in disbelief, after Randson had explained about the purchase of the new warships. "Fleet Admiral Vickers has bought an entire warfleet?"

"It's how things are done in the Gothan Empire," Captain Randson answered. "Everything is for sale there." He then went on to describe in more detail what they had encountered on Kubitz and the brief space battle after they left the empire.

"Fleet Admiral Vickers needs spacehands," Fleet Admiral Tomalson said thoughtfully. "I know some went to Newton with the evacuees, but many elected to stay here with their families."

"How do we get them to Newton?" asked General Braid. "That fleet will be useless without qualified crews."

"We send them and their immediate families," replied Tomalson evenly. "We also have a number of people in the air force and navy who would be well qualified to serve on these new ships. It'll just take a while to round them up and get them to the waiting shuttles."

President Mayfield looked intently at Captain Randson. "When Fleet Admiral Vickers has the defense grid set up around Newton, and once the new ships arrive, will he be able to free Earth?" Everyone looked at Randson expectantly.

"That's the idea," Randson replied. "Once we have the defense grid in place, we'll order a second one for Earth. We'll begin picking off the Profiteer convoys and make their operation here unprofitable. That alone may force them to leave. If not, then we'll have no choice but to bring in our ships and attempt to drive them from Earth orbit."

"But you're expecting them to attack Newton before the defense grid arrives," pointed out General Braid. "Can Newton survive that attack?"

"We'll survive," Captain Randson replied with a nod. "If the Profiteers attack Newton, they'll regret it, as it will be very expensive for them. That's one thing we need to remember. We must not look at the Profiteers as conquerors but as modern-day pirates, looking to turn a profit. If we can reduce or take away that profit, they'll leave."

"I hope you're right," commented President Mayfield with a deep sigh. He then turned to General Braid and Fleet Admiral Tomalson. "Let's begin finding those spacehands for Fleet Admiral Vickers." For the first time in weeks President Mayfield felt maybe there was hope for Earth after all.

-

High Profiteer Creed looked down at the message he had just received from the Australian government. They had offered three hundred bars of gold as payment.

"How dare they!" roared Second Profiteer Lantz in anger. "They are one of this planet's leading gold producers. They have the gold. They're just refusing to turn it over! We should nuke several of their cities as an example."

Creed gazed at the ship's main viewscreen for a long moment. The southern landmass of Australia was surrounded by the deep blue waters of the surrounding ocean. This planet was becoming far more troublesome than he had believed possible. He may have made a mistake in agreeing to leave their major cities alone if they paid the monthly tribute.

"No, contact Clan Leader Jarls. I want to send teams down to find the gold. This time we'll search through their major cities. If they resist, we'll use our ion beams and energy projectors to destroy entire areas if need be. The gold is there. We just need to find it."

-

A few hours later seventy Profiteer and Dacroni shuttles descended on Australia. Their targets were Sydney, Melbourne, Brisbane, and Canberra.

Upon the ground, the Australian military saw the inbound shuttles and quickly triangulated the possible targets. When they realized the cities the shuttles were aiming for, the alert was sent out. From a number of air bases modern F-75 Eagles launched with full weapon loads. Ground-based interceptor missiles were activated and targeted the descending alien vessels. From the city of Canberra a frantic message was sent, offering five hundred gold bars if the Profiteers called off the attack. There was no response, and the enemy shuttles continued to descend.

-

The chief of the air force looked chagrined as he received his orders. "We're to engage the descending shuttles and attempt to keep them from the cities."

"But they have energy shields," protested his second in command. "We'll lose our fighters!"

"I know," the commanding officer said, resigned. "But we have our orders."

"What about the interceptor missiles?" Those were of North American Union design with a very powerful warhead.

"They'll be fired also."

-

In the sky above the Australian cities, eighty-five F-75 eagles climbed toward their descending targets.

"All squadrons, fire upon confirmed targeting lock," ordered Major Hanson. "Once your missiles have been fired, move in and use your cannons."

"That's suicide," protested one of the pilots over the comm channel. "They have energy shields. The South Africans didn't shoot down a single shuttle."

"We have our orders," the major responded. "We also have better fighters and more powerful missiles."

A warning alarm sounded in his cockpit, and, looking out, he saw the contrails of dozens of missiles arrowing up toward the enemy shuttles.

"Interceptor missile launch," he said over the squadron comm channel.

It took only a few seconds for the interceptors to reach their targets, and the sky was suddenly full of bright explosions.

"Did we get any of them?" yelled someone over the comm channel.

"I can't tell," several others responded.

"Look! To the northwest, a shuttle with smoke pouring out. It's going to crash!"

The major looked, and he saw the falling shuttle impact the ground, leaving a large smoking crater.

"Scratch one," someone called out in an excited voice.

Major Hanson said nothing. He knew the warheads in those missiles were much more powerful than the ones in the interceptor missiles the F-75s carried.

A target lock tone suddenly sounded on his console. "I have a target lock," he announced. "All Eagles, engage."

Moments later the sky was full of more contrails and jet fighters screaming through the air. Explosions lit up the sky, but now the shuttles were firing back. Energy beams flicked down, and, whenever they struck an aircraft, it exploded in a ball of fire.

"They got Jenson," called out a frightened pilot.

"Swenson and Gallagher are gone too," another pilot replied. "Our missiles are having no effect!"

Major Hanson breathed out a deep sigh. He knew their cannons would have no effect either.

-

On the ground, the chief of the air force watched as his planes were blasted from the sky. "Call them back," he ordered, as he studied the sensor screens. "We'll lose all of them if we don't, and I refuse to throw away their lives needlessly."

"Sending out the recall," the officer at the comm station replied.

The air force chief looked down at the polished floor, even as the comm channel lit up with a message from the government office in Canberra. "Don't answer," he instructed the comm officer. "I'll turn in my resignation tomorrow."

-

The Profiteer and Dacroni shuttles continued downward unmolested, as the remaining human fighters flew off to escape the fighting. From what the aliens had learned in the smaller cities, numerous small and large stores held huge amounts of gold plus valuable jewels. Those would be their first targets.

On the ground, the Australian army deployed moving tanks and armored vehicles into hastily evacuated city streets. They might not be able to destroy a shuttle, but a Profiteer not within the protection of his ship would be a different matter.

In Sydney nearly two thousand soldiers fanned out, blocking major intersections and setting up choke points. They knew the Profiteers would be looking for gold, jewels, and other valuables, possibly even art. Snipers were placed on the roofs of buildings, covering the entrances to the stores most likely to be hit. Reserves were called up, but it would be hours before they could assemble and be armed. Soldiers checked their assault rifles and crouched down out of sight. Everyone was now waiting to see what the Profiteers would do.

In Canberra, the government was in a near panic. The Profiteers hadn't responded to their latest offer. In desperation another offer was made. This time it included the last offer of five hundred gold bars plus ten thousand carats of other valuable gemstones. The government waited with bated breath, hoping for a response.

-

"Five hundred bars of gold and ten thousand carats of gemstones," gloated Second Profiteer Lantz with greed glinting in his eyes.

"A good offer," replied High Profiteer Creed with a satisfied smirk. "Contact the humans and tell them we accept. However, because of their failure to offer this to begin with, their city of Sydney will be stripped of all its wealth. After all, I promised Clan Leader Jarls he could have 40 percent of anything his mercenaries take from the cities. He'll have to be satisfied with the one. Call back our shuttles and inform Clan Leader Jarls that his own shuttles may strip the human city."

-

In the air above Sydney, a dozen profiteer shuttles suddenly stopped their downward descent and rose into the sky. On the ground, the troops cheered, as the enemy retreated. But then, in the distance, they saw other shuttles coming toward them.

-

Lieutenant Blake Everton stared as two large shuttles landed in a nearby park. A third circled overhead, and suddenly bright beams of light speared down, blowing apart two military tanks. Billowing smoke and flames erupted, blotting out the sunlight. From the two landed shuttles, dozens of aliens swarmed forth. They were of human height but with a bulkier form. They had very short necks, making it look like their heads sat on their torso. Each was covered in some type of dark gray battle armor.

"Let them get close, and then open fire," ordered Blake over his comm, as the aliens made their way cautiously down the empty street. The civilians had been ordered to stay in their homes and to not come out until the all clear was sounded.

"What weapons are they carrying?" asked Lance Corporal Phil Stewart.

"They supposedly have an energy rifle," Blake replied over his comm. "Don't fire until I give the order." Blake had forty soldiers under his command. Half were concealed on the nearby rooftops, and the rest had taken cover behind vehicles, doorways, and down several side streets.

With apprehension Blake watched the aliens come closer. Looking at them, he realized these must be the Dacroni mercenaries he had heard so much about. That greatly concerned him, as it implied they were trained how to fight.

-

The Dacroni worked their way down the street, heading toward the largest jewelry store in the city. Their heads moved from side to side, as they searched for any potential danger. Suddenly their leader motioned for them to stop, while he checked some device he carried. Looking around in what appeared to be anger, he called out some commands, and the Dacroni with him suddenly raised their rifles and began blasting away at the hidden soldiers.

-

"They spotted us!" yelled Lance Corporal Stewart.

"Open fire!" ordered Blake, as he raised his own assault rifle and took aim at the nearest Dacroni mercenary. Blake was inside the open door to a clothing boutique across from a jewelry store.

Weapons fire rang out, and, with satisfaction, Blake saw several of the Dacroni drop to the pavement, unmoving. Then the orbiting shuttle poured down a deadly fire of energy beams, blasting the tops of the surrounding buildings and hitting the vehicles in the street, hiding Blake's soldiers. Smoke filled the air, and it became difficult to see. Occasionally Blake could hear the piercing scream of one of his soldiers as he or she was hit.

Out of the smoke appeared two dark shapes. Blake targeted the first one, firing a short burst into the Dacroni's chest, seeing the alien drop his energy rifle and fall to the ground. The second Dacroni raised his rifle and fired at Blake, who felt a strange numbness and dropped his assault rifle. What happened? He thought. Looking down he saw a smoking hole in the center of his chest. Falling to his knees, he felt dizzy and faint.

"Foolish human," the Dacroni said, striding up to Blake. He raised his rifle and fired one more time.

-

Across Sydney the fighting was much the same. A few Dacroni mercenaries were taken out, but the orbiting shuttles made the military pay a dear price for each Dacroni they killed. In the end, the fighting died out, and the looting began.

The Australian army, realizing they could not stop the Dacroni, ordered its soldiers to stand down and withdraw from the areas the aliens were targeting. The loss of human life wasn't worth it, and the city was already heavily damaged from the fighting. Numerous buildings were on fire, and some of the streets were now impassable. Firefighters were told to wait until the aliens left in their shuttles, before responding to the destruction. Above Sydney a dark pall of smoke covered the sky. The fighting was over, and, once again, the aliens had proved they had control over the Earth.

-

President Mayfield paced in the situation room, while General Braid and Fleet Admiral Tomalson stood nearby. Raul sat at a table, alone.

"At least we know they can be killed, when they're out of their shuttles," commented General Braid, as he turned from a viewscreen, showing a satellite shot of Sydney.

"We already knew that from the incident in Youngstown," replied President Mayfield. "At least the Australians managed to hold the damage down to just one city."

"But who will be next?" asked Raul Gutierrez. "We see a pattern developing, where the aliens are increasing their demands. It seems our monthly tribute's no longer enough."

"It'll be up to Fleet Admiral Vickers to stop this," Fleet Admiral Tomalson answered. Captain Randson had left the previous evening. Already Tomalson was making arrangements to find and locate the necessary people Kurt needed to crew his new warships.

"If we can last that long," replied President Mayfield grimly. He knew it was only a matter of time before the same demands made of South Africa and now Australia were made on the North American Union.

Chapter Seventeen

Fleet Admiral Kurt Vickers watched with deep satisfaction as the battlecruiser *Trinity* exited the large construction bay of Newton Station. She moved out slowly, using her thrusters, while the outside lights around the bay flashed.

"I can't believe she's ready," Captain Randson said, as he stood next to Kurt, seeing the activity on the shipyard.

"I've already spoken to Rear Admiral Wilson about my plans for the *Trinity*," responded Kurt, as he turned toward Andrew. "I'm moving the *Kepler*, *Trinity*, and the *Dante* into a lower geostationary orbit on the other side of Newton. That will put the three ships between the sun and the planet."

Andrew nodded his understanding. "So, when the Profiteers and the Dacroni jump in, they won't detect the ships, which will be hidden by Newton."

"That's the idea," Kurt answered, folding his arms across his chest. "We're also emplacing the rest of the hyperspace detection buoys around the Solar System. If Captain Watkins detects the Profiteers jumping toward Newton, he's to leave the *Newton Princess* and his two destroyers and bring the *Vindication* here immediately."

"Do you think we can stop them?"

Kurt nodded. "From what we learned on Kubitz, their entire motive is profit. If we can destroy enough of their ships in the early part of the attack, I think they'll break off and return to Earth. Before they can call in reinforcements for a more powerful attack, we'll have the defense grid installed. Once that's done, they won't even consider attacking Newton again. It would be too costly."

Kurt looked back at the viewscreen and the *Trinity*. She was almost an exact duplicate of the *Star Cross*, and Captain Cheryl Anniston would be a good commander for the ship. She was strong willed, a good tactician, and extremely intelligent. They had also found enough qualified spacehands with fleet experience to fill the empty billets on the ship.

"Which exploration ship is next?" Randson asked Kurt.

It had been nearly two weeks since Andrew had returned from Earth, and they were hoping the *Newton Princess* would return shortly with its first load of potential crew personnel.

"The *Carlsbad* will be next," answered Kurt.

Kurt looked at another viewscreen, which showed the other four exploration ships in a slightly lower orbit beneath Newton Station. Even as he watched, one of them broke orbit and began moving toward the shipyard.

An alarm suddenly sounded drawing everyone's attention toward the sensor console. This new alarm was set to warn them of ships approaching in hyperspace.

"Admiral, the hyperspace buoys are detecting two inbound ships," reported Lieutenant Lena Brooks as she studied the data. "They're coming from the direction of the Gothan Empire."

"The *Dallas* and the first cargo ship we sent to get more hypermissiles," suggested Andrew, gazing intently at the tactical screen, now showing two red threat icons far outside the system.

They had sent another cargo ship and the light cruiser *Sydney* to Kubitz to get more hypermissiles to replace the ones lost on the *Lansing*.

"It's time for them to return," Kurt said, as he gazed at the screen. "Take the fleet to Condition Two as a precautionary measure."

Andrew passed on the order, and shortly alarms and klaxons sounded, calling the crew to their battlestations.

Kurt hoped it was their two ships and not two Profiteer or Dacroni vessels about to drop in and pay them an unscheduled visit.

Several minutes passed, and the two ships in question dropped out of hyperspace six million kilometers from Newton.

"It's the *Dallas* and *Plymouth*," confirmed Lieutenant Brooks, as her sensors quickly identified the two ships.

"I have Captain Marsh on the comm," reported Ensign Pierce. Her eyes suddenly took on a stunned look. "Captain Marsh reports they have Private Lucy Dulcet on board!"

"Lucy," said Andrew, taken aback "How?"

"I guess we'll find out shortly," Kurt said. "Have them dock at Newton Station, and I'll meet them there."

"Yes, sir," replied Ensign Pierce, as she relayed the admiral's orders.

-

Kurt took a small shuttle to the shipyard and was waiting anxiously at the docking port for the *Dallas*. He had been extremely relieved to hear that Private Dulcet was on board the light cruiser. It was one more loose end that had been tied up from their trip to Kubitz. He was curious to hear how she had been rescued or if the Dacroni had just released her.

Captain Simms came down from the Command Center to watch the docking and to speak with the admiral.

"The engineers have come up with a way to put a temporary energy shield around the station," Simms said, as they waited for the large hatch to open. Four Marines armed with assault rifles stood next to them with wary gazes on the hatch, on alert in case someone other than a human came through.

Kurt looked at them for a moment and then turned toward Captain Simms. "We really need to find a better weapon than assault rifles. Firing armor-piercing rounds on the station or even on one of our ships is just asking for trouble."

"Is there something on Kubitz that would work better?" asked Simms thoughtfully. "Perhaps they have some energy weapon or even a stun gun."

"We know the Profiteers use energy weapons," Kurt answered. "I'll have Lieutenant Tenner check into it. Now what did you come up with on the energy shield?" A noise at the hatch drew his attention, and he saw it open. The Marines tensed, holding their rifles at the ready.

"If we place one of the destroyers against the incomplete hull structure of the flight bay, the ship's emitters will allow us to activate the energy shield. We'll need to make some adjustments to the destroyer's emitters though."

"What if we used one of the exploration ships instead?" suggested Kurt, as the door swung completely open, and Captain Bridget Marsh stepped out. She instantly stopped, upon seeing Kurt, and quickly came to attention and saluted.

"Too big," Simms answered. "It'll work better with a destroyer."

"At ease, Captain," Kurt said, returning Marsh's salute. "I understand you have our lost Marine with you."

"Yes," replied Marsh with a somber look on her face. "However, there's a problem. A Dacroni mind probe was used on her, and she doesn't remember who she is. Grantz rescued her from one of the Kubitz pleasure houses, where she was working."

"A pleasure house," Kurt said, his blood boiling. "How did that happen?"

"They emplaced some false memories to make her think she belonged there. She'd been there for a number of days before Grantz rescued her."

Kurt had to focus to fight down his rising anger. "Where is she?"

"Dr. Jelk is with her, and they'll be out shortly."

"Dr. Jelk," stuttered Kurt, his eyes growing wide. "She's here?"

"Yes, she's been treating Private Dulcet and insisted on coming, since we didn't have anyone familiar with the effects of this mind probe device the Dacroni used. She was very insistent, and Lieutenant Tenner didn't think it would be a problem."

Kurt heard other voices coming toward the hatch, and soon Private Dulcet, dressed in civilian clothes, and Keera stepped through. Lucy looked at Kurt, and, from the look of confusion on her face, he knew she didn't recognize him. He swore silently to himself and vowed that he would make whoever did this pay.

"Hello, Admiral Vickers," Keera said with a pleasant smile. "Do you have a medical facility on this station where I can take Lucy?"

"Yes," Kurt answered. "Captain Simms, will you please escort Dr. Jelk and Private Dulcet to the station's medical center."

"Yes, sir," replied Simms. Motioning toward Dr. Jelk, he said, "If you will please follow me, I'll take you where you need to go."

"I'll talk to you later, Keera," Kurt said, his gaze meeting hers.

"I was counting on that," Keera said, as she turned to follow Captain Simms.

"Where are we?" asked Lucy with a frightened look on her face. "Why can't I go back to the pleasure house? I liked my work there."

"Everything will be fine," Keera said in a soft and reassuring voice. "Just trust me. The people here will help take care of you."

"Don't leave me!" pleaded Lucy. "I don't know anyone else."

"I'm not leaving you," Keera promised.

As the three walked down the corridor, Kurt turned toward Captain Marsh. "Do you have a full report of what happened?"

"Yes," Marsh replied. "Lieutenant Tenner sent a report and interviews with both Profiteer Grantz and Avery Dolman."

"Dolman was involved too?"

"Yes," Marsh answered. "From what I understand, one of Dolman's informants told him about Private Dulcet's location."

"Do we know who did this to her?"

"The Dacroni on the orbiting battleship," Marsh answered. "It left shortly after the *Star Cross* did."

Kurt nodded; his anger faded slightly. If that were true, then the Dacroni battleship that had died with the *Lansing* was the guilty party. Those involved had already met a swift and deadly justice for their crime.

"Did you bring the hypermissiles? We're expecting a Profiteer attack on Newton shortly."

"Yes," Marsh answered. "The *Plymouth* has its cargo holds full of the new missiles."

"Let's go to the Command Center. Get her docked and unloaded as quickly as possible, so those new missiles can be on board the *Star Cross* and *Trinity* today."

"The *Trinity*?" said Marsh with a look of surprise on her face. "Is she ready for combat?"

"Yes," Kurt answered. "You just missed her exiting the construction bay."

"How soon are you expecting the Dacroni to attack?"

"Anytime," Kurt replied. "We've put the hyperspace buoys in place around the system, and we should have a short warning before they arrive."

"The *Dallas* will be here for a month, before we're scheduled to relieve the *Sydney*," Marsh said thoughtfully.

"We can certainly use her," Kurt replied. "Give your crew forty-eight hours' leave and then have them report back to the ship. Requisition any supplies you might need to have your vessel ready for combat."

"We won't need much," Marsh said, pursing her lips, as she considered her ship's supply situation.

Reaching an open turbolift, the two entered and were soon on their way to the Command Center. Kurt wanted to meet briefly with Colonel Hayworth and see to it that the correct hypermissiles were delivered to both the *Star Cross* and the *Trinity*. Then he wanted to find Keera and have a long talk with her. With a deep sigh, he knew he would have to take her to Newton to meet his sister, or he would never hear the end of it.

Kurt and Captain Marsh walked into the Command Center of Newton Station and were quickly ushered by one of the Marines on duty to Colonel Hayworth, who was talking to several engineers.

"I don't care how complicated it is. I want that particle beam cannon operational by this time tomorrow. Put extra crews on it, if necessary."

"The targeting computer hasn't been programmed yet," protested one of the engineers, an older woman. "We need it to calibrate the entire system."

Hayworth frowned and then looked surprised when he saw Kurt and Captain Marsh walk up. "I'll make sure it's programmed by the end of the shift tonight. Will that work?"

"Yes," the other engineer replied. Seeing the fleet admiral, he turned a little pale and motioned for the other engineer to follow him. Moments later they had left the Command Center.

"Problems?" asked Kurt.

"Not really," replied Colonel Hayworth. "Engineers constantly complain. I think sometimes they spend more time complaining about a project than actually getting the job done."

"The *Plymouth* is here, and it has my hypermissiles on it," Kurt said. "I need them unloaded, and then the missile tubes on the *Star Cross* and the *Trinity* loaded with the fifty-kiloton ones."

"All twelve of the missile tubes on the *Trinity* have been converted to handle the new missiles," Hayworth answered. "But only six of the tubes on the *Star Cross* have been modified."

"I'm aware of that," Kurt answered. The large Command Center seemed to be unusually busy with people constantly coming and going. "Load the tubes that have been modified."

"We'll also have to change the missile control system so the missiles will respond to our commands," Hayworth added.

"How long?" Kurt was anxious to get the missiles on board the two battlecruisers.

"Probably only a few hours," Hayworth answered, "if I get the right people on it. And I know just who I need. I've got a young hotshot computer specialist who can work circles around the other programmers. I'll assign him to it."

"What about this destroyer idea Captain Simms was talking about, so we can activate the energy shield around the station?"

Hayworth looked surprised and then answered, "If we bring in one of the destroyers and replace some of its emitters with more powerful ones, and then shove the ship against the hull where we're building the flight bay, it should work. It'll take about six hours to change the emitters and then ground the destroyer to the metal frame of the bay."

Kurt thought about it for a moment. The shipyard needed that energy shield. One well-placed hypermissile and the entire structure would be toast. "Do it," he ordered. While he felt confident he could protect Newton Station, he didn't want to take the risk of losing everything due to a single missile slipping through their defenses.

"Does it matter which destroyer?" asked Colonel Hayworth.

"Use the *Callisto*," suggested Kurt, as he mentally went over the destroyers under his command. "She's one of the newer ones, and its emitters should be the easiest to modify."

Hayworth nodded and turned toward Lieutenant Vargas, who was the station's traffic controller. "Lieutenant, have the *Plymouth* brought into the repair bay and have the munitions specialists present unload and store its cargo. Then contact Captain Deming on the *Callisto*. I want that destroyer in the repair bay as soon as the *Plymouth* exits."

"Yes, sir," replied Lieutenant Vargas, as he contacted the captain of the cargo ship.

"Colonel, the *Carlsbad* has entered the construction bay," reported Lieutenant Jeannine Haley from her sensor station.

Hayworth nodded. "I'll have a shuttle take the necessary missiles from the *Plymouth* to the two battlecruisers, along with a work crew to get the systems working correctly."

"We'll leave you to your work," Kurt said satisfied with the progress Colonel Hayworth was making. "Let me know if there are any problems with the missiles or the *Callisto*. I'm also giving Captain Marsh's crew a forty-eight-hour leave. Can you make the necessary arrangements to transport them to Newton?"

"There won't be any problems, and I'll make the transportation arrangements immediately," promised Hayworth as he saw another engineer with a confused look enter the Command Center.

Kurt made his way to the medical center to find Keera explaining to several doctors what had happened to Private Dulcet.

"What did this mind probe do to her?" Kurt asked, after listening for a few moments.

"If used too long, it can scramble the pathways in the brain used to recall memories. The best way to explain it is to say, everything is just jumbled up. For instance, if she were to smell a flower, she might instead think about the color blue."

"If her memories are that bad, how did she manage to function in the pleasure house where Grantz found her?" Kurt still found it disgusting what Private Dulcet had been forced to endure. This was bound to have a profound effect on the rest of her life.

"The Dacroni used another illegal device, which implants a new personality in her short-term memory."

"Is there any way to bring back her old memories?"

"Yes." Keera sighed. "It's complicated. She will need to be exposed to familiar stimuli, and, over time, her old memories should gradually reestablish their normal neural pathways. She needs to have visits from family or people who know her well. If they just sit and talk to her and describe some of the things they've done together, it will help."

It sounded to Kurt as if Private Dulcet had a long road ahead of her. At least she was back home and safe. "Can you come with me to the surface of Newton?" Kurt asked. "I promise to have you back here within twenty-four hours."

"That won't be necessary, Admiral," one of the doctors said. "We're transferring Private Dulcet to Newton to one of the better medical centers. They can give her the type of personalized treatment and care she needs. I'm afraid that, as her old memories return and she realizes what went on at the pleasure house, she may have some other mental issues."

"I'll help get her situated," Keera said. "Then, once I'm sure she's safe, we can talk."

Kurt nodded. Even though he wanted to talk to Keera, she was correct in making sure that Private Dulcet was taken care of first. The young Marine private was much more important business to deal with.

On his way to his shuttle, Kurt stopped by the construction bay, where the *Carlsbad* was fastened to the metal deck as a safety precaution. Large magnetic grapples were attached to the bottom side of the large eight-hundred-meter-long exploration ship. In hindsight, the North American Union had probably made a mistake in not arming the exploration ships more heavily.

The construction bay was full of dockworkers. Many were moving equipment to the ship, and some were already busy installing scaffolding. It was sad to know that all five exploration ships were now being converted for war. Even when this was all over, if it ever was, the people of Earth and Newton would never look at the galaxy the same again. If they did explore in the future, it would be with heavily armed ships and probably as part of a small fleet formation.

With a deep sigh, Kurt turned to go to his shuttle. He had a few more things to take care of, and then he would head to Newton. It was time to introduce Keera to Denise. He also needed to meet with Governor Spalding and General Mclusky one more time. There was no doubt in Kurt's mind that it might be a while before he could afford personal time on the planet again. He had a prickly feeling on the back of his neck that the Profiteer attack would happen sooner rather than later.

Late that afternoon Kurt walked to the door of his sister's house with Keera following nervously behind.

"Your world is so strange," the young woman said, as she looked curiously around her. "You have no Controllers. Most of your people are unarmed, and there's no pollution. I can't believe how clear the air is. It's actually safe to breathe!"

Kurt allowed himself to laugh. He had picked up Keera at the medical center and then taken her on a quick tour of the capital, finally ending up at his sister's house. "I'm glad you came to Newton."

"Really?" asked Keera, her gaze shifting to Kurt. "I wasn't sure if you would want to see me again. After all we only had that one evening together."

"I definitely wanted to see you again," Kurt assured her. "I planned on seeing you again when I returned to Kubitz."

The door to the house opened, and Denise stood there with a big smile on her face. "Hello," she said. "I'm Denise, Kurt's younger sister. You must be Keera."

Keera looked slightly embarrassed and nodded her head. "I hope I'm not intruding."

"No way," Denise said, indicating for them to come inside. "I'm fixing one of Kurt's favorite meals."

Kurt led Keera into the living room, where a wide-eyed Bryan waited in ambush.

"Are you an alien?" he asked excitedly, walking up to Keera and examining her from head to toe.

Keera laughed and slowly shook her head. "No, I'm just as human as you are."

Bryan nodded with a disappointed look on his face. "I was hoping you had a tail or extra arms."

Sitting down on the sofa next to Kurt, Keera looked at Bryan. "There are actually aliens who have tails and two sets of arms."

"Really?" said Bryan, his eyes shining with excitement. "Can you tell me about them?"

"We can talk about aliens later," Denise said, as she sat down across from Kurt and Keera. "Bryan, why don't you go outside and wait for your dad? He should be home shortly."

Bryan ran outside and took a watchful lookout on the front porch.

"You have a good-looking son," commented Keera, shifting her focus back to Denise. "On Kubitz the children stay indoors most of the time."

"Thank you," Denise replied. "Kurt says you're a medical doctor?"

"Yes, I attended the medical training center on Karash, which is one of the more enlightened worlds and a considerable distance from the Gothan Empire."

"Why did you go to Kubitz? I understand that world is very dangerous."

"I wanted to treat different humanoid species, and there are more on Kubitz than anywhere else in the galaxy. I went there with my brother, and we ended up staying."

"Where's your brother now?" asked Kurt. He had forgotten that Keera had an older brother.

Keera sighed and looked disappointed. "He works for one of the larger Profiteer groups, helping to sell the items they bring to Kubitz."

"The Profiteers," said Denise, as she looked sharply at her brother.

"A different group than took over Earth," Kurt quickly said. He realized he really wanted Denise to like Keera.

Denise nodded. "What was it like to live on Kubitz?"

Keera explained what her life had been like as a medical doctor on the diverse planet, while Kurt listened. He found her revelations highly interesting. He was pleased that Denise seemed to be going out of her way to be friendly to Keera. For tonight, he would just enjoy being with Keera and his sister's family. Once he returned to orbit, he might not have another opportunity for quite some time.

Chapter Eighteen

High Profiteer Creed sat in his command chair and glared at the *Ascendant Destruction*'s main viewscreen, which showed the blue-white world it was orbiting. The latest news from the last convoy he had sent to Kubitz fueled his anger. It seemed the humans were buying every captive he sent to sell on the planet.

"Twenty million credits this time!" he swore in a loud voice, glaring at Second Profiteer Lantz. "Added to the forty million for the first two groups."

Lantz took a step back and then responded. "They paid it to our representatives on Kubitz." His large eyes waited for Creed's response. "We still made credits off the deal."

"With gold that should have been ours, not exchanging it for the slaves," rumbled Creed, standing and striding to the front of the Command Center to stare at the viewscreen. "All over this planet, they've either hidden their gold reserves or sent it to their colony world, and who knows how much they've deposited with the Controllers in our own empire."

"They pay up when we threaten them," Lantz pointed out. "Only last week the leaders of Japan turned over two hundred bars of gold and ten thousand carats in gems."

High Profiteer Creed turned toward Lantz, his light-blue-colored skin turning darker. "I believe most of the gold on this planet has been sent to their colony world."

"Then let's go take it," suggested Second Profiteer Lantz. His eyes glowing with greed.

"We shall," Creed replied. He would need the Dacroni clan leader's battleships if he wanted to take the colony. "I'll contact Jarls and tell him it's time to move on the colony world. He has agreed to 40 percent of the gold we find. That will give him the necessary encouragement and incentive to risk his battleships in the attack."

"Forty percent is a lot," Lantz pointed out discontentedly. "He might do it for less."

"No, Jarls won't settle for less," Creed responded. "We need to plan an attack to hold our losses to a minimum."

"The humans can't have much of a fleet," Lantz said, his large eyes narrowing. "We know they have the one battlecruiser and six or eight escorts. I say we just jump in with some of our ships and half the Dacroni battleships, wipe them out, and then take over the colony. If the gold is on the human colony world, it shouldn't be too hard to find."

"What about that truly large ship that was in their shipyard?" Creed responded, not fully confident Lantz's plan was practical or economical. He looked at another screen, which showed the partially disassembled human station. He had wanted to finish that ship, and sell it and its technology to the arms dealers on Kubitz. "What if they've managed to complete it?"

"The Dacroni will destroy it," Lantz said confidently. "Remember how the humans fled when we returned with the Dacroni battleships? They may even flee from their colony world, once they see we've brought the battleships with us. As for that large ship, I doubt that the colony world has the resources to commit to finishing its construction, considering the costs of buying back their people."

"I wouldn't be so sure," replied Creed, letting out a deep and frustrated breath. Creed pointed to the viewscreen, which still showed the blue-white globe of Earth. "We're meeting constant resistance to our every demand. These humans aren't like other races we've subdued in the past."

"We could make examples of some of their cities," suggested Lantz. "A few well-placed nukes would be the proper encouragement."

High Profiteer Creed was silent for a long moment. He had renewed Clan Leader Jarls's contract for a second ninety-day period, and it already looked as if it would be necessary to renew it for a third time. Each time he did so, it was more costly. It was essential he get the gold from the colony world.

"Contact Clan Leader Jarls and tell him that I want to meet. It's time we paid this colony world a visit."

President Mayfield was once more in the situation room with Fleet Admiral Tomalson and General Braid.

"What's going on now?" asked Mayfield in a tired voice. He had a pounding headache from all the stress he had been under. It was all they could do to keep the civilian population from revolting against the Profiteers. Already a few isolated incidents had occurred with well-armed civilians ambushing the aliens and even killing a few of them.

Over the last few weeks, the tension across the planet had mounted. After the attacks in South Africa and Australia, the entire planet was on edge. Mayfield feared, if there was one more major incident, the lid could blow off everything. He and his Cabinet had even talked about evacuating the major cities, but the sheer magnitude of such an operation was too daunting. If word were sent to evacuate, the civilian population would panic. More people would die leaving the cities than if a Profiteer nuclear missile struck.

"Some of the Profiteer ships and Dacroni battleships are moving from Earth orbit," reported defensive coordinator Colonel Stidham, gesturing toward a sensor screen with numerous red threat icons encircling Earth.

They all watched as a large group of ships assembled and accelerated away from the planet.

"Are they leaving?" asked Mayfield, his eyes lighting up with hope. Perhaps the Profiteers had given up on collecting the remaining gold and other valuables still on Earth, grown tired of the people's resistance and disappointed in not finding as much gold as the aliens had hoped.

Fleet Admiral Tomalson shook his head. "I think they're preparing to attack Newton. It looks as if two Profiteer battlecruisers, six of their escort ships, and ten Dacroni battleships are forming an attack fleet."

"Can we get word to the *Vindication*?" asked Mayfield, looking at the fleet admiral. He knew the light carrier was hiding out in the Kuiper Belt.

"I'm sure Captain Watkins has already detected the ship movements. He'll recognize it for what it is and will jump into hyperspace, so he can warn Fleet Admiral Vickers."

"How many fleet personnel have we sent to the *Newton Princess* so far?" asked Mayfield. Over the last few weeks the military—still under their control—had fanned out across the North American Union, seeking the individuals who Fleet Admiral Vickers needed.

Fleet Admiral Tomalson looked at the president. "Nearly 1,400."

"All fleet personnel?" asked Mayfield. He knew that most of them had families on Earth. That's why they had stayed originally and not gone to Newton during the evacuation.

"Fleet or at least military," replied the admiral. "We promised most of them that we would get their families off Earth shortly, plus look to their well-being until we could do so."

"They're preparing to jump," Colonel Stidham said, as the enemy fleet accelerated rapidly away from Earth. Several alarms sounded, and then the red threat icons on the sensor screen blinked out one by one.

"They've jumped," Stidham said, shifting his gaze to the president.

President Mayfield looked at the remaining red threat icons on the sensor screen. "It's a shame we don't have some way to take out those ships while their fleet's reduced."

"We couldn't take out even one of their ships with our planet-based weapons, as long as their energy shield is up," General Braid said, folding his arms across his chest. "However, with that many ships no longer in orbit spying on us, now would be a good time to gather up more of the people needed by Fleet Admiral Vickers."

"If he can defeat the fleet that's headed his way," said Mayfield with a trace of concern in his voice.

"If I know Vickers, he has some tricks up his sleeve," said Tomalson. "The Profiteers and their Dacroni friends might very well be jumping into a trap."

"Let's hope so," Mayfield said, checking the sensor screen showing the remaining orbiting alien spacecraft. "If he loses this battle, then Earth has no hope. They'll strip us of everything, and leave us with a broken and desolate world."

-

A few minutes earlier Captain Watkins had been summoned to the Command Center of the light carrier *Vindication*.

"The Profiteers and the Dacroni are forming up into a possible attack fleet," reported Lieutenant Anthony Dries, the executive officer, as Captain Watkins stepped through the hatch.

"Bring in the CSP and inform the *Sultan* that we're leaving. Also let Captain Mertz on the *Newton Princess* know."

A few more moments passed as the CSP was recalled.

"The enemy fleet will be entering hyperspace shortly," Lieutenant Julie Jenkins reported from her sensor console.

"CSP is in," added Lieutenant Dries, as he received confirmation from the flight bay.

"Set course for Newton and take us into hyperspace," ordered Watkins. He knew that, at their best speed, they might only arrive a few minutes ahead of the enemy. However, in a battle of this type, even a few minutes of warning could be the difference between victory and defeat.

"Course set," Lieutenant Dries reported.

Watkins heard the telltale sound, as the powerful sublight engines of the light carrier accelerated the ship, and then he felt the gut-wrenching sensation as the *Vindication* jumped into hyperspace.

"We'll go to Condition One twenty minutes prior to emergence," he said to Dries. "Arm our bombers with Hydra ship killers, and have them ready to deploy." The Hydra missiles carried a ten-kiloton warhead, quite deadly to a ship that had lost its energy shield. He had ten Scorpion bombers on board along with ten Lance fighters. All would be deployed as soon as the *Vindication* emerged from hyperspace.

-

Fleet Admiral Kurt Vickers awoke instantly, as alarms sounded and red lights flashed in his quarters.

"Admiral Vickers, please report to the Command Center," Lieutenant Evelyn Mays said over the comm. "We have an inbound ship detected by the hyperspace buoys, tentatively identified as the *Vindication*."

Pressing the comm button, Kurt replied, "I'll be there shortly. Bring the fleet to Condition One and contact Governor Spalding. Tell him we expect a Profiteer attack shortly."

"Yes, sir," replied Mays.

Kurt hurriedly dressed, and it didn't take him long to reach the command deck. There was no doubt in his mind that, if Henry was returning with the *Vindication*, then the Profiteers wouldn't be far behind.

Striding into the Command Center, he saw that Captain Randson had already arrived and was in deep conversation with Lieutenant Lena Brooks.

"It's definitely the *Vindication*," Andrew said, turning toward Kurt. "She should be dropping from hyperspace in slightly over five minutes."

"All ships, except Rear Admiral Wilson's command, are to form up in attack formation Alpha," Kurt ordered, as he sat down in his command chair. "Send word to the *Dallas*, *Birmingham*, and *Johnas* to get underway and take point in the formation. Notify the rest of the fleet to stand by for combat operations."

After a few minutes Andrew notified Kurt that the messages had been sent and that the three light cruisers were moving into their assigned positions in the Alpha formation.

"*Vindication* has dropped from hyperspace," reported Lieutenant Brooks. "Distance is twenty thousand kilometers, and she is launching her fighters and bombers."

"Incoming message," added Ensign Pierce. "Captain Watkins is reporting that a combined Profiteer and Dacroni fleet will be dropping from hyperspace shortly."

"Order the *Vindication* to join our formation," Kurt ordered. "Put her off our starboard side. Move the destroyers *Starburst* and *Kline* to cover her."

"Message sent," replied Ensign Pierce after a moment.

An alarm sounded on the sensor console, indicating the hyperspace buoys had detected more ships.

"Inbound enemy fleet detected," Lieutenant Brooks reported. "Confirmed eighteen contacts."

"Governor Spalding wants confirmation this is an attack," said Ensign Pierce.

"Inform him we have eighteen inbounds," Kurt responded, as he gazed at the tactical screen, which now showed the red threat icons.

Alarms would sound shortly on Newton, and the population would go to their shelters. Around the larger cities, General Mclusky would activate his air defenses to take out any missile that might get through, though Kurt doubted they could do anything to stop a hypermissile.

"Captain Simms reports that the energy screen for Newton Station is operational and functioning as expected," Andrew said, as he listened to various reports from fleet captains plus the shipyard.

Kurt acknowledged the report, relieved that the temporary energy screen idea worked. They couldn't afford to lose Newton Station. Without it, he had no way to repair his ships or build new ones.

"All ships are in formation," reported Andrew, as he studied the tactical screen. It took but a few minutes for the fleet to form up.

"I have ships exiting hyperspace," stated Lieutenant Brooks, as more alarms sounded on her panel. She quickly reached forward and silenced them, looking questionably at the admiral.

"Give me numbers and types," Andrew ordered. He felt his heart hammering in his chest and knew they were about to enter combat.

"Two Profiteer battlecruisers, six escort cruisers, and ten Dacroni battleships. Current range is two hundred thousand kilometers."

Andrew studied the tactical screen and then turned toward Kurt. "From their position they won't detect Rear Admiral Wilson's ships."

"Good," replied Kurt with satisfaction in his voice. "Inform Captain Simms to prepare to launch his Scorpion bombers upon my command." Twenty of the small deadly crafts were in Newton Station's original landing bay. "Also tell him to launch the squadron of Lance fighters the *Vindication* left behind."

Andrew was in constant communication with all the fleet units and the shipyard, so he could pass on each of the admiral's orders.

"Profiteer fleet is moving toward us," reported Lieutenant Brooks.

Kurt nodded. The Command Center was alive with intense activity as the crew prepared for battle.

"Move us out at 10 percent sublight," Kurt ordered. "I want to meet them far enough away from Newton so they can't fire weapons on the planet."

"If they're coming for the gold they think we have, I doubt if they'll risk destroying it," pointed out Andrew.

"Let's hope so," Kurt answered. He was concerned about his family on Newton as was Andrew, as well as the millions of others on the planet.

Kurt could well imagine the fear running through his sister's family and everyone else on Newton when the planetwide alarms sounded. They were all familiar with what the Profiteers had done to Earth.

"Combat range in seven minutes," reported Lieutenant Brooks in a steady voice. She kept a close eye on her sensors and the eighteen approaching red threat icons.

"Instruct our fighters they're to intercept any enemy shuttles that might be launched," Kurt added, as he thought of the possible tactics the enemy might use.

"All weapons are powered up, and the new hypermissiles are on standby," reported Lieutenant Mays.

"I wish bigger warheads were on the hypermissiles," Kurt commented. "If they were of the ten- or twenty-megaton range, we might be able to knock down the enemy shields with the missiles alone." But he didn't have any of the more powerful antimatter warheads. Those had been lost on the *Lansing*, and Lomatz had balked at sending additional ones on the *Plymouth*. He had demanded more security to move the more deadly missiles. Lomatz had promised to send more, once the defense grid was delivered.

"We can speak to our R&D department on Newton Station," Andrew said, agreeing with the fleet admiral. "However, we might not have the technical expertise to construct such powerful warheads."

"We can get the know-how from the right people on Earth," Kurt answered, as he kept his eyes glued to the tactical screen. He didn't like being dependent on Kubitz and Lomatz for these.

"Engagement range in three minutes," reported Lieutenant Brooks.

"As soon as we engage, Rear Admiral Wilson is to commit his ships," ordered Kurt. "Have him here as quickly as possible."

"I'm relaying the message," Andrew replied and then a few moments later added, "He says he can be in combat range in four minutes, once he comes around the planet."

"Very well, order all ships to stand by for combat maneuvers."

High Profiteer Creed gazed intently at the tactical screen and the human ships about to enter combat range.

"Sensors show they have one battlecruiser, one of their carrier vessels, six light cruisers, and what appear to be nine of their small destroyers," Second Profiteer Lantz reported nervously.

"More ships than we thought," Creed said, as he quickly calculated how much this battle might cost him in credits.

If everything went according to plan, he shouldn't lose more than one of two of his lighter units, with minor damage spread across the fleet. If he could find the gold the humans had hidden on this colony world, the attack would be well worth the possible cost.

"Clan Leader Jarls has placed his battleships in a double line just above our ships," reported Third Profiteer Bixt from Sensors.

"Very well," Creed answered. "Put our ships into two lines of four directly beneath Jarls's ships with the *Ascendant Destruction* and the *Crimson Star* directly below Jarls's flagship." The *Crimson Star* was his other battlecruiser.

Creed leaned back in his command chair with a satisfied grin on his face. His large eyes gleamed, as he thought of the vast amount of gold that would soon be in his hands. True, he would have to turn over a large portion to Jarls; but, if his theories were correct, there would be plenty to go around.

"Combat range in one minute," reported Lieutenant Brooks.

"We're at the extreme range for our main KEW batteries," commented Andrew with a cunning look in his eyes, looking meaningfully at Kurt.

Kurt nodded. "Lieutenant Mays, one of those two Profiteer battlecruisers probably belongs to High Profiteer Creed. Hit both with two KEW rounds from our main batteries. I want them to know we're here."

"Yes, sir," Mays answered, as she passed on the orders to her tactical team. Moments later the *Star Cross* vibrated slightly as the large tungsten rounds were fired at 10 percent the speed of light at the two Profiteer ships. "Weapons fired," reported Mays with a satisfied grin.

On the main viewscreen, the energy screens of the two Profiteer ships suddenly lit up with explosions of released energy. When the screen cleared, the two ships were still there, but now they knew, for certain, that the humans were coming.

-

"What was that!" roared Creed in anger. The sudden attack had nearly thrown him from his command chair.

"Kinetic energy weapons," answered Second Profiteer Lantz. "No damage, though the shield was stressed from the sudden attack. Those rounds were coming at 8 or 10 percent of light speed."

"We're in combat range," reported Third Profiteer Talbot from Tactical.

"Well, fire then!" roared Creed, his large eyes glowing with rage. "Destroy the humans!"

-

"Inbound fire!" warned Lieutenant Brooks, as her sensor alarms went off, indicating incoming energy.

The *Star Cross* shook, and the lights dimmed slightly.

"Ion beams and energy weapons," reported Andrew. "Shield is holding at 82 percent."

"Initiate firing plan Beta 3," ordered Kurt. Time to teach the Profiteers that this attack would be expensive. "Contact Rear Admiral Wilson and tell him to commence his attack run."

-

From the *Star Cross* and the six light cruisers, dark blue particle beams lanced out and struck a single Dacroni battleship. In their wake KEW rounds hammered the shield, seeking a weakness. Almost at the same time, six hypermissiles from the *Star Cross* slammed into the battleship's energy screen, and, for a moment, a small hole opened. Instantly a KEW round penetrated, smashing into the hull, blasting a huge glowing pit in the side of the ship. Its power fluctuated briefly, and then several particle beams penetrated, raking the hull and opening up more compartments to space. Almost immediately the shield failed completely, as too many power couplings had been compromised.

The light cruisers *Dallas*, *Birmingham*, and *Johnas* turned broadside and opened fire with their lighter KEW batteries, quickly scoring numerous hits on the now heavily damaged battleship. They continued to pound the hapless vessel, until it suddenly exploded in a blazing flash of light.

-

"Dacroni battleship is down," reported Lieutenant Brooks excitedly.

Another flash of light suddenly lit up a viewscreen, drawing Kurt's attention. "What was that?"

"Destroyer *Kline* is down," replied Lieutenant Brooks, as her jubilation at the destruction of the Dacroni battleship quickly faded.

"They were hit by multiple ion beams and a hypermissile," reported Andrew, as he listened to the reports coming in across the fleet. "Rear Admiral Wilson is inbound and is preparing his Scorpion bombers for a shipping strike."

"When his fleet gets in range, have him order Captain Anniston to target one of the Profiteer escort cruisers with the *Trinity*'s full spread of hypermissiles," ordered Kurt.

"Message sent," replied Andrew.

-

The space between the two battling fleets was full of weapons fire. The dark blue human particle beams and the white flash of Profiteer and Dacroni ion and energy beams filled the void. Occasionally a hypermissile would light up space, as one struck an energy screen.

-

"Three more ships!" roared High Profiteer Creed, still reeling from the shock of one of Jarls's battleships being blown apart by the human fleet. "Where did they come from?"

"They were hiding behind the planet," reported Third Profiteer Bixt. "One of them is 1,200 meters in length. It must be the ship they were building. They did finish it! There's also another human battlecruiser and one of their small carrier vessels."

"Where did they get another battlecruiser?" Creed leaned back in his command chair, deep in thought. This attack would be far more costly than he had originally thought. These humans were full of surprises; he wondered what else they might be hiding.

-

The light cruiser *Blair* suddenly found herself under attack from four Dacroni battleships. Her shields flared brightly under the assault.

"Put all power to the shields," called out her captain, as he saw they were in danger of failing.

"Engineering reports they're giving us all they've got," reported the executive officer. "Shifting all power from weapons and life support."

The ship suddenly shook violently, and an explosion rocked the Command Center. Crewmembers were hurled to the deck, and several consoles erupted in bright showers of sparks. Smoke filled the room, and the acrid smell of burned wiring prevailed.

"Shield is down," reported a grim-faced executive officer.

"Damn!" uttered the captain, knowing this was the end.

-

Several ion beams slammed into the top section of the *Blair*, causing massive explosions; the hull pressed outward, and glowing debris drifted from the ship. Then a Dacroni hypermissile detonated in the damaged area, and the ship turned briefly into a miniature sun. When the brightness died away, all that was left was a few wisps of glowing gas.

-

"Light cruiser *Blair* is down," uttered Lieutenant Brooks in a shaky voice.

"I think it's time for our surprise," suggested Andrew, looking intently at the fleet admiral. "Most of our ships can't go toe-to-toe against those Dacroni battleships."

"I agree," answered Kurt, as he studied the tactical display with a frown. Other ships were damaged, and, if he didn't do something quickly, he would lose more ships. He had already lost the crews of the *Kline* and the *Blair*; he refused to lose any more human lives.

"Rear Admiral Wilson is nearly in combat range, and he's launching his Scorpion bombers," added Andrew. "The *Trinity* is preparing its hypermissile strike."

"Initiate Operation Last Ditch," ordered Kurt. Now he would see if his little trap would pay off. "Order Rear Admiral Wilson to hold off on the *Trinity*'s hypermissile strike for now. We may need those missiles later."

Amid the human fleet, four small computer-controlled cargo ships, posing as destroyers, suddenly accelerated forward under full power. Each ship had been equipped with an energy shield, and nearly all the power the ships had available was directed into those shields.

-

"Four human destroyers have accelerated and are heading toward our ships," warned Third Profiteer Bixt.

"What!" called out High Profiteer Creed, his eyes focusing on the four red threat icons, pulling out of the human fleet formation. "That's suicide."

"We're directing weapons fire toward them," reported Second Profiteer Lantz, "but they're still accelerating."

Creed's large eyes watched one of the viewscreens, which showed a magnified view of the approaching human ships. One of them was hit with an ion beam, blasting a glowing crater in the bow of the ship. Another was hit with several energy beams, tearing open compartment after compartment.

"They're still accelerating!" warned Third Profiteer Bixt. "I think they're going to ram us!"

"Pull us back!" yelled Creed, his eyes suddenly full of fear. Before he could say another word, the viewscreens suddenly filled with light.

-

The four cargo ships were half-destroyed wrecks when they slammed into High Profiteer Creed's support cruisers. The cargo ships' Command Centers had been moved to the rear of the ships, in case the forward sections were destroyed in the headlong attack. The cargo ships smashed through the Profiteer support cruisers' shields, as the sheer mass of the cargo ships overloaded the enemy's energy screens. Massive explosions lit up space as the eight ships died.

"We just lost four of our escort cruisers," reported a frightened Second Profiteer Lantz. "If one of those ships had struck the *Ascendant Destruction*, I'm not sure we would have survived."

"The other three human ships are entering combat range, and they've launched over two hundred small attack craft," reported Third Profiteer Bixt from his sensor console.

"Withdraw," grated out High Profiteer Creed, his large eyes glowing with anger. "This attack has already been too costly, and it's only growing more so. We must jump back into hyperspace, before we lose even more of our ships."

"Jarls will be displeased," warned Lantz.

"He'll be compensated for his losses," growled Creed, turning toward Lantz. "Now get us out of here. We've already lost enough credits as it is."

"Admiral, they're pulling out!" screamed Lieutenant Brooks, her eyes lighting up with relief.

"Calm down, Lieutenant," Kurt ordered, though he felt the same way.

"It's confirmed, sir," Andrew reported, as he listened to the reports coming in from the other ships. "The enemy is breaking off combat and turning away."

"Let them go," Kurt ordered. "I don't want to risk any more of our people or our ships. Have our fighters and bombers follow them just out of weapons range, until the enemy jumps into hyperspace."

A few moments later Kurt allowed himself to take a deep breath, as the red threat icons on the tactical screen vanished one by one, until they were all gone.

"Enemy has jumped and is on their way toward Earth," reported Lieutenant Brooks in a calmer voice. They were showing up on the hyperspace detection buoys, and their course was easy to plot.

"We won," said Lieutenant Mays in a pleased voice.

"It's over now for Newton," Kurt said, addressing the command crew. "But it might have just gotten a lot worse for Earth." Kurt knew that, with the failure of the attack against Newton, the Profiteers would in all likelihood speed up their pillaging of the home planet. "We also lost a few ships along with their brave crews. They died to keep us free, and we should all remember that. A fleetwide memorial service will be held later to honor their memory."

Kurt's heartbeat returned to normal, and his breathing slowed down. In a few more weeks the defense grid would arrive, and, shortly after that, his new warships should be ready. It was nearly time to take the battle to the Profiteers and to make them pay dearly for what they had done to Earth and the people living there.

"Take us back to Newton," Kurt ordered. "We need to get our battle damage repaired."

"Yes, sir," Andrew replied, as he relayed orders.

Kurt would send the *Vindication* back to the Kuiper Belt, where the *Newton Princess* was waiting. The first load of fleet crewmembers should be about ready. This failed attack should have bought Newton the necessary time it needed. Kurt also planned to let his crews have some leave time, even some for him to visit Newton and Keera. He didn't know what it was, but he found something about the young doctor extremely fascinating, and he wanted to further explore that relationship.

Chapter Nineteen

Several weeks passed, and Kurt was at a small restaurant with Keera. They had gone out several times now, and each time Kurt became more at ease in the young woman's company.

"What is this called?" Keera asked, as she used her fork to spear several pieces of food on her plate.

"Fried okra," Kurt answered with a smile. Keera had a way of making him forget all the pressure he was under.

"You have a number of foods here that are quite different from what I'm used to," she said, as she took a cautious bite. She smiled and took another. "I must learn how to cook this!"

"My sister could probably show you," Kurt replied. "She's a great cook."

This restaurant was one of Kurt's favorites, as the food was excellent and the place was not overly crowded. He disliked eateries where the crowd noise was so loud that he couldn't speak to whomever he was with.

Keera put her fork down and looked seriously at Kurt. "You'll be pleased to know that Private Dulcet shows some positive signs of improvement. Her mom and dad have been coming daily, and today they brought her younger brother. She said his name without any prompting."

"I'm glad to hear that," Kurt replied. He was still highly upset about what had been done to her. "How are you adjusting to Newton?"

"It's a beautiful world. Every time I go out, I find something new and interesting. It doesn't have the crowds or the pollution that Kubitz has. Even my home world seems crowded compared to here, and it had strict population controls."

Kurt nodded and cut another slice of the baked chicken on his plate. "When we have more time, I'll arrange for a shuttle, and we can take a tour of the entire planet. Newton has some really big mountains, as well as some beautiful and deep oceans."

"I would like that," Keera said, her eyes focusing on Kurt. "Newton is so different from Kubitz. It almost makes me regret my decision to remain there these last few years."

"What are the other civilized worlds like?" asked Kurt curiously. "We're familiar with Kubitz, of course, but the others we've explored were empty of any type of intelligent life."

"The other civilized worlds are unbelievable," Keera said, her eyes taking on a dreamy look. "Some cities float in the air, using antigravity. On a few of the older worlds, the entire planet is one massive city. Even in space, there are colonies. Huge constructs orbit planets where millions of beings live. Asteroids have been hollowed out to provide living space, and huge space liners travel from world to world."

"Why do these civilized worlds put up with the Gothan Empire?" With the technology Keera described, they should easily subdue the Profiteer worlds.

"They've been at peace for a very long time," Keera explained. Some have recorded histories that go back millions of years. The races in toward the galactic core are some of the oldest. To them war is unknown, and violence is nearly unheard of. I know of several worlds I've read about that don't even have a police force."

"What stops the Gothan Empire from expanding and taking over those systems?" To Kurt it sounded as if they were vulnerable to an attack.

"Not all civilized worlds are so peaceful," answered Keera. "Enough planets are protected by large warfleets to keep the Gothan Empire and others like them at bay. For access to some of the technology of the core worlds, they extend those worlds their protection. Their ships are so advanced that the Gothan Empire wants no part of them."

"I see," Kurt said. "So the Gothan Empire, while it occasionally raids the ships of these worlds, is careful not to become such a nuisance as to provoke any type of retaliation."

"Precisely," Keera said with a nod. "You saw the defenses around Kubitz. A number of other worlds in the Gothan Empire have similar defenses, particularly Marsten, the capital. While these civilized worlds could probably take out the Gothan Empire, it wouldn't come easily or without substantial losses. Much of the technology used to defend Kubitz and Marsten has been stolen from some very advanced worlds."

"You mentioned there were other worlds like the Gothan Empire."

"A few scattered across the galaxy," Keera responded, as she took another bite of her fried okra. "For the most part they leave the more advanced worlds alone and only trade among themselves. They occasionally wage small wars against one another over valuable star systems they come into conflict over."

"I may go to Marsten someday," Kurt said, thinking about what had been done to Private Dulcet and to Earth.

An empire that practices such depravity should be made to pay the consequences for such acts. However, a punitive visit to Marsten was far in the future. He also wanted to learn more about the defenses around Marsten and those at Kubitz. It might not be a bad idea to put together an intelligence team and send them to Kubitz to study the defenses.

"I would stay away from Marsten," cautioned Keera with a concerned look on her face. "No good can come from going there." She paused and took a sip of her tea. "I love this tea. We have nothing like it on Kubitz."

"It's one of our favorite drinks," replied Kurt. "There are a number of different varieties with unique tastes." He could recall his mother making sun tea on the porch, when he and Denise were much younger. Those times were so much simpler than now.

"I want to try them all," announced Keera. Then in a more serious voice, she said, "Kurt, please stay away from Marsten. Very few people who go there in anger ever return."

"That's a long time from now," Kurt assured her. "Presently I have to worry about Newton and driving High Profiteer Creed from Earth."

Those were his highest priorities. Sometime in the next few weeks, the defense system for Newton should arrive. Once that system was installed and tested, this war would take a different turn, as he planned to go on the offensive.

Keera nodded. "Your sister has invited me to go shopping with her tomorrow, once I'm finished at the medical center. While I'm here, I've been sharing with your doctors some of the medical treatments we use. They've been very helpful and are highly interested in what I have to show them. A number of devices and medicines for sale on Kubitz would be so useful to your people."

"Make a list, and I'll have Lieutenant Tenner look into it."

Keera was so generous with her time and her skills and her knowledge. She hadn't indicated any desire to return to Kubitz, and he hoped she didn't for quite some time.

Captain Nathan Aldrich waited nervously for the hatch to open on the Profiteer shuttle, which sat on the runway of the airport. With him was a full squad of Marines, guarding the two armored vehicles, each carrying eighty bars of gold. This was the second tribute payment at the higher amount the Profiteers had demanded.

"We shouldn't be giving them this gold," muttered Corporal Lasher. "We may need it ourselves someday."

Nathan didn't answer, as he looked around the perimeter of the airport. Like all airports it had been shut down since the invasion, and only a few planes left occasionally and then only by permission of the Profiteers. For the most part the airport was empty with very few people moving about. Only a few maintenance and security people were present, and they were keeping their distance from the shuttle. Nathan thought he could see a few people in the control tower, watching the proceedings from its large windows.

"Did you see how the people looked at us, as we drove through the city?" asked Private Malone, cradling his assault rifle in his arms. "There was hate in their eyes, because we're the military and haven't done anything!"

"Look, the hatch is opening," said Corporal Lasher, gesturing toward the shuttle.

The large hatch opened, and a ramp extended until it touched the tarmac. A moment later, half a dozen heavily armed Profiteers emerged and walked to the waiting Marines.

"I have your gold." Nathan spoke in a calm and measured voice to the one who appeared to be the leader.

"Open the trucks," demanded the Profiteer. "I want to see our gold."

Kurt gestured to his Marines, and the large doors were swung open.

The lead Profiteer then checked each truck, quickly inspecting the gold and counting the bars. As always another group of Profiteers brought antigravity sleds to load the gold and take it to their shuttle.

The Profiteer returned to Nathan with a contemptuous gaze. "Next month the tribute will be three hundred bars of gold and fifty thousand carats of gemstones."

"What!" uttered Nathan in a stunned voice. "We agreed upon eighty to begin with, and then you increased it to 160. We may not have that many bars of gold left, and I'm not certain about the gems."

"You will deliver the gold here and the gemstones, or you will lose a major city," the Profiteer said coldly. "The tribute must and will be paid. This planet is no longer yours. It is ours!" The Profiteer then returned to the waiting shuttle, along with his five escorts.

"Let me shoot him," muttered Corporal Lasher in a low voice, as he clicked off the safety on his assault rifle. "We could storm the shuttle and take it."

"No," replied Nathan, wishing they could do as Lasher suggested. "We need to get word of this increase to the government and see how they want to handle it."

"What if we can't produce the gold and the gems?" asked Private Malone.

"We have four weeks to figure it out," Nathan said, as he watched the Profiteer shuttle take off. "Let's get these trucks moving and report back. They won't like what we have to say."

High Profiteer Creed stood in the large hold of the cargo ship *Zental*. Twelve pallets filled the bay, holding gleaming yellow bars of gold, as well as numerous cases full of precious gemstones.

"The humans were not happy with our increase in the tribute," Fourth Profiteer Cade announced. "I thought one of the human soldiers would fire on us."

"The North American Union seems to be the one in control of the majority of the gold and gemstones on the planet, or at least the others are following their lead. I suspect they will pay the tribute."

"I would suggest we send down a heavily armed party and a number of shuttles to furnish aerial coverage when we go to collect," said Cade. "I'm not sure the next time will be so peaceful."

"I'll have Clan Leader Jarls provide support," Creed replied.

He was still irked at how much Jarls had demanded for the Profiteers' failed attack on the human colony world. It had been a very expensive attack with one Dacroni battleship destroyed and four of his own escort cruisers. When this cargo ship left, he would send orders for four new cruisers to replace the ones he had lost. Reparations would have to be paid to the families of the dead crews, plus bonuses to encourage crewmembers to sign up for the new ships.

"There is more resistance each day to our Profiteers on the ground, seeking out this planet's riches," commented Fourth Profiteer Cade. "It's only a short matter of time before the entire planet erupts in open revolt. It may be time for us to move into their larger cities and sweep up any gold or other valuables that might be stored in them."

"I will summon more detainee ships and additional cargo vessels," Creed said. The ships would be needed for what he planned on taking from Earth. "It's time we wrap up our business with this world." Even once they were gone, he planned on returning and making occasional raids against the planet to take more captives to be sold on Kubitz. If he handled things properly, Earth would be a source of income for many years to come.

"We also need more Profiteers to search the cities, if we want to finish this," added Cade. "We're already stretched too thin."

Creed shook his head in dismay at the thought. More Profiteers would mean the profits from this venture would have to be split more ways. However, he recognized the wisdom of what Cade was saying. If he didn't bring in more Profiteers, they might never strip this world of its valuables before it became too tenuous to hold. If he were forced to nuke too many cities, then the expense of extricating the wealth from the planet would go up exponentially.

"I'll add in more Profiteers," Creed promised. It would be simple enough to bring in four or five hundred more at a low pay grade to find the gold and other items of interest on Earth.

Cade nodded his satisfaction and left the cargo hold.

High Profiteer Creed sighed a deep breath of frustration. Every time he turned around, this venture became more expensive. Walking to one of the crates filled with gemstones, he reached down and filled his hand with diamonds, rubies, emeralds, and other precious stones. After a moment he allowed them to fall back into the crate. In just this room alone was enough wealth to pay for this entire venture a hundred times over. Turning, he left the cargo hold, sealing the hatch behind him.

President Mayfield sat once more in the situation room, listening to defensive coordinator Colonel Stidham brief him and the others on Captain Nathan Aldrich's report.

"Three hundred bars of gold and fifty thousand carats of gemstones!" Mayfield echoed, as he heard the numbers from the colonel. His eyes bulged and showed growing anger. "If we pay that next month, then what will they want next time? A thousand bars of gold?"

"It's possible," replied General Braid with a deep frown. "We can make the payment, but it's as you suggested. If we do, they'll doubtlessly raise it again. They're becoming more aggressive across the planet. There are unconfirmed reports that a number of civilians have been killed in recent days, while resisting the Profiteers' demands for admittance to their private homes to conduct searches."

President Mayfield went silent for several long moments, as he thought over his options. "We have four weeks," he finally said, his eyes shifting to Fleet Admiral Tomalson. "Send word on the *Newton Princess* that Fleet Admiral Vickers must move on the Profiteers as soon as possible, or the situation here on Earth may turn into a firestorm. If the people revolt, he might not have a world to come back to."

"If he hits some of their convoys, it may shift some of their attention from us," suggested Tomalson, knowing things on Earth were reaching a tipping point. "He hurt them badly at Newton. They lost five ships, and several of the Dacroni battleships showed battle damage. From the reports we received from the stealth shuttle pilots, Kurt lost one destroyer and a light cruiser in the battle."

"But he sacrificed four valuable cargo ships to achieve that victory," pointed out General Braid. "He can't use that tactic too often, or he'll run out of ships."

"I hate to push him, if he isn't ready, but we can't wait much longer," responded Mayfield with deep worry lines etched across his forehead. "I'm afraid that, at any time, some of our troops will take matters into their own hands."

"I agree," said General Braid. "The dissent is growing, since we're not allowing them to fight back. Keep in mind that the majority of our general army and Marine units were sent home to be with their families during this crisis. Most of them have weapons they could use at a moment's notice. The president's right. This could blow up in our faces any day, from both the civilian and military fronts."

"I'll send the message," Tomalson replied. "The *Newton Princess* is scheduled to return to Newton with her load of fleet personnel in a few more days."

"That should be soon enough," Mayfield said, as he looked at the red threat icons circling Earth.

True, not quite as many enemy ships were in Earth orbit as before the Profiteers and the Dacroni had attacked Newton, but there were still enough to keep Earth in submission. Mayfield just hoped they could hold out until Fleet Admiral Vickers figured out some way to free Earth of its tormentors.

-

Captain Henry Watkins reread the message the communications officer had just handed him. He let out a deep breath and looked up at the main viewscreen in the *Vindication*'s Command Center. The passenger liner, *Newton Princess*, floated in a sea of black under the steady light of countless stars.

"Bad news?" asked Lieutenant Anthony Dries, the executive officer.

"Events have taken a turn for the worse on Earth," answered Henry, as he crumbled up the paper and stuffed it into his pants pocket. "The Profiteers are increasing their tribute demand."

Dries shook his head. "If this keeps up, there won't be any gold or much of anything else of value left on Earth shortly. What do they want us to do?"

Henry gestured toward the passenger liner on the viewscreen. "Fleet Admiral Tomalson wants Kurt to begin hitting the Profiteer convoys. He hopes that will divert some of the pressure off the home planet."

"Or it could make it worse," Dries quickly pointed out. "It could further anger the Profiteers, and they could redouble their efforts to strip the planet."

Henry remained silent, knowing Dries was right. The defense grid and the new warships should be arriving shortly at Newton. Once the grid was operational, and the warships crewed and made ready for combat, it would be a different situation. However, it didn't sound as if President Mayfield felt they could wait that long.

"How many more passengers do we need to fill the space on the *Newton Princess?*"

"One hundred and ten," Dries answered promptly. "Three more days and we should have the liner at 100 percent capacity."

"Tell Captain Mertz I'll have a personal message for him to deliver to Fleet Admiral Vickers when he returns the *Newton Princess* to Newton."

Dries nodded. "Yes, sir."

Henry leaned back in his command chair, oblivious to the activity going on in the Command Center. He knew the enemy had suffered in their attack on Newton and had called it off before incurring even more losses. He also knew that, if the aliens had pushed the attack, the Dacroni battleships would have blown right through Kurt's ships. Every day the situation on Earth was becoming more desperate.

Henry had hoped they would have more time to prepare Newton's defenses and shake out the bugs in the new warships. They had sent some of their own construction engineers to help ensure the ships were properly equipped and ready for human crews. However, they needed several months for the crews to familiarize themselves with the new warships. It sounded as if that preferred time frame was out of the question and it would be more like several weeks instead.

A few days later on Newton, Kurt was inspecting a laser battery set up on the outskirts of the capital. "Does it have enough power to reach low orbit?"

"Yes," General Mclusky replied. They stood in a small field several kilometers from the city. "It's completely computer-controlled and will fire upon any missile it detects entering the atmosphere."

Taking a deep breath, Kurt gazed about. The laser turret sat upon a twenty-meter tower with gleaming twin barrels pointed upward. "What about a hypermissile?" Kurt was deeply concerned about the Profiteers using hypermissiles to bombard the surface of Newton.

"Hypermissiles won't work through an atmosphere," Mclusky replied. "They're designed to operate in space, and, upon hitting any obstacle, they instantly lose their high intrinsic velocity. That's why they explode with such violence when they hit a ship's energy screen."

Kurt wondered why he hadn't been made aware of this before. That explained why the Profiteers had used regular missiles in their attacks against Earth. "How many of these towers do you have?"

"Ten around the capital and a few more protecting some of the other major cities."

"If our luck holds, and the defense grid gets here in time, we may never have to worry about being bombed from orbit." In the distance, Kurt could see several large birds, circling high in the air, looking for prey. There was a light breeze, and it seemed so peaceful out here in the country. "Let me know if you need anything else. We have quite a bit of military construction capability with the manufacturing section we added to Newton Station."

"Yes, sir," replied Mclusky.

—

A short time later Kurt headed back in a shuttle to the *Star Cross*. He had wanted time to see Keera and his sister's family, but Andrew had sent him a message saying the *Newton Princess*, escorted by the destroyer *Sultan*, was inbound and would shortly be docking at Newton Station. Andrew had mentioned that Captain Stephen Mertz had an urgent message from Captain Watkins.

As the shuttle rose through the atmosphere, Kurt couldn't help but wonder about the message. Sometime in the next week or two, he was expecting the ships containing the defense grid to arrive. From what he understood in his original conversations with the arms dealers, they maintained a special fleet capable of moving large constructs and which would set up the grid. Of course all this came with a cost, as stated in the signed contract registered with the Controllers on Kubitz. Dolman and Grantz had both assured Kurt that the contract would be fulfilled, and he had nothing to fear from the crews assembling the grid. Dolman had also mentioned that a Controller would be on one of the ships, to ensure the contract was strictly adhered to. Of course neither Grantz nor Dolman knew about the warships. They had been purchased on a separate contract, which those two knew nothing about.

The shuttle cleared the atmosphere, and, glancing out the viewport next to him, he could see the darkness of space studded with numerous unblinking stars. A few days earlier he had paid a visit to the medical center where Private Dulcet was recovering, and she had recognized him. Much of her memory was still jumbled, but she had known who he was. While there, he had spoken at length with Keera about Lucy's future treatment. Keera was certain that Lucy would, in time, make a full recovery, though treating her mental state—in regard to her "work" at the pleasure house—might take some long sessions with several doctors who dealt in that type of trauma.

A few minutes later the shuttle neared the *Star Cross*, which was in orbit close to Newton Station. Gazing at the shipyard, Kurt could see flashes of white light where welding arcs occasionally flared. Workers were busy on the new flight bay, installing the new weapons systems: defensive laser batteries, particle beam cannons, and the tubes for the hypermissiles. The destroyer *Callisto* was still attached to one section of the flight bay, just in case the shipyard needed to activate the energy shield again. Colonel Hayworth had indicated in their last meeting that, in another two to three weeks, the outer hull of the flight bay would be fully installed, plus the emitters for the energy screen. At that point the *Callisto* could be returned to its regular duty.

"We'll be docking in a few minutes," the pilot announced over the comm system.

Kurt leaned back and allowed himself to relax. He was alone in the passenger compartment of the small shuttle, feeling curious about what was in the message Henry had brought. It almost certainly concerned Earth and the Profiteers. He felt a cold chill run across his back. He strongly suspected that whatever was in the message wouldn't be good news.

Chapter Twenty

Kurt sat in his quarters, staring, worried about the message Henry had sent him. Henry was one of Kurt's oldest friends, and, from the contents of the message, Henry was very concerned about what was going on down on Earth. It looked to Kurt as if the Profiteers were intensifying their search for the planet's hidden wealth, most of which was safely hidden on Newton.

"So what's the plan?" asked Andrew, sitting in front of Kurt's desk.

"President Mayfield wants us to attack the convoys immediately," answered Kurt, with a deep sigh. "He's afraid that the situation on Earth is about to go down the tubes."

"We knew it would steadily get worse, particularly when they realized much of the gold and other valuables on the planet had been removed," responded Andrew. "What do you want to do?"

"I'm not sure. The only problem is, a lot of the remaining gold and other valuables are still in the hands of some of the governments and particularly in the homes of numerous civilians." Kurt leaned back, closed his eyes, and then opened them. He didn't really want to leave Newton until the defense grid arrived. "Some civilians have massive art collections and probably millions in hidden gold and jewelry."

"The *Carlsbad*'s conversion from exploration ship to battlecruiser will be done in another week," Andrew commented. "Once she's out, we could afford to send one of our battlecruisers to hit a convoy."

"I wish we didn't have to weaponize all those exploration ships," uttered Kurt despondently "Someday we might need them again for their original purpose. We never dreamed something like the Gothan Empire might be out there." It saddened Kurt immensely, since he had always wanted to command an exploration ship and explore the galaxy with wonder and optimism, not fear.

"When that day comes, we can build more," Andrew answered. "They will serve us better as battlecruisers for now."

Kurt nodded and looked intently at Andrew. "If we were to hit a convoy and make it disappear, how would High Profiteer Creed respond?"

After a moment of thought, Andrew said, "He'd freak out. He would want to know what happened to the convoy."

"Yes," Kurt said in agreement. "He might be just concerned enough to send some of his ships orbiting Earth to search space for it."

"The fewer ships around Earth, the less pressure from the Profiteers in their pillaging of the planet. But how do we find the convoy once it enters hyperspace? The hyperspace buoys we've put around Newton and Earth can only detect a ship in hyperspace for a distance of five light-years."

"As you know, we partially disassembled one and integrated it into our own sensors on the *Star Cross*," Kurt answered, as he tried to come up with a solution. "Ships in hyperspace can only communicate if they're very close to one another."

"Seventy thousand kilometers," Andrew replied. "That's as far as our communications and short-range sensors will function. Any farther and communication becomes impossible, plus the sensor data is nonsense. Long-range sensors don't work at all."

Kurt looked down at the message from Henry. "The Profiteers normally send one cargo ship, two detainee ships, one battlecruiser, two escort cruisers and one Dacroni battleship in each convoy."

"From what Fleet Admiral Tomalson has relayed to us through the stealth shuttles we have operating, a convoy leaves each month," Andrew said, his brow creasing in a frown. "That should be any day now. Should we try for that one? Not only would we be throwing a wrench into High Profiteer Creed's plans but we'd be getting some of our gold back."

"We don't know if they monitor hyperspace for potential threats," Kurt said, as he unconsciously drummed the fingers of his right hand on his desk. "We would have to follow them, wait until they drop from hyperspace, then jump in, disable the drives on the cargo ship and the detainee ships."

"What about the warships?" Andrew asked with a frown. "They won't be all that easy to take out."

"Hypermissiles," Kurt answered. "If we can hit them before their shields come online, we could take them out."

"That's a big *if*," Andrew said, shaking his head doubtfully. "If I were to lay money on it, I would say the Dacroni battleship is bound to have some type of hyperspace sensors. It may also be several days before they drop from hyperspace. How far do we follow them?"

"I think it's a risk we have to take," answered Kurt, reaching a decision. "We'll take the *Dallas* and the *Johnas* with us, and, if necessary, we'll follow them clear back to the Gothan Empire."

"What about the Profiteers' cargo ship and the detainee ships?" asked Andrew, realizing Kurt intended to take the *Star Cross*. "If we succeed in taking out their hyperspace drives, they'll be stuck in whatever system they're in."

"Once we've secured the enemy ships, we send back one of our light cruisers to return with our own cargo ship and several passenger liners for the captives."

Andrew was silent as he mulled over Kurt's plan. "I don't see anything else we can do," he said finally. "If the warships get their shields up, we could lose the *Star Cross* and the two light cruisers."

"I know," answered Kurt in a solemn voice. "I'll contact Rear Admiral Wilson and tell him of my decision, and I'll also speak with Governor Spalding. If you want to go to Newton for the rest of the day to be with your family, you have my permission to do so." Kurt knew that Andrew had been spending as much time as possible with his wife and daughter. They'd found a house close to where Denise and her family lived.

"If we're leaving tomorrow, I have too much work that needs to be taken care of," replied Andrew, shaking his head. "Emily will understand. I know Lieutenant Mays could probably handle it, but I'd feel better if I took care of the details."

"At least give them a call," Kurt suggested. "We may be gone for a week or two." Kurt intended on speaking to Denise and, of course, Bryan. Anytime Kurt called, the inquisitive six-year-old demanded to be part of the conversation. He would also talk to Keera and let her know he would be gone for a while.

"Let me go with you," suggested Keera over the private comm channel Kurt had set up in his quarters. "With my medical history I could be useful in case of casualties."

"Thanks for the offer," Kurt replied, "but we have a shipboard doctor, and he's pretty protective of his turf."

"I can understand that," Keera responded. "But has he ever treated injuries from the weapons the Profiteers and the Dacroni mercenaries have? I'm talking about energy weapons that will burn completely through a body. I've treated those injuries before."

Kurt was very tempted to agree to Keera going, but the *Star Cross* was a warship and no place for civilians. "No, Keera," he said firmly. "I want you here, helping Lucy. When we return, if your medical expertise is needed, I'll give you a call."

The comm was silent for a moment, and then Keera spoke. "I thought you would say that. I'll be here when you get back. Just be careful and don't do anything too daring. Keep in mind that the Dacroni are trained mercenaries and know how to fight."

"Thanks for the words of advice," Kurt answered. He could tell from the tone of Keera's voice that she was a little dejected with his decision. "I promise when I get back, I'll take you on that tour of Newton we've been talking about."

"We might have to include your nephew," answered Keera with a slight laugh. "I mentioned it to him, after your sister and I went shopping, and he became very excited about taking a shuttle and seeing the rest of the planet."

Kurt was silent. There went the alone time he had planned with Keera. There would be no privacy or even quiet time with Bryan around.

"Don't worry," Keera said, laughing even more. "Denise told Bryan he could go next time and that she would come along also. So the first trip will be just you and me."

Kurt thought over what Keera was saying. "Have you ever gone camping?"

"Out in the wild, like sleeping under the stars?"

"Not quite that wild," answered Kurt, smiling to himself. "There are several resorts in the mountains with some very nice cabins and spectacular scenic views. I was thinking more along those lines."

"And what will be expected of me on this trip?" asked Keera in a teasing voice.

Kurt suddenly realized he didn't have a response.

"Don't worry," Keera said over the comm. "We'll figure it out when we get there. It might be fun. By the way, what's your favorite color?"

"Blue," Kurt blurted out, confused by the question.

"I like blue too," Keera said demurely. "I better let you go. I know you have a lot to do."

"I'll call you as soon as we get back," promised Kurt. The comm went silent, and he knew Keera was gone. He was still a little confused about the color question. Oh, well, he would worry about it later; for now he had a fleet to ready for combat.

-

Slightly before noon the next day Kurt returned to the Command Center.

"The *Dallas* and *Johnas* have moved into flanking positions," reported Lieutenant Mays, as she got up from the command chair, relinquishing it to Kurt.

"Thank you, Lieutenant," Kurt answered. Captain Randson was busy making sure their extra hypermissiles were properly stowed in the missile pod.

Kurt pressed the ship-to-ship button on his comm. "Captain Marsh and Captain Owens, are you ready to get underway?"

"Yes, Admiral," they both replied.

"You will go first. Leave in ten minutes," Kurt ordered. "Proceed to rendezvous with the *Vindication*. The *Star Cross* will follow, so we can see how well the new hyperspace sensor functions."

"See you at the rendezvous, sir," replied Captain Marsh.

"Same here," replied Captain Owens.

-

Captain Randson came into the Command Center just in time to witness the *Dallas* and *Johnas* preparing to make the jump into hyperspace.

"Lieutenant Brooks, make sure the new hyperspace sensor is online," ordered Andrew. "I want to see those two light cruisers on the tactical screen, and I don't want to lose them."

"Yes, sir," she replied, as her fingers moved nimbly across her computer screen, touching different icons. "Sensor is operational and online."

"Ensign Styles, stand by to jump into hyperspace. Lieutenant Brooks will feed you the course and speed of the two light cruisers. Stay on their tail and do not lose them."

"Ready to engage," Styles answered, as he leaned forward a little bit closer to his navigation console.

"*Dallas* and *Johnas* are jumping," reported Lieutenant Brooks.

-

Kurt looked at the main viewscreen, as both ships seemed to shimmer and then vanished. He stared intently at the tactical screen, which now showed two green icons rapidly departing the Newton System.

"Give them a ten-minute head start, and then we'll follow," he ordered. He noted the increased activity in the Command Center as they neared the time to enter hyperspace.

"All systems are powered up and working at optimum levels," reported Andrew, as he took his place at his command console. "All departments report ready for hyperspace entry."

On the main viewscreen, the image shifted to show Newton Station. Several Lance fighters were visible, flying their patrol routes.

"Admiral, Rear Admiral Wilson wishes us good luck on our mission," reported Ensign Pierce from her communications console.

"Tell him thank-you and to keep Newton safe while we're gone," replied Kurt.

A few more minutes passed, and Kurt returned his attention to the tactical screen, still showing the two receding light cruisers.

"Distance is 2.6 light-years," Lieutenant Brooks reported. "Hyperspace sensor is showing a strong tracking signature."

"Stand by to enter hyperspace," Andrew announced. "One minute to hyperspace transition."

Kurt looked at another screen with the blue-white globe of Newton. He wondered if the defense grid would arrive before they returned. Taking a deep breath, he prepared himself for the transition into hyperspace.

"The ship is yours, Ensign Styles," said Andrew, looking at the Navigation and Helm.

"Yes, sir," Styles replied, as he pressed several buttons on his console, including his preset initiate icon.

Almost instantly the *Star Cross* accelerated forward, and then the hyperspace drive activated. Kurt felt a slight wrenching in his stomach, while the stars disappeared from the ship's viewscreens. He checked the tactical screen for the two light cruisers and was surprised to note that the screen revealed the entire Newton System plus the ships in orbit. He came to realize this hyperspace detection system could be quite valuable, if used properly.

"All departments report normal operations," said Andrew, as he listened to the different department heads report in over his comm.

"All right," Kurt said, relaxing a bit. "Now let's see if we can follow those two cruisers without losing contact with them."

"You heard the admiral," said Andrew, looking at Lieutenant Brooks and Ensign Styles. "Don't lose those two ships!" Andrew smiled. "I'm also curious as to how well the new sensors will work."

For the next two hours Kurt watched with interest as the *Star Cross* followed the light cruisers. Several times Ensign Styles made minor course adjustments. What intrigued Kurt most was the hyperspace sensor's display on the tactical screen. The two cruisers showed as brilliant green icons; however, the sensor also showed nearby star systems. He noticed, the farther away they were, the detail was not all that great. But the new sensors should give adequate warning of any approaching hyperspace hazards.

"The hyperspace sensor seems to be working adequately," commented Andrew. "Unless the Profiteers have a better hyperdrive on their cargo ship and the two detainee ships, we should have no trouble following them."

"We'll see," answered Kurt. The Command Center routine had become more normal once they entered hyperspace.

Kurt was curious what the sensors would show as they neared the Solar System. Once they rendezvoused with the *Vindication*, it would be a matter of waiting for the Profiteers to send the convoy on its way. A lot was riding on this mission. If the humans were successful, they could recover a full cargo ship of the riches the Profiteers had stolen from Earth, plus free several thousand captives who were about to be sold into slavery. It might also buy them the time they needed to get the defense grid at Newton up and operational, and perhaps even see the arrival of the new warships.

Kurt sat in the Command Center, while the *Star Cross* dropped out of hyperspace two thousand kilometers from the *Vindication*. It would be two more days yet before the *Newton Princess* returned to pick up her next load of fleet hopefuls.

They had managed to follow the two light cruisers without losing them. It made Kurt feel confident that they would be able to follow the Profiteer convoy when it finally left Earth orbit.

"Message from the *Vindication*," Ensign Pierce reported. "Captain Watkins says the alien convoy is already forming up and may be leaving at any time."

"Crap," muttered Andrew, as his gaze moved to the tactical screen, now showing the Solar System as seen by the hyperspace sensor. It didn't show the system in great detail, but it did show the ships around Earth. It was obviously detecting their hyperspace drive emissions. Even when not activated, the drives still gave off a distinctive energy signature. "I wonder how much time we have."

"Have the *Dallas* and the *Johnas* take up supportive positions on our port and starboard sides, and be prepared to enter hyperspace at a minute's notice. Have them slave their navigation computers to the *Star Cross*, and we'll handle the pursuit for all three ships," ordered Kurt, as he gazed at the tactical screen. "Once the alien convoy enters hyperspace, we have twelve to fifteen minutes to locate them, before we no longer will be able to track them."

Andrew looked over at Kurt with concern on his face. "We've never attempted that type of coordinated navigation before. At the speed we'll be traveling, there won't be time to make sudden course corrections."

"First time for everything." Kurt grinned. "Our navigation computer can handle it. We just need to input the right information. Isn't that correct, Ensign Styles?"

"Yes, Admiral," Styles replied confidently. "With the new hyperspace sensor, the computer should be able to navigate all three ships safely."

Andrew let out a deep breath and nodded. "I'll contact Captain Marsh and Captain Owens, and let them know what's going on." Andrew still had a frown on his face.

"I'll be in my quarters," Kurt said. "I need to speak to Captain Watkins."

"How are things on the *Vindication?*" asked Kurt, once he had Henry on the comm. He leaned back in his plush office chair, enjoying the momentary comfort.

"Boring," replied Henry. "We spend most of our time hiding behind some of the larger ice rocks, waiting for the stealth shuttles to go back and forth."

"Has there been any sign of the Profiteers or the Dacroni detecting the shuttles?"

"No, nothing," replied Henry, sounding perplexed. "Hell, even if I was running a standard sensor sweep, I would have noticed something by now."

"We don't know what their standard operating procedures are for scanning the space around a planet," Kurt answered.

"We've only been landing at night and coming in with the Earth shielding the sun," Henry explained. "We've even used storm systems to hide where the shuttles land. For some strange reason, the enemy doesn't seem to be covering the poles of the planet with any of their ships. We've been coming down over northern Canada."

"They're only interested in stripping the planet of its gold and other valuable metals," Kurt said. Plus the Profiteers were not real military but pirates. However, that didn't explain why the Dacroni mercenaries hadn't detected anything. Maybe they just didn't care.

"And gemstones," Henry added. "I received a report yesterday that several Profiteer shuttles landed at The Louvre in Paris. Dozens of Profiteers emerged and attempted to enter. There was a brief battle between the French security people at the museum and the Profiteers. Surprisingly enough, the Profiteers returned to their shuttles and left. A few hours later the Eiffel Tower was destroyed by an energy beam."

"With the tribute Earth is paying, the Profiteers are supposed to leave the major cities alone," Kurt said in concern. "I'm not surprised about the Eiffel Tower. The Profiteers always seem to retaliate when we offer resistance."

"*Supposed to*," reiterated Henry. "They seem to be ignoring that agreement more every day."

Kurt didn't like the sound of that. President Mayfield was right. Earth was rapidly reaching the tipping point where an actual revolt against the Profiteers could easily happen. That couldn't be allowed to occur, because there was no doubt in Kurt's mind that the Profiteers wouldn't hesitate to use nukes on more Earth cities. They had already nuked the planet once before, and there was no reason to think they wouldn't do it again.

"Hopefully, if you can take this convoy, it will ease the tension on Earth some," Henry added. "Although High Profiteer Creed will be infuriated."

"Earth will only feel some relief if the aliens commit some of their ships to the search for the missing convoy," Kurt reminded Henry.

"Creed will search for it," Henry said confidently. "Each cargo ship he sends off is packed full of plunder. He'll do everything he can to try to recover it."

Kurt talked to Henry for a few more minutes about what was going on at Newton. Henry asked some questions about Kurt's sister and how Andrew's family was doing since the rescue. Finally Kurt signed off and hoped to take a quick nap. At any moment, he expected to be called back to the Command Center. As he lay on his bed, his thoughts turned to Keera, and he soon drifted off to sleep.

-

"Admiral Vickers, please report to the Command Center," said someone in a loud and urgent voice over the comm.

Kurt's eyes flew open and, glancing at the clock next to his bed, he was surprised to see he had slept for nearly six hours.

"Report," he ordered, pressing the button on the comm.

"Enemy convoy is leaving Earth orbit and moving into open space," Lieutenant Mays reported. "We estimate they'll be jumping into hyperspace sometime in the next ten to twenty minutes."

"Very well," Kurt answered. "I'll be there shortly. Let me know if they jump into hyperspace before I reach the Command Center."

Kurt quickly stripped off his wrinkled uniform and changed into a clean one. He spent a few minutes freshening up and then left his quarters, hurrying toward the command deck. On his way he passed several crewmembers also headed to their stations.

Stepping into the Command Center, he saw Andrew was already there and Lieutenant Mays had returned to her tactical station. "Where are they?" Kurt stepped to his command chair and sat down with his gaze shifting to the tactical screen.

"Past the orbit of the Moon," replied Andrew, as he turned toward Kurt.

"They're jumping," called out Lieutenant Brooks.

"Inform the *Dallas* and the *Johnas* to stand by," ordered Kurt. "Also notify Captain Watkins that we'll be departing shortly."

"How long do we wait?" asked Andrew.

"Five minutes," Kurt answered. "Give them a head start but not much of one. We don't know if that Dacroni battleship will detect us or not."

"If it does, we're screwed," commented Andrew in a low voice that only Kurt could hear.

The time passed quickly by, and, at a signal from Kurt, Ensign Styles turned the navigation of the three ships over to the ship's navigation computer. Almost instantly the *Star Cross* accelerated and jumped into hyperspace.

"*Dallas* and *Johnas* have jumped also," reported Lieutenant Brooks.

Kurt looked at the tactical screen, seeing two green icons displayed in close proximity to the *Star Cross*.

"Now we'll know for sure," Andrew said. "If there's no reaction shortly, then I would guess they haven't spotted us." Andrew focused on the tactical screen, his gaze locked on the red threat icons they followed. He also watched the green icons. On the screen they were so close that they seemed to be touching.

The anxiety in the Command Center was high, as everyone took occasional furtive glances at the tactical display. After about thirty minutes, nothing had changed, and the tension gradually receded.

"I don't think they know we're here," Kurt said, allowing himself to relax. It confused him some as to why the Dacroni wouldn't be monitoring hyperspace; surely they had the ability to do so.

"Now we just have to wait and see how long they stay in hyperspace," Andrew commented, as he sat down at his command station. "It could be several days or more."

Kurt nodded in agreement. The Profiteers and Dacroni were more experienced with hyperspace travel than humans were. It was unknown how many times they might feel it necessary to drop from hyperspace during the 1,500–light-year journey to the Gothan Empire.

For five days the *Star Cross* and the two light cruisers shadowed the small convoy. During that time the Profiteer fleet never varied its speed in hyperspace.

"Current distance between us and the convoy?" asked Kurt, as he gazed at the red threat icons on the tactical screen.

"Three point two light-years, sir," answered Lieutenant Brooks.

"What if they don't stop until they reach the Gothan Empire?" Andrew asked from his command station. "They've been maintaining that speed from the very beginning. I'm concerned we might be away from Newton for quite some time."

"They have to stop short of the star cluster," Kurt responded, his brow wrinkling in thought. "They need to drop out to plot their hyperspace course, as the star density in that cluster is too great to enter blindly."

"Admiral!" called out Lieutenant Brooks. "Their speed is dropping."

"Contact the *Dallas* and *Johnas*," ordered Kurt, leaning forward expectantly. "All ships are to go to Condition One!" He was relieved that the convoy was finally exiting hyperspace.

"They're dropping out," confirmed Brooks, as she checked the hyperspace sensor. "They're in a small brown dwarf system."

"I've updated the *Dallas* and the *Johnas*," added Andrew. "They're going to Condition One."

"Ensign Styles, put us two hundred kilometers from the Dacroni battleship. Lieutenant Mays, I want two hypermissiles targeted on the Profiteer battlecruiser, one each on the two escort cruisers and the remaining two on the battleship. Have the tubes reloaded as soon as the missiles have launched. Any enemy warships that survive our initial attack, we target with our particle beam cannon. Lieutenant Mays, it's vital we launch the hypermissiles as soon as we drop from hyperspace and before the enemy can raise their shields."

"Yes, Admiral," Mays responded, as she started speaking to her tactical people.

Kurt pressed the ship-to-ship comm on his command console. "Captains Marsh and Owens, the *Dallas* will target the drives on the two detainee vessels, while the *Johnas* is to target the hyperdrive on the cargo ship. It's imperative that we disable the drives on all three ships. Once you've confirmed the drives are out, you're to come to the aid of the *Star Cross*, if we're engaged with any enemy ships. I'm hoping our sudden emergence from hyperspace will take them by surprise and our hypermissile attack will do them in."

"We'll be ready," answered Captain Marsh.

"I hope this works," Andrew said uneasily. "We have a lot riding on them not having their screens up. We're taking a chance jumping in so close."

"We'll find out shortly," responded Kurt. "The hypermissiles have the speed to hit the enemy warships before they can fully activate their energy shields. We'll only have a few seconds to do this."

"Eight minutes to hyperspace emergence," announced Ensign Styles, as he worked with his navigation computer so all three ships would come out within close combat range of their intended targets.

The Condition One alarms sounded, and Captain Randson made the announcement over the ship's comm. Across the ship, the crew raced to their battlestations. Safety bulkheads slammed shut, and damage control teams put on self-contained suits, in case they had to enter damaged areas no longer in an oxygen environment. Marines retrieved assault rifles from the ship's two armories and took up positions at key locations throughout the vessel.

Andrew turned off the alarms and flashing lights, and turned toward Kurt. "Ship is at Condition One, and all stations report ready for combat."

"Very well," Kurt replied, as he buckled his safety harness. The others in the Command Center did the same. "Stand by for combat maneuvers."

"Hypermissile strike is set up," Lieutenant Mays reported.

"Four minutes to hyperspace emergence," said Ensign Styles, as he double-checked their course and the projected dropout points for all three ships.

Kurt felt his heart speed up, and he took several deep breaths. Around him, the tension increased in the Command Center as they neared the time for battle.

"Enemy ships are holding their position," confirmed Andrew, his focus on the tactical screen.

"Two minutes to dropout," reported Ensign Styles.

"All ships, stand by for combat," Kurt said over the ship-to-ship comm. "Shields up as soon as possible."

The last minute crawled by, and then Kurt felt the familiar gut-wrenching sensation, as they dropped from hyperspace. On the viewscreen a background of stars suddenly appeared.

"Targets!" called out Lieutenant Mays. "Target locks! Launching hypermissiles!"

On the *Star Cross*, six hatches slid open over her converted missile tubes. The missiles exited the tubes and then seemed to blur, as their hyperspace drives kicked in. Two missiles carrying fifty-kiloton warheads slammed into the nine-hundred-meter-long Profiteer battlecruiser. Two fiery glowing suns appeared as the ship was torn asunder. One missile each struck the pair of six-hundred-meter-long escort cruisers, turning them into molten wrecks. The final two hypermissiles hit the Dacroni battleship. However, the ship had its energy shield up, and the missiles exploded harmlessly fifty meters from the armored hull.

The *Dallas* and the *Johnas* both managed to disable the hyperdrives on their targets using their defensive laser batteries. Several pinpoint blasts ensured the cargo ship and the two detainee ships wouldn't be going anywhere soon.

The Dacroni battleship slowly turned toward its attacker. Missile ports slid open, and energy projectors powered up.

-

"Profiteer battlecruiser and both escort cruisers are down," reported Lieutenant Brooks excitedly and then, in a more concerned voice, said, "The Dacroni battleship had its energy shield up, and both hypermissiles detonated fifty meters from the hull. It's turning toward us!"

"Crap!" swore Andrew, looking intently at the tactical screen. "I was afraid of that. We'll have a fight on our hands."

"Targeting battleship with our particle beam cannon and main KEW batteries," reported Lieutenant Mays, as she swiftly passed on new orders to her tactical team.

"Captain Owens and Captain Marsh are reporting that their targets have been disabled," added Andrew, as he listened to the two captains over the ship-to-ship comm. "They're moving to assist us against the battleship."

-

In space, a dark blue particle beam flashed from the *Star Cross* to strike the Dacroni energy shield. It was followed by number of large KEW rounds from the ship's bow batteries. Brilliant flashes of light lit up the battleship's shield as the rounds struck at 10 percent of the speed of light, releasing massive amounts of kinetic energy.

The two light cruisers moved up and added their own weapons to the attack. Two more particle beams lashed out and more KEW rounds hit the Dacroni energy screen too.

From the Dacroni battleship, four white energy beams leaped forth to strike the *Star Cross*'s energy shield.

The *Star Cross* vibrated sharply, and warning alarms sounded on the damage control console.

"Energy beam penetrated the shield," Andrew reported, as reports of damage came in. "We have several compartments open to space."

"I'm having all three ships fire their particle beams at the same spot on the battleship's energy shield," Lieutenant Mays reported. "I'm hoping we can overload that one section. We'll follow up with a barrage of KEW rounds."

"Do it!" ordered Kurt, as the *Star Cross* shook violently. Kurt could hear his ship crying out in protest from the onslaught of Dacroni weapons fire. The hull seemed to ring with every strike to the energy shield.

"That was a fifty-kiloton hypermissile," reported Lieutenant Brooks, her face turning pale.

"Energy shield is at 70 percent and dropping," warned Andrew with concern on his face. "We're not designed to take on a fully armed battleship with an active energy shield."

"I know," answered Kurt grimly. "But what other choice do we have?"

"Firing particle beams," called out Lieutenant Mays.

On the main viewscreen, three particle beams stuck the same section of the enemy battleship's energy screen. The shield glowed brilliantly in cascades of exploding colors, and then a single KEW round struck the side of the vessel. The impacted section of the ship blew apart, and debris scattered.

"We got a hit!" called out Lieutenant Mays, as she tried to fire more rounds into the damaged section, only to see them explode harmlessly against the energy shield.

"Hypermissile tubes are reloaded," reported one of the other tactical officers.

"Sir, the *Johnas!*" called out Lieutenant Brooks in alarm, pointing toward the viewscreens in the front of the Command Center.

Looking at the indicated viewscreen, Kurt saw the ship under heavy attack from the battleship. A hypermissile suddenly slammed into the stern of the light cruiser, and the ship vanished in a fiery explosion.

"*Johnas* is down," reported Lieutenant Brooks in a stunned voice.

"Firing all hypermissiles," Lieutenant Mays said in a steady and commanding voice.

Almost instantly the Dacroni energy shield lit up under the massive release of energy. At the same moment, the *Star Cross* fired her particle beam cannon. The dark blue beam struck the fluctuating energy shield and penetrated, drilling deep inside the enemy battleship. A huge section of the hull split open, and secondary explosions rattled the vessel. More KEW rounds penetrated the shield, opening up compartment after compartment on the enemy ship.

"Enemy energy shield is down," reported Lieutenant Brooks, as she read the information coming in over the short-range sensors.

"Firing all weapons," said Lieutenant Mays in a vengeful voice.

A few moments later the Dacroni battleship exploded, as her power reserves were compromised. A huge blast ripped apart the ship from the inside, leaving the vessel a torn and mangled wreck.

"Dacroni battleship is down," confirmed Lieutenant Brooks with relief in her eyes.

"Cease fire," ordered Kurt, taking a deep breath.

"It's over," Andrew said, his face still white from witnessing the *Johnas*'s destruction.

"Secure from Condition One and take us to Condition Two," ordered Kurt. "Shuttle some Marines to board that cargo ship and the two detainee ships ASAP. Capture the crew and don't harm them unless they offer resistance."

"Shuttles will be leaving shortly," Andrew replied, now speaking to the lieutenant in charge of their flight bay, where four small shuttles were.

Kurt unfastened his safety harness and looked around at his command crew. Many had shocked looks on their faces from the loss of the *Johnas*. It had always been a risk that one or more of the enemy ships might have their shields up. Captain Owens had been a good commander. He had brought the warning to Newton, when the Profiteers had first struck Earth. He had just barely made it to Newton in his heavily damaged light cruiser. His perseverance had held the shattered ship together until they could warn the colony.

"Once the convoy ships are secure, we'll hold a brief memorial service for our people we lost today," Kurt announced. "Their deaths will be remembered."

Leaning back in his command chair, Kurt watched as three shuttles left the *Star Cross* and docked with the convoy ships. There was no resistance, and shortly all three were under the Marines' control. Once the memorial service was over, he would dispatch the *Dallas* to Newton to escort the waiting cargo ship and the two passenger liners here to the disabled ships. It would take fourteen to fifteen days before the *Dallas* and company could return to this system. During that time, the *Star Cross* would keep a protective watch over the captured convoy ships.

Kurt knew, sometime shortly afterward, High Profiteer Creed would learn that his convoy fleet had vanished. If the High Profiteer responded as expected and sent ships out searching for his missing convoy, then it might buy Earth and Newton the time needed to prepare for the next step in the war: the freeing of Earth from the Profiteers.

Chapter Twenty-One

The *Star Cross* dropped out of hyperspace just two million kilometers from Newton. Moments later the *Dallas*, the cargo ship *Graham One*, and the passenger liners *Empress* and *Stardust* also put in an appearance.

"All ships have emerged from hyperspace," reported Lieutenant Brooks, as she gazed at the green icons on her sensor screen.

Kurt nodded. They had been gone for nearly twenty-eight days, and he was relieved to be returning to Newton.

"It's good to be home," Andrew said, as he listened to the different departments check in over his comm.

Suddenly Lieutenant Brooks looked over at Kurt with growing alarm on her face. "I'm picking up additional contacts around the planet! I have what appear to be ten large cargo ships of Kubitz design, four battleships, and ten battlecruisers, and two other ships I can't identify."

"The defense grid and our new ships," Andrew said, his eyes lighting up. "I thought the ships would come at least a few weeks to a month after the defense grid arrived." Andrew was pleased to see them, as it meant that shortly Newton would be safe and so would his family.

Lieutenant Brooks looked relieved after hearing Andrew's announcement. "I believe you're correct, sir."

"I don't know why they're here so early, but I'm glad they are," said Kurt, as he looked at the tactical display and the numerous new icons showing up in orbit around Newton.

"I've got Rear Admiral Wilson on the comm," reported Ensign Pierce. "He's confirming the large ships are Kubitz cargo ships, two construction ships, and the others are the new fleet."

"Take us in, Ensign Styles," ordered Kurt. He was anxious to inspect the new ships personally. "Ensign Pierce, inform *Graham One*, *Empress*, and the *Stardust* that they're to proceed and dock with Newton Station."

"I wonder how long it will take them to install the defense grid," Andrew said, as he shifted his gaze to the viewscreens.

On the main screen one of the massive cargo ships suddenly appeared. The vessel was nearly two thousand meters in length and four hundred meters in diameter, shaped like a giant cylinder, with engines on the rear and a Control Center in the slightly curved bow.

"That's a big ship!" commented Lieutenant Mays, as she glanced at the viewscreen in awe.

"I'm detecting energy screen emitters on the cargo ships," reported Lieutenant Brooks in surprise. "Earth and Newton cargo ships don't have energy shields."

"As big as those ships are, I'd bet they're armed also," commented Andrew, looking at the ship on the screen. "I'm sure the arms dealers on Kubitz wouldn't want to risk losing one. I would hate to think of the cost of them."

"Captain Randson is correct," confirmed Lieutenant Brooks, as she studied additional sensor data. "I've detected two powerful energy projectors on the bow of the ship, plus twenty missile tubes that probably contain hypermissiles."

"Rear Admiral Wilson reports that a Controller named Nirron is on board the lead cargo ship and requests a meeting with you at your earliest convenience," said Ensign Pierce.

"Inform Rear Admiral Wilson that the *Star Cross* will be in orbit shortly. I'll be glad to meet Controller Nirron on Newton Station."

"I wonder what he wants," Andrew said.

Kurt looked over at Andrew and then replied, "I guess I'll find out when I talk to him. Get us into orbit at our best speed. I'm going to my quarters to send a few messages and prepare for this meeting."

-

Once in his quarters, Kurt contacted Rear Admiral Wilson to get a better understanding of what was happening in orbit.

"They arrived three days ago," Wilson explained. "The hypermissiles have already been transferred to Newton Station, and Colonel Hayworth has been meeting with the cargo fleet engineers about where the different units of the orbital defense grid are to be placed. General Mclusky has also flown up to the station to discuss the ground emplacements."

"I see," Kurt said, his brow creasing in thought. "Have there been any problems?"

"No, none that I'm aware of. Captain Simms does have a large Marine contingent on the station to ensure security, but, so far, all the people from Kubitz have been quite amicable. An individual called Lomatz keeps asking for a tour of Newton Station and has been very quizzical about the weapons systems we're installing."

"Lomatz?" responded Kurt in surprise. "He's one of their chief weapons dealers, and the one I made the deal with for both the defense grid and the warships. I wonder what he's doing here."

"From what you told me about conditions on Kubitz, he's probably looking for something more to sell us."

"What about the warships? Has anyone gone on board one?"

"Yes," Wilson replied. "The engineers we sent to help on the interior design have taken a number of people on tours of the ships. I haven't gone myself, but Captain Deming of the *Callisto* toured one of the battleships and one of the battlecruisers. He was quite impressed by what he saw and didn't foresee any problems with us operating the vessels. I did speak to several of our engineers, and they confirm the same thing."

"Very well," Kurt said, satisfied with Rear Admiral Wilson's report. "I need to speak with Governor Spalding and Colonel Hayworth before I go to Newton Station for this meeting."

"I'd have Hayworth attend the meeting also," suggested Wilson. "He's had the most contact with these people since they arrived."

"General Mclusky also," added Kurt. He had to get the defense grid up and functioning, and then begin work on his new fleet.

After talking briefly with Governor Spalding and Colonel Hayworth, finally turning off his communicator, Kurt leaned back and sighed. He had hoped for a few days of rest after returning, but that was not going to be the case.

Stepping from his shuttle on Newton Station, Kurt found Captain Simms waiting for him with two heavily armed Marines.

"Marines?" asked Kurt curiously.

Simms nodded. "We have a number of the Kubitz cargo ships' technicians on board. We've been allowing them to eat in the large mess hall on C-deck. The Marines are just to ensure they don't wander into unauthorized areas."

As they made their way toward the briefing room where the meeting would be held, Captain Simms filled in Kurt on the Newton Station construction.

"The outer hull is in place for the flight bay, and the *Callisto* has been returned to duty," Simms reported. "We have the energy shield emitters in place and have even tested the shield. Everything worked perfectly."

"What about the particle beam cannons?"

"Coming along," Simms replied. "We finished one more while you were gone. A curious thing, the cargo ship engineers have been very interested in our particle beam weapons. Surely, as advanced as they supposedly are in the Gothan Empire, they can build them if they want?"

"You would think that," Kurt answered, as they arrived at the hatch to the briefing room.

"I should warn you," Simms began, as Kurt opened the hatch. "Your pet Profiteer is in there too."

"What?" Kurt asked, as he heard a loud gruff voice call out his name.

"Fleet Admiral Vickers, you're here!" Profiteer Grantz bellowed, standing up and walking quickly over to the hatch to greet Kurt.

"Why are you here?" Kurt demanded. Grantz was supposed to be helping Lieutenant Tenner on Kubitz.

Grantz gestured toward Lomatz, already sitting at the large conference table. "When I heard Lomatz and some of his people were coming to your colony world, I thought I should tag along to make sure they didn't take advantage of you and your people. I'm the best negotiator you have."

Kurt nodded, though he strongly suspected that Grantz was working some angle to get his hands on more gold. "We'll see," he replied.

"Admiral Vickers," Lomatz said, as he rose and nodded toward Kurt. He gestured toward the Controller next to him. "This is Controller Nirron."

The Controller nodded his head. In front of him were several paper documents and the normal computer pad that all Controllers always carried with them.

"What can I do for you?" asked Kurt, speaking to Lomatz. "I wasn't aware that you would be involved in delivering the defense grid."

Lomatz smiled widely. "After you left Kubitz, I got to thinking of other items that might interest you. I've brought a few samples along on one of our cargo ships."

"I'll take a look," Kurt promised, as he walked over and took his seat. "How soon before we can begin installation of the defense grid?"

"We have a full Class Two defense system on board the cargo ships," Lomatz said. "We can begin installation tomorrow, if you so desire. On board the ships are sixteen Class Two Orbital Defense Platforms, sixty-four satellites with dual-firing energy turrets, a Class Two Command and Control Center, and eight Planetary Defense Centers with top-of-the-line direct-energy cannons that can hit anything in orbit or shoot anything down that enters your colony's atmosphere. With this system you have complete space control of all that comes within forty thousand kilometers of your planet's atmosphere."

"That's a little bit more than what I agreed to," Kurt pointed out, cocking an eyebrow. He wondered what Lomatz was up to.

"It seems you've made some powerful enemies on Kubitz," Lomatz responded calmly. "Both the Profiteers from Marsten as well as the Dacroni are very displeased with you. There is also the matter of the supposed rescue of a human woman from the Brollen Pleasure House by your friend Grantz here with assistance from Avery Dolman."

Kurt kept an impassive look on his face, as he listened to Lomatz. He didn't know if Lomatz was speaking the truth or if this was just idle speculation.

"Considering the enemies you've potentially made, I took it upon myself to bring the extra units for the defense grid. I can promise you that, with this system in place, your world will be 100 percent safe from attack."

"How much?" Kurt demanded with an icy stare.

"Forty-eight million additional credits," Lomatz replied with a smile. "Controller Nirron has the new contract ready for you to sign."

"If I agree to this, how soon can you have the grid ready for full activation?"

"Five days," Lomatz answered promptly. "My people on the cargo ships are very good at what they do. I also have two construction ships that can make any modifications that might be needed."

"How did you finish the warships so quickly?"

"Ah, I was hoping you would ask that," Lomatz said with a pleased grin. "Since I knew you would want a stronger defense grid, I assumed you would want the ships as quickly as possible as well. I arranged for extra shifts and crews to hurry the construction."

"How much?" asked Kurt, suspecting there was a price involved.

"Not that bad," Lomatz answered, his eyes meeting Kurt's. "Only an additional twelve million credits."

Kurt groaned softly to himself. This man was a scoundrel, but, thanks to his greed, he might have solved several of Kurt's pressing problems.

"Is there anything else that we can do for you?"

"I noticed a lot of work being done on this shipyard. Am I correct in assuming you're installing weapons systems and other crucial elements to help in this system's defense?"

"Yes," answered Kurt in an even voice, almost dreading what he knew would come next. "We're upgrading the station to better suit our needs."

"My cargo ship engineers can help complete this station," offered Lomatz with a crafty gleam in his eyes. "We can offer construction methods far in advance of what you're currently using, plus several advanced power systems. On the same cargo ship carrying the samples that I wish to show you are additional defensive energy beam turrets, long-range energy projectors, and ion cannons. I'm willing to place my engineers under your command and provide whatever assistance you may need to complete this shipyard."

"Careful," cautioned Grantz, gazing angrily at Lomatz. "He wants all your gold."

"What would it cost to complete the shipyard as you suggested?" asked Kurt.

"Twenty-two million credits?"

"Twenty-two million credits," roared Grantz, standing up and glaring at Lomatz. "What's the entire cost of what you're offering?"

"Eighty-two million," answered Lomatz. "That includes the overtime for finishing the ships, the extra units for the defense grid, and completing this shipyard."

"Sixty," roared Grantz.

"Eighty," countered Lomatz.

"Seventy-five and not a credit more," snarled Grantz.

"Seventy-eight and we have a deal," Lomatz responded.

"Done," said Grantz, nodding his head in agreement.

"Wait a minute," interrupted Kurt, shaking his head. "I'll decide if we have an agreement or not."

"Seventy-eight million and, when my ships leave here, this system will never have to fear the Profiteers or anyone else from the Gothan Empire bothering you again," promised Lomatz. "I'll spread the word that your system is so heavily defended that it would be tantamount to suicide to attack it."

Kurt looked over at Controller Nirron, who had remained silent during this entire exchange. "Will he do as he says?"

"Yes," Nirron answered passively. "It will be entered into the contract."

With a deep sigh of resignation, Kurt turned back toward Lomatz. "Agreed."

Lomatz's mouth turned up in a wide and satisfied smile. "As soon as the contract is signed, I'll give the orders to begin the work."

"Prepare it," Kurt told Nirron. "Do we need to pay the credits now or from our account on Kubitz?"

"Forty percent now, and the rest from your account on Kubitz," Nirron answered. "I can calculate the weight in gold needed for the payment. Tell me when, and I can come to this station and collect it, and I'll bring you the updated contract to sign at the same time."

"I'll make the arrangements," Kurt answered.

Part of the gold he had taken from the Profiteer cargo ship would be used to make that payment. He found it slightly humorous that the gold that High Profiteer Creed had stolen from Earth would now be used to make Newton impervious to any future attacks from the Profiteers.

For the next several hours, Controller Nirron watched silently, while Lomatz, Kurt, General Mclusky, Colonel Hayworth, Captain Simms, and even Grantz discussed their different needs and what was to be done. They made up a list of priorities and set up a time schedule. When they finished, Kurt felt drained of energy. Between Lomatz and Grantz, Kurt had to stay on his toes and guide the conversation in the direction he wanted. The others in the room had numerous questions about the defense grid and what would be done to the station. General Mclusky, Colonel Hayworth, and Captain Simms asked detailed questions about the systems to be installed and what they were capable of.

When it was finally over, Kurt left the conference room, intending to take a shuttle to Newton to brief Governor Spalding.

"I did good in there, didn't I?" said Grantz, as he followed Kurt into the corridor. "I saved you millions of credits with my negotiating skills."

Kurt wasn't so sure of that. "I do want to thank you for rescuing Private Dulcet."

"It was the least I could do," Grantz responded, as the two walked down the corridor.

"I suppose you want a reward?"

"I wasn't expecting one," Grantz answered with a gleam in his eyes. "Why did you not mention the fleet you purchased? With my negotiating skills, I could have saved you millions of credits."

"Keep an eye on Lomatz. I'm not certain he's completely honest about why he's here."

"A Controller is here," Grantz quickly pointed out. "Lomatz wouldn't dare try anything with him around."

"I know that's what you think," Kurt answered, "but keep an eye on him nevertheless."

"All right," Grantz agreed huffily. "I'll do it."

-

Kurt took his shuttle and flew to Newton to meet with Governor Spalding. For nearly three hours, he described to the governor his battle with the enemy convoy fleet and his meeting with Lomatz on board the shipyard.

"I'll be glad when the defense grid is operational," Spalding said, as he walked over to the large window in his office and gazed out at the city. "It will ease a lot of people's minds. When the cargo ships and your new warships arrived, it nearly caused a panic. I had to go on all the airwaves and explain who they were. Hell, I nearly panicked when Rear Admiral Wilson told me the size of some of those ships. Two thousand meters!"

"They're big," admitted Kurt, watching the governor. "They have to be, considering what they're carrying."

"It's so hard to imagine the ship manufacturing capability that's available at Kubitz. I don't know if we could ever build something like that."

"It's just a difference in needs and technology," Kurt explained. "I suspect, if we ever decide we need really big ships, we'll find a way to build them."

"Or just order them from Kubitz," Spalding said with a grim laugh. "I know you told me anything could be bought on Kubitz for the right price. I guess I didn't really believe you until those ships arrived."

"I'll sign the contract in the morning and deliver the necessary amount of gold to Controller Nirron. Within five days the defense grid will be operational."

Spalding nodded. He left the window and walked to his desk. "With the defense grid up, Newton Station being finished, and your new ships, we have only one more thing to worry about."

"Earth," Kurt said evenly. "We need to decide how to go about freeing our home planet from the Profiteers."

"We have a lot of refugees who would like to return home someday."

"Also a few are building good lives here," Kurt reminded the governor. "More may want to stay than you think."

"I hope so," Spalding replied. "We have a good world here. I just want it to stay that way."

"It will," promised Kurt. It would be expensive, but Newton would continue to be the pristine and peaceful planet it had always been.

–

Kurt had called Denise and told her that he would stop by for a few minutes. She had been excited to hear his voice and promised to cook him a quick meal. He also tried to reach Keera, but the staff at the medical center informed him that she had already left for the day. Disappointed, he had his driver drop him off at his sister's with instructions to return for him in two hours. He needed to return to the *Star Cross* and arrange for the gold transaction, plus monitor the installation of the new defense grid. Kurt also wanted to get some crews on the new warships, so they could start becoming familiar with them.

As Kurt walked up to the door to Denise's house, he couldn't help chuckling to himself. Denise's home had everything but the white picket fence. He could remember when, as kids, she had always dreamed of living in a big fancy mansion with servants and everything. Now, here she was, living in a modest home with her son and husband.

He wasn't quite to the door when it was flung open, and Bryan ran out.

"Uncle Kurt!" yelled Bryan, his face lit up with joy. He launched himself and wrapped his arms around Kurt's waist, giving him a big hug. "Mom said you were coming. She's making meat loaf with mashed potatoes and gravy!"

Sounds great," said Kurt, laughing as he untangled himself from Bryan's grasp. "Let's go inside and help."

"Keera's here too," Bryan said, as he took Kurt's hand and led him inside the house.

Entering the living room, Kurt saw Keera, sitting on the sofa, talking to Alex.

"Hello, Kurt," Alex said, standing up and shaking his hand. "I'm glad you could come by."

Keera stood up and came over and gave Kurt a hug with a big smile. "I hear you have some visitors up in orbit."

Kurt sat down next to Keera with Bryan coming to sit on his lap. "Yes, the ships from Kubitz brought the defense grid and my new warships. Lomatz even showed up."

"The arms dealer," said Keera with a distasteful frown. "He only shows up when there are credits to be made. How much did it cost you?"

"A lot," Kurt confessed. "But if he carries through with what he has promised, it'll be worth it."

"Is there a Controller with him?"

"Yes," Kurt answered. "Controller Nirron came on board one of the cargo ships. I met him earlier today."

"Good," Keera said with relief in her eyes. "That will keep him honest."

"More aliens," Bryan said with wide eyes. "Can I meet them?"

"When you're older," promised Kurt.

"Are these Controllers really that powerful?" asked Alex, looking over at Keera.

"They are," Keera said, nodding her head. "You have to realize the entire economy in the Gothan Empire and particularly on Kubitz is based on these signed contracts the Controllers oversee. They also control all the credit accounts and have a vast amount of resources available to them. No one dares break a contract for fear of the consequences."

"How is Lucy doing?" asked Kurt.

"Better," Keera said with a gentle smile. "She's gradually getting more of her memory back. She has had several breakdowns over the realization of what she did at the pleasure house."

"What's a pleasure house?" asked Bryan, his ears perking up at the unfamiliar term.

"It's nothing," said Alex hastily. "Why don't you see how close supper is to being ready?"

"All right," Bryan said, sliding off Kurt's lap and vanishing into the kitchen.

"Does she remember any of her military career?"

"Some," Keera answered. "Bits and pieces. Her memories are still pretty jumbled up. She vaguely recalls the attack, being on board the Dacroni battleship, and part of what happened at the pleasure house. As the weeks go by, she'll remember more. It's important right now that her family stays close by. They're her anchor to sanity."

"Supper's ready," called out Denise, as she stepped from the kitchen. "I hope everyone's hungry."

"I know I am," Kurt said, as he stood up and took Keera's hand, helping her up off the sofa. He held it longer than necessary, before letting go.

Keera looked at him with a timid smile. "What's *meat loaf?*"

"You'll love it," Kurt promised.

"Denise makes a great meat loaf," Alex added, as he headed for the kitchen.

"I wish you didn't have to return to your ship so soon," Keera said in a suggestive voice.

Kurt felt his heart flutter. "I do too, but someone has to keep an eye on Lomatz."

"We'll have time later," Keera said with a smile. "Let's eat. I'm sure Bryan is full of a thousand questions he wants to ask you."

Kurt nodded, as he led her into the kitchen with its wonderful smells. He wished he could stay longer, but he knew that, as fleet admiral, he had to put his job first and his personal life second, at least for now.

Chapter Twenty-Two

Kurt stood in the Command Center of the *Star Cross*, watching as another of the large Class Two Orbital Defense Platforms was put together directly over the north pole of Newton. The platform was one hundred meters across and twenty meters thick. On top sat a massive ion cannon, four large energy projectors, and eight smaller defensive energy turrets. There were four pods containing six hypermissiles with an automatic reloading system. Everything was computer-controlled, and a crew of six could operate the entire platform. However, the living quarters were set up to hold a crew of twenty, to allow for routine maintenance and crew rotation in the small Command and Control Center.

"That's the last one," Andrew said, as he stepped to Kurt's side. "All sixteen ODPs are finished, and the sixty-four defensive satellites have been deployed."

"The Command and Control Center should be finished tomorrow," added Kurt, drawing in a deep breath.

He was glad everything was going so smoothly. For the first time in a long while, he felt the pressure of command recede, as he knew now than Newton would shortly be safe from attack. His sister and her family would be protected, as well as the other eight million people who called Newton their home.

"How are the Planetary Defense Centers coming along?"

"Nearly done," Kurt answered. "General Mclusky is very satisfied with what he's getting to defend the planet with. He seems quite excited at the weapons he'll now have at his disposal." Kurt had spoken to Mclusky earlier, allowing the general to give him a detailed report of the progress being made on the surface of Newton.

"What about the station?" Andrew asked.

"That's a little different," replied Kurt, sounding a little perplexed. "Lomatz is becoming more insistent that we turn over to them the designs for our particle beam weapons."

"Why?" asked Andrew, sounding confused. "Surely they have particle beams of their own."

"Not in operation," replied Kurt, turning from the viewscreen. "I think the problem once again is costs. An ion cannon or a large energy projector is much cheaper to operate than a particle beam cannon. Also our recharge time is quicker than what they're used to. Lomatz thinks it's some quirk in the technology we're using and so is highly interested in obtaining it."

"What's he offering in return?"

"That's the interesting part," Kurt answered. "Lomatz said, if we give him an operational cannon and the schematics to build more, that he would be willing to complete the flight bay on the shipyard free of charge. He's also offering to revamp our ship construction bay to decrease the time to build a battlecruiser by nearly 70 percent. Of course, for that, there would be a charge. And we'd make sure the contract states he can't use our technology against us, anywhere in the universe."

"You'll take him up on the offer, won't you?"

"I think I have to," Kurt answered with a slight nod. "We don't know what will happen when we attempt to free Earth. With what's already occurred on the planet, it may be years before they're completely back on their feet. It's very likely the responsibility for defending both Earth and Newton will fall on us."

"Can we order another defense grid for Earth?" asked Andrew, knowing that would help alleviate part of the problem.

"It's a possibility," Kurt answered. He had discussed it briefly with Fleet Admiral Tomalson several months back.

"Another Profiteer cargo ship should be leaving Earth shortly," Andrew continued. "Captain Watkins sent word on the *Newton Princess* that he thought another one would be leaving in a few days."

"I'm sending the *Trinity* and the *Carlsbad* both this time," Kurt said. "As well as the light cruisers *Alton* and *Birmingham*. We've installed a hyperspace sensor on the *Trinity*, so she should be able to trace the convoy."

"If the convoy leaves," said Andrew, raising his eyebrow. "If High Profiteer Creed receives word that the other convoy didn't reach Kubitz, he may decide to hold this one until he learns what happened."

"That's what I'm hoping," Kurt said. "We've already placed crews on all four of the new battleships and the ten battlecruisers."

"Partial crews," corrected Andrew with some concern. "We still need a number of crewmembers to fill out the ship rosters."

"How long did Colonel Hayworth say it would take to modify our last six missile tubes for the hypermissiles?" Kurt wanted all twelve tubes on the *Star Cross* to be capable of firing the new missile. He had been hesitant until now to put the ship inside the repair bay to have it done.

"Two days," responded Andrew. "They'll also need to modify two missile storage pods and set up an automatic reloading system for all twelve tubes."

"Schedule it," Kurt ordered. "Inform the new crews they have three days to become familiar with their ships, and then we'll do some shakedown cruises. In two weeks I want them ready to go to Earth."

"Two weeks!" said Andrew, his eyes widening in alarm "I'm not sure they'll be ready by then. There are some pretty raw recruits on those vessels."

"If we have to, shift some crews from the destroyers to the new ships. The destroyers won't be of much use in a battle and will serve better if they stay here at Newton."

"That's a good idea," said Andrew, nodding his head in agreement. "We have seven destroyers, counting the two with the *Vindication.* That would fill all the important positions with trained crewmembers, including most of the officer positions. If we shift a few other people around, we should end up with decent command crews for all fourteen of the new ships."

"I'll explain to Captain Anniston on the *Trinity* that she's to send the destroyers *Sultan* and *Deimos* back when they reach the *Vindication*," Kurt said. "We're still not certain how High Profiteer

Creed will react when he learns that his convoy never reached Kubitz."

"He'll go ballistic," predicted Andrew, folding his arms across his chest. "I wouldn't want to be around him when he does find out."

"Let's just hope he sends ships searching for the missing convoy and doesn't take out his anger on Earth."

"I guess we'll know shortly," Andrew replied and then continued. "I think he'll go hunting for the convoy. That cargo ship was packed full of gold and gemstones. He won't want to lose it. Not to mention all the potential slaves he's taken from Earth to sell." Several passenger liners under escort had already returned to Newton from Kubitz with humans that Lieutenant Tenner had freed.

Kurt shifted his attention to the viewscreen and the defense platform. He knew he should probably send a message to President Mayfield, briefing him on the readiness of the new defense grid over Newton. He would also indicate to the president that he was preparing to initiate offensive operations against the Profiteers.

Captain Nathan Aldrich was once more on the tarmac, only this time in Western Oklahoma at an abandoned military airbase, dating from the Cold War between the then United States and the former Soviet Union. It still boasted a long airstrip used occasionally for training purposes. He saw a tumbleweed blow across the wide runway, but, other than that, there was no movement out here.

"I wonder why they wanted to land in the middle of nowhere?" asked Private Malone, peering at the high clouds drifting over the area.

"The cities are becoming too dangerous for them," Nathan responded. He heard a loud noise in the sky, and, looking up, he saw the shuttle descending. A second one was with it and took a higher orbit above the former airbase.

"We're late with this payment," Corporal Lasher commented, as the shuttle landed fifty meters from the four large armored trucks.

"We got them to agree to the delay, claiming it was taking us longer than expected to round up a sufficient quantity of gemstones," explained Nathan. "It was hoped, by making it seem that we were having a difficult time meeting this tribute, they wouldn't increase it again."

When the shuttle hatch opened and the ramp touched the tarmac, ten heavily armed Profiteers came forward with another group behind them pulling a number of antigravity sleds.

"It's hot today," complained Corporal Lasher, hoping the Profiteers hated the heat as much as he did, especially when wearing that gray body armor. The temperature hovered in the low one hundreds with a strong gusty wind blowing from the south.

"You have the tribute?" demanded the lead Profiteer.

Nathan thought this was the same one he had spoken to the last several times. "Yes, it's all here."

The Profiteer motioned to the others with him, and the doors to the four trucks were opened, and they rapidly began transferring the bars of gold and the gemstones to the antigravity sleds.

"You were late with this month's tribute," the Profiteer stated with a scowl on his face.

"It was a large amount of gold and gemstones," Nathan replied evenly. "It takes time to gather up such wealth."

"Next month the amount is doubled," the Profiteer said in a cold and harsh voice. "No delay will be accepted or you will lose cities. Do you understand?"

"Yes," responded Nathan, his anger rising. He wanted nothing more than to pull his pistol from its holster and put a 45-caliber bullet between the Profiteer's large pale eyes.

"I see your anger at our demand," snarled the Profiteer, gazing directly into Nathan's eyes. "If any harm comes to me or any other Profiteer, the orbiting shuttle will nuke this landing site!"

"No harm will come to you," promised Nathan, drawing in a deep breath and reining in his anger.

The Profiteer turned and went to the others, who were loading the gold and gemstones; they finished shortly and returned to the shuttle, pulling the antigravity sleds behind them. A few moments later the shuttle took off and headed toward space.

"Double," muttered Corporal Lasher, his face turning grim. "Can we do that?"

"I don't know," replied Nathan, as he looked around the desolate airfield. "Let's get back, so we can report." Nathan had a feeling that everything was coming to a head. The Profiteers were increasing their demands to take the last of Earth's wealth. Nathan had a suspicion the Profiteers might have just received their last tribute.

A few hours later High Profiteer Creed glared at Third Profiteer Bixt in shock. Two detainee ships had just dropped from hyperspace into Earth orbit and sent a message that the last convoy fleet dispatched to Kubitz had never arrived.

"Impossible!" roared High Profiteer Creed, shoving Second Profiteer Lantz to the side, as he made his way to the communications station. "What do they mean, *the convoy never made it to Kubitz?*"

"First Profiteer Hiltol is confirming the message," Bixt replied, as he listened anxiously to his comm. "The convoy was fourteen days late when he left Kubitz with his two ships."

"Could another group of Profiteers have captured it?" asked Lantz.

"Someone has interfered with it," muttered Creed, knowing his profits had just taken a huge hit. "I'll contact Clan Leader Jarls and have him send three of his battleships to Kubitz on the same course the convoy was supposed to take. Perhaps they can find out what happened."

"Could it have been the humans?" asked Lantz.

Creed stood still for a moment, deep in thought. "I doubt it," he said finally. "They're too concerned about defending their colony world."

"Could they have hired some mercenaries to hit the convoy?"

Creed gazed at Lantz in surprise, and then anger spread across his face. "That would make sense," he said. "They don't have the forces or the technology to track the convoy and then attack it. They could have hired someone to do it for them. Just a split of the gold and gemstones on that cargo ship would make such an agreement worthwhile."

"What should we do?"

"I still think we should send the Dacroni battleships to search, but it would also be a good idea to have our people on Kubitz ask around, see if the humans have hired anyone to hit us. It would have to be a good-size contract, and word of it may have leaked. I'll tell them to see if anyone is spending large sums of credits at the pleasure houses. If mercenaries hit us, stealing our gold, someone will be bragging about it."

"How do we go about replacing our losses?"

Creed's eyes narrowed, and he shifted his gaze to a viewscreen, which showed the blue-white globe of Earth. His accounts on Kubitz were already swollen with the profits he had made from this world. Perhaps it was time to leave, before his fortunes turned. This missing convoy might be an indication of that. "Tomorrow we'll send messages to all Earth's countries. Additional tribute will be levied on each of them. And it will be due in two weeks, or they can face the consequences."

"Some will attempt to resist," pointed out Lantz.

"Then they will die," Creed answered coldly. "We'll hold the current convoy until we ourselves can escort it safely to Kubitz."

President Mayfield stared bleakly at Fleet Admiral Tomalson, General Braid, and Raul Gutierrez, who were all gathered in his office. "Two weeks to raise double what we did this past month?"

"We have it," commented Raul. "But a lot of others don't. The Chinese Conglomerate has indicated they will not pay. The same for the Russian Collective."

"What about the European Union? What will they do?" asked Mayfield. He was greatly concerned that this latest demand from the Profiteers would bring about the war he had been hoping to avoid.

"Unknown," Raul answered, as he glanced down at several messages he had recently received from various world governments. "They have indicated they will consider following our lead."

"The Profiteers have made demands of every country," commented General Braid with a scowl. "Hell, some of those countries have no gold!"

"This is it then," said Fleet Admiral Tomalson with a deep sigh. "They have four big detainee ships currently in orbit and several cargo ships. One is full or nearly full, and the other is for what they are expecting to gain from this next tribute."

Mayfield let out a deep breath. "Fleet Admiral Vickers indicated the defense grid around Newton is complete." Mayfield looked intently at Tomalson. "Is there anything Kurt can do with the ships he currently has?"

"Possibly," Tomalson said with a deep frown. "If Newton is secure from attack, he could lead the rest of his fleet against the Profiteers. The problem remains with the Dacroni battleships. Kurt's battlecruiser and carriers wouldn't stand a chance."

"If he could only take out a few of them, they might withdraw," suggested Raul. "We know the aliens are hesitant to take losses, as it affects their profit margin."

General Braid shook his head in disgust. "A culture that fights wars based on profit ... it's just beyond my understanding."

"How many do you think he would have to down in order to get the Profiteers to pull out?" asked Mayfield, looking intently at Fleet Admiral Tomalson. Perhaps a limited battle was all that was needed.

"At least one Profiteer battlecruiser, a couple of their escorts, and maybe one or two of the Dacroni battleships," answered the fleet admiral.

"Is there any way he can do that?" asked Mayfield.

"No," Tomalson replied, shaking his head. "I'm afraid any attack against the Profiteer fleet could also result in them nuking Earth. Even without an uprising, once they get all our gold and gems, I just don't see them leaving our home planet intact. We could rise up one day and retaliate."

"The admiral's right," General Braid said gravely. "They'll nuke us when they leave. They don't dare leave our technology base intact, in case we come hunting for them some day. They'll blast us back to the Stone Age."

"If their fleet is under attack by Fleet Admiral Vickers, perhaps they couldn't get off enough nukes to permanently damage the planet," suggested Raul, seeking a solution to the problem. "We do have some assets to defend ourselves with."

"I would be willing to take that risk, *if* we could get rid of them once and for all," replied Mayfield grimly. "We can't go on much longer like this." He looked over at General Braid. "Can we stop their nukes?"

"They won't take us completely by surprise this time," said General Braid. "We do have a large number of interceptor missiles and jet fighters to knock down the missiles before they detonate. However, I fear that, no matter what we do, a few will get through our defenses."

President Mayfield looked over at Tomalson with a desperate look on his face. He greatly feared he might be overseeing the end of the world as he knew it.

"I'll send Fleet Admiral Vickers a message on one of the stealth shuttles, outlining High Profiteer Creed's latest demands," Tomalson said with a heavy sigh. "I can't promise anything."

"Do the best you can," Mayfield replied.

He leaned back in his chair and took a deep steadying breath. He realized there was a good chance that he might be the last president of the North American Union. Even if they met the Profiteers' latest demands, he fully expected them to nonetheless strip the planet and then nuke it as they left. General Braid would do his best to defend the North American Union, but Mayfield feared that, in this instance, the general's best would not be enough.

-

Several days later Kurt was on Newton Station, meeting with Governor Spalding and several others who had flown up to inspect the newly finished defense grid and to observe the work being done by Lomatz's engineers to the shipyard.

"I'm impressed," Governor Spalding said, as they stood in the Command Center, where numerous viewscreens showed activity around the station. Small work vehicles were everywhere, and defensive energy turrets were being installed at strategic locations on the outer hull. Larger weapons, which he was told were ion cannons and energy projectors, were also being installed to give the station a powerful offensive punch.

"It was costly," Kurt said with a heavy sigh. He was almost afraid to think of the amount of gold he had spent in the last several months.

"But worth it," said Colonel Hayworth, coming to stand next to Kurt. "The engineers from Kubitz are doing the work in days that would have taken us weeks."

Looking at one of the viewscreens, Spalding saw one of the huge Kubitz cargo ships. One of its cavernous bays was open, and small shuttles flew back and forth, carrying equipment.

"I wonder if we can trust them," General Mclusky said. "Yet I've inspected the PDCs they've put on Newton, and they're perfectly designed. They're everything we could hope for to defend the planet."

"Same with the defense grid," commented Colonel Hayworth. "Everything functions just as they said it would, and they've taken the time to show us how everything works."

"It's the Controller system," explained Kurt, looking at the others. "If it's in the contract, they'll carry it out to the letter. We even have a Controller on board one of the cargo ships that's ensuring Lomatz stays true to his word. Once they're done, the Controller will inspect the work and then check with us to ensure it has been completed to our satisfaction. If it is, we'll sign off on it, and the cargo fleet and Lomatz will return to Kubitz."

"I saw some of the smaller weapons that Lomatz brought," commented General Mclusky, looking at Kurt. "They have energy rifles and even energy cannons that can be mounted on vehicles. For handguns they have a stun weapon that has a range of nearly forty meters."

"Yes," Kurt said. "We purchased a few of those to try out. I informed Lomatz that, if we're satisfied with their performance, we might come to Kubitz later with a cargo ship to purchase more."

"What about Earth?" asked Governor Spalding, his eyes narrowing sharply. "I understand you received a new message from Fleet Admiral Tomalson."

"Yes," Kurt answered with a grim look on his face. "The situation has taken a drastic turn for the worse. High Profiteer Creed has made outrageous tribute demands to every country on the planet. The escalated tribute is due in less than two weeks."

"Can they pay it?" asked Spalding. "With much of Earth's wealth here."

"Some countries can, but most won't be able to," Kurt answered, his eyes taking on a haunted look. "Fleet Admiral Tomalson expects them to collect what they can, nuke Earth, and then leave."

"Then our plan to take the convoy to force them to take some pressure off Earth failed?" said Colonel Hayworth dejectedly.

"Not completely," Kurt answered. "Three Dacroni battleships left Earth orbit to travel the same route as the missing convoy."

"What does that leave around Earth?" asked Captain Simms.

"Fifteen Dacroni battleships, three Profiteer battlecruisers, and six escort cruisers. There are also four large detainee ships and two cargo ships in orbit as well."

"So what will we do?" asked Governor Spalding. "We can't let them nuke Earth!"

"We might not be able to prevent it," answered Kurt, meeting the governor's gaze. "I'm giving the crews on the new ships eight more days to prepare, and then we're setting out for Earth. Whether we can stop the attack or make a difference is unknown. A lot will depend on how many losses the Profiteers and the Dacroni are willing to suffer before they withdraw."

Spalding was quiet as he digested this news. The governor knew they had no other choice but to attempt to help Earth, or Newton would become home to the last survivors of the human race.

Chapter Twenty-Three

Kurt sat on the front porch of his sister's house with Bryan next to him. Kurt had taken a shuttle for a quick visit, as the fleet would shortly be departing on their mission to Earth.

"So you'll fight the aliens," Bryan said with an excited look in his eyes. "I'll bet they'll fly away when they see the *Star Cross* coming after them."

"I hope so," Kurt said. Denise had gone to pick up Keera at the medical center while Kurt watched the six-year-old.

"I'll be a fighter pilot someday," announced Bryan, as he stood up and spread out his arms, as if he were flying. "I can be your second in command of the whole fleet."

"You need to finish school first," Kurt reminded him with a smile. "You have to do well in school, if you want to become a pilot."

Kurt really loved being around Bryan. His nephew was full of energy and had so many big plans. Kurt could remember his own childhood. His dreams had been simpler, becoming a firefighter, and then, for a while, a race-car driver. Denise had constantly followed him around, normally carrying a doll and demanding that Kurt play with her. Now here they were together on another world.

A vehicle pulled up, drawing Kurt's attention, and he saw Denise and Keera get out.

"They're here!" yelled Bryan, running over and grabbing Keera by the hand. "Uncle Kurt's over this way!"

Keera laughed and allowed Bryan to pull her to Kurt, now standing. "I wish I had that much energy," she said, grinning.

"Don't we all," commented Denise, carrying several small bags. "I picked up some chicken, so we could have something to eat. I hope you're hungry, big brother."

"I'm always hungry," Kurt replied.

"Come help me with the chicken," Denise said to Bryan.

Kurt watched the two go inside and then turned to Keera. "How are things at the medical center?"

"Better," answered Keera, taking Kurt's hand. "Lucy has more of her memory back and is in treatment for the issues she's dealing with as far as her actions at the pleasure house go. I think she'll be okay."

"That's good to hear," responded Kurt. "How's it coming explaining some of the medical practices to the other doctors?"

"Slow," she admitted with a slight frown. "The medical center doesn't have some of the more modern equipment that I had available on Kubitz."

Kurt nodded in understanding. "I sent your list to Lieutenant Tenner. I'm sure he can find what you need and have it sent here."

"That would be great," Keera said, stepping a little closer to Kurt.

Without thinking, Kurt pulled Keera to him, putting his arms around her, and kissed her. For a moment, Keera seemed to hesitate and then responded fervently.

"Yuck!" said Bryan from the doorway. "That's germy! Mom said the chicken is ready."

Kurt stepped back from Keera, who had a slight blush on her face. "Let's go inside and eat."

"Just remember," Keera said in a demure voice. "You promised that, when you return from Earth, we could go to the mountains."

"We're definitely going to the mountains," answered Kurt, his heart pounding. Keera had a powerful effect on him anytime they were close.

"And your favorite color is blue?"

"Yes," answered Kurt, still confused about why she wanted to know that. "It always has been."

Keera nodded with a satisfied look on her face. Taking Kurt's hand again, they walked into the house.

The next day Kurt was back in the Command Center of the *Star Cross*. In another few hours, they would leave the Newton System and fly to Earth. He just hoped they all made it back.

"The Kubitz cargo ships are jumping into hyperspace," reported Lieutenant Lena Brooks.

"That only leaves the two Kubitz construction ships and the one cargo ship," said Andrew, as he looked at one of the main viewscreens showing Newton Station.

On the screen two massive construction vessels nearly the same size as the Kubitz cargo ship were holding position in close proximity to Newton Station. Hundreds of engineers and construction people from the two ships were busy working on completing the shipyard and installing a new ship construction facility.

"Lomatz is still here," commented Andrew. "Do you feel safe leaving Newton with the arms dealer still around?"

"Grantz is keeping a close eye on him," responded Kurt. "He doesn't get his particle beam cannon and the plans to build one until this contract has been completed." It was one way Kurt felt confident that Lomatz would do as he said, as he really wanted that cannon.

He had met with Grantz earlier and had given him another bar of gold in payment for rescuing Lucy. The Profiteer had sworn to Kurt that he would make sure the arms dealer didn't pull a fast one while Kurt was away.

"I also had more Marines assigned to Newton Station to ensure we maintain tight security," Kurt told Andrew.

"Rear Admiral Wilson reports that his task group is ready to jump," Ensign Brenda Pierce informed Kurt from Communications.

"Have him proceed to the jump coordinates and initiate entry into hyperspace," ordered Kurt.

Rear Admiral Wilson's task group included his flagship the *Kepler*, the light carrier *Dante*—plus the *Vindication*, once he rendezvoused with Captain Watkins—and light cruisers *Dallas*,

Hampton, *Alton*, and the *Birmingham*. In total he would have seven vessels in his small fleet.

Kurt's own task group would consist of the *Star Cross*, *Carlsbad*, *Trinity*, eight of the new battlecruisers and three of the new battleships. The exploration ship *Himalaya* had been refurbished into a battlecruiser and would remain at Newton with the other two new battlecruisers and the remaining new battleship, plus all the destroyers.

"Move us toward the jump point," ordered Kurt. He was anxious to get this mission started. "We'll jump ten minutes after Rear Admiral Wilson's task group does."

It would take two days to reach the Kuiper Belt where the *Vindication* was waiting. That was one day before the Profiteers were supposed to pick up their tribute from the nations of Earth. Kurt planned on them receiving a tribute, but not the one they expected.

"Rear Admiral Wilson's task group is jumping into hyperspace," reported Lieutenant Brooks, as the seven green icons vanished from her sensor screen only to reappear on the hyperspace sensor.

"Ten minutes until hyperspace entry," reported Ensign Styles, as he started a timer.

"Did you say good-bye to Emily?" asked Kurt, looking over at Andrew, who stood near him.

"Yes," Andrew answered. "I called her early this morning. I spoke to her and to Alexis."

Kurt nodded. "I told Denise good-bye this morning as well."

"What about Keera?" asked Andrew with a knowing look.

"Her too," Kurt admitted. He didn't tell Andrew that he had spoken the longest to Keera.

Looking around the Command Center, Kurt watched the crew, busily preparing for the hyperspace jump. He had a good crew, and he was confident they would do their best to get through whatever was ahead of them.

"Hyperspace entry in five minutes," Ensign Styles said.

"The hyperspace sensor is tracking Admiral Wilsons's task group," confirmed Lieutenant Brooks.

"All stations report ready for hyperspace entry," reported Andrew, as he listened to the different departments check in.

Kurt watched the counter on the helm and navigation console continue its count down.

"Hyperspace entry in one minute," reported Ensign Styles, as he reached forward and turned control of the *Star Cross* over to the ship's navigation computer.

"All task group units report ready to jump," Ensign Brenda Pierce informed the admiral.

The final seconds ticked by, and then the *Star Cross* suddenly accelerated and made the jump into hyperspace. Kurt felt the all-too-familiar gut-wrenching sensation in his stomach; even his eyesight blurred briefly, and then everything returned to normal.

"Hyperspace entry successful," reported Ensign Styles.

Kurt leaned back in his command chair and relaxed. They had a two-day trip to Earth's solar system and then a brief war council before they launched their attack.

-

President Mayfield was in the situation room along with Fleet Admiral Tomalson, General Braid, and Raul Gutierrez.

"I just received word from Captain Watkins on the *Vindication.*" The president paused, making sure he had everyone's attention in the room. "Fleet Admiral Vickers will be launching a full-scale assault against the Profiteer and Dacroni fleets the day after tomorrow."

Everyone in the room looked at each other with sudden hope showing in their eyes, except for defensive coordinator Colonel Stidham. He stared at the president with a confused expression on his face. "I don't understand, sir. I thought Fleet Admiral Vickers didn't have the ships to take on the enemy."

"He does now," Fleet Admiral Tomalson answered. They had received a message over a week back detailing the completion of the defense grid above Newton as well as the arrival of the new warfleet Kurt had purchased at Kubitz.

"What are your orders, sir?" asked Colonel Stidham, standing a little bit straighter. The room had grown so quiet as to hear a pin drop.

President Mayfield turned toward General Braid. "Put us on a war footing, General. It's time we showed these Profiteers that they came to plunder the wrong world."

"Yes, Mr. President," General Braid replied. He then turned to address the men and women in the room. "I want all primary military units activated and ready to engage in combat operations at a moment's notice. There's a good possibility the Profiteers will attempt to nuke us, when they see they're losing the battle. It's imperative that all our interceptor missiles are operational and ready to launch. Have all our F-75 Eagles ready to take off, plus our K-14 Vulture fighter-bombers with full interceptor missile payloads. We have thirty-six to forty-eight hours to prepare for all-out war. Let's not waste any time."

"What about the tribute payment?" asked President Mayfield, looking over at General Braid. He had nearly forgotten about that, since receiving Captain Watkins's startling message.

"I have a plan for that," Braid replied with a wolfish grin. "I believe Captain Aldrich will be quite pleased with my idea."

-

On the day of the tribute, High Profiteer Creed looked with relish as numerous shuttles descended to Earth to pick up the gold and gemstones to be turned over. This one tribute would more than double everything he had taken from the planet so far. Surprisingly the North American Union had volunteered to meet the tribute for the entire planet. It made him wonder just how deep their coffers ran.

"How much gold do they have hidden?" asked Second Profiteer Lantz, his eyes gleaming with greed.

"Evidently more than we had thought," Creed answered. "And here on this planet."

"Then it wasn't all taken to their colony," Lantz said. "It was hidden here all this time."

"Not for much longer," Creed answered. "Once we have today's tribute, I want all four detainee ships filled with the best-looking women and enough able-bodied young men to fill our accounts from what we'll make at the slave auctions."

"Are we going to nuke the planet?" asked Lantz. "If we do, we can't return for more humans for the auctions."

"We won't completely destroy the planet," Creed replied with a smug grin. "I've selected a few island nations to spare. With the rest of their world in ruins, we can return at a later date and take those we want from the islands." This would ensure him a lucrative slave-selling income for years to come.

Lantz nodded his appreciation at the idea. "All of us will be very wealthy from what we have taken from this planet. This world was a good find."

Creed nodded his head in agreement. He would buy the land on Marsten he had always wanted. His status as a Profiteer would be assured for all time. Profiteers for generations would talk about how High Profiteer Creed had made his fortune and rose to prominence. Yes, Creed was quite satisfied with how this would turn out.

At an abandoned airstrip once called Area 51 in the desert some eighty-three miles north-northwest of Las Vegas, Captain Aldrich and his Marines waited. The large military airfield next to the southern shore of Groom Lake was the site of considerable activity. Nearly one hundred armored vehicles were lined up just off the runway, waiting for the Profiteer shuttles to land.

"Is everyone ready?" asked Captain Aldrich.

"Yes, sir," answered Corporal Lasher. "All armored vehicles are at their assigned locations."

"Here they come," announced Private Malone, as twenty Profiteer shuttles appeared.

Nathan tapped his comm device, which instantly put him in touch with the two hundred men and women now under his command. "Let them land and exit their shuttles. We have a plan, and let's stick to it. No firing until I give the order."

Nathan, Corporal Lasher, Private Malone, and four other Marines stood just on the periphery of the large runway, when the first shuttle landed directly in front of them. Exactly where Nathan had hoped they would land. His trucks were lined up in groups of ten, and, as expected, a shuttle landed directly before each group. The other shuttles took up a high orbit around the airfield.

The shuttle before Nathan opened its hatch and out came ten heavily armed Profiteers. Behind them came another group, dragging the antigravity sleds.

The leader stepped toward Nathan and gazed at him arrogantly. "Is the tribute ready?" the Profiteer demanded.

"Yes," Nathan said, very pleased to see the same Profiteer who had come for the tribute the last three times. Looking up and down the airstrip, he saw all the shuttle hatches were open with some, if not all, of their alien crews outside, ready to receive the gold. "Open fire!" he yelled over his comm. Instantly the back doors to the armored vehicles swung open. Small railguns mounted inside on heavy metal tripods fired at the Profiteer shuttles.

Without a moment's hesitation Nathan drew his 45-caliber pistol from its holster and fired one shot right between the eyes of the stunned Profiteer leader, who promptly dropped to the ground, dead. Nathan heard Corporal Lasher, Private Malone, and the other four Marines with them open up with their automatic weapons. Other Marines along the runway added their weapons fire, and the Profiteers died in mass.

Railgun rounds slammed into the open hatches of the shuttles, causing explosions inside. Other rounds tore gaping holes in the hulls. Black smoke came from several of the shuttles, darkening the sky. A large explosion shook the ground when one of the shuttles exploded, throwing debris into the air.

After a moment the stunned Profiteers began firing back, and the hissing noise of energy weapons was heard. However, the sudden surprise attack by the Marines had already eliminated most of the Profiteers. In less than a minute, the battle was over.

Dead Profiteers lay sprawled across the runway as well as a few unfortunate Marines, who had been hit by energy weapons fire.

Nathan looked up and down the line of grounded shuttles; several were burning, and the rest emitted billowing clouds of black smoke. There was a gaping hole in the runway where one shuttle had exploded. "Implement operation Undercover!" Nathan ordered, as he turned and ran. Corporal Lasher, Private Malone, and the other Marines were right behind him. No doubt the orbiting shuttles would shortly retaliate for the attack against the grounded shuttles and Profiteers.

"Damn, that felt good," yelled Corporal Lasher, as they ran toward a small concrete building with an open door. The rest of the Marines arrived there as well, with a few carrying wounded.

Nathan stopped at the entrance and looked back at the runway, then pressed the switch on the remote control detonator he carried. Instantly the preplanted explosives detonated, blowing several more of the shuttles apart. Fire leaped high into the air, and secondary explosions racked the remaining shuttles. Satisfied that none of the alien shuttles were going anywhere, Nathan entered the building.

Once inside the Marines quickly made their way to a wide stairwell and went down.

A few minutes later, they were inside an old Cold War bunker, buried deep beneath Area 51. Marines milled around, as they found places to sit, while the massive entry doors were shut and sealed.

Suddenly the ground seemed to heave up, and the lights went out. Nathan could hear people yelling, and then the emergency lighting came on.

"They nuked us," commented Corporal Lasher, as he looked nervously around. The shelter appeared to have held up. A little bit of dust was in the air, but the walls and ceiling were intact.

"It was a small nuke," Nathan said, as he sat down with his back against a wall. He knew that the surface above them would be a burning inferno.

"What do we do now?" asked Private Malone.

"We wait," answered Nathan. "We should be okay down here. When it's over, someone will come for us."

"What if we lose?" asked Corporal Lasher with worry in his eyes.

Nathan didn't reply. He didn't have to. If they lost, then no one would be coming, and this old Cold War bunker would become their tomb.

"They did *what?*" yelled High Profiteer Creed, his large eyes growing even wider in shock.

"The humans attacked and destroyed the ten shuttles that landed. One of the orbiting shuttles nuked the site."

"What about the tribute?" snarled Creed. They shouldn't have nuked the site without contacting him first.

"I don't think there was any," replied Second Profiteer Lantz. "It was a trap."

Creed considered that and finally nodded. It all made sense. That was why the North American Union had volunteered to make the entire payment. It lured all the shuttles to one location, so they could destroy them.

"They will pay for their insolence," he growled, his growing anger turning his eyes red. "Give the order to nuke all their major cities! Once we've destroyed their pitiful world, we'll return to Kubitz. We're done here!"

Alarms suddenly sounded, and red lights flashed on the sensor console. All the Profiteers in the Command Center turned to look at Third Profiteer Bixt with concern on their faces.

"What now?" demanded Creed, as he turned toward Bixt.

"It's the human fleet," called out Third Profiteer Bixt with fear in his eyes. "It's returned!"

"Contact Clan Leader Jarls and tell him to destroy it, while we deal with the planet," ordered High Profiteer Creed, his eyes focused on the blue-white globe on one of the viewscreens. The humans were in revolt, and they had called in their fleet from the colony world. They would all die together.

"I don't know if he can," responded Bixt in near panic, as numerous red threat icons showed up on his sensor screen. "There are too many of them!"

-

Fleet Admiral Vickers felt grim satisfaction as his ships emerged from hyperspace within combat range of the Profiteer and Dacroni ships. On the main viewscreens, the images shifted to show the enemy vessels.

"Energy shield is up, and weapons are online," reported Andrew. "Condition One is set, and the crew is at their battlestations."

"Send word to the *Hampton* and *Dallas* to disable the hyperdrives on those two cargo ships and the four detainee ships. Rear Admiral Wilson has the go-ahead to launch his fighters and bombers. Instruct our fighters that their first priority is to stop any missiles aimed at Earth," ordered Kurt, as he stared at the tactical screen.

"Fleet is engaging," reported Lieutenant Lena Brooks.

"Opening fire!" reported Lieutenant Mays with a vengeful grin on her face.

Kurt and his crew had known many of the fleet personnel who died in the original surprise attack. Now was payback time.

The battle to free Earth had begun.

-

The light cruisers *Dallas* and *Hampton* closed rapidly on their unsuspecting targets. Dark blue beams of energy shot out, as the two cruisers fired their particle beam cannons at the hyperdrives of the two cargo ships. The beams penetrated, tearing through the hulls and cutting holes completely through Engineering. The power in both ships died, and they began drifting in space.

Turning to the four detainee ships, the *Dallas* and the *Hampton* sent KEW rounds, which smashed into the hulls of two of them, as it would be forty seconds before the particle beams cannons could be fired again. Each round penetrated deeper and deeper into the ships' hulls. Moments later large explosions blew apart the engineering sections, leaving the front two-thirds of the ships intact.

The other two detainee ships accelerated away, trying to escape; however, the particle beam cannons were now ready to fire, and two more dark blue beams flashed out, and both of the fleeing ships' hyperdrives were destroyed.

-

"Both cargo ships and all four detainee ships have been neutralized," reported Lieutenant Brooks. "Two of the detainee ships suffered significant damage. I think they both lost their engineering sections."

The *Star Cross* shuddered violently, and red lights blinked on at the damage control console.

"Multiple energy beam hits to the screen," reported Andrew, as he swiftly checked for damage. "There was some bleed through, and we have slight damage to the outer hull in section fourteen."

Kurt nodded and, reaching forward, pressed his comm button to allow ship-to-ship communication with his two task groups. "All ships press the attack. The more we can hurt them, the more likely it is they'll break off and withdraw."

A bright light suddenly filled one of the viewscreens. "What was that?" demanded Kurt, fearing the worst.

"The *Hampton*," replied Lieutenant Brooks in a shaken voice. "They were too far inside the enemy fleet formation, and two Dacroni battleships blocked her withdrawal. The *Dallas* managed to return to its fleet position unharmed."

-

In space, dark blue particle beams and white energy beams fought a duel. The beams crisscrossed each other, seeking targets to destroy. Particle beam fire from the *Trinity* and *Carlsbad* penetrated the energy screen on a Dacroni battleship and slammed into its armory, setting off powerful explosions and hurling glowing debris into space. Moments later the screen failed completely, and a hypermissile blew apart the battleship in a massive fireball.

In the human fleet formation, one of the new battlecruisers was under heavy attack from a Profiteer battlecruiser and two of its escort cruisers. The new battlecruiser's energy shield glowed brighter and brighter, as energy beams and hypermissiles pummeled it. With a brilliant flash, the shield failed, and moments later a temporary sun appeared where the cruiser had been. The cruiser and its human crew died instantly.

"Battlecruiser *Taggart* is down," reported Lieutenant Brooks.

"Press the attack," ordered Kurt resolutely, knowing more would die before this was over. They were fighting for Earth and for their freedom. They would either win this battle or die trying.

"Profiteer ships are launching missiles at Earth," warned Lieutenant Brooks in a frightened voice, as her sensor screen suddenly blossomed with new threat icons. "I'm picking up close to two hundred missiles, all with nuclear warheads."

"They must have emptied their tubes toward Earth," muttered Andrew, his eyes filled with worry, as he gazed at the tactical screen, now showing numerous amber icons heading toward the planet.

"Our fighters?" asked Kurt. He knew if the fighters could get there in time, they could shoot down most of the missiles.

"Almost in range. It'll be close," reported Andrew, as he watched the small green icons attempting to intercept the deadly missiles.

In the bunker in Canada, President Mayfield and the others huddled together in the situation room, watching the battle in space intently.

"Admiral Vickers has more ships," commented Colonel Stidham in confusion.

"Yes, I was going to tell you about that," said General Braid with a grin. "The ships that Fleet Admiral Vickers bought at Kubitz arrived early."

"What ships?" asked Stidham in confusion.

"I'll explain later," Braid responded.

"We can win this then," Colonel Stidham said, realizing what this meant.

"Enemy missile launch," reported a lieutenant. "We're detecting 182 inbounds."

"Crap," muttered Raul with fear in his eyes. "Now what?"

"We try to shoot them down," answered General Braid calmly. "We have our fighters in the air, and our interceptors are ready. From what I'm seeing on the tactical display, the carriers have launched their full squadrons of Lance fighters to also intercept the missiles. Let's see if we can help them."

All over Earth, interceptor missiles rose from their hidden silos and accelerated toward space. Fighters and fighter-bombers climbed to the extreme limits of their flight capability and fired their smaller interceptors at the rapidly descending targets. Above them in space and in the atmosphere, brief fiery explosions of light indicated the successful interception of some of the enemy missiles.

In space, Captain Craig Jenson heard his targeting computer give off a firm tone, as it locked on a dropping alien missile. He pressed a button on his flight controller, and a small interceptor ejected from the wing of his Lance fighter and darted toward the enemy missile. A few seconds later, a bright fireball indicated a successful intercept. "Got one!" he called out over his squadron's comm frequency. "Everyone, target those missiles. We can't let them get through!"

All around Earth, the Profiteer nuclear missiles were blown apart. From the European Union, the Russian Collective, and the Chinese Conglomerate, interceptor missiles and fighters targeted the alien missiles. The nukes died by the dozens, and soon their number had been reduced to less than forty. However, these last ones weren't normal missiles; at a signal from the *Ascendant Destruction*, the remaining missiles suddenly came apart. In their places were ten small targetable nuclear warheads, each with a ten-kiloton yield.

In desperation, the Earth fighters tried to shoot them down; more interceptors were launched, and even the Lance fighters came into the atmosphere, following the warheads dangerously close to the surface. There were numerous successful intercepts, but there were just too many warheads. Suddenly, on the surface of Earth, mushroom clouds appeared.

-

"Nuclear detonations detected," reported Lieutenant Brooks, her face turning white. "I'm picking up dozens of nuclear explosions on the surface of Earth."

Kurt's face turned pale at the news. "Keep me informed. We need to finish this battle and then see what's left on Earth." This was his greatest fear: that the Profiteers would nuke Earth, destroying all life. Kurt wouldn't know until the battle was over just how badly Earth had been hit.

-

With renewed fury, the two Newton task groups closed on the Profiteer and Dacroni ships. Two of the new battleships promptly blew apart an escort cruiser with their powerful ion beams. Hypermissiles pummeled the enemy energy screens with a fury not yet seen in the battle.

A Profiteer battlecruiser tried to move in to support a Dacroni battleship under heavy fire. The attacking human battleship and two battlecruisers cruisers promptly turned on the battlecruiser, which was a weaker opponent.

The battlecruiser's energy screen was compromised by two particle beam strikes and an ion beam hit. A hypermissile slipped through a momentary gap in the screen and slammed into the bow of the battlecruiser, obliterating one-third of the ship. Its power failed, and the two human battlecruisers quickly finished it off with their energy projectors. Then the three vessels turned to the Dacroni battleship, which had pulled back. At that moment the ten squadrons of Scorpion bombers from the human carriers swept in, each releasing two Hydra missiles with ten-kiloton warheads. Nuclear fire washed across energy shields of the entire Profiteer and Dacroni fleet formation. Several failed, and the attacking Newton warships promptly blew apart another Dacroni battleship and two more escort cruisers.

-

"We're hurting them," Andrew said jubilantly, as he saw three red threat icons, representing the Dacroni battleship and two escort cruisers, vanish from the tactical screen.

"Battlecruiser *Kraken* is reporting heavy damage," reported Ensign Pierce. "The captain is requesting permission to pull back to initiate repairs."

"Permission granted," responded Kurt, not wanting to lose the ship and crew.

On one of the viewscreens a brilliant light suddenly appeared. Kurt looked intently and could see a human battlecruiser under heavy attack from three Dacroni battleships. "Is that the *Kraken?*"

"Yes, it is," replied Lieutenant Brooks.

Even as Kurt watched, a hypermissile penetrated the ship's energy screen, and a massive explosion tore through the forward third of the ship. Then secondary explosions blew open compartment after compartment, until the ship seemed to come apart in a violent explosion of raw energy.

"*Kraken* is down," reported Lieutenant Brooks.

Kurt felt the pain of losing another ship and its crew; this battle would be costlier than the previous ones, but he had no intention of pulling back. The Profiteer fleet and the Dacroni had to be nearing their breaking point.

-

High Profiteer Creed picked himself up off the deck. His right arm was bleeding, and he had a darkening bruise on his forehead.

"We have compartments open to space, and our sublight drive is damaged," reported Second Profiteer Lantz with a panicked look in his eyes. "We need to withdraw!"

"But the cargo ships," roared Creed. One of those cargo ships was loaded with a fortune in gold and gemstones. How could he abandon it?

"We're taking too many losses," Lantz informed him. "If we stay, the humans will destroy all of our ships. There's nothing we can do about the cargo ships. Both hyperdrives have been destroyed."

Creed let out a deep and frustrated breath. He had already sent enough gold and gemstones to Kubitz to make this a highly profitable venture. If he remained, he would be risking his own life. "Do it," he ordered. "Contact Clan Leader Jarls and tell him that we're withdrawing."

High Profiteer Creed gazed in anger at the now not-so-quite-blue-white world. Even as he watched, it receded, and then the *Ascendant Destruction* jumped into hyperspace. His occupation of Earth was over.

-

"Remaining Profiteer and Dacroni ships are jumping," reported Lieutenant Brooks elatedly. "We won!" The entire Command Center broke out into cheers and yells of jubilation.

Kurt nodded and allowed himself to take a deep breath and then spoke over the ship-to-ship comm. "Rear Admiral Wilson, recall your bombers and fighters, and then secure those two cargo ships and the four detainee ships. Take their crews as prisoners." Kurt looked at one of the viewscreens. Earth was prominently displayed, and he could see dozens of small mushroom clouds dotted across the planet. Had they won only to lose the home planet?

-

President Mayfield looked grim, as the reports continued to come in. Fourteen nuclear warheads had struck the North American Union. A number of major metropolitan areas were in ruins. Fortunately the nukes were quite small, as nukes went, and the country would survive. Early casualty figures indicated over six million people had died and many more were injured.

"The Profiteers and the Dacroni have jumped," confirmed Colonel Stidham.

"Fleet Admiral Vickers has control of Earth space," added Fleet Admiral Tomalson. "We won. It's over!"

President Mayfield appeared to have aged years over the last hour. "Yes, it's over, but they still hit us pretty hard. Six million are dead. And those nuked cities will take time and manpower to clean up. We need to get aid to those areas immediately. Get help to the injured and food and water to the homeless, so we don't lose more of our people."

"I'm on it," Raul said, as he went to talk to several military officers.

"All the Profiteers on the planet have either been captured or killed," reported General Braid, as he listened to the numerous reports coming in.

"There were 112 confirmed detonations of thermonuclear devices," reported one of the other officers in the room. "The European Union and the Chinese Conglomerate were both heavily hit."

"I'll contact their leaders and offer what help we can," Mayfield said. He didn't know exactly what they could do to help the other countries, as the North American Union had their own dead and injured to deal with.

For several long moments, he gazed at the large tactical screen that for too many months had shown a myriad of red threat icons orbiting Earth. It felt strange to only see the friendly green icons of Newton's victorious fleet.

Standing up to his full height, he looked around the situation room and then he spoke. "Let none of us forgot today. Millions of people have died because, in our ignorance, we assumed we might be alone in our galaxy. We now know that isn't true. I promise all of you this. We will never be caught unprepared again, and someday we will have our full vengeance against those who brought this carnage and suffering to our planet."

Chapter Twenty-Four

President Mayfield stood outside the presidential bunker in southern Canada. He took in a deep breath of the cool fresh air. It was a little chilly, and he shivered slightly. The mountains around him were covered with snow, and, in the distance, he could see a herd of elk grazing in a small meadow where a few sprigs of grass still poked through the snow.

"Cargo ships from Newton will be arriving the day after tomorrow," Fleet Admiral Tomalson said. He stood next to the president. "It's nice being out in the sun after weeks of underground living."

The president just smiled and nodded.

"I've checked with the colonies on the Moon and Mars, and they'll need supplies shortly."

"It still amazes me that the Profiteers left them alone."

"No money to be gained in messing with them," Tomalson explained. "They were more interested in the looting they could do on Earth."

"The scientists say it will be years before all the radiation from the nukes goes away," Mayfield said glumly "It's hard to believe that there'll be so many areas of our planet devoid of life for decades."

"Perhaps not," responded Tomalson. "I had a long conversation with Fleet Admiral Vickers earlier, and he suggested that we send a team to Kubitz to see what they have to clean up radiation."

"Kubitz?"

"Remember what Admiral Vickers said. Everything is for sale on Kubitz. If something will clean up radiation, it will be there."

"So many people died. So many cities destroyed," Mayfield said with a deep sigh. "We've lost a lot of our future and our past, our history. Raul estimates the casualties from that last attack will exceed forty million worldwide."

"It's a hard lesson we've learned," admitted Tomalson gravely. "We became too complacent."

"How do we ensure it doesn't happen again?"

"We acquire a defense grid, similar to the one that Admiral Vickers put around Newton, then we must rebuild our shipyard. We need to complete our fleet and secure our own planet before we even consider a retaliatory strike against the Profiteers."

"Why not just purchase the ships at Kubitz, like Fleet Admiral Vickers did. Wouldn't that be faster?"

"Strange thing about that," Tomalson said. "While it's true that the ships Admiral Vickers purchased are very powerful, they still are only moderately armed for their size. I think we can come up with a much more powerful design on our own that will be better suited to our defense. Kurt plans on completely reworking his new ships. Also a clause in the ships' purchase contracts prevents their use against any world of the Gothan Empire. To attack one world with a ship built at Kubitz is the same as declaring war on the entire star cluster."

Mayfield remained silent for quite some time; then he turned toward Fleet Admiral Tomalson. "This is a new day and age," he said in a somber voice. "We're not alone in the galaxy. It's full of numerous human and alien races. We'll have to learn to cope with that or fade away into history."

"We won't fade away," promised Tomalson. "Not when we have people like Kurt, who can help to lead us into this new future."

Mayfield nodded. Perhaps Tomalson was right. "Let's go back inside. We have a lot of planning to do."

-

Several days later Kurt was back on Newton. He had left Rear Admiral Wilson in the Solar System to see to its defense. In another week, Kurt would be going to Kubitz to see about purchasing a defense grid for Earth. A special team would be going along also to see what they could find that might help clean up the radiation from the nuked sites. With any luck, Earth would shortly be free of radiation, and it could begin to heal.

"What are your plans?" asked Andrew, as he and Kurt walked toward the flight bay.

"Down to report to Governor Spalding and then off to the mountains for a few days."

"Rest and relaxation," responded Andrew in understanding. "I may do something similar with Emily and Alexis. It would do us all some good to get away for a few days. I promised Alexis to take her to the beach and teach her how to surf. The only problem is, I haven't done any surfing in years."

"I think some R & R would be good for all of us," agreed Kurt. "We've been through a lot these past seven months."

"I don't suppose Keera might be going with you on this trip?"

Kurt allowed himself to laugh. "Yes, she really wants to go. I promised to show her the mountains and the snow."

"She's good for you," Andrew said with a smile. "Don't mess it up. Also stay away from Newton Station. I understand Grantz is looking for you."

"He has probably come up with a new way to earn more gold." Kurt grimaced. "I'll put him off until I come back from the mountains."

"We could always take him back to Kubitz with us," Andrew suggested. "I'm sure Lieutenant Tenner could use his services. That's where he's supposed to be anyway."

"Sounds like a plan to me," Kurt answered with a nod. "I'll be sure to tell him that the next time I see him."

-

A few days later Kurt and Keera were in the mountains; they had elected to stay at one of the large ski resorts, as it offered so many amenities. They had spent most of the afternoon sitting in the lounge of the resort, taking it easy and talking about what was ahead for Newton and Earth.

"You have no idea how fortunate you are to be this far out from the big civilizations," Keera commented, as she sipped yet another tea that she had never tried before.

"Why is that?" asked Kurt, pausing to take a drink of his coffee. "I would think it would have a lot of benefits."

"The big civilizations look down on those of us who aren't as technologically and socially advanced," Keera explained. "It's one of the reasons the Gothan Empire has flourished for so long. The midrange civilizations seem to serve to keep everyone in check. They have the space navies that limit aggression and help to keep the Gothan Empire—and others like it—under control."

"That didn't help Earth much," Kurt pointed out.

"Earth and Newton are in a backwater area," Keera explained. "There haven't been a lot of exploration ships out this way. That's one of the reasons the Profiteers search out worlds like yours to exploit. Most of the civilized races of the galaxy are gathered farther in, toward the galactic center, where there are more stars. You also find some in the larger star clusters. My own home world is inside a star cluster where the stars are less than half a light-year apart."

"I wonder how many other undiscovered worlds are out there." Kurt asked.

"Probably quite a few," Keera answered. "After all, the galaxy is quite a big place, and most of the outlying areas remain unexplored."

Kurt nodded. He wondered if it would be too soon to resume their exploration program to look for those other worlds and races. It might be wise to search out and find a few allies against future threats.

Keera looked over at Kurt with a mysterious smile. "Why don't we go up to the room? It's been a long day."

"Go ahead," answered Kurt. "I'll make arrangements at the front desk for some ski lessons for tomorrow. I think you'll love skiing."

"Okay," Keera said, as she stood up. "Just don't be too long."

Kurt watched Keera walk off, and, after quickly finishing his coffee, he arranged for the lessons. Then he took the elevator to the fourth floor, where their suite was. It had a balcony with a fabulous view of the mountains. If he timed it right, they could sit outside and watch the sunset.

Placing his key card inside the lock, he heard it click open, and he went inside, locking the door behind him. He didn't see Keera anywhere, but he could hear the shower running. Walking over to the balcony, he opened the doors and stepped outside. Looking up, he knew that the *Star Cross* was above him. Lomatz had left the day before, along with his ships. As per their agreement, Kurt had furnished the arms dealer with an operational particle beam cannon and the plans to create more. For the first time in many months, Kurt was at peace with himself. The war was over, at least for now; Earth was free, and his sister and her family were safe here on Newton.

He wasn't sure if anything would be done about High Profiteer Creed and his attack on Earth. That was something to be decided in the future. For now Kurt just wanted to enjoy the peace and quiet of the mountains, plus spend some quality time with Keera. He heard the shower stop and then, after a moment, footsteps crossing the floor. Turning around, he saw Keera standing there in a blue gown that left very little to the imagination. Kurt felt his breathing quicken and his heart beating faster. Keera looked stunning!

"You said your favorite color is blue," she said demurely, as she stepped up to him and put her arms around his waist.

"Yes," Kurt answered. "It always has been and always will be."

Keera smiled. "Then kiss me, silly. We have all night to discover what your other favorite things are."

Kurt did as she asked. He was glad the night was still young, and, for once, he felt that the future looked very bright.

The End

If you enjoyed *The Star Cross* and would like to see the series continue, please post a review with some stars. Good reviews encourage an author to write and also help sell books. Reviews can be just a few short sentences, describing what you liked about the book. If you have suggestions, please contact me at my website, link below. Thank you for reading *The Star Cross* and being so supportive.

For updates on current writing projects and future publications, go to my author website. Sign up for future notifications when my new books come out on Amazon.

Website: http://raymondlweil.com/

Other Books by Raymond L. Weil
Available on Amazon

Moon Wreck (The Slaver Wars Book 1)
The Slaver Wars: Alien Contact (The Slaver Wars Book 2)
Moon Wreck: Fleet Academy (The Slaver Wars Book 3)
The Slaver Wars: First Strike (The Slaver Wars Book 4)
The Slaver Wars: Retaliation (The Slaver Wars Book 5)
The Slaver Wars: Galactic Conflict (The Slaver Wars Book 6)
The Slaver Wars: Endgame (The Slaver Wars Book 7)

-

Dragon Dreams
Dragon Dreams: Dragon Wars
Dragon Dreams: Gilmreth the Awakening
Dragon Dreams: Snowden the White Dragon

-

Star One: Tycho City: Survival
Star One: Neutron Star
Star One: Dark Star

-

Galactic Empire Wars: Destruction (Book 1)
Galactic Empire Wars: Emergence (Book 2)
Galactic Empire Wars: Rebellion (Book 3)
Galactic Empire Wars: The Alliance (Book 4)

-

The Lost Fleet: Galactic Search (Book 1)
The Lost Fleet: Into the Darkness (Book 2)

-

The Star Cross (Book 1)

-

(All dates are tentative)
The Lost Fleet: Oblivion's Light (Book 3) December 2015
Galactic Empire Wars: Insurrection (Book 5) February 2015

ABOUT THE AUTHOR

I live in Clinton Oklahoma with my wife of 43 years and our cat. I attended college at SWOSU in Weatherford Oklahoma, majoring in Math with minors in Creative Writing and History.

My hobbies include watching soccer, reading, camping, and of course writing. I coached youth soccer for twelve years before moving on and becoming a high school soccer coach for thirteen more. I also enjoy playing with my five grandchildren. I have a very vivid imagination, which sometimes worries my friends. They never know what I'm going to say or what I'm going to do.

I am an avid reader and have a science fiction / fantasy collection of over two thousand paperbacks. I want future generations to know the experience of reading a good book as I have over the last forty-five years.

Printed in Great Britain
by Amazon.co.uk, Ltd.,
Marston Gate.

13675530R00188